GAIL STRICKLAND

ORACLE OF THE SONG

THE ORACLE OF DELPHI TRILOGY, BOOK TWO

CURIOSITY
QUILLS PRESS

A Division of **Whampa, LLC**
P.O. Box 2160
Reston, VA 20195
Tel/Fax: 800-998-2509
http://curiosityquills.com

Cover Art by Ricky Gunawan
http://goweliang.deviantart.com

ISBN 978-1-948099-02-8 (ebook)
ISBN 978-1-974097-87-6 (paperback)

For my best friend and beloved husband~
Michael Joseph Flynn
who walked beside me every step of the way
through the bleak Underworld.

TABLE OF CONTENTS

ADVANCE PRAISE
FOR ORACLE OF THE SONG:

"For an established professional, *Oracle of The Song* would be a brilliant accomplishment. For the second novel of a first trilogy, it's astonishing, in every sense of the word... I can't wait for the third book - it will take me that long to catch my breath and recover from my envy."

—Peter S. Beagle
Author of *The Last Unicorn, The Innkeeper's Song, Summerlong* & many others

"Thaleia is destined to be more than just the Oracle, her fate is intertwined with the fate of Greece, with the passion of a God, with mysteries that are beyond our understanding. Ancient and enchanting, a journey into the unseen world of prophesies, of clashes and bravery. **The strength of a girl who stands her ground.**

Will the song of the God save Thaleia? Will it echo in those who treated her in disbelief and threatened her existence?

Marvelously readable, The Oracle of the Song, is a mesmerizing story of a time when the divine and mortal were entwined around a common fate."

—Angeliki A. Pateli, Archeologist Msc.

"Everything I love about Greek myths—wild monsters, power-crazed gods, and breathtaking adventures—come to life in this story of a young priestess's odyssey through the Land of the Dead to save a friend. A terrific story well told! I loved it."

—Vicky Alvear Shecter
Author of *Cleopatra's Moon, Curses and Smoke* & many others

"Strickland gives readers a thrilling twist on the dark journey to Hades' Underworld with Thaleia's quest to save a friend from its monsters and entrancing yet deadly visions."

—Catherine Stine
USA Today bestselling author of *Witch of the Cards*

"Vibrant prose, rich in ancient myth, Gail Strickland's *Oracle of the Song* will transport you to ancient Greece and the terryfying, beautiful experience of a girl who becomes a spokesperson for the gods. I highly recommend!"

—Eva Pohler
Author of *The Gatekeeper's Saga, Purgatorium, Storming Olympus* & many others.)

PRAISE FOR NIGHT OF PAN
(BOOK ONE OF THE ORACLE OF DELPHI TRILOGY) & OTHER WRITINGS BY GAIL STRICKLAND:

"Thaleia battles and befriends gods, leads her city to oust failing religious leaders, and deals with situations that call for wisdom beyond her 15 years. The historically inspired details in this novel—such as the cheese bags hanging in the trees, the elaborate ceremonies, and the mythology—are joyous and enthralling."

—*Kirkus Reviews*

"*Night of Pan* is head and shoulders above most of the young adult novels now being published."

—Peter S. Beagle

Author of The Last Unicorn, A Fine and Private Place, and *The Innkeeper's Song*

"A stirring and evocative journey."

—Linda Watanabe McFerrin

Author of *The Hand of Buddha* and *Dead Love*

"A new twist on the Joan of Arc story, and the feminist aspect is interesting."

"Gail Strickland's writing will take your breath away. ...her prose is gorgeous. Thaleia is a strong role model."

—Debra Goelz

Mermaids and the Vampires Who Love Them

"Thaleia has always been a wild one. She's always in the mountains... defying all the rules that are set in her village... I'm a fan of Thaleia's POV. It's a mix of mischief and innocence... **I recommend Night of Pan for older fans of Rick Riordan's novels...** Any mythology fans will find *Night of Pan* fascinating... with rich characters and setting and lovely writing. I can't wait (to see) how this series goes!!"

—Paula Micahella Bulos

Reviewer

"As a butterfly, helpless and fragile, I learned to be fearless when confronting the gods."

Thaleia, Oracle of Delphi

MEDUSA'S CAVE

PALACE
OF
HADES

EREBOS

CASTALIA
SPRING

12

⟩ARMENIDE⟩
⟨REEK ⟨ORACLE ⟨OF ⟨ELEA

5th Century BCE

You can't kill the song.

That is the first thing you must understand.

There was a girl. And a satyr.

An army... a million strong.

But that doesn't change anything. Because it *is*. It cannot *not* be.

And this poppy? Just a simple meadow flower? There are hundreds. Thousands. A million like the Persian army... but I stray from my thought.

The Song. It is Pan's song. It is the gods' song and the stars and sun and earth and wind. And most importantly, it is all of us.

At all times and in all worlds, I hear the Song. They ask me if it is happy. Sad? Wise?

It is all those and more.

The vital thing is to never stop listening for it.

Look at the flower, next to its petals... behind. *There*... do you see a light? Like a leaf shadow? Be the heart of the color. Feel with color. Find color in your body and hear its song. There you will find your power.

She did.

The girl... her name is Thaleia. It means to blossom, to burst with life. Her destiny is to hear the Song. In the poppy. The wind. Trees. The wine-dark sea. She thinks the Song will die, and she has to save it... to save us all.

But... as I've already mentioned—you can't kill the Song.

What is *is*—un-generated and imperishable. Whole, single-limbed, steadfast, and complete. Nor was it once. Nor will it be, since it is *now*. Altogether. One continuous.

But once again I digress with big words and metaphysical ideas. All I really need to tell you is the story of the girl's *Night of Pan*. Why she travels to the Underworld. And what... no *who*... she is looking for.

And, of course, why I hear the Song in *your* dreams.

My name is Parmenides. I am a dream healer. Shaman. Oracle.

I first met the girl Thaleia in the sanctuary of the Temple of Apollo at Delphi. She was fifteen at the time.

The girl is brave. She wants to claim her friend and bring her back. She doesn't know it, but as she steps into the Land-of-the-Dead, she may lose her way.

She doesn't know that she risks everything.

Her life.

Her soul.

True love.

But here, let Thaleia tell you her own story:

CHAPTER ONE
THE ORACLE'S INFERNO

I **am here. My feet planted wide on a black marble threshold** deep underground. This cave hides beneath a stone-circled pond, receptacle for the Kastalia Spring. Sacred water, holy to Apollo and his nymphs. Here I died, drowned by priests. Here the satyr-god Pan returned me to life.

On this day, I challenge death again... not for myself, but for my best friend Sophia. Guilt led me to dive beneath the spring water; to grope in the dark, until my hands encountered the opening to this stone chamber. My first gasp found dead air, putrid with slime and rotting fish. But a place to stand. To breathe. A womb in the earth between life and death.

A massive stone gate towers high. The carved rock, scabbed by dark moss, glows with a pulsing green light.

Beyond the gods' gate, vultures fly like dark wraiths across a starless Void. Whispers of the dead catch in a rush of the river. Shades, the spirit shadows of those not at rest, writhe from the black current, then disappear only to reemerge as an arm, a gaunt face, a screaming mouth.

This arch is the gateway to the River Styx and Erebos—the Land-of-the-Dead. The Lord-of-Many-Names—Zeus' brother Hades, so feared that none will call him by his true name—rules this desolate land.

As I hesitate, unsure whether to cross into the dark lord's realm, a flash of knowing hits me, leaves me shaking. Sophia's Shade is close, hovering nearby in the fog.

Bitter bile and a memory assault me—a sword's flash, a cry... and blood.

"Sophia, come home with me." I keep my voice low and steady, like talking down a skittish horse.

Her laughter surrounds me. It is mocking and bitter, without joy.

"Please, Sophia, take my hand."

Kneeling in black grit before the threshold, I bow my head. "Gods, you claimed my life before. Now I claim Sophia's."

I stand and turn in circles, strain to hear one voice among the Shades'. "Lord Hades, I call upon you by your true name. Relinquish Sophia! Return her to the Land-of-the-Living."

"Help us! Honor us!" The spirits' sobs tangled in the racing water are my only answer.

"Sophia, I've come for you!" My whisper is strangled by hope, by fear.

I pull panpipes from my sash and stare at the yellowed reeds. This flute, gift from the satyr-god Pan, summoned an earthquake. My music stopped King Xerxes and his entire army. Can Pan's flute destroy the fabric of this Underworld?

There! Her laughter seems to come from one Shade that drops and flits above. But it quickly escapes beyond the great stone gate, growing faint—and fainter.

"No! Sophia. Come back. Please, Sophia... forgive me!"

For an instant, I can't move or breathe.

Hoping I can draw Sophia to me, my fingers fly across the pipes' carved holes, coaxing the music to sing lament and power.

The notes swoop low, like a swallow diving from a cliff.

Sophia's laughter fades, and still I play. I would reach into the darkness to claim her hand, but she is lost in an ill wind.

Straining to hear her once more, I stop playing and peer into the mist. Nothing. Wind and water... I wait. Something shifts just beyond the portal. I can't make out the shape, but it's massive. A menacing growl rumbles. I stifle my scream.

Six fire eyes glow like brands in the night. Kerberos, Hades immortal dog, looms out of shadow and mist, shifting his bulk warily side to side. The three-headed hound slobbering through sharp teeth, guards the god-gate to the Underworld. Green serpents crown his shoulders, writhe and ripple down his back. His breath steams between yellow teeth rank with rotting flesh.

The beast glares at me as if he knows me for who I am: Thaleia, Oracle of Delphi, Initiate into the Mysteries... Intruder.

I adjust my hood to cover the poppies that sprouted from my head the night of my initiation into Persephone's mysteries. In a fire-lit cave, Pan revealed my destiny to join gods and mortals for time everlasting. That night I claimed my powers as Pythia.

With a slow, deep breath, I ease closer to the hellhound and play once more, summon the music's magic. *Sophia, I can get you past Hades' guard dog with my music.*

Stark notes crystallize like shards in the night air. I see them tear the dark-veil surrounding me and scatter the spirits.

Kerberos' breath blows steady and even like a blacksmith's bellows. He doesn't back away.

Colors—red and orange and a soft, warm white—swirl from the notes like a bright wind dancing around the beast.

Three mouths snarl.

These notes that can rip apart a mountain, can they soothe this hellhound, so I can rescue Sophia? And Parmenides?

The canine's flaming eyes, rooted deep in scaled sockets, glare at me.

Parmenides was my mentor. He led me in dream-healing, helped me challenge Apollo and save the fake Oracle's life. He taught me to heal, to forgive... to hear the Song.

Red tongues flick in and out of the reptile mouths as if scenting the air. Scenting me.

It's my fault. I abandoned Parmenides. And Sophia. I take another step and keep playing. So close, I could stroke the dog's slobber-flecked muzzles.

After the Battle of Thermopylae, with the Persian Immortals

chasing us, I left him deep in the Underworld beside the river of fire and haven't seen him since.

I urge my music to sing like the River Pappadia that flows near the Sanctuary between sweet-smelling laurels. The notes cry like a lullaby and calm Kerberos.

There has to be a way I can save Sophia and Parmenides. I must be fearless.

Not wanting to break the music-wrought trance, I'm careful of any sudden movements. Iridescent blue and wine-red notes settle around the dark snakes like a blanket. The serpents lower their heads, close brittle eyes, and sleep, wrapped across the great dog's back like ripples in a windblown sea.

Abruptly, the wind stills, as if time herself has wound down to listen. The beast-dog doesn't stir at my feet. I slowly lower my panpipes.

"Thaleia." I jump as a deep voice whispers, hoarse and tense behind me.

Kerberos jerks and lunges. I jump back, as one fanged mouth snaps at my bare arm, another snarls and lowers, ready to spring. The third roars with deep barks like the earth's rage.

"Look out, Thaleia!"

I know this voice. It's Valmiki—the Hindu poet who freed me from the Persians, who helped me return to Delphi—my village under siege. I feel him next to me as if bound by a gossamer thread, singing and thrilling to my core. The dark and wild man I'm not supposed to love.

I am Pythia. No man must love me.

The guardian dog growls.

"Don't say another word!" I hiss, terrified that he startled the beast. I don't turn to look at him, though I want to.

The hound's heads are tense and aware.

I play again.

The dog stops statue-still, one paw lifted; the serpents flare like Apollo's sunburst around his thick neck. The creature's heads loll side-to-side, but still the six eyes stare—Past, Present, and Future—three monsters to tame. His quivering muscles slacken.

Valmiki takes another step behind me and says, "Thaleia, please let me help you. Let me go with you. Let me protect you."

His voice, low and sweet as honey melting in the comb from summer's heat, fills me with longing. I straighten my shoulders and refuse to look back. "No, Valmiki. I can take care of myself."

There's more I would say—that I need to rescue Sophia by myself and beg her forgiveness. That he would only be a distraction. That an Oracle must never love a mortal man, only her god. Mama betrayed Apollo. Gave birth to me—her child of shame. I... must... not... be weak. But only the one word snakes between my clenched teeth—"No."

Kerberos growls again. Three heads twist left, right. Their throaty rumble shakes the ground, echoes around us like Zeus' thunder.

I bring the panpipes breath by breath to my lips and begin with a low, gentle note, never taking my eyes from Kerberos. The melody of Pan's meadow swells with sunlight, grasses, and laughter.

The beast's thick shoulders slump. He lies down again, but his alert heads swing to watch us.

Valmiki keeps his voice low. I strain to listen but never stop playing. "And Parmenides?" he says and then stops, as if hesitant to say anything more. He clutches my free hand. When I try to pull away, he squeezes tighter.

A memory washes over me of the Oracle's head, pale with death resting on my mud-spattered *chiton*.

"Thaleia, don't go alone into Hades' realm! Take me with you."

Kerberos lunges. Sharp teeth sink into my arm. I will myself not to move. I lock eyes with the beast's yellow orbs, malevolent and red-veined with rage.

Valmiki lunges forward and grabs the dog's neck; wraps scaled snakes around his left arm with a quick twist and chokes with his right.

The beast doesn't back away, but his teeth release my arm. We stand frozen: Hades' guard dog, a Hindu poet, and the Oracle of Delphi.

Kerberos scores us with firebrand eyes. He's poised to strike again. The time is now.

Fate brought the poet and me together in the Persian camp, where I was King Xerxes' prisoner. Valmiki set me free.

Hand-in-hand, we cross the threshold.

Time shifts. Everything is black.

I am alone.

I cannot feel Valmiki's hand in mine or see any part of my body. I am a soul, a spirit, alone.

A hissing assaults me, intensifies, a crescendo like the roar before a volcanic eruption.

I gag on a smell rife as the python's carcass.

Darkness congeals before me into a massive head, a shaggy-haired god with a gold crown; fiery eyes stare at me beneath a craggy brow.

"You dare enter my realm?" He bellows.

"Lord-of-Darkness, Hades, I've come for Sophia, my friend."

"None may leave who cross into Erebos." His enraged words are the rumble of earthquake deep in bedrock.

"Her death was a mistake..."

"None may leave." The god's disembodied head floats in the darkness. I try to find Valmiki's hand, but it's as if he vanished. There is only Hades to confront. To make listen.

"She's an innocent. Thanatos claimed the wrong girl."

"The Fates declare your time of death before your birth. Death never makes a mistake."

"The Fates are ever wise, dark Lord. But *I* made a mistake... and I've come to beg for forgiveness."

The god's sigh is a warm wind sweetened with narcissus and summer. He closes his eyes and is quiet for a long time.

At last, his eyes fly open. With a challenging stare, he says, "A price will be demanded."

I bow my head. "Whatever you wish, Lord of the Underworld."

"Honor your word, Pythia. Honor your word. Honor..." His voice fades as the darkness unravels and with it the Lord-of-Many-Names.

Once more I stand with Valmiki holding his hand just past the high gate to Erebos.

"Valmiki, did you see him?"

"Who? What do you mean, Thaleia?" He looks quickly around.

"No one. It's nothing. I think Sophia is close."

The moment we take a second step in, repulsion and fear seize me. I take a deep breath and remember Parmenides' words the last time I was in Hades' domain with him. "Death and the Void do not exist. There is only Being. There is only life. Your fear makes this land of death real."

I scream as rock and stone crumble beneath us. We spin, tangled and helpless into a tunnel black as the Death Hag's eyes. Faster and faster, we fall into the earth's bowels. Like a thousand angry snakes, a hissing throbs in my chest and head.

This isn't real.

Valmiki and I crush against each other, and I try to seize his arm, but we are torn apart and thrown against sheer stonewalls.

This isn't real.

Time and reality shift as memories assault me, each one so vivid, I can't discern past from present.

Is this death? Our life's worst fears come alive to torture us?

One memory hits me sharp as a rock: I cower behind a doorframe watching my parents whisper to each other, their faces tense with guilt, doubt, horror. Despair overwhelms me. Nothing matters. Not that I defeated the Persians. Not that I saved the Greeks.

Like a nightmare, the memory won't let me go. It drags me into the Void tangled with a boy I love.

I fall. I remember every detail:

"We have to tell Thaleia that Sophia's gone up the mountain," Mama says.

Two candles flicker faint shadows across Papa's face. Running his fingers through graying hair, he peers up at Mama. Doubt and anger flash in his eyes, before he looks back down and wraps his large hands around a goblet of wine.

I see myself push into the room and shout. "Did she go to the fertility festival? We promised each other not to go to the Agrionia. Why did she go? How could she?"

Mama backs away and looks a question at Papa. When he doesn't answer, she turns to me, her eyes dark and uncertain. "You know how it is, Thaleia. Dancing under the stars and fortune-telling games. The search for the god Dionysus. Such is our way." Mama picks up Papa's goblet and gulps the wine.

Papa stands, paces to the hearth without looking at me, and gathers a clay platter with cold chicken, boiled eggs, and soft goat's cheese in the crook of one arm and another mug of wine. He settles heavily on his bench.

Mama rests a hand on his back.

Papa chooses an egg and peels it.

Rock walls rush past. Sulfur mist mingles with fragmented memories of Mama and Papa.

"She's not of the Minyan family. She'll be safe."

"Like I was safe?"

Guilt strips away any hope of helping Sophia, until there is only my fall into the Land-of-Darkness. Guilt shreds my courage, my belief that this time I will be able to help her. Fear reveals my shame.

I batter rock walls and careen off Valmiki. He grabs my arm. Our spinning—as if we're swept down through a vortex—pulls us apart. Grabbing for him, I scream his name.

My stomach heaves. Blackness sweeps across my eyes. I strain to not lose consciousness.

"No! She promised... *we* promised each other."

CHAPTER TWO
THE UNDERWORLD

When I force my eyes to focus, I become aware of shifting light. Shadow-Shades—like spider webs sticky against our skin—scream and moan. I flail, trying not to fall through them, but their grappling arms carry us down slower and slower.

The stone chamber widens. At last, we crumble against solid ground.

The Shades encircle us, but keep their distance. Their vaporous bodies mingle with a yellow mist steaming up from cracks and vents, swaying like flames in the death wind that lifts off a wide river flowing just beyond burnt tree stumps.

There is only wind all around, and birds, shadow vultures casting their wings in this unseen wind. It blows through me, and I am chilled and afraid. My body is gone. There are shades here in the currents—the men who went before. Women wailing in childbirth, moaning to leave behind their child. And when they are gone, there is no one to give sweet milk to the babe; no one to plead and throw themselves at the father's feet in supplication if he decides the child is to be abandoned.

They are all here.

But not.

The air reeks of rotten eggs and death.

Black snakes slither between the spirits and wind around our ankles. For a breath, the air thick with hissing and sobbing overwhelms me. Through it all, there's the rushing black river.

Snakes swarm over each other to reach us, as if our warm blood attracts them. I grab my panpipes from my belt and play like I never have. I try to imagine Pan's meadow, where the god first gave me his *syrinx*, the flute named after the snakes' hiss. Here in this dark world, I summon sunlight and warmth. I mingle my soothing music with the song of the reptiles, so light and dark spin like sunlight shafting between bitter storm clouds.

The serpents crawl up my legs; their scales cool my skin. I play the poppies, startling in the sun; my panpipes whisper the shadow behind the soft petals, the power in the dark.

The snakes slide away between the Shades and are gone.

Still I play. Step by careful step, I work my way over to the river shore.

Valmiki follows close behind, staying clear of the Shades. They back away, as if they fear the racing water. The wide river froths and churns and crashes over submerged rocks.

I kneel and let the current between my fingers. "Valmiki, it's cold!"

"Thaleia," he kneels beside me as I splash water on my face, "how do we cross?"

"Kharon, the ferryman, will come for us." I turn to look carefully at Valmiki. "Once we cross the River Styx, the sacred river on which the gods swear their binding oaths, there will be no turning back. Do you still want to go with me?"

"I will never abandon you, Thaleia."

"Never is a long time, Valmiki." I want to discourage him, convince him to turn back. But I don't have the heart to say more. Let it be in the gods' hands if this poet stays or leaves. I try to smile as I say, "Not the smartest decision you've ever made."

A boat prow thrusts through the mist. Dressed in a red girdle barely covering his loins, a solitary figure steers the empty craft with a long-poled paddle. He is ancient with stranding white hair and a tangled, greasy, gray beard that whips in a wind rising from the churning waters. He glares at us with black eyes, almost hidden by bushy eyebrows. He's lean but strong, his bare chest and arms muscled but pale, white as bones.

I raise my arm in greeting, and he shouts back. There's menace in his growl.

"Undead, who are you? Who is your family? From what rocky soil are you birthed?"

"Thaleia, daughter of Icos. Pythia of Delphi. I would pay for crossing for myself and my friend." Valmiki steps up and stands tall beside me.

"I ferry the Dead across. Only one way. Go back to your hearth and family. Go back to the land of your birth and treasure your time there. This is no place for the living."

Shades press closer. The ferryman's oar slips a stroke and splashes a spray of black water.

"I left behind a night sky filled with stars, a waning moon and my village, my parents... but my mentor Parmenides and Sophia are here in this dark land. I will not turn back."

Valmiki rests his arm across my shoulder. I keep my gaze on the old boatman. "*We* will not return to the land of light, until we speak with The-Lord-of-Many-Names."

"Go back, girl." The old man glances up at Valmiki but returns his gaze to me. "Even if you find the dark lord... he will never again let you leave. Return home." The boat eases against the muddy shore.

Behind me trembles a long exhalation, as the Shades sigh as one.

Kharon turns his attention to those doomed spirits. "You may not cross! You came here without honor. If you would find peace, convince this girl to return to your homes and beg sacrifice and cremation for you. Away! Until then, you may not pass over this river."

"Most noble Kharon. I can pay you. I must cross and find Zeus and Poseidon's brother."

"How can you pay?" His eyes narrow, and he edges closer to the prow, a carved serpent that dips and tips unsteadily.

Without taking my eyes off the ferryman, I reach inside my sash and withdraw three pomegranate seeds—gift at my initiation, my Night of Pan, with the satyr-god. I unfold my fingers and stretch my arm toward the ferryman. His eyes widen, when he sees the seeds of Persephone. He looks at me as if with new understanding but doesn't say anything.

Pulling the long oar from the water, he stows it in the boat across the plank seats then steps with care over the vessel's worn side. His robes drag through the current. The old man's withered feet leave deep prints in the muddy shore, as he eases closer and extends his long fingers.

One by one, I place two red seeds in his pale palm. One for each of us. The last seed I tuck back into my sash. With only his calloused fingertips, Kharon guides me to the boat, then waits while I step inside and settle onto the bench.

My heart beats wild like a caged bird. *Turn back*, it cries. *You will never leave this Land-of-Shades once you cross the river.*

The ferryman eases to the stern and stands as still as a statue.

Valmiki joins me. The scow tips uneasily side to side, before he eases onto the seat beside me, leaving some distance between us. The boat steadies.

Kharon glares at us, looks from Valmiki to me. "I thought you said you are the Pythia, dedicated to Apollo. Do you lie to me, girl?"

I move as far away from Valmiki as the wooden side-slats, weathered and splintering from the water, will allow.

The old man pushes his sleeves up thin and muscled arms. "This is your last chance. Once I take you across, there is no turning back."

My throat is so tight, that I can only nod.

Kharon leans into his long oar and pushes us off the shore. We glide, our prow slicing across black waves and a swift current that roars in my ears.

Waves crash against our boat and over the sides, until our craft sloshes and spins. Kharon fights the raging water, steers us diagonally across. Towering cliffs line the river. Cursing and screaming against the white-frothed waves, the old man deftly guides us downriver, past rocks and half-submerged logs.

A large red-veined boulder looms before us. Water, whipped into a fury by the blistering wind, crests over it. Just as I'm sure we will crash into it, Kharon jabs his oar into the river directly before the massive rock and swings us around it.

I lose all sense of time. There is only heat, and the angry current, and Shades, as if we will never leave the Styx. Here is our hell. I won't ever leave this river. I won't find Sophia or my mentor. It will be one wave after another against our bow, water filling the boat, and vultures, and the old sailor fighting his way downriver.

The cliffs grow taller, funneling us into a treacherous, narrow channel. The current races us on and on, faster and faster.

Everything is black—the river, cliffs, sky high above. I feel consumed by the water's roar. The boat tips wildly side to side as it pushes its prow through the waves.

Beneath the churning flow, I hear a whirring that feels like words, like a warning, but I can't make it out.

The air is suffocating, bitter with sulfur. Suddenly, fire flares across the sky, silhouetting the cliffs, and then nothing. Wind whips my face. Crashing waves echo against close stone walls. Another flare reveals the river widening.

Our boat slows at last, and eases against a black sand beach.

Kharon jumps out and tugs the boat higher on land. His smile is bitter. "Welcome to your new home. Your *last* home." One long finger points to a faint trail that leads up and away from the shore and disappears between two crags silhouetted by a distant flaming sky, orange-red and green fire that lights a barren land. Rock and dust. Stones stubble the slope like the mountain vomited.

Sophia's somewhere beyond... up? *Where is she?* My chest aches as I take in the charred branches, the ash-dusted boulders. Death every direction I look.

The boat dips. I grab the side, step out, and help Valmiki to follow. The long hull is tugged by the endless rush, while the dragon front grinds and scrapes the sand's grit. The river snakes off to black clouds to our right. To the left, the fire-sky lights burnt tree trunks; stumps of limbs scar the flames like rips in a quilt stretching away from us. The river's breath smells of ancient stone, like water flowing deep inside a cave never warmed by the sun.

Kharon shoves his pole in the mud and pushes off. "Girl, you will regret this decision."

The boat pulls back from the rocky shore. The river's raw power sweeps the prow around, carrying the hunchbacked old Kharon off to the current's center.

He doesn't look back.

Valmiki's breath—fast and shallow—veils white vapor between us. Despite the blistering sky, I shiver as river cold seeps beneath my skin, evil and rotting. Rising beyond, carved between high crags, snakes a path. Bats sweep high across the flame sky, but here on the riverbank, there is no life or light, only tendrils of despair misting from the water. I take a deep breath and glance back at Valmiki. He's looking around, bewildered and unsure.

I shouldn't have let him come. Be brave, Thaleia. For him.

"Sophia would have passed here." I point to a trail wound between high crags. "That way."

Valmiki lifts the slingpack from my back. I take one step away from the River Styx and another. Each step loosens the feeling of dread that engulfed me. Away from the river, the heat becomes unbearable. But it's good to feel the stones through my sandals. Good to look ahead and claim a direction. Good to believe Sophia walked here.

After a long time, the trail winds up, always up and away from the river; the land becomes flat meadows of asphodel flowers, spiky, white as old ash, as far as I can see in all directions. Their stalks are rough against my bare legs. The narrow path leads straight across. I pull off my cloak and wipe the back of my neck. My poppy hair hangs limp over my shoulders, but I force myself to plant one foot in front of the other. Valmiki is close behind me. We don't talk. It's enough to keep going.

Just when I think we will never leave the death-flowers, they change to rushes and finally a long expanse of black sand. A bog. It's eerily silent. I would expect frogs and birds and insects, but there's only water soughing through dead reeds.

I motion for Valmiki to wait.

"No, Thaleia. We should stay together."

"Stay here and watch the trail. I've heard stories of this place—The Stygian Marsh. Who knows what creatures or spirits roam here."

Valmiki peers back down the track, up to the sky, narrowing his eyes against the flares of fire and a green wind, before he nods and squats down in the middle of the trail.

I step from log to jutting boulder, try to find solid ground in the marshy water. It smells of rot and putrefying flesh. Dead trees, half-sunken branches jut from the brown slime.

At last, I reach a small island of solid dirt caught against a massive log. I'm unbearably thirsty in the scorching heat. Kneeling, I draw my hand through the water. No, too putrid too drink. And it's hot! Wails and moans lift from the ripples. I jerk my hand out and sit back. The cries stop.

An acrid smell like rotted flesh gags me. *Sophia. I won't leave you here. I won't. Parmenides, please, where are you?*

I wipe my mouth with the back of my hand and look around. Patches of mist lift from eddies swirling around sword-blade reeds clinging to jutting rocks. What is up in this Underworld? Why is there sky in a land beneath the earth? Delphi is above me. Mama and Papa are up... but this trail? Where will it lead? This swamp feels a lot like my state of mind.

I look back and can just make out Valmiki still crouched down, waiting tense and alert.

A scream cuts the silence.

Faster than seems possible, Valmiki is beside me.

Greek and Persian soldiers rise from the water. In bronze and wicker breastplates, they press close. One young boy, a slash bleeding at his neck, drifts like fog around Valmiki. Reeds and dead water plants show through his translucent face and chest and muscled arms.

"Help us. You must help us claim our honor." His voice crackles with youth... or with fear.

"From what rocky shore do you come? By the horsehair helmet crest, I'd name you Greek."

"I am Spartan by birth. Sacrifice the fat of a bull! Sacrifice for our immortal glory."

"Give us rest," a ghost with a wicker shield pleads, his eyes sunken in a gaunt face, his hair curly and long. Persian.

"Are you from the Battle of Thermopylae?" Three hundred brave Spartans died defending the pass. Shoulder to shoulder with King Leonidas, they held off the Persian Army for four days... four days of blood and death and honor... until Brygos, my betrothed, the man I despise... betrayed them. Four days defending Hellas, holding off the invaders while Athens evacuated.

The eidolon-soldiers look from one to another. They weave in and out and around, surrounding us. A whir of swords and greaves and shields... and fear. Palpable and bitter fear.

"We are warriors. Greek. Persian. Kings. Generals. What does it matter now?"

"Help us."

"Give us peace and honor."

"Return to the Land-of-the-Living and ask our families to bury us and burn sweet hecatombs to the gods."

"What does it matter if the gods are Greek or Persian. Zeus or ram-headed Amun?"

"We died without honor. We are forgotten."

"Did you die at The Hot Gates?"

I kneel to the Spartan. "Did you die at King Leonidas' side trying to save Greece?"

Deep, angry voices sob, and plead, and roar, gathering like glowering storm clouds.

"We would return to our homeland. Give us sacrifice and an honorable burial."

Scrambling to stand, Valmiki and I press our backs together so we both face the soldiers. They circle us, mingle together so there is no division between Persian and Greek. Only rage and loss and fear.

"Blood. Give us form. Give us life. Give us blood." The laments grow more desperate.

"Ratnakara... Ratnakara." A gaunt Shade, an old man with tattered embroidered robes, a wealthy stranger with eyes only for Valmiki breathes one word: "Ratnakara. Ratnakara." Gray, bloodless fingers clutch Valmiki's robes. Two other men, younger, also dressed in shreds of wealth, hear the cry and join him. One man's throat is gashed deep as if by a sword, the other is stabbed in his chest. The wraiths push between us, then drift back, when I pull Valmiki close beside me.

Warriors circle us by the hundreds, thousands. Like water gnats, they rise from the gloomy deep, their diaphanous bodies swaying and swirling with their laments.

A dark soldier, bare-chested, stripped of armor and shield, so I do not know if he is Greek or Persian, closes in. "No longer are we warriors. No longer do we care for victory or courage. Better to be a slave and live on the wide-browed earth than drift in this heartless land." He kneels before us and grabs my knees in supplication. "Pity us. Help us."

The soldiers' cry is oppressive, suffocating.

"Thaleia?" Valmiki's voice is tight.

They push and shove to get closer to us, to our breath and heat. To our aliveness.

"Blood. Give us form. Give us life. Give us blood. Ratnakara... Ratnakara."

"Brave warriors, you deserve eternal glory. You gave your lives for your city-state, your families... your hearth."

There's barely room to move my arm, but I bring my flute up and blow one loud, strident note. It quells their cries. They back a short distance away. Once more there is only the wind's breath rattling the reeds.

"I will play to honor you."

I play a lament. The melody twines with the Shades' breath and river's current, lifting and sighing, honoring the soldiers' deaths. As if the music is a salve to their bloody wounds, they drift away to the rush and sigh of the wind. The wealthy merchant—the last to leave—turns back to glare at Valmiki. "We will meet again, Ratnakara." His form scatters and is gone.

Valmiki and I are once again alone. I stop playing and try to smile at him, but I'm shaking. He strokes my cheek with the back of his hand. I can't look at him. The air above the river shimmers, neither sunlight nor deep night, like tattered smoke.

"Why did that old man call you Ratnakara? Why does he look at you that way?"

"My name." He looks away, then as if he's decided something, as if he refuses to hide a truth, he stares at me a long moment and says, "They were looking for me. I killed them."

Unconsciously, I back away. "Why?" It's hard to ask, but I have to know.

"I was born to wealthy Brahmin parents, but when I was very little, I wandered off and lost my way in the forest. A hunter couple found me and took me in. They named me Daku Ratnakara."

"Ratnakara..."

He nods but hurries on with his story, as if he will not be able to tell it if he stops. "My foster father taught me to hunt. I was very young, when he married me to a neighbor's daughter. And our children? Children born to children. Hunting made me restless and hard. But you know this already. The first time we met in the Persian camp, you said..."

I sigh. *Another good reason not to fall in love with this man.* I repeat my words. "You were not always a good man, Valmiki. When you first grew hair on your face, you had a wife. Soon two children. But you had no way to feed them, so you robbed innocents. You murdered for gold. Now is your time to redeem yourself. This is your chance."

He takes both my hands, but I pull them gently away. "Those were the men you murdered."

There are tears in his eyes. He clears his throat and finally gets out one word. "Yes." He waits for me to say something.

Here in Erebos, we are surrounded by death. "I'm no better,

Valmiki." I don't want to accept him as murderer and thief. "Valmiki, all is the will of the gods."

"No, I won't blame the gods, because I killed. It is my shame. My burden."

"You're not the only one."

"What do you mean? You are honored by the gods. I... I destroyed lives from greed."

"Sophia's here because of me." I blurt out. I can't look at him. Instead I stare at the path as it winds up the hill, around boulders and dead trees, until it fades into the mist and void.

He waits for me to explain. I feel it. My gaze finds his. "Where is your family now?"

He's surprised. I see it in his wide eyes, but he tightens his lips and looks at me, as if trying to decide what to tell me. At last he rests his hand on my shoulder. His words rush low and steady, as if only the truth can free him.

"One day in the forest, I attacked the sage Narada Muni. He was not afraid of me like all the others had been. Instead, he asked me why I killed." Valmiki smiles at me. "Just as you asked. I gave him the same answer, but he wanted to know if my wife and my children and my parents shared my shame, since I murdered to bring them wealth. I tied the wise man to a tree and went home to ask my family. They told me the guilt was mine and mine alone."

"No! You did everything to support them. How could they say that?"

He smiles a small, sad smile and continues. "I returned to the forest and untied the mystic; begged him to teach me how to change my existence... I never returned to my home."

After a long awkward moment, I finally say, "Who gave you Greek clothes? Last time I saw you in Delphi, you were dressed like a Persian." I try to keep my voice light and bend the subject away from what I'm really feeling. *He's a murderer. A thief. How can I have these feelings for him?*

Valmiki looks down and picks at his ivory sleeve. "What? Oh, your father. When I headed up the mountain to follow you, he grabbed me.

He thought it would be better if I didn't wander around at night in a Persian army uniform." Valmiki looks back toward the river, touches my hand. Smiles tentatively. "You despise me now."

His gentle touch sends a thrill up my arm.

"You know I am a thief... and worse."

His smile warms my belly and chest. *I am Pythia. I will not love this poet. I cannot.*

My throat tightens with the answer I would say. The answer I can't say. I look at him too long before placing my right foot, then my left, one after the other, walking away from Valmiki.

CHAPTER THREE
MASK OF SHAME

He quickly catches up to me, though he leaves some distance between us and doesn't touch me... to my great relief. We walk awhile side-by-side, then veer off, up toward the flame-filled sky. Our path is rubble, winding up a rock-strewn hillside, barren and studded by black stumps as if a firestorm swept across the mountain and left no will for trees or brush to grow.

Mist creeps over the mountaintop high above. Yellow and reeking of sulfur, it swirls and thickens, until we've walked inside. I can barely see Valmiki. Choking and coughing, I place one foot in front of the other, determined to keep going. Out of the smoky haze, I hear singing. High ululations weave through a second voice low and rusty like an iron gate clanging in a breeze. And another—rich and heartbreaking to hear. Smooth like honey. Sorrowful as lost love. The song drifts down. But there is nothing to see. Only smoke wafting between black trees, wretched and charred.

"Valmiki, do you hear that?"

I stop, squint my eyes.

The music is haunting—filled with yearning, like a lullaby to a small child. I pull my panpipes from my sash and mix my song with theirs.

They stop. There's a rustle of feet in the grass, whispers... a cough wet with phlegm.

"Who's there?" A creaky whisper slips through the mist. A woman's voice. Old. "Grandmother?"

"Is your grandmother here in Erebos?" Valmiki squeezes my shoulders and turns me to look at him.

"The god Apollo murdered her." I can't hide my rage.

"What..."

"Who are your parents?" the ancient voice says.

I strain to see who's speaking—to no avail.

"From what rocky shore do you come?" Their questions spatter like cold rain. It's not my grandmother. There are three distinct voices... three women. All old. One high and cracked like splintered wood. One low and smooth as a stream. The last is angry. Bitter.

I motion to Valmiki. We take a quiet step uphill.

The way winds around a large boulder. Just before us, huddled together are three ancient crones, shriveled and stooped, with long gray hair, matted and wild. As one, they look over their shoulders to confront us.

"Give it to me! I want to see!"

"No, not yet."

"Deino, now! You've had it too long!"

One hag jerks around to face us. Craggy wrinkles scar her features like brown and rutted pine bark. She has one dark eye, sunk deep. It darts side to side and finally lands on us. As if scorched by her gaze, Valmiki wraps his arm tightly around my shoulder.

The eye locks with mine. I'm stunned with its rabid need to take me in, an intruder threatening from a misty shroud. Her unquenchable desire to *see* scores my spirit.

"Valmiki, her eye socket is just flabby skin... it's empty!" I hope the old woman doesn't hear my whisper.

"Look, Enyo! Will you just gaze there! There are strangers from the outland. Just look!"

"I *can't* look. You have our eye! Pass it here. It's my turn... my turn!"

"Fine. Here it is then, sister." With cracked talons for fingernails, Deino digs into her face and removes the eye. As if this is normal as passing sweet butter to a friend, the crone rests the eyeball in her open palm and holds it out.

The eye looks straight at me.

My scalp tingles and my hair-poppies stick out like papyrus stalks. The one called Enyo reaches with wrinkled fingers and gently takes the eyeball. With horror, I realize that she and the other woman hunched beside her in deep, yellow veils that drape over her head and shoulders and down to the ground, diaphanous as liquid sunshine... so beautiful... except they both have empty eye sockets. "Look! Are they all really sharing one eye?"

Enyo pops the eyeball—looking like a peeled egg with red and yellow veins—into the socket. She flutters her feathered lashes as if to settle it and leans forward to peer at me. "It's just a girl and a boy. Huh." She shuffles slowly around us, glaring with the one eye, while the others lean in as if they can claim some knowledge from the current eye-holder. "What are you doing here? You aren't dead yet."

The other two mutter their assent and step closer, holding onto each other.

"Go away!" She frowns at us.

The eye glares.

Her voice is deep and gravelly. It's clear she's the sister with authority.

I pull away from Valmiki and step up, hoping to persuade her to let us pass. How much trouble can three old women be, with one eye between them?

The third sister pushes aside veils shimmering like a hummingbird's wing and twists around to peer up into the mist, then back at us. "My turn, Enyo. You've had our eye too long. Please, may I have it?" She smiles an attempt at a winsome smile, revealing one long tooth. "I'll give you our tooth, sister, so you can taste that sweet apple in your pocket." Tugging on her sister's veils, she holds out her hand. "My turn for our eye, sister."

As she steps in front of Enyo to block her view, her back to us, I realize that their upper bodies are old women, but their lower halves are black swans. Long-feathered wings protrude from the veils and drape the ground. I can't see the feet. Are they swan or sandaled human?

"Alright, Pemphredo, but first, give me the tooth. If for only one moment, I want to feel whole. To see. To tongue something other than gums." Huddled together, feathered wings touching feathered wings, an exchange takes place with much sighing and disputing. When they turn back, the last sister stares at me with the eye, her yellow robes startling against gray hair and skin.

"Who are your parents? Go back to whatever shore spit you into the vortex of death. You do not belong here!"

I sense Valmiki trying not to laugh beside me. Revolting as these sisters are, there's nothing about them to scare me away.

"You were singing. It was a beautiful song. Will you please sing again?"

"Go away! We will protect her."

"Yes, you must leave her alone."

"Who do you protect?" I look around, try to see past the women up the path, but the mist is thicker than ever.

"Just go home now!" They wave arms and wings, stirring the dust.

"Your music was lovely." I play a lively melody, the flute notes laughing and dancing.

The crones surround us. Without missing a beat, I segue my melody to a lullaby, soothing and gentle... I hope. Can I change their minds with my music?

The old women join hands and lift their arms high and circle us. Slow at first, then faster and faster, until they are a blur of gray and flapping black wings. At last, they sing. Their song is throaty and hoarse. They sing wordless notes that hum and soar. Whirling and singing and panting and laughing, we weave a melody that flames with the power of the fire sky. Finally, their melody shapes words, unintelligible at first. Then, as the sisters stomp their feet and swing their arms up and down and high, I realize what they chant is the name of a goddess: Hestia.

"Hestia, the hearthstones strong." Their arms lift high.

"Hestia, goddess of our home." They swoop down once more.

"Hestia, goddess of hearth." Swing up. Stomp. Turn. Stomp. Sing.

"Hestia! Fire in our soul!" Stomp and turn. Their veils swirl and spin. Faster and faster to my flute melody and their song and laughter. "Hestia! Hestia!" Their circle unfolds and they dance and stomp and sing in one line with their arms linked over one-another's shoulders.

I play loud and fast and glance at Valmiki without stopping my music. We dance past the two sisters with no eyes. Ease up the path. When we put some space between us, we run as fast as we can, around a twist in the path so we're out of sight. I bend over panting and chortling.

Valmiki laughs so hard that he sinks to his knees. When he finally looks up at me, his eyes swim with tears. "Who are those crazy old women?"

"Papa told me stories, when he wanted me to behave, about three sisters—the Graeae. Born old and gray, ancient from the beginning. They are sisters to the fierce and hideous Gorgons."

"Who is Hestia?"

"Firstborn to Kronos and Rhea... and lastborn as well, since she was the last to be disgorged when Zeus saved his brothers and sisters from their father. A hearth goddess who tends our fires. We pray to her to keep our home safe. When several families band together to colonize elsewhere, they always take with them a firebrand from the communal fire."

"She must be powerful, indeed."

"It's always seemed strange to me, they honor her greatly, but at the same time think of her as an old maid, a humble homebody." I take Valmiki's hands and pull him to his feet. "We'd better keep going. The Graeae seem harmless, but I'm not sure I trust them not to stir trouble. They said they are protecting someone. I can't imagine they make good guards, yet I am worried."

Focused on keeping on the faint trail, I almost miss the statue. White as old bones, it looms out of the fog. A warrior with raised arms protecting his face, mouth grimaced in fear, torso twisted away, caught in flight.

"Valmiki!" I point up the trail at the next sculpture, an old man crouched behind a boulder, peering over the top, also facing uphill. "There's more. There... and there!" The hillside is scattered with stone men, all staring at the same point. Caught in a moment of terrifying death.

We stop at the same time. It's hard to see clearly through the mist that obscures then reveals. A strong wind rips aside the vapors, and I peer uphill. Dark against dark, gapes a cave—a dark maw, like the mountain's mouth.

I shiver when Valmiki takes my hand, but don't pull away. We wind our way up the steep slope, until we reach the closest statue.

It's limestone, a Spartan warrior with breastplate and grieves. One muscled hand grasps the once-leather strap crossing the curve of his shield. His head is thrown back like he's screaming.

Everything about this place forces a whisper. "This is no art sculpted by man. Valmiki, this *is* a man. *Was* a man, his life turned to stone." I touch the warrior's cheek. Despair and rage course through me. For one horrible moment, I am trapped. Connected to the Spartan.

"Pythia, I'm here. What are these statues? There's a myth..."

Valmiki's voice brings me back. I pull my hand from the rock. "These were men, Valmiki."

"Some god passed here?" Staring at the stone man in horror, he reaches out but does not touch the sculpting.

His words remind me of the old woman. That's what she said over and over after the elderly priest Diokles drowned me in the sacred Kastalian Spring... but with the grace of the gods, I didn't die. I returned to my home, to my life, returned to fulfill my mission: Save Hellas from the invading Persians. And I did. I stopped a million soldiers and their golden king. Guilt washes over me, mixed with my pride... and determination. *I must bring Sophia back to the Land-of-the-Living.*

I step around the warrior and stride straight toward the cavern. A shadow moves just inside its ragged mouth. Hissing fills the mountain air and slithers up my spine like vile music. I never slow down. *Sophia.* I let her memory carry me uphill. The closer I edge to the opening, the more despair threatens to engulf me. *I'm worthless, selfish. Sophia wouldn't be here if not for my pride. She wanted to marry Timon and have babies. I dragged her up to the forbidden Sanctuary. My hubris brought her to Hades.*

Overwhelmed, I stop.

"Thaleia!" There's urgency in Valmiki's voice. "Something moved over there. Someone's watching."

We're out in the open. There are only mist and stone men between us and the watcher.

A near-palpable hatred washes over me. I struggle against it, try to push the memory from my mind, but I'm consumed by self-loathing.

"It's this dead land, Valmiki. It's poison. I can't... I can't do this."

"Fight it, Thaleia. You can... you have to. Think of Sophia."

I close my eyes and remember the satyr-god's words, when I stood in his sacred meadow, tasked to choose between immortal life and my struggle to save Greece. "Be the heart of the color," he said. "Feel with color. Find color in your body and hear its song. There you will find your power."

Where do I find power in this death land? Is it only in a flower and Apollo's brilliant sun? Or is there power in this dark land? Power I can claim?

Though the hissing swells and threatens to overpower me, I fling my arms wide and stride boldly up the trail straight toward the waiting maw. Gray lichen spots the stones like leprous scales. Black tendrils of dead vines almost obscure the entrance.

Valmiki catches up with me. "Don't go in. There's someone..."

A hand thrusts from the shadow, clutches the jagged rock. The skin is withered, gray as stone, with fingernails so long, they curve back like talons. A woman emerges from the shadows. Her hair is writhing snakes—the Gorgon Medusa.

I scream and shove Valmiki behind me. "Don't look at her!"

Now I understand the statues. They turned to stone when they met Medusa's gaze—one look that transforms men to solid rock—Athena's curse.

Medusa eases from the cave mouth, stooped and ancient, clinging to the ledge. Her tongue protrudes between purple, chapped lips, curled around boar tusks. Snakes crown her scaled face, hissing and straining to sink sharp fangs into my flesh.

I cringe but meet her gaze.

Her eyes bulge from her head, dark with death.

Valmiki's breath is hot on my hair as he cringes behind me. My blood freezes, coursing from my heart down my legs and neck, screaming through my veins.

"Keep away!" she shrieks.

Her hatred scalds me. For a moment, death sounds inviting. My arms and legs feel heavy, rooted to the mountain.

But the stone surges with its own power, vibrating through the soles of my feet: *Be the heart of the mountain. Feel with the rocks. Find stone-power in your body and hear its song. There you will find your power.*

I look deep into the Gorgon's gaze. There's surprise there, faint and tenuous. Time shifts, and I see her as she was. Scaled eye sockets, cracked and scarred, become large eyes framed with thick, curling lashes. Her haggard face changes to the beautiful woman she was before the goddess cursed her—hair black as night, lustrous and long and swept back over olive-skinned shoulders. Inviting, high-proud cheekbones.

For an instant, the present struggles to reassert itself over the past. A young virgin shimmers beneath the deformed hag. Both there. Vibrant. The moment lasts a seeming eternity; then...

Athena's Parthenon Temple.

A devoted priestess.

A jealous goddess.

There is love and devotion in this beautiful *kore*—virgin maiden dedicated to the gods. She bows before Athena's altar. Towering above her is a massive gold and ivory statue of the warrior goddess. Broad shield held close before Athena's virgin breast. A javelin clutched in her right hand. The goddess seems to keep an eye on the girl, but in the shadows another god watches and lusts—the sea god Poseidon.

He ravages her.

She runs from the temple, but there is no escaping the god's revenge.

Sudden as Zeus' lightning bolt, Medusa's eyes widen with panic. She darts down the temple steps. Athena screams from its porch.

The girl's long hair thickens and transforms to vipers. Black scales writhe across her eyes, their red mouths fanged, forked tongues flicking and seeking a victim. She tears at her face, her nails scratch long wounds, but nothing stops Athena's curse. The girl's skin thickens with scales. Boar's tusks protrude from cracked lips. Her eyes bulge white and terrified from their sockets. The snakes hiss and seethe and thrash from her skull.

Kore is now Gorgon—death's daemon.

Once again time shifts. Facing me is the Gorgon, whose dark glance turns men to stone. But I've seen the beautiful girl trapped within the beast. My body relaxes, surges with wonder. "How could Athena do that to you? You were her devoted priestess. You did nothing wrong!"

Tears course her face, now ashen and weather-plowed, as rigid and stony as the mountain.

"You're beautiful. You are not a monster." Without thinking, only wanting to comfort, I step close and touch her shoulder. She jerks back as if my touch hurts her, but then covers my fingers with her scaled hand and crushes them as if she will never let go.

A shiver runs through me and tightens my throat, but I force myself to remember the beautiful *kore* and don't move.

Valmiki steps around me.

Horrified she will kill again; Medusa covers her eyes to protect him from her gaze.

I try to peel her fingers away.

"No! I will destroy him! It is my curse. My shame. Leave now!"

"It is not your shame. What blame is yours? How can this be your fault?"

I gently pull her hands away from her face.

This time she lets me, but averts her gaze.

"Tell us, Medusa. Tell us how it happened."

Without looking up, as if her life story is carved in the dark stone at her feet, she tells her story: her devotion to the goddess Athena whose jealousy and "evil eye" claimed her beauty, lets it spill from her in a tide of grief. Though I'd seen it in my vision, I remain silent. She needs to talk.

"I was priestess to the warrior goddess Athena in the great Parthenon Temple in Athens. There were many suitors who wanted to claim me as bride, but I shunned them all and dedicated my life to my goddess. My life changed one day as I lay narcissi across the altar at the foot of Athena's towering statue—as tall as ten warriors, carved in ivory and gold..."

Her voice breaks. Her snake-hair twists and struggles with the memory. The vipers strain to bite me, but I step back just out of their reach.

Her next words are so soft, I can barely hear her. "Poseidon. He waited in the column shadows. He stole my maidenhood. My life as priestess. Cursed by Athena to live forever alive but banished to this land of ghosts and monsters... she believes *I* am a monster."

Medusa stares a long time at her hands, fingernails cracked and pointed like raptors, skin scaled and gray.

I want Medusa to look at me. I want to heal her, but she's not ready.

"Instead of protecting me, Athena banished me."

With a groan of anguish, she throws her head back. "Look what she did to me!"

I wait for her to continue, but she is spent. We stand together in an awkward silence.

At last I say, "You turned those men to stone."

Medusa grimaces, her lips snarling around the boar tusks. "They desired me. I had to protect myself."

"You must not believe Athena's curse. You are beautiful. You are powerful."

"No." She glares at me. "For the crime of being seduced against my will, I lost my status, my beauty... I can't even look at a man without killing him!"

Gently, I squeeze her shoulders, willing her to listen to me. "I still see you as you really are: devoted, kind, lovely."

"How can you say that? Look at me!" Her bulging eyes stare into my own, their rage like fire.

"I see someone deeply hurt. Someone who would do anything to keep that pain away. You accept Athena's curse; turn any man who approaches you to stone... anything, anything to cover your shame. But you don't need to. The shame is not yours. It is Poseidon's. You have been judged and exiled by society, turned into a vile monster in the eyes of men, because you were ravaged by a god." I take her face in my hands and kiss her heinous brow. Hold my breath, when the snakes curl against my neck.

I pull the hood off, so my poppies dance in answer to her hissing vipers. For a moment, red flowers mirror the open snakemouths, red as wine. Red as blood.

A god's curse. A god's blessing.

The serpents twine among poppy stems. Medusa and I stare at each other like shadow sisters. The dark. The light. Understanding blossoms in her eyes.

And with it, comes a transformation. Slow at first, twining snakes change, a shift as subtle as gray sky melting into iron waves, strand by strand each viper becomes soft hair flowing over sun-blessed shoulders. Medusa's violent face transforms to the olive-skinned *kore*; bitter hands and mouth and yellow tusks smooth to a young ravishing girl.

Her beauty is reclaimed.

Valmiki steps around me.

In one frantic moment, Medusa and I both react. She whirls around, and I jump between them. "Valmiki, no!"

He shakes his head, disbelieving his eyes. "How...?"

"Don't look at her."

"But I saw. The curse is gone. You did it, Thaleia! You saved her." He pushes me aside gently. "Trust me... no, trust yourself." He steps across the distance between us and rests his hands on Medusa's shoulders. "Medusa, look at me."

"No! Valmiki! No!"

He smiles back at me. "It's alright. I'm safe. You've destroyed the curse."

"What if you're wrong?" There's no time to say more, to tell him I can't lose him. He whispers in her ear. "Medusa, trust me. Look at me."

The girl straightens her back. Takes a deep breath. As if forcing herself to dive into a lake fed with frigid, melting snow—she whirls around.

"Valmiki!"

CHAPTER FOUR
WHY IS NYSSUS DEAD?

My eyes burn. My throat constricts. *No.* **I grab his arm to** pull him away, but Valmiki jerks free.

Face twisted by terror, Medusa tears her gaze from his, doubtless horrified she will once more see a man turn to solid rock, condemned mid-step by Athena's curse. No man may look into her eyes without paying the price. She is unclean, unworthy. Shamed by gods and man.

Valmiki lifts her chin, so she looks directly into his eyes. And then he does something amazing—he smiles.

Where do you find the courage?

Medusa's smile, tentative and tight, bursts into a wild laugh. "You... you're alive!"

And then we're laughing and crying together. She drops to her knees before me and kisses my feet. "Who are you? You defied the goddess. You lifted my curse." Tears pour down her face, her soft and lovely... *human...* face that is no longer the death mask of a plague victim, scaled and crusted like a gangrenous reptile.

She is beautiful. Her innocence could not be stolen by the sea-god. Devotion and love overflow from her eyes—eyes that turned away from her home, her role as priestess—eyes that turned men to rock and lime.

"Who are you? Are you a goddess? Queen Persephone?"

I pull her up to stand before me. "No, I am no goddess... or a queen. I am Thaleia, Oracle of Delphi. I am here to find my friends and bring them back to the Land of the Living."

"How can I thank you?" She glances a shy, sideways glance at Valmiki.

Why does it hurt so much when they look at each other like that? I shrug off the feeling. *She's beautiful. Why wouldn't he look at her with those eyes... I'm the Pythia. What difference does it make?*

But it does make a difference. I look away, so I won't have to see them. *Thaleia, don't be ridiculous. And selfish! You're the Pythia, dedicated to Apollo. That is your destiny. Not this poet.* I square my shoulders and turn just in time to see Medusa return his smile... faint at first as if she doesn't believe. As if she's waiting for the curse to claim him.

Shaken, I release her hands and step back.

Valmiki seems lost in thought.

There's a sound from the cave. A sigh?

I squint to see through the mist. *Did something move? Was Medusa alone in the cavern?* I turn my attention back to the beautiful *kore* waiting before me.

"Thaleia, you saved me, but do you know what you've done?" She looks from Valmiki and back to me. "Athena will pursue you."

I shrug. "Many gods would turn me away. Right now, it's Hades..." Medusa gasps when I say his name. "I'll scream it in his face. If I must face him, I claim the right to call him by his real name. Which path do we take to find the Lord Hades?"

"No one can leave once they've crossed the River Styx."

"No man can ever look into your eyes and live." I grin.

The girl returns my smile, but hers is tinged with sadness.

"Can you tell us which way to go?"

"There is only one path. And it leads to The-Host-of-Many. He will welcome you as he did his queen... but you must beware, he..."

A scream, a blood-curdling death cry shatters the quiet. As fast as a lynx, Valmiki wraps one arm around me, the other around

Medusa and pulls us down to the ground. We form a circle and peer up at the sky, back to the cave, and downhill toward the river... Filled with hatred, the shriek seems to be everywhere, cascading off the black cliffs.

Untangling my limbs from Valmiki, I look around and scramble higher up the rock-strewn hill. At last, I see a man crouched above the cave, half-hidden by a scorched tree, fog caught in its black limbs like spider webs. The man wears a priest's yellow robes, but his face and arms... his entire body is diaphanous.

A cliff stone shows through his chest.

A Death-Shade.

He throws his head back and howls, then charges down the cliff at me. His face. The hooked nose and scowling brow. *I know this man! The priest I shoved off the mountain to his death.*

He stops a few feet away. "Thaleiaaaa..."

I gag on his smell: rotting flesh and hatred.

"You! Nooow you come for your friend? Nooow you care about her?"

The sky flares red above the cliffs. Heat sears my face and scalp. His viper mouth is scarlet. Blood red of goats and lambs... virginal girls sacrificed to satisfy the gods and priests and fathers who give away their baby girls to men twice their age.

I sink to my knees with a shameful memory—blood everywhere... my best friend's life spilled onto boulders; the pale limestone stained deep red; her face blanched white. Her body lifeless in my arms. "Sophia." Her name catches in my throat.

My heart aches with memories: the day of Sophia's betrothal—a pig pushing its nose in the dirt looking for grubs, while we stood scrubbed clean, five and six years old, waiting to hear the naming of her betrothed, Timon. The moment he stepped up to the family altar and spread a laurel branch across the marble shelf and glanced over at my best friend. His chest not yet filled out, but already tall at fifteen. Sophia smiled as he placed a gold band on her finger. She touched it with her thumb and spun it two times, pleased with her father's choice for her.

How could she be happy? Even at six, I hated the very idea of arranged marriages. Our fathers bartering us off like sheep and bags of grain.

Wicked and grim-faced, the priest smirks at me as if reading my thoughts.

I scream and rush at him. But there's nothing to attack. I run through his Shade, gritty as sand scraping my shoulders and face. Nothing is flesh and solid in this dark world. Now that the priest is between us, even Valmiki wavers like water.

"Yessss, you think you can kill Nyssus, little girl?"

His voice hisses like a snake coiling in black wind.

"You mussst ask, 'Why is Nyssus dead?'"

I can't say he smiles. Nothing tainted with such venom can be described as a smile.

With careful purpose, he turns to peer at me, then twists his shadow-body to stare back at the cave, before easing closer. He smells of sulfur and mold and rot.

"You deserved to die."

"Ah, death. Yesssss." He raises a bloody sword high, so the flaming sky casts back—red to red against the burnished blade. "Sssacrifice for honor."

I try to grab his wrist, but there is nothing to seize. Only shadow. Only whispering smoke.

"I am change, little girl. I follow. I lead." He looks once more back over his shoulder and frames his ghastly smirk.

"Not change, you monster. Death!" Do I imagine it or does he shuffle away from me?

"Yesss... I kill for the godsss. I follow. I lead. All for the godsss."

"The gods? Not the gods. The priests. Diokles." My words spill like the rapids in the River Styx, filled with hate and rage. I hardly know what I'm saying. "For the gods? The *gods*?"

"I change."

"You're dung, a rotting corpse...vile! What do you change?" I *ache* to throttle his smile off.

"Whooo will change? Not whaaat."

His lips drop to a smear of red across his sallow skin.

He lifts the sword and studies it. "Yessss, who is to blame?" He glares at me.

I swipe at the sword. He floats into the air over my head and lands behind me.

"You will defy Thanatosss? You think ssso? Hubrisss! Ask whooo will change, not whaaat."

I clench my fists and push closer, but it does me no good to press the shadow-priest.

"The god of Death brought the girl through the Gate of Shadesss. You will change Life and Death? Return your friend to the Land-of-Living? Do not blame the godsss. Do not blame the priestsss."

I try to grab his wrist, but it slips through my fingers.

Nysus grimaces. "Whooo will change? Whooo will defy Thanatosss? Know thyself, Pythia."

He dissolves with the wind. I'm left shaken, tight and hard as the towering stone. I glare into the cave. My muscles scream with fury.

"Who was that, Thaleia?" Valmiki wraps a protective arm around me.

I can't look at him. I can't move away, though I know I should.

"He hates you." Valmiki drops his arm.

I glance up. Is he blushing?

He clasps his hands behind his back as if he doesn't know what to do with them. "He wants to kill you... why?"

Medusa slips between us. "Who was that?"

"I don't know."

Valmiki lifts my chin so I have to look at him. My faces burns, and I pull free. "There's no time." My words are desperate, forced; I try to steady them. "We have to find Sophia."

"Thaleia." One word. One command and with it, I begin to shake uncontrollably. Valmiki doesn't take a breath or speak or look away. At last he insists, "Why does that priest loathe you?"

"I murdered him!" I shout over and over, until my words tear my throat. I jerk my hood back and turn away. I can't stop shaking. Over and over I see his blade shine in the moonlight. "I shoved him off a cliff. He deserved to die! He was trying... they're all... it doesn't matter. Nothing matters anymore except finding Sophia and bringing her home!"

Valmiki strokes my back like he would calm a horse.

Black mist rises up the mountain.

"It's the River of Lamentations," Medusa says. "Shades that wander its banks want one thing: revenge."

The fire sky flares, shadowing her face red and orange.

"The priest turned into a snake-man. Why?" I say, haunted by his insolent grin.

"In this land of darkness, the Shades suck their true natures from the earth's deepest heart. If their *psyche* is poisonous like venom, then they claim the soul of a snake. Your land of light and trees and meadows of flowers—all things are rooted deep in the Underworld. Even a great oak anchors in black mud. Here we cannot hide our true nature."

"Erebos reveals our truest nature?" Valmiki takes up both my hands.

I fail to stop their trembling. The priest's words snake through my veins.

"Why do you hurt so, Thaleia? What does this death world reveal about you? You couldn't... I can't believe... why would you kill that priest?"

Pulling away, I stare at my feet and try to shut out the memory, the shame. When I finally look back up at Valmiki, there's nothing but kindness, patience, and understanding in his eyes. I want to tell him everything. Be done with it. I look from Valmiki to Medusa and open my mouth to speak... but it's too horrible. There is no place to begin. No way to explain.

Valmiki sighs as if making up his mind and says, "There is a thirst for blood." He drops his arm to his side. "I know." His eyes darken as if remembering.

"You're a poet now. That was before. That was to survive and to feed your children." I touch his bare arm, feel his muscles. *He could easily kill.*

He pulls away, when I mention his family. I wait, unsure what to say.

"No. I will not make excuses. I slaughtered men for gold. And there was more... I remember the power that consumed me, when I stole another's life."

"You enjoyed murder? For gold?" Medusa says.

"It's not that. The money was blood money. I hated the way it felt in my hand and gave it to my wife as fast as I could. I tried to live simply. I didn't want embroidered robes, gold chains around my neck."

"What power did you claim then?" I need to understand. This poet. This man.

"You never forget the blood spurting from the neck vein; the power like flood waters overwhelms you. That moment when a life shifts, a body abandoned because you claim the soul."

Medusa steps back and stares at Valmiki.

I look down at my hands, my heart divided. Then up at the sky as if there I might find answers. "That was long ago, Valmiki. You wanted to feed your children, your wife...you wanted to survive." I try to reassure him, but I'm not sure I believe it myself.

"Does that justify murder?"

"Does anything?" My chest aches with the meaty thump of the priest striking cliff rocks.

My self-loathing is so overwhelming, I feel like *I* could turn to stone. Valmiki roughly shakes my shoulders. "We can't give up. We have to find Parmenides. Maybe he knows where Sophia is in this wretched land."

I whirl away and head toward the cave, focus on climbing over boulders and avoiding snags. Anything to get away. Anything but stand beside Valmiki and imagine him killing women, children, and old helpless men for gold coin.

"Wait, Thaleia!" Medusa rushes up, grabs my arms, and turns me to face her. "You helped me. Now let me help you. The Land-of-the-Dead is huge—fire river, endless bogs, no night or day. How will you find your friend in this land of misery? You need the gods' help... there's someone... a great goddess..."

Before she can finish, a dark cloud comes to hover above us—bleak and damp, a mist as cold as Poseidon's sea. The fog seeps into rock scars and covers trees, dead branches jutting above it, creeping closer.

It silences the rush of the River Cocytos far down the ravine; swallows the wind and the flames' heat... until there is only silence. A dead, heavy silence. This is no ordinary sea mist. It sidles lower, obliterates scraggled trees protruding from boulders and the scree and dirt. Closer. Thicker. Engulfing flames and mountain, until it hovers over us only an arm's length away.

CHAPTER FIVE
NYX—GODDESS OF NIGHT

t first, I'm drawn to the mist. It feels like it's alive and loving. And something I can't explain. It *waits*. Stretching my arm out, I dip my fingers into the swirling gray. They disappear.

Valmiki rushes to my side and clutches my hand.

This time, I don't let go.

Long-drawn laments shatter the quiet—wails that seem to echo from inside the cave, as if the mountain's mouth, rock primordial, cries out.

"Don't be afraid, Thaleia." Medusa's voice is calm and quiet. "It is Nyx, Goddess of Night, older than the Olympians. Older than the Titans."

"Nyx? Mother of earth and air?"

A woman's voice, deep as the sea, groans, trembling the ground. "No mortals or gods dare disturb me." Her moans rise and fall, cloaking us with fog, denser with each cry. Louder. Closer. The air throbs around us, so poppies at the cave entrance sway. Blood seeps from the opening, a rivulet scoring gray dust; spreading gouts of red soak the soil to mud. The rock bellows with her words. "Not even Zeus of the thunderbolts will cross me!"

The mist is so thick that I still can't see the goddess. Valmiki and Medusa disappear in the dark cloud. It devours me. My throat tightens.

I try not to panic. Breathing deeply with the pulse of the living fog, I inhale, then exhale.

Only Valmiki's grasp is solid and warm. There is ground beneath my feet, the cold mist against my cheek, a smell of cinnamon, but my eyes betray me. Is this how Death sneaks up on us? Is this how *Thanatos* will claim me and transform me to a Shade? First sight, then smell and hearing, until nothing is left?

Abruptly, Nyx parts the fog and emerges from the cave, massive blue-black wings cast twin shadows over us. Her face is smooth like moonlight across a summer sea. She wears a crown of poppies. Beneath her towering figure, vapors moan and swirl, alive with spirits—night creatures: lynx, owl, and rats. Snakes encircle the goddess.

"You are intruders in The Land-of-the-Dead."

The air is charged, dense and crackling like a thunderstorm. Stars trail from the goddess' shimmering wing feathers, forming constellations.

"Adrasteia!"

Nyx's shout summons a girl from the cave. I can't decide if she is young or old. Everything about her is pale in comparison to the goddess' black robes and hair. White hair feathers her bone-pale face. She reminds me of the fake Pythia, the girl I brought back to life... the girl I killed. The Child of the Clouds. Though she seems frail, when she crashes two cymbals together, the music is raw and commanding.

"Medusa, who is she?"

"A nymph, born of the Sky God's blood."

Nyx chants with the rhythm and sways side to side. Stars swirl above her.

"Her song controls the tides and stars, planets and the boiling rock of the earth's core. The kosmos dances to her music."

"And Nyx commands her."

I drop to my knees in supplication. "Goddess of night with woven poppies for a crown, immortal Nyx, child of Chaos, wiser than all the Olympians and the Titans, feared by Zeus, I implore you. Allow your supplicant to honor you."

Valmiki kneels a little behind me and says, "Here let us all for Death prepare."

The music, screams of owl and lynx, snake and rat grow oppressive. I can barely draw breath.

The goddess wraps her wings around me. Her heart beats like the pulse of the universe.

Nyx's feathers are soft and warm. I will sleep. Rest in this ancient power. She will protect me. I will let the struggle go—the priests, the gods... just drift asleep in the nest of her arms.

No. I fight my desire to surrender. If I dissolve into her power, I will never save Sophia and Parmenides. *Think. Think. What would Parmenides do?*

Panic rises in my throat; I taste fear's bile. Pull away from her embrace.

Nyx draws a *tympanon* from the cave mouth; closes her vast eyes and strokes the taut skinhead with her long fingers, wrinkled and large-knuckled with age. The air thrums with cymbal and drum.

She lifts her wings above me—no longer the black Void, but a goddess carrying the heavens on her widespread feathers.

"Sister, you are Pythia, dedicated to Apollo."

Struck speechless, I nod and draw back my hood to reveal my poppy hair.

She smiles and takes my hand, then lifts me to my feet. I would follow her anywhere.

"Why are you here in this dark land?"

"I must find Sophia. My best friend. She died because... and my mentor."

Adrasteia drops the cymbals to her side. The fog drenches the fire sky, leaving the night still and calm, waiting and breathing with the goddess' power. Strand by strand, the mist lifts to reveal a firmament dancing with more stars than I have ever seen. Constellations shift and swirl—the Great Bear and Leo the lion, Draco the mighty Python—summoned by the goddess' will.

Nyx towers over me. Her flowing robes smell of cave damp, asphodel flowers... and honey? I feel like I will fall into her piercing gaze, but say, "You are the goddess of all: Gaia, the earth mother and Uranus, father sky. Your power is so vast, even Zeus, king of all the Olympians fears you. Time cannot bind you. Wise Oracle, will you tell me where I can find them in this vast and unknown land?"

"Come inside." She turns sharply to stare at Valmiki, then shares a slight smile with Medusa. Turning back to me, her voice lowers. "Only you, Pythia." Without another word, she crosses her wings and stoops to enter the cave.

I look back at Valmiki, then follow the goddess.

It's so dark inside that at first, I see nothing. There's cold, damp, a smell of stone and dead fires. The chamber fills with light as she points with a black fingernail, long and curved, from candle to candle, nestled in crevices and crannies of the cave wall. Each taper bursts into flame.

When they flare, I see a floor covered with deep red tapestries. Several skulls hang on the rough walls. I identify goat and bear. The air is cloying and as I look around, I realize that dried poppies and asphodel are suspended everywhere, from stalagmites jutting from the floor and the dead tree branches, bare and black, leaning against the rock walls, decorated with flower bunches hanging upside down, gathered together with a strip of cloth, even from the goat skull.

I remove my sandals by the entrance and step onto the thick rug. What I thought was a spiraling design, moves. Snakes. *Thaleia, don't show fear*. I back away carefully and wait while they slither off into the shadows.

"Follow me." Nyx's command forces me to step once more on the rug. I place each foot where I see red, watch for movement out of the corners of my eyes. The goddess disappears into a cleft at the rear of the cave. I hurry to catch up.

Though I can't see the ceiling where it fades into darkness, there is wing flutter and chirps high above me. Bats. I stand still trying to give my eyes time to adjust. A new smell, cloyingly sweet, fills the chamber, reminding me of home. *Why?* I smile. *Mama's honeycakes*. This massive chamber reeks of honey.

Suddenly, like the outcry of an invading army, the walls shudder with a loud snore. It echoes and rumbles, harsh and moist. Whoever is snoring must be huge. There's a catch, cough, then a roar, low and steady like a rogue wave rushing from the farthest recess. I tense, wishing I could see past the black goddess. Chains rattle, scattering bats that flit and swoop from the shadows.

Nyx ignores it all and adds a couple of logs to a small fire and sits cross-legged before it. The snoring grows louder, bouncing off the stone.

I glance a silent question to the goddess.

She nods for me to go see for myself.

With my first step, the rasping ceases. The stillness is somehow more unnerving than before. I take another step and glance side to side at the rug, but there is no sign of the snakes. A cough. Sigh. Heavy shifting accompanied by a rattle of chains.

I stop in my tracks and whirl back to face the goddess. "Who's in there?" My voice comes out so faint, I'm sure she didn't hear me. I clear my throat. "Who..."

"My grandson."

I search my mind for the lineage: Nyx, born of Chaos, coupled with the wind and birthed an egg. A silver egg, suspended in the Void and glowing from within, surrounded by utter darkness. The shell cracked in two. The upper half became the sky—the god Ouranos. The lower half the Earth—Gaia.

"Gaia and Ouranos birthed the Titans," I say more to myself than the goddess. The snoring starts again, mid-cough.

"And whom did I raise? Whom do I cherish above all others?" In that moment, she appears more beautiful than before. She lifts her wings and spreads them like a black sunray above her head. The feather tips brush the ceiling. Stars on her gown spark like a shifting night sky. Everything about her shimmers and glows with a current of love and power.

"Kronos? The Titan? Zeus' father?"

"Among others. Zeus is the youngest. Demeter, Hestia, Hera, Poseidon, Hades... all the Olympians are their children. There was a prophecy that one of Kronos' children would seize the scepter of power. Just like he seized it from his own father. One by one, the moment each was born to Rhea, Kronos devoured the baby."

"He ate his own children? That's horrible. What did Rhea do?"

"What could she do? She tore her hair as she carried each child for nine months, only to see the baby ripped from her arms. Her cries shattered the earth, but she was helpless to stop her husband. At last... desperate... she tricked Kronos. Wrapped a stone in swaddling cloths and handed it to the Titan, telling him it was the newborn Zeus. He swallowed it whole; content he had secured his power."

"I raised the boy in the Cave of Dicte on Mt. Ida," Adrasteia says as she enters the chamber and stands beside Nyx. She stares back toward the grumble of the Titan's breathing. "May the gods curse him! We kept the boy safe. The divine goat Amalthea suckled him. The Kuretes danced, stomped their feet, and crashed bronze swords against their shields to hide the child's cries."

"When Zeus was safely grown, he gave Kronos a magic potion, a strong emetic that caused him to throw up all of his mother's children in the reverse order Kronos had swallowed them. The stone first." Nyx casts me a knowing look. "You have seen it—the *omphalos* in your Sanctuary of Apollo on Mt. Parnassos? That's the very rock Rhea fed Kronos."

I gape. Never did I expect to hear this, a firsthand account. My mind swims with questions. "Why didn't she save her children sooner? How could she bear to watch her husband devour them? For what? Power? Greed?"

"She was afraid. Remember, he was the king of the Titans. She could not challenge him... for many years. So she lost her children one by one. Until the birth of her youngest. Filled with rage and despair, no longer caring what happened to her, she defied her husband."

"And were there no children after Zeus, her youngest?"

"Her fury was boundless. She found the courage to no longer allow Kronos close."

"After Zeus saved his siblings, how did he claim power?"

"The Olympians banded together, even raised the Cyclopes and

60

powerful *Hekatonkheires* from Tartaros, the deepest region of the Underworld."

"Three monsters, each with one hundred arms and fifty heads." Adrasteia shudders. "With Hephaestus' help, they forged thunderbolts for Zeus, Hades' helmet of darkness, and Poseidon's trident to help them overthrow the Titans."

With a flash of triumph in her eyes, Adrasteia brushes the cymbal with her fingertips. For a moment, the shadows above her shimmer with stars, green and blue lights, iridescent as a dragonfly's wings and a pale whisper of a song—a subtle melody that settles like a cloud. She rests her palm across the bronze and everything fades. "Zeus defeated the Titans and chained Kronos here."

"Are all the Titans prisoners in the Realm of Hades?" I say.

"Not all. Not Atlas and Oceanus. Especially not Prometheus. He helped Zeus defeat Kronos."

This doesn't make sense. The goddess hides... something.

I let silence sit between us, add a branch to the dying fire. It's not my place to question Nyx, but I can't stop from asking. "Why is Kronos here? How can you help a monster that eats his own children? Your great-grandchildren?"

The goddess lifts her wings and drops them, staring at me.

"You still love him after all he's done?"

"Fear can make even a Titan do evil things... More than any other, he was my child of earth and starry sky. He was always the one who found me at night to wander together and name the stars, listen to the wind blow across bold rock face and whistle through rough-barked pines. We mostly walked side by side comfortable we knew each other's thoughts... and he's my grandson. Someday you may understand."

I don't think I will ever understand helping... caring for someone as horrible as Kronos.

Then I think of Valmiki. Poet. Murderer. Maybe I do understand.

A shadow crosses the goddess' face. I think better of pressing her for answers.

"He sounds like he's drunk."

Nyx slowly nods. "Zeus suggested he be my... *guest*... after he overthrew him and claimed the scepter of power. I give him honey to keep him content. Evidently, the sweet nectar makes him intoxicated. I feel sorry for him. At least if he's drunk, he may forget he can never be free."

I stand and face the opening to the back cavern.

"You may ask him your questions. He knows all things of all times." Nyx smiles. "You *may* get an answer."

The giant roars a sound like thunder and a raging waterfall. It goes on a long time, as if anguish could shatter the Titan's stone prison.

Valmiki rushes into the cave. I push him back. "No. If we both go in, it might anger him. I have to ask him where I can find Sophia and Parmenides. Wait here." His face is dark with a fear that melts my heart. "Please, Valmiki. I don't know why, but I *know* I have to go in there alone. Trust me." Without waiting for his answer, I stride forward. There are garbled words I can't understand as if the Titan talks in his sleep. Humming, laughter—deep and moist—echoes off the craggy walls. Chains rattle as the Titan shifts his massive body.

I take one step toward the sounds, but stop when Nyx says, "Thaleia, he was ruler of all the universe. He controlled heaven and earth, gods and goddesses."

I nod, step around a jutting rock, and see the giant.

CHAPTER SIX
DESTINY

His smell gags me—onions and sweat and the all-pervasive honey. As revolting as the odor is, nothing prepares me for the massive, slug-like man slumped against the cave wall slick with green slime, splattered with white bat guano. *This is the goddess' favorite grandson?* There's no time to think about it.

He's awake.

I edge closer one cautious step at a time, putting off the moment I'm noticed. He tilts back his head tangled with long, gray hair, oily and lying limp over bare shoulders. With a flourish of a thick-knuckled hand, he pours honey into an almost toothless mouth. The few teeth remaining are yellowed and jagged. His tongue licks the amphora rim and his full lips. Flesh, fat and ebony-black, sags from his forearms and over a bearskin loincloth. He has jowls and a double chin. Two pendulous breasts droop over his belly.

This was the ruler of the Universe? The king of earth and sea and the vast Void? A laugh swells inside my chest, but is cut off when the Titan casts his dark gaze upon me.

He lowers the jug and straightens his back, leaning in. "Who are you? Who are your parents? From what land do you travel?" His words slur, but each is black with menace and power. Rage.

My muscles tense to run, but I stand completely still. Gather my breath and my courage. "I am Thaleia, daughter of Icos and Hipparchia—the last Oracle of Delphi. Now, *I* am Pythia of Delphi, the most sacred Sanctuary of Apollo."

Kronos scoffs. Takes another slurp of honey and hiccups.

I wait for him to speak again but as if already dismissing me, he launches into a song.

I kneel before the monstrous man and bow my head. "Wise father of Zeus..."

His roar cuts off my words. I jump to my feet and back away, into the cave wall.

"You would speak his foul name to me?!" He curses, until the rocks threaten to shatter.

When he is spent, the deep cavern echoes his cries. They career off slick rock, scattering back, cavern-to-cavern, and sinking down into the mud-crusted earth. His dark gaze feels like it will devour me. I take a step closer.

Kronos staggers to his feet and lunges at me. His honey jug shatters, hurled against the stone behind me, but the bonds hold. I jump back and cringe against the wall; my palm finds the sticky nectar. He jerks his chains, taut from his wrists and ankles, screams and roars, but he can't reach me.

His gaze, filled with hatred, feels like it will pierce me, but I walk straight up to him.

"You can read the breath of the Kosmos and tell the future. You are wise beyond time."

His answer is a scream that is blood and death, a rage so violent that my bowels twist in fear. But I kneel once more and wrap my hands around his knee, so wide that even with both hands, my fingers don't touch. I bow my head to honor him... and to show him I'm not afraid. *Will he destroy me?* With one hand, he could break my neck and crush me like a twig. I keep my head low and stare at his foot, cracked and filthy with jagged nails. *Now he will kill me.*

His big toe moves up and down. Up and down. With a rush of relief, his voice washes over me soft, filled with restrained fury.

"What would you know, Pythia? And what will you do for me if I share my knowledge?"

What can I possibly give to this Titan? As I stare into his gaze, the doubt and mistrust there, I understand what he wants above all else.

"I can give you freedom."

"You're weak. A girl! You will give *me* my liberty?" When he strains against the iron chains, I sit back.

I hold my breath and wait for him to calm before I speak. "Yes. I offer you a chance to persuade your son to set you free."

He slumps against the wall. "What do you want to know? Can't you see? I'm a prisoner in this filthy cave. How can I possibly help you?"

"Tell me how to find my friend and my mentor. They're here, wandering among the Shades, lost in Hades' dark realm."

"If I tell you, how does this grant me my freedom?"

"Zeus and Hades are brothers in constant feud. The Lord-Thunderer is always looking for ways to prove he is superior. You will help me steal something Zeus' brother wants. If you mock Lord Hades and please Zeus, he may grant your release."

At the mention of the Thunder-Bearer, Kronos screams so bats shriek and fly helter-skelter across the cave recesses, spinning and whirling between stalagmites.

Only when they settle, do I say, "Kronos, this is your chance to claim your freedom from those who imprison you."

The giant rubs his large hand across his mouth, sticky with honey and seems to consider.

"Why should I believe you?"

"I give you my word as Pythia, priestess to Apollo."

"Huh... what good is that? Our destiny is carved in stone. You cannot change what the Fates unwind with their thread. Not even I can. Look at me! Murderer! I deserve to be chained here in Erebos. How can you claim my release from this cave?"

A thought comes to me. I don't know how or from whom... the gods? Apollo? But I trust its power and speak it aloud. "I promise to bring the scythe to you. The one Gaia created from stone and urged you to steal your father's manhood with. Present this to your son Zeus. Ask his forgiveness for castrating his grandfather and swallowing Zeus at birth... he may forgive you. And free you."

He snatches up another honey jug and tips it back, rests it on the cave floor next to him. "Follow the path over this mountain, down to the Valley of the River Lethe... and listen well, girl. Do not drink! Though thirst may scream at you to sip from the swift-flowing waters, you must not. Cross the river and continue as the road widens and the cobblestones glisten with gold. You'll know. Then you will be close to the House of Hades. There you will find Sophia. Parmenides is more of a mystery. He comes and goes between the Lands-of-the-Living and-the-Dead. You will not find him. He may find you."

He knows their names. He knew all along.

Bowing in supplication, I touch my forehead to the cold floor. "Freedom will be yours, wise Kronos. I will steal my friends from the Lord-of-Many-Names."

"Yes, I know."

I back away, never taking my eyes off the towering figure, but pause at the tone of his voice. There's no anger, no boundless power as king of the kosmos. He sounds sad... lost. "Girl, remember me. Will you do that?" He rubs a hairy hand across his eyes. "Ah, but I know you won't." He mumbles beneath his breath.

"What did you say, Lord Kronos?"

With sad eyes, he says, "Just remember me, Thaleia."

The last thing I hear is the Titan slurping honey in rapid gulps. Easing along the wall, I feel for the opening and slip through backwards. Nyx still sits by the fire. Her eyes burn with an unspoken question.

Valmiki wraps his arm around my shoulder and squeezes.

I lean into his warmth. Tears fill my eyes.

Nyx arches one eyebrow, looks from him to me.

Though every fiber of my being orders me not to, I pull away from Valmiki.

Behind me the Titan mutters. Sings. And before long snores.

"What happened? What did he tell you?" Valmiki says.

Looking around the fire-lit room, I want to tell them we will find Sophia, explain to them about the path to The-Lord-of-Many Names, but I'm mesmerized by the Titan's last words. I shake my head. *Remember me. That's what he said. Remember me?*

The high-carved ceiling, its hollows and crevices spark with planets and constellations. Pinpricks of light wink on and off—Ursa Major, Mother Bear; Lynx; Draco, The Giant Serpent, twists and swirls, pointing its snout down toward me, toward Nyx, toward the Void.

I'll find Sophia in the House of Hades, the dark heart of the universe.

I slowly become aware that Medusa is shaking my arm. "What did he say, Thaleia?"

"He told me where to find Sophia. There's a path, but first we must cross the River Lethe."

"Thaleia..." Nyx stops.

"Goddess of Night? Is there something you would tell me?"

She smiles a quiet smile. "No. Trust that you will find your own way. You don't need me to meddle."

"Valmiki? Medusa? Kronos sends me to Hades, to the darkest depths of the Underworld. I'll go alone. Sophia's lost here because of me."

"Why is it your fault?"

"I only know I need to be the one to find her."

"Alone? You must have lost your senses!" Valmiki grasps my shoulder.

"You returned my life to me, Thaleia," Medusa says. "Now you think I will just walk away when you're in danger?"

"Medusa, we defied Athena. She will come looking for me... for us. Will you stay here and face her? Can you do that? I don't know if I can take on Athena and Hades both. If you can at least slow her down... maybe there's a chance."

Anger and pride flash across Medusa's face. "Athena dishonors all that is feminine. How could she turn on me? Blame me? Take Poseidon's side and curse me? I will stop her here, Thaleia. One thing about turning men to stone, I learned a little of my own powers." She smiles shyly at Mother Night. "And I have a powerful ally."

"Valmiki, will you stay here and help Medusa?"

"No."

"No?"

He doesn't bother answering. There's conviction in his eyes. He doesn't look away.

I have a feeling that nothing I say or do can move him from my side.

The goddess smiles a faint, wistful grin.

I glance one last time at the ceiling, but the constellations are gone. There is only shadow.

"Rest awhile beside the fire. I have a barley tea and honeycakes that will give you strength. Your journey will be long. There are many monsters, daimons, gods who would lead you to death... rest and gather your will."

There should be night and day, some division from one moment to the next, but when at last Valmiki and I leave the goddess' cave, heat assaults us. I force myself to scramble up the narrow path, grabbing jutting boulders that sear my palms. I strain up, always heading toward the mountaintop. Tangled thickets get in our way—dead berry brush whose thorns tear at my bare legs and force us to stray far off the dirt path. I put one foot in front of the other and push through. Valmiki is close behind. I have to stop more often to catch my breath than he seems to need. His bronze skin is dark with exertion, but while sweat pours down my face and neck and between my breasts, he doesn't seem to be bothered at all.

"How can you tolerate this heat?" I bend over, gasp for air, wait for my heart to stop beating like a caged bird.

"Just like the desert in Persia." He looks around. "Well, we didn't have flames in the sky, but it was so hot, so parched, so unrelenting... Speaking of parched, how about sharing some of that water in your pack?"

When I pull out the goatskin, it feels light. I shake it. "We'll have to only sip. There's not much left." I look far down the ravine to the River Cocytus winding like a snake through the gray landscape. We've climbed farther than I realized. "Guess we'll have a ways to find more water." I hand the bag to Valmiki. He tips back his head as if to gulp, but I have the impression he is pretending. He doesn't really swallow any.

"Here, you should drink as well. This heat will steal all your energy."

He reaches out to touch the necklace I always wear—spun lamb's wool, twisted to shape a delicate spider web. "This is beautiful." He lifts it with two fingers and looks closely at it. My throat contracts.

"A gift from Sophia." My breath is tight as I try not to cry. I take the necklace from him and tuck it beneath my chiton.

"You never told me how she died."

"It was the day I defeated King Xerxes' army. Everyone was celebrating, dancing in the streets, singing. Remember? I left you and went home to rest?"

"I'll never forget that day." He laughs. "I drank too much wine. I fell asleep down by the blue gate." His brow furrows. "I'm sorry, Thaleia."

There's an awkward silence between us. He takes back the water skin and tucks it back into the backsling. Without looking at me, he says, "I should have been with you."

"How could you know? How could either of us... she promised me she wouldn't go."

"Where? Where did she go, Thaleia?"

I cover my eyes with both hands trying to block the memory.

Valmiki pulls them gently away, so I have to look at him. "What happened? You saved us. Defeated the Persians. That slime king Xerxes ran away with his tail between his legs... but what happened to Sophia?"

"I was exhausted. More like I was unconscious..." I try to laugh but start to cry instead.

Valmiki brushes the poppies from my face and wipes off my tears. Gives me time to steady myself.

"I'll never forget the look on their faces."

"Who?"

"Mama and Papa... it was late. They were sitting together at our table drinking wine, eating boiled eggs and bread... their voices woke me up. Loud and frightened... I can't, Valmiki. I can't talk about it!" I turn away. "We're wasting time. I have to find her!"

He catches up to me, pulls me around to face him. "Please, Thaleia? Maybe if you tell me…"

At first I can't find the words to explain, but at last I say, "I remember I was stunned that Sophia had gone alone up the mountain. I remember each moment. Papa wrapped his arm around Mama's waist. She leaned against him without looking away from me. 'How can you say she'll be safe?' she said. 'Sophia will join the other maenads at the Agrionia. The priests tell us it's necessary to insure fertility. Of the fields. Our women… but she is just a child!'"

I wrap my arms tight around my chest, tight with the pain. "Papa pushed against the table and jumped to his feet. Our heavy table, its grained wood stained with wine and lamb fat, it tipped, then righted itself. Eggs and cheese and wine crashed to the floor. 'I know where they are. I'll go get her,' he said. 'Icos, no!' Mama gasped. 'We should wait. The priest is already furious with us. With Thaleia.' I can't forget the terror in her eyes as she looked down at her hands clutched together. 'With me.' 'Wait for what? Wait for the damn priest to apologize for his sacrifice of an innocent girl?' Papa said. Mama seized his shoulders and turned him, straight toward the fire in her gaze. 'She's not of the Minyan lineage. Only a girl from that family may be chosen. She'll be fine.' It seemed as if Mama spoke with the insistence of winds falling off the mountain above us. 'Wait… until… you… can forgive. Revenge will not persuade the gods.' I don't want to remember, Valmiki! Don't make me!"

"We'll find her, Thaleia. I promise."

He touches the spider web once more and looking to the mountain crest, shakes his head. "Looks like we have a steep climb ahead."

CHAPTER SEVEN
THE RIVER LETHE: RIVER OF FORGETTING

fter that, we don't talk much. The unbearable heat feels like we walk straight into a dragon's mouth. I pace myself. Try not to look up too often, try not to gauge how far we've walked; I just place one foot in front of the other. It looks like no one has walked our path for a long time. Asphodel flowers grow from the middle. They are beautiful in a way: white six-petaled blossoms cluster around a stalk as gray as the dust they sprout from. A budding crown tops the stems like a pinecone or the tip to my *thyrsus*.

I stop and breathe deeply as if to catch my breath, but really, it's a memory that stops me dead in my tracks: the night Parmenides dressed me in spotted fawn-skins and walked me up Mt. Parnassos to my initiation. He placed the fennel stalk carved with a twining snake, crowned with a pinecone in my right hand. His words, I can still hear them so clearly in my mind that it is almost as if he stands beside me on this path, heading deep into Hades' Realm.

This will be your initiation to womanhood and marriage. You will marry the god, Thaleia. Only then will you truly be Pythia.

How does that power help me? What good does it do if I am Pythia but cannot save Sophia? I wish Parmenides were here. Kronos said he'll find me. I hope it's soon.

Valmiki never stops walking. He's far ahead of me. I hurry to catch up.

The trail finally begins to level out to a gradual incline, and we get a second wind, striding faster across meadows of asphodel and bold poppies, studded with smooth boulders and stunted pines, clusters of needles sprouting from the tips of scraggly, black branches.

My swollen tongue feels like it's stuck to the roof of my mouth. Valmiki and I walk without speaking, conserving the little moisture left. All I can think about is water. I try not to let my mind wander to the Kastalia Spring, sparkling and cold and clear. Or the Kassotis Spring rushing its sacred waters through Apollo's Sanctuary. Or the sea! I shake my head to clear it and stare into the flaming sky. At last, I force myself to think only of my feet. One step. Only one step.

"Thaleia! Look!"

Ahead of us on the narrow path, there is an old woman. Small. Frail. Her back stooped, a cane in her hand. She's walking straight toward us, pacing the path with one deliberate step after another. A blue scarf is wrapped over her head and shoulders and covers most of her face. There are only her eyes. Her eyes and the jolt of familiarity. I don't know why or where or how it can be, but I'm sure I know her. I hold my arm out to stop Valmiki and wait.

"Who is she?" he says as he watches the woman take step after step, purposeful and slow.

It takes forever for her to reach us. The sun is unbearable. Sweat drips from my temples. My chiton is soaked. My throat and tongue are parched. My lips cracked, and I'm so dizzy, I nearly faint. Still I wait. I have to know who she is.

Three more paces, and she stands directly before me. My height exactly. Her eyes fill with tears as she smiles at me. "Thaleia."

"How do you know my name?"

"Burst with life."

"How do you know me?" I want to wrap my arms around her, protect her... from what? She's a Shade. Like the others. Lost and confused.

"Thaleia. Granddaughter. Beautiful."

As my legs lose all strength, I drop to my knees. My heart leaps with hope.

"Granddaughter? Why do you call me granddaughter? Who are you?"

She rests her wrinkled hand on my head. I see her do it but can't feel her touch. I've never wanted to feel anything more in my life.

Valmiki grabs my hand and pulls me to my feet.

"Talk. Hard. No words." She taps her cane on the path. Red dust swirls up and dances through the transparent folds of her cloak, her arms, the worn, wrinkled face.

I cringe to see it, to know this fragile elder is only spirit. A shadow resemblance of someone who walked her fields, rocked a baby... now a Shade. She looks so sad.

Unable to even hold her withered hands in mine, I collect all the love I felt as a child for the grandmother I never knew—all the love I could never share—I gather in my smile. "Are you *my* grandmother? My mother's mother? The one I longed for?

Her eyes shine. "Yes."

As if we both need a quiet time to contemplate one another, neither of us says a word. But our gazes say everything.

My mind is a jumble of questions. "Did Apollo really shove you off the cliff to your death? That's what Hestos said. But it was Diokles. The priest tried to kill me, and I came back to life. It was that old priest, wasn't it? He pushed you off the cliff."

She shakes her head no and stares hard at me as if willing me to read her thoughts.

"It really was Apollo?"

"Yes."

"Was it an accident?"

A shadow crosses her eyes. "No."

"No? Why did the god murder you?" To my horror, without answering, she begins to fade. The dust swirls grow bolder and brighter, until I can barely discern my grandmother's form. I reach out. She jumps back, but not before I feel cold and a tingling that shocks me. "No. Wait. Please."

Her faded form drifts back up the trail.

"Hestos said Apollo was jealous..."

I can barely see her. She is dust and a sighing wind.

"Mama was pregnant. With me. Why would Apollo be jealous of Papa, a mortal? Hestos said that Apollo was jealous of another god. What does it mean? You know. Tell me!"

My grandmother fades into the flame-filled sky and heat shimmers. She's gone. As if she never stood before us.

"Please, only you can tell me. Is Papa my father?"

Rage sweeps through me. *How can you just leave me here? You're my grandmother!*

"You can't go! Who is my father? Come back! Tell me who my father is."

Valmiki kisses my palms and holds them to his chest. "She's gone, Thaleia. We'd better keep going. Come on, let's get out of here. Let's find Sophia."

There's nothing to do. No way to learn more. I search the path and sky. The fragile lady with her cane and blue scarf and gentle smile is gone. Grandmother was here. Now she isn't.

Valmiki walks the path beside me without a word as if he understands that in this, he can't help. For now, there's nothing he can say that will pull together my empty heart.

I'm jolted from my confused thoughts, look up just in time to keep from running into Valmiki. He hands me the near-depleted goatskin, a broad smile flashing across his face. I shake the skin to see if there's any water left and hand it over to Valmiki to have the last little swallow.

He points... downhill! We are at the top! Below us, not too far... I scan the path that twists away to the bottom of a ravine. A green patch there. Another meadow that leads to living trees. Heavy branches so covered in dense foliage that I don't see it at first. Don't see the reason for the green and the growth and the towering oaks... a river.

I collapse on the ground. "That must be the River Lethe. Kronos told me I have to cross it to find Sophia.

"Water. Thaleia, at last, water!"

"No, wait Valmiki! Kronos warned me..." Laughter. I jerk around with the gut-wrenching feeling that the laugh is Sophia's. The path rises behind me, empty to the mountain peak. Down to the lapping river, it is also empty. "Valmiki, what was that? Someone laughed."

He kneels beside me. "I didn't hear anything."

I squint my eyes against the flaring light and peer along the river's edge.

"Thaleia?"

Another laugh from down the trail. This time I'm sure.

"It's Sophia!" I jump to my feet. "Sophia? Where are you?" Scrambling down the trail, I lunge forward, catch myself, and run faster. Valmiki races after me.

"Here, I'm here."

Slowing my steps, I strain to listen. I still don't see her, but her voice seems to come from farther down the path. With tender, careful steps, I take the trail toward the river. Step by step, trying to follow her breathing, her occasional giggle.

"Thaleia, you must be hot." Sophia whispers. "Very thirsty. Come to the river and refresh yourself. Drink and rest, Thaleia."

"I can't drink from this river, Sophia."

"So, do not drink," she says airily. Her voice fades as if she also rushes to the water's edge. "Beat you to the river!"

Valmiki and I run side-by-side.

At last we reach the wide oaks.

"Sophia, where are you?"

"Here, Thaleia! Here I am!"

"Sophia, I'm coming! I'll bring you back to the Land-of-the-Living!"

"Yooou can't get me..." Her voice taunts me from the middle of the river, but Sophia is nowhere to be seen. "The water's perfect. Jump in and have a drink!"

"I can't, Sophia! It's the River of Forgetfulness... come here to me! I'll take you home."

Her laugh fades, as if coming from the far riverside. Swept from me by the current.

"Sophia!"

"You never loved me, Thaleia. It's always the same. You only care for yourself."

"No! It's not true. I've come to bring you home."

"Goodbye, Thaleia."

The sky rips with a thunderclap, closely followed by a second. A god's warning?

"Goodbye." Her voice is faint.

"No!" I plunge into the river. Valmiki jumps in, grabbing for me, but I pull away and swim hard for the far shore. "Wait, Sophia!"

I choke and cough, sputtering as water fills my mouth.

A feeling of complete contentment sweeps over me. A lifting of every worry. Every fear. Every loss. One small thought nags at the corner of my mind. I came here to find something. Someone? I shake my head. Oh well.

Valmiki and I splash each other, laughing and shouting, then sit side-by-side on the grassy bank, letting the sun dry our tunics. The sky is clear blue reflected in the quiet river, so slow and lazy that it seems more like a lake. The expanse across is so wide that, though the far bank is also studded with massive trees, they shimmer in sunlight. I'm lightheaded and dizzy.

Dragonflies flit over water, their translucent wings purple, blue, and iridescent green. They skim just across the calm surface, so close that their shadow-reflections sweep along beneath them. A bird sings from a nearby branch, long trills followed by several short chirps. Silence. The entire call repeated again. I pull the panpipes from my belt and mimic the bird. Call and response. Call and response. The water laps against the shore. I lie back on the grass and close my eyes. "I wish we could stay like this forever."

Valmiki settles back beside me; leans on one elbow and smiles at me. He folds his arms behind his head. Stares up into the branches and chuckles. "Be careful what you wish for."

"What do you mean?"

He throws his arm over his eyes to shade them. He's peaceful. Silent.

I move away from him a little to settle the stirrings I feel when he is near, close my eyes, and listen to the wind and water. Birds sing from the branch just above my head. The sun warms my body, but it's a gentle heat now.

We fall asleep.

When I wake up, white clouds shadow the sun. Gray like the inside of a cave. A cave. Why does that thought feel dark with threat? A memory of screams. A warning.

I jolt upright.

CHAPTER EIGHT
"WHERE AM I?"

A **man lies beside me on the grass. His muscular chest** lifts and falls in a rhythm of deep sleep; the arm draped across his eyes is sun-bronzed, covered with a down of black hair. I have a feeling I know him. He doesn't make me afraid, but who is he? For that matter...

Who am I? I am disoriented, my mind blank. I'm sitting beside a wide river. My tunic and a scarf covering my head are damp. I must have been swimming. *Why can't I remember?*

It is peaceful here—slow, rolling current; a light breeze rustles oak leaves, clustered on a heavy branch sweeping over the water; two swallows swoop and dive for insects—but there is a black void. A void that is me.

I wrap my arms around my shoulders and hug real flesh. I'm just a girl relaxing beside a river... with a man? Why don't I know him? Is he my husband? My love? Surely not my enemy. We wouldn't be lying together... are we together? There's space between us. We do not lie in each other's arms. My questions fly at me. I do not have a single answer. It's as if all my knowledge of my past is wiped away. "Blessed gods!"

The man rolls to his side at the sound of my voice but doesn't open his eyes. Soon, his breathing slows. I can look at him more closely. We are dressed in similar clothes: loose tunics gathered at each shoulder with metal clasps. His are bronze birds... herons I think. Mine are gold spiders. I have a strong feeling that this signifies something, something important. I almost know, but it's gone. Like a memory dipped its toes into my brain and fled.

Heat rushes to my face as I stare at his body. Muscular arms. Strong legs, his calf muscles taut like a buck's, poised to run even while he sleeps. The sandals on his feet look like they've walked a few leagues.

While I stare at him, hoping some memory will return and tell me what's going on, he opens his eyes. "Where are we?" His voice is deep, quiet with wonder and confusion.

For a moment, I'm afraid of him, afraid of this unknown land. Afraid because I have no idea who I am. My fear makes me defiant. "Who are *you*?" I scramble to my feet and face him.

My question seems to stun him. His dark eyes—a brown so deep, they seem black—un-focus. He looks around, as if the twilight sky or slow-running river could tell him, before turning back to me. There's honesty in his answer... and to my surprise, no fear. "I don't know. I have no idea where I am or who I am." Then he does something I would never have expected. He smiles. Warmth rushes through my body. I pull off my hood to let the breeze cool me.

He gasps and reaches out to touch my hair. Kneeling before me, he bows his head. "Are you a goddess?" As if he cannot resist, he pulls his gaze from the ground and stares at my hair.

I feel a tugging, strands pulling from my scalp. But when I try to brush my hair back, my fingers touch a writhing, living mass. Are there snakes tangled in my hair? With a shudder, I freeze; don't move my hand; don't breathe.

He comes to my rescue. Stands and pulls me to him.

I burst into tears. "What is it? It *moved*." It's all I can do to not scream.

"Poppies. Your hair is woven with beautiful poppies."

I relax. "Oh. I have poppies woven in my hair? But I thought I felt something move." I step back, embarrassed at this stranger's closeness.

"Not exactly *woven* in your hair... uhh... they're growing..."

Then I do scream and rush to look at my reflection in the river. A frightened *kore* stares back at me. Wide eyes. Mouth tight. Hair twisting and twining like snakes, but it's flowers. Dark red poppies lift and fall, dance and sway, framing my face. It's haunting and beautiful. But why? *Am I a goddess? It can't be. I would know, wouldn't I?*

I have no answers. All I can do is throw my head back and laugh. Twine my fingers behind my back and dance side-to-side so my reflection twirls and twists in the river.

Before long, the man stomps the riverbank, shouts and hums a song, a rhythm for our feet. The melody blends with the wind and current, taunts me with a memory of a meadow filled with sunshine and poppies and yellow daisies. A vivid image of a gnarled, burnt pine is there... Gone.

I'm laughing so hard that I finally sink down onto the sand and sit back on my heels. He still wonders if I am a goddess. I can see it in the way he looks at me. *Am I?* When he lowers himself before me, I study his face—high cheekbones above a strong, bearded chin. His black hair long and swept over his shoulders. He doesn't once take his eyes off me. I'm the one who has to look away.

"I don't know who I am." His look is bewildered as he looks upstream and down, peers across to the opposite trees, but a smile hides just behind his eyes.

"Looks like we'd better settle here for the night." The boy... no, man... what do I call him? He heads along the bank, gathering rushes still humming the same melody. When he comes back, his arms are full of long, feathery reeds just going to seed. "What do you think? Maybe up under those oaks a little away from the river? It seems safe enough here, but I suppose there may be water snakes." He laughs. There's a moment of uncertainty in his gaze as he glances out at the wide expanse of water. "What am I talking about? I have no idea where we are or what animals live here." He shifts his load of reeds and walks uphill.

"What should I call you?" My question sends another jolt of fear up my spine. It's crazy we're here. Together on this windblown beach with no idea who we are or where. Even, when. It's just *now*. I start laughing again... a little hysterical this time, unable to stop. I laugh so hard that tears fill my eyes, and I collapse onto a half-submerged log. My laughing is contagious.

He drops his rushes and sits beside me. It takes a while for us to stop. Every time we look at each other, we start up again. I finally take a deep breath. "Fine. If you insist I am a goddess, you can call me Thea. I like it. Did I always like it? What do you want me to call you?"

Our laughter broke the barriers between us, but suddenly I feel shy and look away. It doesn't really help. I feel him beside me. I know when he's looking at me... most of the time... and when he looks across the river to think....

"I don't know," he says after a long pause. "Would it please you to give me a name?"

The answer jumps into my mind, unbidden—Poet. "May I call you Poet?"

He seems pleased. With a nod, he gathers his rushes and heads back to the oaks.

I wander upstream, looking for food. I've seen fish in the slow current, flashing silver and blue just beneath the water, but I can't think of any way we might catch them. Just watching them swim by, my mouth waters, as if my blank mind holds a memory of roasted fish and figs steeped in wine, barley soup, and goat's cheese. *I'm hungry!* I walk faster away from the river, heading for a tree I spot in a clearing beyond several gnarled oaks.

It's farther than I thought, but when I enter the small meadow, an apple tree grows in the middle, its branches sturdy and spreading against the darkening sky. I peer up through the deep green leaves. There are apples! I take off my scarf and create a sling that hangs across my chest. Slipping my sandals off so I can climb better, I jump for the lowest branch. It holds my weight. Branch by branch, I pull myself up, picking the pale yellow apples and nestling them in my sling.

When I'm almost to the top, I see one long shoot—the volunteer shoot, the god's shoot. A single apple, lush and fully ripened, grows from the branch, high above all others. It alone has a blush of red. "That one is for the gods," I whisper and shimmy carefully back down the tree.

"Look what I found." Poet has woven two thick nests for us beneath the oaks. I'm pleased he put them a little ways from each other, but not too far. "Apples for dinner?"

"I filled our water skin. Do you think it will be cold tonight? How does this look?"

The melody of the river and wind, the sweet apples and Poet's humming. It occurs to me that it's strange that I feel this way, but I can't imagine anywhere else I'd rather be. Though I don't remember, I must have traveled far today. My muscles ache, and I'm still a little dizzy.

We wait for day's end. Wait for the sun to dip beneath the tree line. Wait for the sky's blue to fade, but it never does. At last, exhausted, we fall sound asleep under towering oaks on soft nests made by a poet.

It's not a restful sleep. My dreams are peopled with images, flashing chaotically through dark mist—a woman's face, scaled and withered, long boar tusks protruding from full lips, bulging eyes. Vipers for hair. A three-headed dog, foaming from fanged mouths, growling and straining. When the dog lunges at me, I jerk awake and scream. Poet rolls over to my side, holds me while the dreams vanish, nothing left but a vague unease. He rocks me side-to-side and murmurs in my ear, until I'm calm, then without a word, he goes back to his bed of rushes.

The morning is still clear. Blue sky. Light wind scented with grasses and redolent earth. Grabbing my scarf with several apples wrapped inside, I head to the river. Poet is asleep, sprawled on his back, his arm thrown over his eyes to block the sun.

I'd tossed our apple cores in the rushes, but notice they are gone, when I go down to splash water of my face. So, there must be some animals around... maybe birds. But I don't see any against the morning glare lighting the water. My dreams follow me along the riverbank, a background melody that tugs against the day's sunshine.

"You alright this morning?" Poet joins me, unobtrusive and welcome.

"Sorry I woke you with my dreams."

"Bad?"

"It seems that way, but I don't remember them now."

"Guess there's a lot we don't remember. What do you think? Should we leave, travel some, try to figure out where we are?"

"Don't you mean try to figure out *who* we are?"

"That too." His laugh is nervous.

"Let's not, Poet. It's beautiful here." I pull an apple from my sash and toss it in the air. "And we've even got these!" I don't want to tell him that it feels like my dreams, the dark mist... terror is out *there*. And I'm not ready to face it.

"Thea..."

I erupt into laughter. "I don't know if I can really deal with you calling me goddess every time you want to talk to me."

"You can get used to that if I can get used to Poet. Why in the world did that come to mind? Me, a poet? More like a shepherd, I'd say. Want to go for a swim?" He gives me a meaningful look that I, of course, completely misunderstand. When I finally do, I blush.

"Oh, right. I'll head back to the old apple tree for provisions and let you have a little privacy... but then it's *my* turn."

That's how our days pass. Swimming. Climbing the apple tree. Laughing. Sunshine on the river in the mornings and always bold sun at what should be night. Once I hear an owl and always the wind that rises up, washing the river against our beach. Sometimes it dies away. Sometimes the water reflects clouds and an occasional crow.

I don't know how long we stay beside our river, but as time passes, we grow more accustomed to each other's company.

Returning from the apple tree one time, I idly wonder what other food we might find. Of course! There're acorns scattered everywhere. I collect a scarf-full and sit beside the river, so I can watch Poet swimming in the river, diving and turning with the joy and ease of an otter. I grind the acorns, pounding them with a stone into grainy flour. I add some river water and as a final thought, chop up an apple and add it.

"What do you think, Poet?" I say as he drops beside me dripping wet and scoops some of the mush into his mouth.

"Not bad." He edges closer.

"Hey! You're wet!"

"Though, really Thea, I'm not all that concerned about what I eat, as long as I can take long walks with you, as long as we can be together."

Unable to resume casual conversation, we eat without a word and watch the river flow by, listen to the wind rustle the reeds, laugh as two herons spin and twirl in the ever-blue sky, dancing their love.

Time passes, I suppose. There is no way to tell. We sleep. We eat. We laugh. We swim and the sun never sets. The days are never hot or cold.

One morning, he is out there in the river having way too much fun. I jump in. He doesn't see me swimming out to meet him, because he is underwater. Finding his bubbles, I tread water close to where I think he'll come up. He does, sputtering and coughing.

"Thea." His eyes are solemn. He touches my cheek. The current rushes around us, cool and gentle. His face is so close. His breath. The soft caress as his lips find mine. The river roars in my ears. I see only his eyes, dark and wild and happy.

With a laugh, I shove him away and swim for shore.

He's stronger than I am and is quickly beside me. Our feet hit the shallows at the same time. We walk hand in hand across river stones, between rushes sharp as scythes, and up to our pebble beach. In silence, as if neither of us wants to break the moment, we settle onto a log he dragged over for us last night.

Poet cradles my face in his strong hands and turns me to him. "Thea. You are a goddess. You must be. You have me under your spell." He looks serious, yet a smile flickers in his warm eyes.

"I would never want to be a goddess... too much responsibility." I rest my hands over his. The silence stirs between us. My breath stops. The river flows around tree trunks stretching to water; a hawk cries, sharp and eager as it dives for a trout; the wind rustles rushes. Every sound is crisp and loud. The world echoes through me, dancing with a throbbing undercurrent. My vision blurs as I focus on the beat, wonder if I'm hearing the pulse of the earth.

It's my heart. I'm listening to my own heartbeat.

Some quiet voice whispers, *No*.

I don't want to listen to its warning... or understand.

I lean close so my lips brush Poet's. "I don't want this to end."

CHAPTER NINE
TYPHON

Then we'd better learn how to fish. Don't think that tree will give us fruit forever." He twists a strand of my hair around his finger and tickles my nose.

The days are a blur, timeless, drifting peacefully by, like the river. The season doesn't shift. The apple tree provides us sustenance, replenished each morning... and puzzlingly, there's always the apple on the god's shoot, reaching to heaven, tempting and perfect.

One morning, Poet is up and off just as he jumps from his bed.

I should get up and help, but I feel lazy. Content. I roll over on my nest and smile.

"Thea. Wake up."

I sense him sitting back on his heels and waiting... smiling? I want to tease him and pretend I'm still sound asleep, so I try to keep the smile off my face, try to lie completely quiet.

"Thea, I have a present for you."

I can't help myself, my smile erupts and my curiosity forces my eyes open. He's holding out the most perfect apple—pale yellow, with just a blush of red.

His eyes fill with pride. "I did it. I picked the god's shoot apple for you."

Is he blushing? There's a distinct likeness between the color of his face and the fruit. He looks closely at it for a moment and then deep into my eyes. I feel shaken and warm and... loved.

"I climbed to the very top." He hands me the apple proudly. It is cool in my hand, without blemish, the stem with one leaf all that is left of its connection to the parent tree.

I take a bite. The sound is like a crunch of new-formed ice. The juice bursts on my tongue like honey fresh from a beehive. It's as if there's never been an apple as sweet, as perfect as this one, gift of my beloved.

He moves so our knees touch, and I hold out the apple for him to try. There's a flash of his smile. His white teeth close just at the apple's red. He takes a large bite, the sound flies around us like bees swarming. My head spins. I feel weightless, as if I've lifted off the ground and float.

A boy and a girl sit close together beside a wide river. There is laughter. Sunshine. A rush of love between them so potent, the strands of red flow from one to the other. The girl throws back her head and laughs, and I fall once again into my own body.

"You climbed to the very top... for me?"

Poet holds forth his right hand, palm facing me.

"Poet, that apple belongs to the gods."

"It is my gift to you, goddess."

"You shouldn't say that. *Hubris* infuriates the gods."

I can't stand that he looks so crestfallen. I spread my fingers so my smaller hand fills his. "Palm joined to palm," he says. We both smile, our shared breaths fast and shallow.

But the gods are prescient; the gods see our moments of glory, our lapsed moments of overweening pride. At first I don't feel the change. It's only when lightning flashes and thunder roars just above our heads that I look around.

The sky turns murderous black. A violent wind whips the river into frenzied whitecaps. Even the sturdy oaks thrash as if their heavy limbs will rip away from the trunks. Poet and I jump up. The apple, bitten by our two mouths, falls to the dirt.

Wind pulses like massive drums pounded with a hundred hands. In the storm, in the throbbing beat, a roar grows around us. Raging like a forest fire, louder and closer. My head feels like it will split. I press my hands against my ears and whirl in every direction, trying to see past the tempest. The wind picks up sand, its grit stinging my eyes, so I can barely peer across the water.

There is a cry, as if the earth is ripped asunder and the anguish of rock and fire and molten lava escapes to the heavens. It's coming from above us, lost in storm clouds and gale. I force myself to look higher, beyond the tree-covered hills across the river, above the black clouds whirling and gathering, beyond into darkness.

A massive black-scaled viper thrusts through the billows. It opens its fanged mouth and blood red flashes among swirling mists. And there! Another viper, as large as the first, twisting and screaming and hissing, its forked tongue lashes a way through the storm.

Poet and I pull back beneath the cover of our oak.

The vipers snake from huge thighs and the heavy torso of a god. Black wings sweep aside the clouds. The monster's hair is dirty gray, matted, and wind-tangled. Pointed ears jut through. But it's the eyes that terrify me. They flash fire from his human head... and countless other heads looking wildly in every direction—lions, leopards, boars, black raging bulls, more serpents, each breathing fire. As I stare, horrified, he screams and molten lava flows from his human mouth. He must have a hundred arms hurling red-hot rocks into the river; the water hisses as it cools their lava crusts.

"You betray the gods!" The giant's voice rages like thunder. He lifts his broad wings and plummets straight for us. The vipers slither through the sand. When they are just in front of us, they stop, their heads swaying side-to-side. Their forked tongues lick in and out as if they would taste the air. The heads tower over the trees.

"Great father Zeus sent me to punish you."

Poet drops my hand. Takes one step closer to the viper and peers up at the giant.

I grab for him but miss. "Poet, no!"

"What did we do? How is it you say we betray the gods?"

"You!" The boars and leopards, all the godly animals roar at once.

Then the giant bends at the waist so his man-face is directly before Poet. His teeth are yellow; his greasy hair brushes the ground. The giant's voice is low and menacing. "You... picked... the... god's apple." With his accusation, the wind lulls and all the animals rooted to the giant's muscled torso are still.

In the quiet, I step up to stand beside Poet. "What god are you? What is your lineage? What rocky shore do you call home?"

The giant turns his head to peer down at me. He raises his eyebrows in surprise. The animal heads are restless, grunting and hissing and yowling in their eagerness to attack, but the giant bellows, "Typhon! I am Titan born of Mother Gaia. Kronos is my brother."

At the mention of the Titan's name, a certainty strikes me that Kronos sent us to this riverbank. "Your brother was the one. We do his bidding. He sent us here."

"Why?" The Titan rises to his full height; rips the clouds with his massive head; shatters the air with animal cries.

I can't think. Can't remember. I have no idea why we came here or where we were going. There's only a dim memory of a dank cave, another foul Titan... *that* one drunk. There was something he warned me about, in regards to this river. Did he warn me about his brother?

Suddenly, Typhon laughs. The sound is raw and mean. "You can't remember? The little girl can't remember? Of course you can't. Meet Lethe, the river of forgetfulness. Did you drink from this river, pitiful mortal? And now you wonder that you can't remember? You trespass *and* you steal from the gods. I think I'll bring you back with me. You shall be my plaything... *little girl*."

His mocking terrifies me more than the raging, but I know better than to show my fear.

Poet eases close beside me, so we stand shoulder touching shoulder.

"You want to play? A riddle then, godly Typhon." Poet tenses beside me, but doesn't speak, lets me talk myself into a cruel torment or freedom from this brute.

"Typhon, let us be clear. If you can guess my riddle, I will go back to your dreaded home without protest. But..." I step closer and look high up to the animal heads, to his hands with hundreds of fingers and torn, black nails, the only semblance of man he has—his beetle-brow face. Inside, I shudder, but I don't let him see. "Hear me Typhon, if you cannot guess my riddle, then you let me and my friend go free... never to pursue us again."

He vomits more molten boulders that steam and boil the river. As one beast, the animal heads roar their fury.

I do not move back. I fold my arms across my chest, glance sideways at Poet, then look back and wait for his answer. The world waits with me. No birdsong or wind, even the lapping water calms.

"I vow in the name of all the gods that I will set you free if I cannot answer your riddle."

Does mockery gleam in his eyes? I know my riddle, so close to his life. Let him try!

I take a deep breath—and another step away from Poet, until I am arm's length from the vipers' thick scales, deep-sea green etched with black.

"What is without beginning or end?
Is beloved by gods and man alike?
And is the source of all life?"

The boar and bull, leopard and serpents are deathly silent. Together they wait for the Titan's godhead to easily answer my riddle. But he looks up at the sky, downriver. He waves his hundred arms through the air, until the beach and river are windswept with raging whitecaps and whipping oak branches.

Poet eases closer and wraps his arm around my shoulders. I look over to see if he knows the answer to my riddle. Yes. It's there, shining in his eyes. Will Typhon know as easily? I shudder at the thought of him dragging me off to his vile den. I wait for what seems a very long time.

The Titan throws back his head and roars. All his animal heads hiss and bellow... one united raging of frustration.

Have I defeated him? He doesn't know?

The Titan's viper legs wrap around us. Their scales are slick and cold against my thighs. One massive snakehead stares into my face, one at Poet. Their tongues flick our necks and faces. "Time is your answer! No, Love!"

Though reluctant to move an inch, I shake my head and whisper, "No. That is not the answer."

With one last roar, the vipers slither away and carry the Titan back to the river's middle. "There's a trick! You would deceive me. If there is an answer, tell me then!"

"There's no trick, Typhon. You gave me the answer yourself. You told me that you were born of Earth and Sky. Your mother Gaia is the answer to my riddle. The Earth is round—without beginning or end. She is beloved by gods and man alike. She is the source of *your* life... indeed, the source of life for mortals, immortals, mountain, and clouds, even the fearful Hekatonkheires of a hundred arms, the vengeful Erinyes, who weave the fates of mortals and the lovely Meliai nymphs of wooded glens. She is indeed the source of all life." I step to the very edge of the river and lift both hands high above my head. "Be gone! Never trouble us again! You vowed by the gods."

His roar is deafening. He pushes his massive body into the water and thrusts upward. As if swallowed by the Void, he lifts up. His heads, flailing arms, and viper legs are absorbed and gone. Lightning flashes from the bleak hole his body cleaves in the storm clouds.

He rips a hole that tears the sky; roars as boar and lion and serpents. Their howl destroys clouds and winds, until Typhon reaches the heavens. In a brief whisper of time, he is gone. There is only a deep stillness and stars. More stars than I've ever seen filling the black sky that shimmers in the ragged hole.

Will he return with others, looking for revenge?

Poet pulls me close against him. Only then do I start shivering, shaking so violently that it seems I will never stop. He wipes the tears from my face. The clouds knit together above us, hiding the Void, swathing us in gray mist, so dense, the river fades out. Our world that was sunlight casting off the ever-flowing water, sturdy oaks and the apple tree... that world is gone. Everything is vague and gray, as are we.

"The gods want to destroy us, Poet. Where are we? *Who* are we?" I take both his hands and stare at his palms as if I could discover an answer. "Where do we go now?"

We both turn and peer across the river. The water rushes by at our feet, sighs and courses over jagged rocks we know are there, but I can't see anything.

A voice seeps from the fog. "Where is your friend?" A man's voice filled with venom. It echoes and carries across the rushing water. "You will defy Thanatossss? You think ssso? Hubris it isss. Ask who will change... not what."

I strain to see but there is nothing but swirling haze. The voice fades away, before I can locate its source. It leaves behind a bitter taste of loss. Suddenly, all I want is to leave.

"Poet, we have to cross the... Lethe? We have to find out who we are." I look around at the skeleton branches disappearing into vapors, listen to moans in the tendrils of cloud cloaking us. "What is this place?"

Without a word, Poet turns away and heads back into the trees. That's one of the things I've come to love about him. He trusts me. If I say we need to do something, he makes it happen.

A memory, one of many we have made in this place, settles over me like a blanket.

Many cycles of sleeping and waking ago, a sparrow tried to escape a hawk and flew directly into a high granite boulder. "We have to help her." I wasn't really talking to Poet, more to myself, but before I could say another word, he scrambled from our beach up a field of scree and out onto an overhanging ledge. He lifted the limp form and gently carried the bird down to me, placing it in my cupped hands, while the hawk circled above. "Is she alive?"

Poet leaned close. I closed my fingers lightly over the tiny body to lend it my warmth. "Please let her live." My fingers tingled with heat. The belly feathers felt soft against my palm. Her black feet pricked my skin. Wait. Did the bird's talon twitch? I leaned so close that my head touched Poet's. The bird's black eye opened and stared back at me. She didn't struggle or move, just turned her head from side to side. Poet and I smiled back. "Are you alright, little one?" The heat from my hand intensified, the little bird seeming completely content to rest, cupped there.

Poet stepped away and glanced skyward to be sure the hawk had flown off.

"That bird. So close to death." He shook his head side to side as if to clear it. "I remember another time... a dying bird." He squeezed his eyes shut and clasped his fingers behind his neck, then shook his head again. "I don't know. It's gone." His sadness rent my heart.

Opening my fingers, I smiled as the sparrow spread her wing feathers and cocked her head. She waited so long that I wondered if she had broken a wing. I didn't want to startle the bird. My look questioned Poet. He nodded his uncertainty. Just as I was about to close my fingers over the frail body, with one cheep, the bird flew up to the oak's highest branch, flitted to another branch closer to us, then flew off.

While I'm remembering the sparrow, Poet returns; his arms loaded with sturdy branches and vines. He spreads them across the sand, thicker ones fashioned into a square frame and thinner—woven across to form a mat.

A raft!

I head uphill to gather more branches and supple vines that grow up the oak trunks. We work the rest of the day, while the mist lifts from the water, the sky darkens, and I watch for Typhon to return. At last, bone weary, we make a supper of apples and water and stumble back to our nests for one last sleep.

In my restless dreams, I stand between massive marble columns on the broad temple steps. There is a girl in a white *chiton* running uphill away from me. Always away. She scrambles up a rocky trail between towering limestone crags. I chase after her but can never reach her, though I run until my breath is raw and ragged. Her ghostly form seems to melt into gray. Gray stone. Sky. Ragged oaks. A black form silhouettes in the moon. A man's arm raised as if to strike. A sword catches the moon's light and glints back, evil and cold.

At lassst...

I jolt awake and sit up. The sun shafts bold light across the river, now silver and peaceful. A voice taunts me, as if from my dream's edge.

You will defy Thanatossss...

I shake Poet awake. "Poet, we have to go."

There is no sleep left in him. He is fully aware. Gathering our pack and the broad paddle he made by splitting a branch, he takes my hand without a word and leads me to our raft pulled up on the sand away from the river current. Grasping my hand tighter, he helps me step onto our craft, keeping it steady. With a shove of his foot, he wades out into the water, climbs on. We're off.

The apple tree and beach, our sleeping mats beneath the grove of oaks disappear as the current sweeps us downstream and around a bend.

The voice snags in the breeze like smoke tendrils.

Not what will change, little girl. Who will change?

There is no escaping the voice. It is everywhere. The laughter cuts through the storm clouds. Cries out in the river's rush, like thousands of snakes hissing and warning. I grab the second paddle.

Mute, Poet and I pull our way downstream. Our oak grove falls behind, replaced by charred skeleton trees and black sand beaches more like ashes from an ancient fire. Even the sky is gray clouds and cries and wails of the Dead, as sad and lost as a mother whose newborn never took her first breath.

We pull with the current rushing faster and faster toward what we hope will reveal where we are. Who we are. We trust the river will bring us answers. We have no one better to trust.

The Shades' sorrow sits heavy on my shoulders. Their sighs batter my heart. But as if she is a white beacon that draws me ever forward, I remember the girl in white from my dream.

You will defy Thanatossss...

I stand up on our boat. It lurches side to side and almost pitches me overboard.

"Thea, be careful!" Poet drops his paddle onto on the raft's floor and grabs my leg to steady me. "Sit down."

I'm too angry to listen or care, and lift my oar over my head with both arms, plant my feet wide to steady the sway. "Yes! I *will* defy Thanatos. I'm not afraid of you or Death." Our boat spins round and round with the current and careens wildly, almost flipping over. It throws me down, tossing me into Poet's lap. He wraps his arms around me, so I'm not pitched into the water. The raft spins once more, tangled in the swift current, but finally steadies and races with the water's force.

I turn to look at Poet's face inches from my own. He's silently laughing! His breath is soft like a bird's wing against my cheek.

I lean forward without thinking and kiss him. Just a light brush of my lips. A thrill like Zeus' lightning jolts time to a standstill. I pull back; blood rushes to my face. There is the wind. The water's rush. A moan from the clouds of Shades and loss. There's his lips, soft and warm.

Fire rushes through my body. In that instant, I'm overwhelmed with hope and loss, a cry deep within me that feels like the tiny bird, warm and comforted and safe in my hand. I want that. Something deep inside me tells me it will never be. I shake my head to deny the thought.

Poet wraps his hand around my neck and pulls me to lean gently against him.

"I'm not, Poet. I'm not afraid of Death."

CHAPTER TEN
THE ELYSIAN FIELDS

The river soon claims our attention. We pull apart and shove our oars into the swift current; pull in tandem without a word; urge our craft to stay to the middle and skirt around boulders that would rip it apart. Gray pebble beaches pass in a blur. Lightning tears apart the storm clouds to reveal a fire sky. The scorching heat rises, always rises. Sweat drenches my chiton; my poppy hair wilts, so the flowers hang limp over my shoulders. Flames turn distant mountains to lava red.

As the river merges with another current., a raging torrent breaks over our brow. The waves sing lament—songs of fallen heroes, wives who paced tide-torn shores not knowing their warrior husbands were already food for the birds. Once again, we're surrounded by the *eidolons*, Shades lost in woe. Like the weight of boulders, their loss is crushing. It takes tremendous effort to keep pulling my oar against the waves.

I look back to see if Poet hears their cries. His face is dark and frightened. He doesn't meet my gaze. "Poet?" My voice is quiet and weak. "Poet?" I shout over the raging water, but look back quickly as one wave catches our prow and swerves us sideways against the flow. We both shove our oars into the water that turns us back. "Poet, are you alright?" This time I try to get his attention without looking around.

He doesn't answer for a long time—time enough to listen to the cries grow louder; time for the hot wind to scorch my face and bare shoulders and white thighs where my chiton is hitched up.

"We need to get ashore," he says at last and without waiting for my answer, angles his paddle so we veer toward the closest shore. I glance up to see where we're headed. Grasses grow all the way down to the river's edge. They are golden and flowing, whipping shiny and supple in the wind. There's a cove where the currents eddy, and I guide our craft toward it. Leaning my back into each pull of the oar, we make swift progress. Sand and rocks grind against our bottom. I jump out and grab the vine we use for rope, tugging Poet up onto the shore.

He alights, and together we pull the raft farther onto land, away from the water's flow. When it's lodged safely between two rocks on high ground, I grab the pack with our meager supplies, walk back down to the stream and fill my water skin, and then return to stand beside Poet. "Now what?"

He twines his fingers with mine, lifts my hand to his lips, and kisses each finger. My eyes lock with his. His gaze flickers from worry to a smile, then dances and simmers with joy. Behind me, the lapping water still moans with lament. The sorrow is palpable, but nothing can tear me away from Poet's eyes.

"Let's get away from this river." He nods uphill. With our two clutched hands, he motions toward a line of pine trees towering dark against the fire sky. "Up there?"

There's not the slightest chance I can answer him. My throat is choked with happiness, so I smile back. Hand in hand, we leave the riverbank and head toward the copse.

The slope is gentle. With each step, the cries and moans fade. Their sorrowful pull weakens, but the sky-fire whips around us, until my arms and face feel blistered with the heat. We hurry, and it doesn't take long to reach the line of towering trees. The moment we slip between two massive pines, silence surrounds us. No wind. No fire-heat. No laments.

We step into a lush meadow filled with grasses and red poppies swaying back and forth in a gentle summer's breeze. The earth is redolent with thyme and garlic.

I look around. "I know this place."

"What do you mean?"

"I've been here before." As if to prove me right, a hummingbird flitting from flower to flower lands on my shoulder. Its wing tickles my neck. It buzzes twice before my face, before it's off again to suck nectar from the flowers.

"When?"

I smile at Poet; slip my fingers from his. "I don't know." Sinking into the soft grasses, I run my hand back and forth across the gold tassels.

The rest of our day is filled with gathering pine nuts and dandelion greens for our supper.

I pick sweet yellow kernels from the open pinecones, careful not to prick my fingers. My hands are sticky with sap.

Poet sits beside me in the grass and helps.

I make an effort to distract my mind from the lightheadedness and heat. My skin prickles, as if it yearns to touch him, to swallow the air between us. I want to talk, but my words choke. I swallow and try again. "Poet, where do you think we are?"

He looks around the meadow. I try to see it as he does, without this lingering sense that this is a familiar land. Dark pines encircle us, form a powerful barrier that protects us from Outside. This magical glade is the opposite of that woeful river with the moaning Shades adrift in the storm winds and the heat... such a relief to have deep blue sky and gentle breezes, smells of fertile earth and herbs and garlic... and wine? Why do I smell wine? And goat? I whirl to look behind me toward an old charred pine.

I'm struck by the feeling that someone is watching us. I startle, when a lizard slips off a rock where it soaks in the sun's warmth and scurries beneath a clump of poppies.

Poet wraps his arm around me and laughs. "A little jumpy?"

"Where are we? What is this place?"

"I've been thinking about that. Why don't we have any memory of who we are... or where we are?" He plucks and chews on a long blade of grass.

"When Typhon mocked me, he said we drank from the River Lethe. Said that's why we can't remember. I've been trying to remember— River Lethe. It's there in the front of my mind. I can feel it, but just can't hold on to it. Every time, it seems like it floats to the surface like a water lily just out of reach. Poet, I think I know where we are. I can't tell you who we are or how we came here, but I may know where we are. Just think about it—fire and misery and hundred-headed monsters with viper legs? Shadow people who threaten us? Look at you! Look at me." I lift his hand and trace his palm lines. "Everything about this place is alien to us... to the way you make me feel."

I stand up and turn in a slow circle. The afternoon sun is warm on my uplifted face. "But not here. And we're safe here. I don't know how I know that... but I do." I pick a poppy, kneel before Poet, and tuck the stem behind his ear. "There, now you have poppies in your hair too."

He rests his hands on my shoulders and squeezes. "Where do you think we are, Thea?"

Sitting back and crossing my legs, I look closely into his eyes. "The way we feel about each other." I kiss the inside of his palm. "Part of me thinks that we must be man and wife." I can't help it; I blush and turn away as if suddenly interested in finding a lizard.

"I think so too." He cups his hand beneath my chin and turns my face back to look at him. "But where are we? You know, don't you?"

"I believe we both died. I think this is the afterlife." I hold my breath and wait to see what he thinks, but he doesn't speak, so I continue. "It makes sense. My memory is fragmented, but there are shards, like broken pottery. I've been trying to put the pieces together. There's a memory of a woman... my mother? She walks beside me down a path to a crystal spring."

There's more that I'm reluctant to say. There's a feeling of holy communion between the woman and me. A glimpse. Nothing more.

But it's a dark communion that holds fear. I don't want to spoil our moment, but I must.

I press on. "I remember something about a holy spring being the mouth to the Underworld. I think I remember a warning that I should never swim in the spring?"

I shake my head and pull away from Poet, rub the back of my neck. "It's so frustrating! They're glimpses, but I can't make sense of them... and I still don't know who I am!" Tucking another poppy behind his ear, I say, "Or who you are."

I'm not sure I want to share my last thought. I just want to wrap his arms around me and ignore it. It's beautiful here. We have each other. "What difference do memories make?"

He takes my fingers and holds them to his lips. "Poet?" My eyes fill with tears. There's only our knees touching and a soft breeze warm on my wet cheeks. And somewhere... is it close or far away? I hear a flute. My poppies lift and sway. Five lilting notes. Silence. Five more that sing in my heart and fill me with a yearning that urges me to tell Poet everything that I feel. That I know.

"Poet, I think we died. I believe we are in Erebos, the Realm of Hades... and this?" I pull my fingers at last from his lips and sweep my arm to take in the glade. "Are we in the Elysian Fields? Is this our reward for a life well lived?"

I sidle over to lean my head on his shoulder. "If you're my reward, I don't care if I'm dead." A fragrant wind sweeps past us; tangles my poppy hair; wrinkles my nose with the smell of rutting goats. Why? I look around, but the meadow is filled only with sunshine, rustling grasses, thyme, and wildflowers. And peace.

"If this is the Underworld, life after death... why do you feel like you've been here before?"

I sit up straight and move away. "I don't know, Poet. It doesn't make sense. But... I might have met someone here. Someone important. There's a memory, just at my mind's edge, but there's a barrier."

The towering trees rustle in a gust of wind. "Like these pines keep out the fire sky and storm. And, Poet?" An uneasiness urges me to move away, so there's some space between us. I study my hands clutched in my lap.

"What is it, Thea?"

I'm distracted by the flute. The music is closer now. Quick, percussive notes that call to me. "Poet, do you hear that?"

"What?" He jumps to his feet, turns in a slow circle. "I don't hear anything." He kneels before me. "But you do, don't you? What am I listening for?"

"I don't know. Maybe it's nothing. Just a bird." I smile. The music fades, but a feeling sweeps over me like a cloud covering the sun, and I know I have to explain everything. Words spring unbidden and demand to be said. "There's something else about this meadow, Poet." I take a deep breath, not sure I have the courage. "My destiny is here... but I don't think it's with you."

He takes my hands and squeezes. There's fear in his eyes, but he lets me go on.

"I... I hate it. And I have no idea what this means, but... I know. I wish I did not."

"Thea, no, you don't. Neither of us does. But I'd rather be right here beside you than anywhere else. Right here. *That's* something I know. It feels right." His eyes urge me to trust him.

"I want to believe you, Poet." I stand up and look down at him, try to give him a smile. Let's just take each moment as it comes..." I laugh. "Who knows? Any moment might bring a snake-man or a Titan."

Time passes quickly, while we gather mustard greens, dandelions, sweet mint, and figs off a scraggly tree we find at the meadow's far end, rooted in a patch of dirt caught between limestone boulders.

The longer I wander searching for edible plants, the stronger the feeling that I know this place. It's a comforting feeling. Like I belong here. Poet disappears once more to the pines' shadows and returns, his arms full of sweet-smelling laurel that he dumps in a heap before turning slowly to look at me.

"Thea?" His voice is low. "I don't want you to ever leave me. A destiny where we're not together is unacceptable." He smiles. Holds his hand out to me. In a daze, I cross the two steps between us and take it. His hand is warm and strong, gentle and irresistible. He pulls me to sit beside him and cradles my face with his hands. Resting his forehead against mine, he holds himself completely still. We sit back on our haunches as a sun-storm surrounds us, sparking motes of blue, yellow, and indigo in a dancing cloud.

A whirring fills my ears, like spinning chariot wheels or a thousand hummingbird wings stroking the air.

"Thea, the gods brought us together."

"No. The gods did not," I say before I have time to think. "I can't explain how I know, but my destiny is to stand alone before the gods. There's something I have to do. It's here in this magic meadow and the wind and the rushing river." I look around hoping for a sign. "It's here. And it will find me. My destiny will seek me out..."

A hurtful shadow crosses his eyes.

"Please understand."

"Thea, what are you saying? You know..."

"You must not!" A deep, male voice behind us forces us apart. We jump to our feet and whirl around.

CHAPTER ELEVEN
ORACLE, HUMMINGBIRD, AND A SATYR

A **man stands before us with arms crossed and sandaled** feet planted wide in the meadow grasses. He's tall, massive in height and shoulders, dressed like a foreigner. In his middle years, yet somehow young and old at the same time, he has dark, curly hair and a black beard. Thick, red robes drape from strong shoulders and gold braids rope around his taut neck and across his chest. His frown softens. I'd swear I see a smile in his eyes, but he remains stern.

My skin prickles. I jump to my feet to face him. Like a great wave that comes thundering in at the mouth of some heaven-born river, I understand that I know this man. From before. When I knew who I was, he had power over me. I struggle to remember more but fail. I take a deep breath, square my shoulders.

"How do they call you?"

"Parmenides."

"From what rocky shore do you come? Who are your parents?"

"Many rocky lands I've called home. As for my lineage, it is without end. None ever called me child, for my time on this earth spans many lifetimes. I step through Death's Veil beyond Time."

"Through Death's Veil? Then we *are* in the Elysian Fields?"

"What do you think?"

My voice shakes as I whisper, "Please, tell me if you know. Where are we?"

He grabs my shoulders and squeezes. "Think, child. Who are you? Why are you here?"

But I can't think. The moment he touches me, images rush through my mind. *A high mountain, glaring light casts off limestone cliffs. A temple with columns alive with bark and gnarled oak branches. Racing clouds above the letter E carved into wood and mounted on the lintel.*

"How do I know you?"

Dropping to one knee, I seize the stranger's knees in supplication. Who is he? I have no idea, other than he is Hierophant, a man of wisdom and power. Poet must sense it as well. He kneels beside me and bows his head.

The man rests his hand on my head. "I'm here to help you find your way."

"Where?" I'm not sure I want to hear his answer.

"Where you must go." His eyes warn me against further questions.

Standing slowly, reluctantly, I search the stranger's eyes for knowledge. Understanding. Answers. "You know who I am, don't you?"

With a long look at Poet and back to me, his stare is awkward, angry. At last he answers with a question instead of the response I'm hoping for. "Don't *you*? How do they call you? What rocky shore do you call home?" A longer pause, while his eyes rake mine. "And why are you here... both of you?" He glances at Poet again but turns his gaze back to mine as if reluctant to look away. "In this land of Death. Shades. Do you know why you're here with poppies dancing in your hair?" He lifts one flower between his fingers. A slight smile lights his eyes and fades.

I look away. What can I tell this Oracle? What does he have to do with me? My heart pounds, my breath threatens to choke me. Unable to meet his gaze, I pull my hood over my unruly hair and sip from my water skin.

The stranger lifts my chin so my eyes meet his and rests his left hand on my chest. Warmth spreads through me at his powerful touch, flushing my face. This stranger's touch is home. Safety. Love. Before I can question him, there is a flash of light. Too fleeting. In that blinding light, I see—*a girl scrambling over boulders. She looks back at me. The terror on her face is raw. I hear hoarse panting as if she is pursued. A sword cutting through the night air over her head.*

And it's gone. I return to my senses shaken and confused. Looking up, I search for meaning in the stranger's gaze. His eyes are so dark, they look black like coal, like a midnight sky. He knows.

"What..."

His whispered answer is gruff. "Do you know who you are now?"

I shake my head, numbed by what I saw. By a truth I can't comprehend.

"We must leave. Follow me." Without another word, he turns his back to us and heads off toward the meadow's boundary.

I glance at Poet. We gather the water skin and trail the stranger to the meadow's edge. Stopping beside the charred pine, I resettle my pack and push off my hood. The hummingbird returns; flits from poppy to poppy. The meadow behind us is filled with its whirring wings and laughing chirps.

A branch snaps off to my right.

I glance over. Nothing. "Poet, did you hear anything?"

He nods, but looking ahead at our guide, doesn't reply out loud.

A deep laugh erupts behind me.

I whirl around. Nothing. *Why do I know who this is?* But I *don't* know. Flute music trickles like a chuckle through the grass.

Parmenides freezes and turns slowly to look at me. His eyes bore into mine with a smile, a question he doesn't ask. He glances at the flute tucked into my sash.

The music erupts. Black branches on the charred pine sprout twisting poppy tendrils. Green and alive like snakes, the stems twine round the ruined trunk. Huge poppies burst in the sky, towering overhead, filling the air with a cloying sweetness, until I think I will faint with the smell. The flute music races staccato and wild through the poppy forest, sweeping with it a smell of garlic and musky wine.

The hummingbird slips between the soft, red flowers. Dips its beak into one black center. Flits to another. Races high above the massive blooms and turns to dive straight at me. At the last second, the tiny green bird, straining its fragile red throat to lift its head, lands lightly on my shoulder.

My vision blurs. Buzzing like a bee swarm fills me and tingles from my chest to my head. I clutch my ears, but that only seems to trap the music and bee screams inside.

Louder. Louder.

The giant poppies twist around me. The smell is overwhelmingly sweet. I drop to my knees.

A trance overcomes me.

A spider web strands from each of my fingers, my toes, my head and shoulders—a great web sparkling with dew and light.

The Oracle chants as if from a great distance. Toi pant' onom' estai—Its name shall be everything.

A sun-bronzed hand thrusts from the shadows, grabs my shoulder. Ebony-black fingernails dig into my forearm. Panic fills me. My feet feel like they grow tendrils snaking into the dirt, rooted with poppies and wild grasses. I can't breathe or cry out.

A hoofed leg steps from behind the pine. I don't move.

A satyr squats before me, his muscled thighs matted with bristling fur that curls over hooves. His broad chest—sturdy as an old oak—heaves.

The air between us is charged with light and a hum like a swarm of bees.

I gasp.

I understand.

He is the god Pan, his eyes full of me. They know me. As no one understands me, this god, smelling of goat and thyme and garlic, his eyes laughing, scheming... this god sees into me. I smile back at his gap-toothed grin. His tongue works a hole where one of his front teeth is missing between full, smiling lips.

When I open my eyes, a satyr squats in the high grasses before me, both hands linked behind his back. His broad smile reveals a gap in his front teeth. The tiny green hummingbird with long black beak and scarlet throat flits around first one of the satyr's stumpy horns, then the other before deciding to land on his curls, golden bristles between the two.

It's not a dream.

"Pan."

He rests his palm against my chest. "Yes, this is true. But do you know who you are?"

There's a burning where his hand rests. And longing. And for a faint flicker, a thought: *I am...* but it's gone before I can clutch it. "No. No, I don't."

"Don't you remember? Know thyself? And now nothing?"

Shames sweeps over me as if in some way, I've failed.

Parmenides steps beside me and raises his arm in greeting. "Pan, it is an honor."

"Ah, Parmenides, I see you're leaving? Why so soon?"

The satyr steps away from me and bows, dancing his feet... well, his hooves. For this is the goat-man—hairy legs with cloven hooves, small horns that grow from his wrinkled forehead, pointed ears. My vision brought to life.

I kneel before him and bow my head. The poppies in my hair are frenzied and wild.

One step, hoof against dirt. Pan is so close that I smell his breath, warm with garlic and wine and wild thyme. He takes my hands and draws me to my feet. "You need not bow." He must have seen the confusion on my face, because he bursts out laughing and releasing me, leaps around us in wild circles. The hummingbird swoops and dives above him, landing at last on his bare shoulder when the satyr stops before the Oracle. "You found her. I planned to keep her here." He smiles over at Poet who drops to one knee. "Keep them both... they make a lovely couple, yes?"

"Why would you do that? There's the prophecy... *your* prophecy, Pan. Why stop her now?" the Oracle says.

"And why not? She's fulfilled her destiny. She stopped the Persians. Delphi is safe."

"And Athens? What about the Acropolis? The League? Her work is not done."

I gasp. "What do you mean, *my work*? What do you both seem to know about me that I don't? You have to tell me! Who am I?"

Instead of answering, the Oracle steps around me to stand before the satyr. "They drank from the River of Forgetfulness."

Pan crosses his arms and smiles. "Clearly."

"She needs to know."

"There's nothing you can do."

Parmenides rests his hands on my head. "Know thyself, child." My poppy hair wraps around the Oracle's wrists, but he doesn't pull away. "Think, girl!"

Slow and sinuous, the poppies unwind. The hummingbird hovers between us—mesmerized by our waiting—then darts off.

"Parmenides, I sense you are my friend... but I have no memory of you. I feel... no, I *know* destiny links us... You ask me who I am. With all my heart, I would answer you, but I don't know. Wise One, can't you tell me? You know who I am."

Parmenides looks at the satyr before he says with a low and broken voice, "It would do you no good. Your name, your identity, your destiny is for you to know. No one can give that to you. No one. Not even the gods." The Oracle starts to turn away but looks back when the satyr speaks.

"Where would you take them?" Pan says.

"Away from temptation."

"Is it not nature for a boy... a girl?" The satry wraps a forelock curl around his finger and stares up at the Oracle.

"She is destined." He scowls back.

"And of what importance is destiny? Tell me that. Doesn't she get to choose?"

"She chose. It was you who gave her the choice. She *chose* Pan."

"So, that's it? One choice, and her life is one endless path, predestined to only go one-way? Never again can she decide to go left or right?"

"She is the child, blessed to the gods, beloved by Dionysos. She cannot destroy that honor, that trust."

"And what is she, a scrap of rotted meat." Pan stomps his hoof. "Thrown away? Left as carrion for the birds? What...is...this...girl?"

Parmenides grabs my hands.

The moment he touches me, memories and scraps of my life flit through my thoughts. *My head fills with buzzing like a bee swarm; flute music; girls chanting in high cadence. And visions of death—soldiers falling off high cliffs into a broiling sea; priests' burning bodies tumbling from the wall of a polis; screams. Screams. Death howls like scavenger coyotes ripping flesh and screaming to a night sky that doesn't care.*

"No! Why am I seeing this?" I whirl in circles desperate to be free. Everywhere there is death, shrieks of the dying, a smell of blood. "No!"

"Now? *Now* you know?"

"No. Leave me alone!" I square my shoulders. "And I don't *want* to know. I want to stay here, with Poet!"

The Oracle looks back at Pan. "She *must* remember."

"Leave her be. Let her rest. Let her stay."

"Pan, you know Hellas needs her. Can't I just tell her who she is?"

"Not here. That may work in your temple, in the land above where the sun rises and birds sing as winter strays to spring... but not here. There is no order in Erebos. No time. No logic." Pan cracks his knuckles and looks away from us. "No hope."

"No, I don't accept that. I cross the boundaries of Life and Death at will. The rules in this Land-of-Shadows don't apply to me!" Parmenides' voice rises in anger, and he snatches up my hand.

"You cannot return the girl's identity to her. She must discover it on her own."

"How? How does she do that?" The Oracle steps away from me and stands a breath away from Pan but he doesn't back down.

"Let the girl be. Let her stay with me. She's done enough."

Parmenides rests his hands on the satyr's shoulders. "Pan, I know. No one appreciates more than I that this girl has suffered. That she could live here in your magic meadow, with you and this boy. With beauty and love. But, Pan, she's needed in the land above. She will face death and indescribable horror, but maybe, just maybe, she can make a difference. You have marked her as the chosen one. The one to bind gods and mortals. You *know*, Pan. She can't hide here in Erebos."

The Chosen One? What are they talking about?

Pan sighs and says, "Ask Tiresias. Ask the blind seer."

"Ah, then they must travel to Tartaros to find him."

"Yes. Tartaros. In the blackest, deepest region of Erebos, you'll find the man who twice lived—the wise one born as man who lived seven years as woman. He, only he, can guide the girl."

I'm... angry, now. Scared, yes. But anger is thick. "Stop talking about me as if I'm not here! I may not know who I am, but don't ignore me. Don't decide what I should do as if I have no say!"

Startled, both Pan and the Oracle turn and look at me, eyes wide.

"Well, child, what do you suggest?" Parmenides is the first to speak.

Pan plops down on a rock, an amused tinge to his gaze, settles in as if he'll wait all day.

"Poet and I were fine before you two showed up." As if to prove my point, I smile at Poet. "We found food, water... we liked being together." I shake my head to clear the buzzing that starts again as I think about the visions. "It's beautiful in this meadow. We were happy... until you found us. Just leave us alone!" I shove my hood back as if that will clear the buzzing and the screams.

I feel dizzy, and gag. A black cloud sweeps across my vision. But I shake my head to clear it and refuse to fall into a trance. Throwing my arms wide to the blue sky, I scream. "Leave me alone!"

But it's pointless. I am powerless as long as my past is a blood-spattered fog. The death I saw in my vision still haunts me. I sink down on the path and stare at the hummingbird flitting from poppy to poppy.

Tears fill my eyes. "Tell me what I must do! I'll do anything to stop that horror. But who am I? What is the prophecy... my prophecy?" I look from the satyr to the Oracle. "Why me?"

"First, you must remember who you are, child. Let us seek the blind seer. Only that." Parmenides touches the top of my head, a gesture that sends a jolt of energy through my body.

It stuns me and I don't move a muscle, just try to hold on to the grass. "Don't you want to know who you are?"

He's right. I want to know. I *need* to know. I look at Poet. Without a word, we move over and stand on either side of the Oracle.

He nods and brings his fingertips to his chest and bows his head to the satyr then strides up the narrow path.

We step, across an invisible boundary from the sun-filled meadow into a dead forest. As if a great fire swept through and destroyed everything, our path leads through charred trees and gray skies and a heavy silence.

Mist swirls, obscuring the path. Poet and I follow close behind Parmenides as the trail winds between scorched pines. I look back over my shoulder hoping to see Pan again, but he's gone.

We head downhill through a misty land, shadowed with ghost tendrils of moss draping from scrub oak. It grows hotter with each step as we twist down beneath a bleak sky licked occasionally with flame and smoke, only to clear momentarily to reveal heavens like a blood-red wound.

Pacing step by step in Parmenides' footprints, more than anything, I want to take Poet's hand. If only we could walk together through this dismal place. Then I could manage, maybe even feel brave. But instead, we walk stiffly apart past charred trees and withered asphodel with drooping stems, and work for each breath.

There's a note, then another. A faint whisper of music fractured by wind and the sky-fire roar. I slow my steps, calm my heart and breath; I pace down and down, focus on nothingness to try and hear with something other than my mind and ears. I feel only laughter. It bubbles in my chest, deep and lusty, warm and kind. Is Pan following us? What is my prophecy? There are too many questions. If they know who I am, why don't they just tell me? Why am I here? Who is this stranger I'm following? I'm trusting? I glance at Poet striding beside me, always careful to not touch me, but always close. Always *here*.

And who are you, Poet? Why does my hand want to hold yours but won't?

CHAPTER TWELVE
SEEKING THE BLIND SEER

I **don't know how long we follow Parmenides. Sometimes it** feels like we're walking in circles, spiraling down. Nothing changes. The Oracle's back remains just ahead on the narrow path. There's almost no vegetation. Gray cliffs, streaked with red, tower over us. Dead vines trail the steep rock. Roiling thunderclouds finally fill the sky, claps of thunder and lightning replacing the flames, cooling the blistering heat. We pass a husk of a tree that looks all too familiar.

"Poet?" I keep my voice low. "We passed this one before, didn't we?"

"You may be right, but Parmenides knows this land, doesn't he?"

"I hope so."

We walk a long time without talking, until the Oracle stops and says, "We'll make our camp here for a few hours."

I collect stones for a fire ring. Poet gathers sticks, while Parmenides sits with his back to us and whispers words or a chant that I can't understand. The Oracle rubs two stones together to spark the brush into flame. We eat the last apples. Without a word, exhausted, I wrap my cloak around me to cover my face from the endless twilight and fall into a sleep deep as death.

My eyes open to study the back of my hand, gritty with soot, black soil under my nails. The moment suspends. Solitary. Silence so stony, I'm not sure my breath is my own. It lifts and falls with the shawl wrapped tightly around me like a cocoon. Now I remember.

Poet sleeps a little distance away, between us trammeled asphodel flowers, grit, and gray rocks. The Oracle sits beside him, his back to me. Chanting the same words over and over, in with a deep breath and out. "*Toi pant' onom' estai. Toi pant' onom' estai.*" Its name shall be everything.

Is that what woke me?

No. My dream—I walk through charred forest that levels to a sandy beach. A broad river, black and boiling, acrid steam lifts from whitecaps, roaring like a sea monster before me. Poet stands close. We both stare at the seething water as if waiting for the gods to intervene. In my dream, I know I need to cross... but how? A hummingbird is the only spot of color—iridescent green chest and ruby red throat—like a fire's spark against the bleak rocks and dead flower stalks. As dead as time. As dead as hope.

As if he knows I'm awake, the Oracle stops chanting and turns around to smile at me. "You're awake."

"Yes."

"Feel better?"

I look around at a gods-forsaken land, where deep black shifts to muted gray. Mist rises from cracks in gray stone, tendrils that blend with a smoky sky. Gray against gray like a dawn that refuses to come. Gods-forsaken. But it's not. Pan is here.

"Was I right? You found us in The Elysian Fields, didn't you? What else could be so beautiful in this bleak world?"

He watches me as if waiting for me to say more. To understand more. He nods.

"And the satyr-god Pan... he lives there?"

"Sometimes."

I sit up, cross my legs, and tuck my tunic over my knees, trying to think. At last I look up. "I've been there before. I have met Pan."

"Yes. This is true."

"Except, this is The Underworld. Why would I have been here before? If I was... I must have been... I would have died?"

"You're not dead now, and you were in the sacred meadow with the nature god."

"Why? You know. You do. But you're not telling me the truth."

"What is truth in this land without time? A land of shadow-truths. What can I tell you that will explain this?" He sweeps his arm wide gesturing to flames shooting high above distant mountain crags. Mist swirls around his arm.

Poet stirs and rolls over; looks from me to the Oracle and props himself on his elbow. "Oracle, tell us, please, who is this Tiresias? Why does Pan want us to find him?" He stands and brushes dirt from his tunic. Kneels between us. "Why is he blind and yet a seer?"

The Oracle presses his palms together and bows slightly to me and then once more to Poet. "Many have sought advice from Tiresias. Even Odysseus, the wily warrior who fought for the Greeks at Troy. When he could not find his way home to Ithaka after the war, the goddess Circe told him to travel into this world of death and find Tiresias. She told him that only the blind prophet could tell him precisely how to return to his homeland."

At the mention of death, Poet sidles closer. Our shoulders touch, but our eyes don't meet.

"Why is he blind?" Poet says. Warmth like sweet honey strands between us. Without looking at him, I move a breath away.

"Was it the gods?" My words are angrier than I meant. Taking a deep breath, I try to calm myself. "The gods have their plans. But Tiresias. He's blind. And dead. *Was* it the gods plan?"

"It was Hera. She blinded Tiresias. I'll tell you the story from the beginning, but first, I'm hungry. How about some of those apples in your bag? And just over there..." He points back down the trail, mist almost obscuring it. "I didn't expect to find it here." He sweeps his arm indicating the charred land. "But there's a small spring. Beside it I found mint, bright green plants tucked beneath a rock-ledge. You can't miss them. If you'll bring me some, I'll make some tea."

Before leaving our warm circle, I add sticks to the fire. Evidently, the Oracle has kept it burning. "Parmenides, did you sleep?"

He laughs and looks at me long enough to get me to stop fussing with the fire. "What is awake? What is asleep? Which is the dream? Which do you call true?"

I smile back and don't even attempt to answer. He has a point. When we're asleep and dreaming, does that feel any less real than what I know with my waking senses? I look around and laugh. "My dreams certainly feel more real than this strange land."

He doesn't say anything, just lets the mystery hang between us.

I head back down the path to look for the mint. *Everything about this stranger, this Parmenides, is a mystery. Why am I certain I know him? Why is he guiding us? What is the prophecy he spoke of?*

Too many questions... all unanswered. But in my gut, a feeling kindles that he's my friend.

I don't see anything alive at first, only more blackened trees. Stark cliffs disappear into smoke like a soot-leavened cloud. At last, a bright green bush peeks out from beneath an overhanging rock. I pluck a leaf—fresh and alive; its sweet smell overwhelms me, as if the plant juices have their own memory. A vision sweeps through me like ice in my blood, until I shake and the forest swirls with red and orange: *Screams cut the air. A young girl curls into a tight ball. Is she a water nymph? She covers her head with her arms and cries out for mercy. A tall woman, radiant and powerful, pulls the girl's hair and kicks her with vicious thrusts to her ribs and arms and head. Though the maid begs and cries out for mercy, the woman overpowers her and screams in a rageful voice. "Minthe, keep your gaze off my husband! Hades is mine. Stay away from him!"*

Queen Persephone!

The girl digs her fingers into the dirt and tries to pull her battered body to the stream. To end it all? To find escape in death? The moment her hand touches the water, she transforms into a mint plant.

The battering stops.

With a fearsome smile of triumph, the goddess bends and with one graceful movement, picks one leaf from the plant. Draws it to her nose to inhale deeply, before turning away.

I shiver back to my wakeful self, shaken and angry. Why would a goddess want to destroy a helpless girl? What is it between the gods and us? Parmenides says all is the gods' will. This cruelty? If the gods will not help us, if they struggle with our same mortal jealousies and anger, how can we hope to find our destiny?

I see the mint leaf in my hand with new eyes. The girl gave her life to save her soul. She lives in this simple plant.

I cradle the leaves in both my hands, grateful for her gift.

But why did the goddess hate her? Destroy her?

Was it love of life or fear that changed the girl into a fragrant plant? The goddess' attack seems senseless, horrible. Yet, from it the girl changed to this herb that brings comfort to many. Must we suffer to transform? Is it worth it? And is this delicate weed, is it still the nymph Minthe, her soul? I smell it once more and am swept up with sadness.

I am here. I am alive. I will find Tiresias. I will survive this Land-of-Death.

My shoulder itches, so I tuck the flute away and scratch my back against a jutting rock. Happy to find some relief, I sit back against the stone, close my eyes, and hold the mint bouquet up to my nose.

"Issss the little girl sssssad?"

I jump to my feet. A figure drifts from the steam—wavering with the pale light—a priest in formal robes. Recessed eyes glare at me over a hooked nose, his lips a red snarl. My poppy-hair writhes and flares like vipers... a warning.

But if there's one thing I've learned in the Underworld, it's best not to show fear.

I straighten my back and take a step toward the Shade. "Who are you? From what dark land do you come? Who are your parents?"

"Would you not want to know who you be, little girl?"

My throat tightens. I can't answer. Only nod.

He laughs a sigh. A moan. A shriek. "Know thysssself. Only you can ssssay who you be."

"No! You know who I am."

"Know thysssself, little girl. In your heart. What be your nature. Know thysssself..."

An angry itching on my back distracts me.

The priest smiles his poisonous smile and nods as if understanding something I do not.

"Tell me!"

"Why are you here, little girl? You tell me. In this land of death and losssss. Did you lossssse something? Are you maybe looking for ssssomething? Sssssomeone?"

"I'm looking for the blind seer Tiresias."

"Ahhhhh, the old man, hated by the godssss. Loved by the godssss."

"Do you know where he is?"

"Yessss, he be wisssse. He tell you who you be, little girl?"

I don't like the sneer in his voice. His mocking tone. My answer is loud and determined. "Not yet, but he will!"

"Who gave you that necklasss you wear around your pretty neck? Tell me that, and look in your heart, little girl."

I touch the woven spider web. Someone I love gave me this necklace.

"Issss ssssomeone dead? Maybe it be you to blame?"

Is he right? Did someone die because of me? I would know, wouldn't I?

"I am change, little girl. I follow. I lead."

"What will you change?"

"Not what. Who. Who will change?" With that, he turns his back to me and fades into the vapors. His voice dies away. "Know thysssseellf..."

I bring the herb bouquet to my nose, wanting... no, *needing* something real. The mint smells like deep forest, alive with hope. I shiver with a thought—*If I ever learn who I am, wandering this black and charred land, will I be glad?*

My feet carry me back to our circle hearth. I settle between Poet and the Oracle. Hand him the mint and wait, while he tears the leaves into boiling water. I should tell him about my encounter, but I don't even want to think about the Priest.

"Oracle, when I gathered the mint, I thought I saw a nymph."

He stops ripping the leaves and looks up.

"Well, a vision of a girl. I think she was a nymph. A goddess attacked her."

"Minthe, a naiad of the River Cocytus. Hades loved her. Jealous, Queen Persephone attacked the girl.

"I hate her! How could she? Minthe was just a girl. Why blame her? It was Hades' fault. How could the queen be so vicious?"

"Was her anger directed at the wrong person? Was it not also the Lord-of-Darkness who kidnapped his queen; forced her to live in the Land-of-Death? Is she not also to be pitied?"

"But that poor girl..."

"From the queen's dark fury, we have mint to carry us both to the dark side of death and to divine light." He holds up the torn leaves. "This sweet-smelling plant takes us to unseen worlds."

Parmenides sings low over the steaming water and continues ripping the fragrant leaves.

I can't understand the words, but I can feel them. They rumble through my chest like my body is the thunder following lightning.

I take Poet's hand. We lace our fingers. Unsettled, I inhale a deep breath of mint, wood-smoke, and river moss, moldy and damp.

Parmenides stops chanting, and I pull my hand from Poet's. Blood rushes to my face, when the Oracle kneels before me and presents the cup with both hands.

"Never forget that mint is a gift from the nymph of the river that flows through the dark Underworld. Here, sip this tea. It is used in the sacred kykeon drink mixed with fermented barley for initiates in the Eleusinian Mysteries. They carry it to the gods to grind into a paste with rosemary and myrtle for our death rites."

"What will happen if I drink this tea made for the gods? Will I die? The gods can be vicious." A tightness in my chest grows as I remember Queen Persephone kicking the girl.

"There's no point in fearing a god's brutality. If the gods have plans for us, worrying about them ahead of time won't help."

I hold the warm cup against my cheek, then take the first sip. My body flushes with warmth; a jolt courses my spine... but it's over so abruptly, I might as well have never felt it at all. I take another sip. Nothing. The black rocks tower over us like jutting teeth. Vultures swoop and circle. "Parmenides, you were going to tell us more about Tiresias."

"And so I was." The Oracle gifts me with a twisted smile. "One day, walking on Mount Kyllini in Arkadia, Tiresias came upon two snakes copulating. He struck the two serpents with his staff. Furious with Tiresias, Hera, queen of the Olympians, cursed him."

"What was her curse?" Poet says.

"She turned him into a woman."

"And that's a curse?" I cross my arms and wonder, not for the first time, exactly what the priests and gods think about women.

The Oracle's smile spreads across his face, until at last, it's so wide that he breaks into laughter. "Well, Hera thought it was! At any rate, Tiresias spent seven years... or so the legend tells us... in the body of a woman. With a woman's heart and thoughts... and desires. There are those who say she became a priestess to Hera. Others say she bore a son and daughter. Still others... and they claim to have personal knowledge... they say she was the finest prostitute there ever was! Time passed. One day, out of boredom, Hera and Zeus were arguing to pass the day. Hera insisted that men gained the most pleasure from... well, intimate matters. Zeus argued that women did. To settle the matter, they decided to ask Tiresias."

"Because he has lived both as man and woman," Poet says.

"Exactly."

Something rustles just beyond our fire's light.

Is it the priest-Shade?

My breath comes fast and shallow, straining beneath my ribs. I look up to see the Oracle staring at me, and try, try with all that I am to focus on his words. Try to push the Shade from my mind. "What did Tiresias say?"

"He sided with Zeus. Should have been more careful."

"Why?" I whisper my question.

"Hera blinded him for disagreeing with her."

"Hera blinded Tiresias. Persephone assaulted Minthe. Are these our gods? The ones we trust?"

But before Parmenides can answer, Poet interrupts. "What does all this have to do with Thea?" There's an edge to his voice.

The Oracle ignores him. "Zeus was sorry that Hera blinded Tiresias. He felt responsible, because Tiresias sided with him. So, he granted him the gift of sight—the gift to see the future. He also granted him seven lifetimes. Tiresias lived long ago. He walked with Cadmus and followed the new god Dionysos up into the mountains in Thebes." The Oracle's voice drops with the memory. "He warned King Pentheus not to mock the god. He foretold the king's death. I haven't seen him... hmm... I'm not sure... is Tiresias still a woman? At any rate, I've heard he or she lives hidden away in Tartaros."

Parmenides seems distracted. He takes both my hands and looks a long time into my eyes.

His gaze stirs something in me. *A smell of incense burning. A dark chamber... beneath a temple? Bittersweet fumes.*

A moment, a breath only, then it's gone.

"Now do you remember?"

"I want to remember." *If only to find out what the Shade-priest knows that I don't.*

"Oracle?"

He drops my hands and leans back to look at me. "Something happened to you when you left to find mint." He squints as if he would peer into my mind. "Not something. Someone. You met someone... and didn't tell me?"

A shiver courses my spine as I think of the priest, his smile.

"Yes..." But I can say no more. Shame washes over me, though I don't know why. I don't want to tell Parmenides about—

"A Shade. A priest." Of course, the Oracle knows whether I tell him or not.

I nod. "He hates me."

The Oracle raises his eyebrows but says nothing.

Poet rests his arm across my back as if to say—I'm here. We'll face it together.

"He knows who I am. He despises me... but I have no idea who he is. Do you?"

"I think I know who he must be. Have you seen him before?"

"I think I have, but..."

"We need to hurry."

"To find Tiresias?"

"For you to know who you are."

I sling my pack on my back and kick dirt on the fire. "Show us the way to Tiresias."

"I don't know the way."

Stopping mid-kick, I look at him. "What do you mean, you don't know the way? Pan said Tiresias is in Tartaros. You are hierophant. You *have* to know!"

"You must lead us to the seer."

"But, Parmenides—"

"Tartaros is a luminal land. The horrors reside in each person's mind. No *one* path leads between rock cliffs, beneath fire skies, across lava rivers. Each of us has our own path to the deepest realm. Your mind creates the junction of time and space in which Tiresias can tell you your destiny."

Cravenly, my eyes flood with tears. It's hopeless. "I don't know who I am. How can I possibly guide us to Tartaros?"

CHAPTER THIRTEEN
TRANSFORMATION

With your permission," Parmenides tells me, "I can transform you. You will become your essence. Your soul. Your *psyche*. In this land of darkness, we become our hearts, our core."

I think about the priest. "If in life we murder, could our *psyche* transform us into a snake?"

"Yes, any beast of earth or heavens. Even rock or light. It might be dangerous. I can't promise what you will turn into. But I believe it's your only hope."

"Oracle, I don't know who I am... or was. A liar? Murderer?" I stare up into the fire sky. Watch broad-winged vultures swoop and dive. "Maybe one of them? I can't let you change me."

"What other choice do you have?"

Poet and I look at each other, struck dumb by the truth of his question.

"And you can trust me. I know who you were... who you are."

I'm struck with the thought that the gods also tell us to trust them. Did Minthe trust? Or Tiresias? Where did it get them?

I take the Oracle's hand a look a long while into his gaze. *He says he knows who I am.* I nod without ever drawing my eyes from his.

"So, that's yes?"

I take a deep breath. "Yes."

There is a moment—just a moment—of confusion, when the Oracle holds his long fingers above my head as if to bless me. A moment only—of gray and wind crying in blood-red sky, and in that moment, I'm certain I made the wrong decision. I look to the hierophant but no longer see a wise seer in grape-dyed robes with god flashing from his fingers and the pennant hanging from his neck. That man smiles at me, but just to his side, a pale girl with blue eyes like pools of calm water, sits on a creature I don't know—dragon legs and wings, leathery like a bat's, and an eagle's head. Its bird stare is cautious and wild, as if daring me to question its existence. Also lurking behind him like a shadow is a massive snake, its cobra head fanning above the oracle's like a crown of gold.

Is this real? That *it* or *they* are there. And *I* am here.

I blink to clear my eyes and they all disappear. Oracle, griffin, cobra. Dissolved like salt in warm water, leaving me cushioned in a night sky, surrounded by stars and red and orange and deep green mists that swirl down and down to one black point. I am pulled and tugged toward that solitary black hole as stars rush past.

In the entire kosmos, I am alone.

Until Parmenides passes his hands over my head and rests them on my heart.

My mind clears.

The Oracle chants. *Τοι παντ ονομ εστει... toi pant onom estei*

Can I simply sink into this compassion I feel from the earth at my feet, skyfire... even the soaring vultures? I don't understand where this feeling of love and safety comes from, as if the Oracle's strong arms hold me up. Maybe I can let go and just *be*... not worry about the Priest-Shade or why I'm here with Poet, and why a spider web necklace hangs around my neck.

Just as I relax and a smile pushes to the corners of my mouth, just as I feel safe and calm like moonlight across a temple sanctuary, Poet whirls around at a sound in the tree shadow. An olive-skinned *kore*, more beautiful than my heart can imagine, walks into the clearing and straight up to Poet. Am I imagining her? Like the cobra and griffin?

"I found you," she says.

Poet looks confused. "Do I know you?"

"Of course you do." Her dark eyes caress him as she touches his cheek.

"I don't remember." Their smiles lock. "I think I would."

My chest tightens, stabbed with bitter jealousy. *No! Poet, what are you doing?*

It's too late. Parmenides' spell has begun its work. *Τοι παντ ονομ εστει.*

Her last words chill me. "I've been looking everywhere for you. Someone's following me. An armed warrior. I think he wants to kill me. Please, you must help."

With a rush, I shrink, until I am the size of a river stone.

My last thought as a girl is both jealousy and an overwhelming desire to help. But what can I do? The mint leaf and clay cup and my shawl loom like mountains, until there is only blackness.

I am trapped. There's nothing I can do to help the girl or even to help myself. Soft and warm, silk strands cocoon me in a dark place to hide and become. Become what? The Oracle said I would become my *psyche*—my deepest being.

Myriad insect legs scratch against my tomb. A segmented torso writhes and expands and contracts.

What am I? What did I become? No, not this. Not this!

I am a caterpillar.

We become what we think. Jealousy created me: a fat, green slug with legs curled into a ball of waiting. The last image I have, seared onto my mind's eye like a burning brand, is Poet and the girl staring into one another's eyes as if they can't resist.

Doesn't Poet see what's happening to me?

And then nothing. I am in a chamber so black, so empty of light that I have no sense of what is me and what is outside.

Does time pass? It must, but there is no light and dark of days to measure its passing. There is only my moment-to-moment disgust.

For what seems like an eternity, I wait helpless. Emotions whirl around me like dead leaves in a winter wind. This is Poet's doing. He's responsible for this. Black is lack of light. And love. Black is this bleak Underworld where anything can happen. The Shade knew. "Who will change?"

The cocoon crowds in on me. I'm like a fly wrapped in spider silk. Sticky and suffocating, the strands trap me. My mind shrinks to an insect's needs. Eat and procreate—the raw and primal insect desires that would eat and grow and consume again—overwhelms me.

I push back against the savage inevitability that I'm losing the last vestiges of a girl who yearns toward the gods. Soon there will be no room for love or jealousy. There is only hunger in darkness.

So this is who I am. I won't accept it.

"Think!" I hear Parmenides' voice like a faint whisper outside the cocoon.

The Shade said, "Not what changes. Who changes?"

"You are the girl who blossoms. Think! Set aside your jealousy. You are more."

The itching returns and with it, pulsing growth.

"The Song. Find the Song of the universe. You can't kill the Song."

My torso shrinks, scrambling legs change to four, two antennae, at last two wings, wrinkled and fragile, unfold to push against the silk cocoon.

"It is! It cannot *not* be! Find the Song!"

I'm distracted by smells in the dark—earth and mint.

"Do you see a light? Any light?"

I start to panic. *It's dark. Black. Suffocating. Parmenides!*

"Find color in your heart—the shadow of color. It's there. It's always there. Like a leaf shadow? Be the heart of the color. Feel with color. Find color in your body and hear its song. It's there you'll find your power. You can't give up!"

Segment by segment, I focus on my body. This writhing, green, furry body repulses me. I force myself to calm and breathe... and accept. All is the will of the gods. Can I still trust the gods? What would the gods have me learn from this? *Not who will change. What will change?*

"You must understand. You *must* remember. You can't kill the Song!"

A caterpillar crawls the earth, finds a tree, and weaves its own tomb.

Millions of caterpillars listen to the Song to travel thousands of leagues, to spin and sleep. To become. To become! Not what will change...who will change!

With sharp mandibles, I rip the soft strands. A gap widens to reveal light—green and red cast from a world beyond the dark.

I tear and push with my stick legs.

The smell of mint and a wind strokes my antennae.

I rip the silk strands and push and scramble with my legs. One thought—to be free. The opening widens.

I shove my way out.

Clinging to a leaf that smells sweet, filled with juices and life, I quiver my antennae to understand where I am... who I am.

My vision is the first to understand. Parmenides shimmers before me. A hundred images of his worried face, faceted like honeycomb. Each Oracle face surrounded by light: red, orange, yellow, green, blue, lavender, and indigo. Bold, true colors unlike any I've seen. With the colors comes compassion. Connection. And a truth that stuns me: I was never alone. Every twig and leaf and stone coruscates with light—shades of white and yellow and sweet lavender—and all I feel, as if a laughing song—is boundless love. I sensed it as caterpillar. And now? I'm a brilliant butterfly with black and white wings scalloped in bold black with red teardrops. I was never alone. Never abandoned in my silken cage. The song of the universe hums through me.

I rest on a small, barren branch and quiver my folded wings.

Poet and the *kore* stand side-by-side, peering at me. But my jealousy... for the moment... has loosed its claws from my heart. *I'm not going to return to the cocooned body of the caterpillar... or worse!*

The Oracle's words break into my thoughts. "Tiresias. You must find the seer. There is no time to waste. You can fly now, and no one will suspect that you are a mortal girl wandering this Land-of-Death. Find Tiresias. Find who you are."

I spread my wings and move them slowly up and down, trying to find the air beneath them. It's amazing, when I push against the current, how easily it lifts my light body. For a breath, my stick-like legs lift off the twig. I settle. Then lift. When finally I begin to comprehend the feel of it, with one strong sweep, I fly up to face level. Circle Parmenides and Poet and the *kore*, then flutter along the path and higher, toward the breaking rock face.

My landing isn't exactly graceful. A little skewed, tipping right, then left. I spread my wings, admire the red teardrops along the scalloped edges. I imagine that's what happened to the poppies in my hair. Deep indigo shimmers, outlining the black. It glows and pulses as I try to focus.

Lovely. Definitely lovely.

I'm tempted to marvel longer at my new form, until I realize that I'm so close to the fire-sky, that it feels like my leaf-thin wings will shrivel and burn like pine straw added to a fire. It's better when I push off and soar back down to my friends. The currents toss me a bit, and I feel queasy, but it's not bad at all. I like flying.

For a joke... and I suppose to reclaim his attention from the rapturous beauty still standing close beside him... I land on Poet's nose. It's pretty funny, when he stares cross-eyed down his nose to see me better.

"I must say Thea, you make a beautiful butterfly." Poet holds out a finger.

I fly over to perch on it.

"Can you hear me?" Parmenides draws my attention.

I lift off Poet's finger, circle the Oracle a couple of times, and land on his shoulder.

"Zeus' thunderbolts. Yes! But look what you've done to me now! And how exactly is this supposed to help me?"

"Have you not noticed that you can fly?"

"And?"

"Do I have to explain everything to you? Like I told you, there is no one path to Tartaros. It's your need to find Tiresias. It's your need to know who you are... ahem, I might add... a need because you were fooling around with that boy and forgot you weren't supposed to drink from a certain river... I might add."

"Great, well where were you, when I needed you? Just wandering around Erebos having a grand time ignoring me? Aren't you my mentor? My friend?"

"Just because I'm your mentor, doesn't mean I'm your slave. There are certain things you have to do and learn by yourself."

I flap my wings slowly open. Closed. My antennae quivers with annoyance. I was quite happy, having Poet again all to myself.

"You're very beautiful." The Oracle touches my wingtip with his finger.

"That tickles." I move away. "I assume you have a plan? Or did you just think it a fine jest to see me change into an insect?"

"Don't quite know how to ask this..." The Oracle clears his throat, nearly dislodging me from my perch.

"Oh, please, you already turned me into a butterfly. And now you're worried about hurting my feelings?"

Flitting off Parmenides' shoulder, I land lightly on Poet's. His smile is filled with questions but warm.

"Fine! I will ask. What happened to you? You've changed. You were... yourself before. Respectful."

"I can't believe you are criticizing me now?" One look at the Oracle's face though, and I'm sorry I've been so short. "I know you're trying to help me. Really I do. So, what next?"

He turns his back, kneels in the dirt beside the makeshift fire-ring, and pokes at the coals.

"Parmenides, you do have a plan, don't you? Please, tell me that you didn't change me into a butterfly for no good reason."

He remains quiet, his back turned. Long enough for a quiver to ripple through my wings.

He's smiling, when he twists back to look at me. "Had you worried, didn't I? Of course, I have a plan. By the way, I liked you a lot more as a girl."

"Well, at least we both agree on that. Now, would you care to share your plan? Which, I hope, includes turning me back into a girl. Sooner, rather than later."

The Oracle moves close, so we are eye-to-eye. We stare at one another as the *kore* heads back into the trees, picking up twigs and small branches for the fire.

With a shudder, I watch Poet follow her. "So, this woman with eyes for Poet, who is she?"

"Medusa. She... well, you changed her... it's a long story. Let's focus on important things right now, like how you find the blind seer so you can discover who you are." He chuckles. "Well, besides a butterfly."

"Funny, very funny." I beat my wings at him in futile disgust. "Now about the changing me back into a girl part...?"

Parmenides' face seems to turn still as a marble statue. He focuses his fire gaze on me. The one I feel to the core. "You must discover your place in the kosmos yourself. When you know that, you will be able to regain your human self. Only then."

"What are you saying?" I fly frantic circles around Parmenides. "You turned me into this cursed insect. Do something! You can't leave me like this!"

"Trust the gods. They will carry you through all there is."

"Gods? Oh indeed!" I flutter to eye level with Parmenides. "You can't leave me like this, Oracle. Change me back!"

Διος δὲτελειτου βουλη... Dios deteleitou boulei are his last words as his form fades. His mint tea sits on a rock by the fire; steam swirls up from the cup, sweet with crushed leaves, a nymph's love destroyed by a jealous goddess.

The path back into the pines is still shadowed and empty. There's no sign of Poet or Medusa. I understand now why Queen Persephone would destroy Minthe. I'd go after Medusa if I could, if not quite like *that*. The Medusa, who, it occurs to me, is very conveniently here now that I have become an insect.

I square my... mandibles? *Which, I suppose, means, I ought to get on with morphing back into a girl.*

CHAPTER FOURTEEN
DON'T CROSS THE GODS

ust for history's sake, let me tell you it's hard work being a butterfly. Not what I'd thought at all. Flying from flower to flower, sipping sweet nectar... sounds pretty good, doesn't it? Lies, all lies. Have you ever thought about how much nectar you get from one flower? Then, it's on to the next. And the next.

So, that's all I do. Stay low enough to not burn my wings in the flames and high enough to see where I'm going. I head off. Only the gods know where. I certainly don't. Gray rocks and rubble change to fields of ghost-white flowers, asphodel like ocean waves as far as I can see. Stalks as endless as time. I fly from one flower to another, sipping my fill of nectar. My heart aches. Over and over I see Poet wander off into the trees following that girl... Medusa? Yes, Parmenides said she is called that. She's so beautiful. Too beautiful!

I must say though that flying is everything I dreamed.

I'm tempted to forget this know-thyself-nonsense. Who cares anyway? When I can swoop down, diving between the snow-white flowers like dancing between clouds.

Why would I want to turn back into a girl... a girl who has no idea who she is? A girl whose love is off flirting with a gorgeous *kore* who just *happened* to show up.

What was that she said? Someone was following her? She was afraid? Well.

And really, it's not so bad, being a butterfly whose only concern is nectar and not flying into those nasty flame-filled skies. Who cares about Poet anyway?

One thought of Poet, and I see him vividly as if he stands before me. As if he turns his back to follow the *kore* into the forest. Turns his back. Again and again and again.

Hoping to outfly my anger, I head toward a dense, sweet smell. Clustered white flowers so thick, they look like snow on Olympos. Home of the gods. Refuge.

Why do I still believe that? Are the gods our refuge? The gods have a way of granting us a sunny day and a light breeze to lift our spirits, before they descend like thunder and storm clouds to strike us down. I know I should remember this and be careful, but oh, it is fun, being a butterfly.

Concentrating, I try to only think of nectar. Food and flight. Dip low. Alight. Sip sweetness from the flower's heart and do it all over again. Forget I was a girl. Forget I loved Poet.

With a steep right sweep, I whirl away, flying a scattered path like Zeus' zigzag thunderbolt.

I twist and dip and fly a circle beneath the flower stalks. A sharp turn, a circle, then a straight flight, pushing as strong as my fragile wings can take.

Just ahead are sturdy oaks. Dark with shadows.

I flip and climb, twist and turn. Two more random dips, and I slip into the forest.

With shuddering wings, I light on a branch and look around. Gnarled oaks that pulse with lavender light surround me. Their rough bark breathes as if alive.

I stare in disbelief as my vision of the trees shifts. A trunk transforms to a man's heavy thigh. Twisted branches entwine one another in a desperate embrace. Off to my right, a tree's limbs become a woman's arms. I try to focus and look at them directly. Try to convince myself that they are not human. Only ancient oaks, rooted in ash and rock.

As a wind that reeks like corpses burned on funeral pyres quakes the spiked leaves, I quiver with an awareness that death won here. Thanatos stalks these people.

With a shudder, their pain jolts me from my self-absorption. How could I think for a moment that anything in this land is fun?

Turning slowly on the branch, I look out at the asphodel field. The flowers beyond the dark woods shimmer lavender, soft yellow, and green.

But silence shrouds the forest shadows like a *bardo* land.

I'm crushed with certainty that these trees were once human. "I am here to help you!" There is a slight tremble beneath me as the oak shudders, but then nothing. "I transformed from girl to caterpillar to butterfly. I can save you."

I strain to hear an answer.

A whisper in my heart tells me to be careful.

"Your fear makes this land real. Your fear traps you. I can help you."

A raging wind whirls abruptly through the branches. There's a loud crack as the limb beneath me splits and crashes to earth. I just manage to crawl between some snaking roots and fold my wings. Above me, boughs thrash, dumping twigs and dead leaves onto the ground as I shelter beneath one branch and peer out into the storm.

Through tree shadows loom a face and red eyes. Hades. He's stalking me. Defiant, I lock my eyes with The Lord-of-Many-Names. His face becomes a knot in an oak's rough bark.

Did I imagine the god? I turn in a slow circle.

"I can free you!" I shout to the oaks.

The only answer is a roar like fire and thunder and a storm sea. Like a rogue wave, it threatens to overpower me. Every vibration shudders through my wings and my body's core.

How can I help them as a butterfly? If only I could play my panpipes. A dense mist shrouds me, convulsing with screams. It closes in, so that I no longer see light through the branches.

Suffocating and thick, the air fills my lungs, stinging like nettles every time I draw a breath. I force myself to take one deep inhale, ignoring the searing pain, and push against the wind to fly back up and spread my wings across the branch.

I close my eyes and let Pan's melody swirl through my mind, until it sweeps away my pain. When at last I can breathe again, I hum along to the music filling me. *You can't kill the Song. You can't kill the Song. It is Pan's song. It is the gods' song, and the stars and sun and earth and wind. It is all of us.*

The roar intensifies, until my wings tremble with it.

A face twisted in anguish stares back at me. Another. And another. Every oak—as far as the dark edge of the woods beyond—traps, roots in an unforgiving soil, a human form. This branch a leg. That long one, stretching horizontal to the earth, an arm. That knothole is a mouth open in an unformed scream. I'm sitting on a woman's naked form encrusted and enslaved by bark for eternity. The forest is oppressive with unformed screams.

I fold my wings and stare.

Here is death. Here is eternity. Here is my end.

No! I won't give up. Death will not claim us today.

"I will help you." My whisper seems to wake them and stir some life and hope.

I spread my wings across the rough bark. A slow beat vibrates through me—the tree's heartbeat and breath and will to survive. Allowing the ill wind to fill me, I let go of everything except a vulture's call high in the fire-sky, the slumping squall, a smell of decay and mud and rotting soil.

A deadly quiet settles around me. Sulfur steam spits and sprays from crevices that split the forest. I want to believe Hades gone, but jump at a raucous cry and turn to look. There! At the bottom of one crack, a decaying goat carcass is draped across pitched stones jagged like sharp knives. Vultures fight for a place to feed, claw and tear at the flesh. They want to live. Nothing will stop them.

My wings quiver.

Everything these butterfly eyes see refracts and reflects, splitting my world into bold colors and fractured smells.

The god-wind and storm sky and the trees' pain pour through me like wildfire.

I spread my wings and close them. *Parmenides, where are you?*

The Oracle's voice whispers an answer: *You must not be afraid.*

How does a butterfly defy Thanatos? But I try. I have to try. For these tortured trees. For the girl I was. I have to defy Hades, who enslaved them. I must not be afraid. I will not...

"I am not afraid." My voice is fragile.

Parmenides' words fly at me. *Trust me. Yearning will carry us... eternal longing of life for life.*

You can't kill the Song. It is all of us. You can't kill the Song. I hum Pan's melody over and over so it rides the shrieks and fury, like a small bird letting the winds carry it.

The dark Lord is in the storm, but Pan's song is older and stronger. It is wind rustling through olive trees. It is a hummingbird flitting from poppy to poppy and landing on a river rush.

I keep my eyes closed and hum. The winds shift and calm. Focusing on my melody, I imagine hundreds of small birds chirping and singing, flocking across a sunrise sky. I hum my heartbeat, the drumbeat of the kosmos.

Pan's melody is the earth. The wind. It is who I am. Whether I am a butterfly or Shade or girl... it is my song. This ancient song of the universe is stronger than you, Hades!

I smile and open my eyes.

The storm is calmed.

Brilliant colors radiate from every charred branch and twig and brown leaf. There's life in the trees. I look closely where rough bark touches a bold red and try to discern where the tree ends and its essence begins. Studying the roots, knobby and twisting down into rocky soil, I look back up along the sturdy trunk to the first massive branch, soon splitting to another and a rounded knob... *by the gods!*

I feel a thrum and pulse beneath my stick feet. One beat faint and faltering. One tree over, I hear a sigh. Answered by another, until the forest around me shudders with one will to defy the gods. To deny death.

"Hades and your brother Zeus, most powerful of all the gods, why do you allow one human soul to be trapped like this?" My anger lifts me from the branch. I fly from tree to tree, fluttering my wings frantically, as if I could revive them. "Why would any god change these wretched souls into trees? This is how you use your power? No! I. Will. Not. Accept. This." I can barely stand to stay among the oaks. Their trapped anguish licks at me like the fire-sky scorches my wings.

"If this is the gods' will, then the gods are vicious. Cruel!"

Until that moment, I didn't understand.

At last, I do.

This is my purpose here. I *won't* accept this pain.

With that realization, the oaks' moaning joins like one breath and carries me up higher and higher, until I'm looking down upon the vast and dark forest. Colored winds swirl up from the limbs. Lavender. Indigo. Pale yellow.

The winds turn violent and threaten to rip apart my wings. The moans become a chant, deep and rhythmic like drums. A song filled with power.

Through spinning smoke and ash, something stirs.

My fragile wings rip in the storm of embers, but I fly higher, fighting the air currents that threaten to dash me to the ground.

Over there! At the forest edge, a branch moved. The chanting throbs through my body. With all my will, I flap my tattered wings as fast as I can. Louder and darker, the unending beat entangles my heart, stokes my anger.

Summoning my breath, I shout against the wind. "Hear me Zeus, Hades. Hear me well. There is a song that connects us all. It is the wind and stars and... yes, even gods and butterflies!"

A sudden gust shoves me just a breath above a branch, but I push up and away. "It is blue sky in the land above and dark night below. It is all that and more!"

The massive oaks sway as the gale thrashes them. The chanting grows harsher, louder, until it is one shriek.

Suddenly, the scream and storm die to complete and utter stillness.

I fly slowly back to the closest oak and gasping for breath, land on the thick-barked branch. Draping my wings across the limb, I say, "Please."

Death is all around me—heavy and almost overpowering.

I can't defeat Thanatos. Not here in this dark land. Why do I try?

An image of Minthe defeated by Queen Persephone fills me with rage. I can barely breathe, but force myself to focus on the trees. "Don't give up. You can't." *Am I talking to myself or them?* "Don't give in to the gods."

From the very end of the smallest branch, a pale green leaf sprouts. Then another. I turn in circles to see the forest bud to life. The branches straighten and grow, until the entire forest is shimmering with green and a song more beautiful than any I've ever heard.

The song is without end. Without beginning. And while the trees sing in concert, they transform to men with stained, earth-tillers' tunics and women with flour-covered aprons. One girl with raven hair tickles a child in her lap. The stolid trees' suffering is gone. Transformed to a laugh. Or a cry.

I finally understand it doesn't matter which. They're here and free and that's enough.

"What have you done?"

I don't see Hades, but his voice ricochets from tree to tree, battering me.

"I set them free."

"It is forbidden."

"How can freedom be forbidden? What god would trap souls in bark, rooted to rock so they can never move? Never hold a child, a wife. Stare out at this world unable to touch or laugh? What god would want this? It is heartless."

"I destroyed Asklepios, because the healer brought one man back to life," the god rumbles. "I stole his immortality. Do you understand what you've done?"

CHAPTER FIFTEEN
THE WRATH OF ZEUS AND HADES

You will pay for this." The disembodied voice shouts from** the towering cliffs. The stone deepens from gray to blood red and echoes and scatters the threat, so it washes over me like a tide of nightmares.

"We will have revenge. We will have revenge. ... revenge." Until it fades, leaving bitter fear mixed with my triumph.

I freed the trees!

An ill wind threatens to blow me off the branch.

Once more butterfly sight reveals flaring eyes, like an angry firebrand, glaring at me from behind an oak. Massive arms and strong fingers clutch a branch. I gasp for air, but my body fills instead with scalding mist. There! The Lord-of-Many-Names and another god who blinds me with searing bolts of lightning.

Hades and his brother Zeus.

Zeus gave Hades his own daughter Persephone as bride. They war. They divide the spoils. Now they've come for me. And then I remember...

This is not the first time. Hades tried to stop me before. How did I escape?

Before I can decide what to do, Hades' massive body rushes me. Light flashes off his gold breastplate.

Zeus roars, "This time you've gone too far!" The lord of all gods expands, glowering over me like a black thundercloud, his eyes, livid with rage, sparking from the fire-sky. Hurtling down alongside his lightning bolts, his cries echo off the cliff. "There is too much of the gods in you."

"You must not bring life from death. Never!" Hades growls.

"Why did you enslave them in trees? What vile deeds did they do in the sun above that you've made them suffer so?"

"Will you challenge a god?"

The ground beneath me shakes. Boulders crash from the cliffs.

I tense for my death. The final death.

Parmenides' voice whispers: *Your fear makes this land of Death real.*

Hades' wide face glows with victory. His breath smells of cloves and blood.

Time stills.

The god attacks with wild howls. Filled with rage, they shatter and fragment off the land.

The next instant takes an eternity.

There is no way I can stop the god.

A dark wind rages around me, whirling and screaming with Shades who would claim me.

I see a girl run up a cliff pursued by a priest in yellow robes. Over and over, as if time loops back upon itself, the god shows her death. The sword. The strike. Blood. The scenes whirl again and again around me, caught in a moaning wind.

I'm trapped between the horror of my vision, and my fear of the divine brothers. There is no place to escape. Something in me lets go.

"Will you fight me?" Hades' taunt vibrates to my core. "Will you defy a god? Lord of this dark unknown? With what? Look at you! Frail and helpless... you, *you* will challenge me?"

Shades laugh and mock. Their fingers and hair caress me like ice smoke, until I shiver, barely able to move. One Shade swoops close. A crone with withered arms and tattered rags for clothes reaches for me. When she opens her mouth to speak, her teeth, cracked and yellow— several missing—frame utter blackness, as if inside her wraith body, she holds the Void.

The Shades pull back, swirling in an ever-wider circle, as one, an old woman in a blue shawl wrapped over her stooped back, strides between the others and waves a cane as if stirring the air. Her dark eyes dart from shadow form to shadow form to warn them off. When she almost reaches me, her eyes lock on mine with love. With determination. Who is this old one who would help me?

"Granddaughter."

A young warrior Shade, still clad in shining armor, slashes a shadow-sword between us and steps close before the old woman, his back to me. "She lives. Do not talk to her."

With a quickness I can't imagine, the woman sidesteps the warrior and looks longingly at me. "Burst with life, butterfly."

"Who are you?"

But the soldier slices his sword over and over through the woman's shadow-form. She shatters and disappears in mist.

I know my own death is close. Thanatos is here. Not to be denied.

For a moment, Hades body grows and swells like a tidal wave that sucks back from a desolate beach, stealing remnants of life—a cod, crab... a child's wooden toy.

The god towers over me. His blood-red eyes devour me.

I draw a sharp breath and wait for my end.

The dark lord smiles in triumph. His smile jolts me from fear to fury.

What is there to lose?

I will die and never challenge the god's cruel injustice. Or—I will die and fight to free all these souls. Either way, I will die.

My wings spread wide, I fly to meet the god's assault. "I do not fear you!"

Zeus rushes to his brother's side. The lord of lightning and lord of the timeless dark confront me.

My wings barely move, just flicker in the mist, so I hover before them. "You have no power over me. I have no fear."

We form a circle: Hades and Zeus and one insignificant black butterfly.

The brother-gods speak as one; their voices echo from cliff to cliff, like thunderbolts clashing and storm winds howling a response.

The sound batters me. I fall back against an oak, one of few that never trapped human life. I cling to its rough bark.

"Leave. Go and never return!" The gods bellow.

"This is my realm. Do you question me? I am king here! Go back to the Land-of-the-Living while you can." He lifts his hands like meaty claws on both sides of my wings. "You do not belong here! What would you claim? Why did you cross the River Styx? Why did Kharon bring you across?"

The heat is blistering. I can't move.

A fractured memory rushes back, and I say, "Kharon carried me across the broad river, beyond the Veil, because I gave him two pomegranate seeds. One for me. One for my friend. The great god Pan, older than even you, Zeus, gave me three seeds."

The men and women, those once trees, form a circle around me. Singing a low song, they dance round and round. Lifting their arms and lowering them, singing, laughing, and stomping, raising gray dust that powders bare arms and sandaled feet.

A heavyset woman cringes away from the gods, squats down before me. "Who are you, butterfly, that you give us life again?"

A man of the earth, his face wrinkled from days in the sun, his hands strong and calloused from tilling fields of barley or wheat or gathering black olives to press for oil, sits in the dirt beside the woman. "Who are you?"

The brother gods rise to the sky, loosen hold of their earth-bound forms. Lightning bolts sear the mist. White light followed by roaring thunder. Earthquake.

I will not let fear conquer me. Spreading my wings to hold on, I dig my frail feet in the dust and try to listen to the farmers. *I saved them. Here is my power.*

"Who are you that you can rescue us from our torture?" The young woman, her toddler screaming and staring wide-eyed at the storm, joins us.

"Who are you?" The gods mock me. Their question ricochets off the cliffs.

"I don't know." Is my answer for the gods? For me?

"You must." The mother takes my hand. "You do. Your heart knows."

Another thunder roll, and a memory stirs of soldiers' boots thundering across sacred land and high rock faces shuddering and crumbling at my feet. An assault by an army a million strong and a king encased in gold riding in a shining chariot.

A memory of cheers of triumph.

A memory of my power.

As if the invaders come alive, boulders crash down from the cliffs. I flutter in circles. The villagers huddle together, their faces tight and pale.

A black spider web strands from my wings to the men and women crouched around me. There is a stirring in my core. Blood red teardrops on my wings become poppies in hair. Scalloped wings become my arms and legs. A whirring burns through me. A song of what was and what will be. The oaks sway and thrash, glow with reds and orange and brilliant indigo. My head is light. Filled with colors and laughter. Wind and a sunburst of light.

I stretch and burn with life, until once more I am a girl.

I'm no longer a fragile butterfly, but she is not gone. The butterfly is my heart.

Power and joy surge through me.

With my transformation, my return to a girl, memories dance through my mind. But they are jumbled and confusing—carved figures dancing on a firelit cave wall. Apollo shapeshifting, furious and filled with a desire for revenge, at last shamed into helping me.

I can defy the gods.

Memories flit through my mind like fireflies on a starless night: my Night of Pan when the satyr-god made me initiate into the mysteries of Persephone and poppies sprouted in my hair... and Poet helping me escape the Persians! I knew him before we came to this Land-of-Shadows.

I crumble to my knees.

I love him.

My fear whispers that I am a fool.

I ignore fear's small voice. My power grows like a seed. As butterfly, helpless and fragile, I learned to be fearless when confronting the gods. My heart tells me to hold out my hand, to wait and listen and understand.

The wind expands and swirls with thunderclouds. Hades' breath is the blacksmith's fire scorching my face. His eyes the bellows.

A pomegranate tree grows from my palm, its roots tingling through my skin and veins and muscle.

The sky and ground tremble, pierced by Zeus' lightning bolts. With a roar like a volcano, both gods appear before me. Hades curses, stomps his feet.

Fear urges me to clench my hand closed. Quiet my heart. But I don't. I hold my arm straight before me, palm up to the storm-blazed sky.

Ripe pomegranates—red like a sunrise, bold like a poppy—sprout from the branches, fill with life's juices. A raven, messenger of Apollo, lands on my shoulder and plucks the lush fruit.

I stare at the tree and bird. The pomegranate is sacred to Demeter and Persephone. It is their power I carry. *Is it enough?* This human body I return to has power. It's there in my palm, prickling with the tiny tree growing from my flesh—a message from the Goddess.

"The goddess Demeter helps me. Will you defy your sister?"

Hades' eyes burn into me.

Like an ancient hermit of the mountains, Zeus straightens his strong shoulders. The cords in his neck tighten. Even his broad brow and deep-set eyes can't hide his surprise.

I see his father Kronos' imprisonment in his eyes. I see a thirst for power, an unquenchable desire to control the world. As I fall into his gaze, lost as if I fall into a vast night sky, I see a son betrayed and a father who betrayed. In that moment, I know what I must say to this god.

"Zeus, father of all the gods. Wise counselor to the Olympians. You betrayed your daughter, Demeter's daughter. When the Lord of this dark land, this land of Shades and emptiness, wanted Persephone for his bride, he came to you. He asked for your permission."

The godly brothers raise a strong wind. Tree limbs flail, whipping and striking my face. With a sharp cry, the raven struggles against the wind, twists his body left, right, and thrusts high with the god's breath, disappearing between the cliffs.

I plant my feet wide and stare down one god, then the other. "Lord-Thunderer, you gave her away to be your brother's queen. Did you believe your sister wouldn't know or care?"

"I am ruler of all. Demeter must heed my will," he roars.

Rocks shatter and fall, but I keep my words steady. "So you said... but she didn't. She left the fields and land parched, thirsting for rain. Brown and scorched and lifeless. Persephone, the *kore,* is our hope, our spring. You allowed the Lord-of-Darkness to steal her, while she gathered sweet narcissus."

"Do you challenge my decisions?" This quiet chill of his is more unnerving than his rage.

"Yes!"

"Who are you to question me?" A starry wind rushes from his mouth and spins around us.

"I am the child of Pan's prophecy. I am a seeker and wanderer."

Heads lowered and jaws tight, the farmers hold hands and dance around me, their faces filled with a certainty that I will save them from the gods' wrath, because I am the girl who set them free.

Zeus and Hades turn their backs to me and lean their heads close. Their argument rumbles like thunder and earthquake meeting. A few words escape. "Honor. Cheated. King of all..."

I can sense their anger, but not the meaning of it. I hold my arm steady, while the pomegranate tree grows taller and sturdier. An almost unbearable energy flows from the earth to my core, raising the hair on the back of my neck. Its power surges into my hand and claims the tree's weight. Gives me strength.

I turn to the sound of men and women and children dancing in a semi-circle behind me. As if they hope to give me courage, their feet beat out a rhythm. They lift their voices with a song so filled with joy that it brings tears to my eyes. *Don't they understand? I freed them from the trees... but they will never leave this dismal land.*

"Persephone is my queen!" Hades roars. "I honor her above all others. She is neither slave nor captive." Anger burns in his gaze, a fury that rekindles my fear, but I quiet the shaking in my arm and lift the pomegranate tree higher.

"This, then, is your queen's sacred tree. You gave her three seeds from this tree of life to ensure she must stay at your side. Did she know? Did she understand that if she ate these blood-red seeds, she must always spend three months of every year at your side? Did she know her mother and the earth would mourn and blacken to dark winter with her gone?"

"Yes, she chose. She loves me and wants to remain at my side. It's that mother of hers… Demeter. She won't let her go. Won't let her reign as queen. Wants her to be a child forever by her side. She ate the pomegranate seeds of her own free will!"

"You say she chose to stay here as your queen? I don't believe you. I think you tricked her."

I've angered him, I know, but I don't care. "If you didn't force her, prove it. Show me that all souls wander this Underworld unconstrained like your queen. Let these farmers go. Let them dance and sing and find whatever joy there is here, far from home and rocky shore."

Zeus rests a hand on his brother's shoulder. The air is charged with his power.

Hades nods in deference. "I free them… but you!" He points a finger as thick as a tree branch at me. "You are mine!"

The farmer, maiden, mother, and boy circle us. "Leave the girl to us, Lord Hades. Let her wander your dark halls. Let her help the lost and fearful. Great Lord, she does no harm." They bow before the Lord-of-Many-Names.

"You are feared by many. Named by few." I blow a breath on the pomegranate tree and it disappears. Shaken, I bow to the brother gods.

Hades glowers at us, but Zeus raises a hand to calm him. "Be still, my brother. What does the girl bring to your realm? A breath of narcissus? A song of the wind and sun, summer light warming this bleak land? Let her stay awhile. What harm? What harm?"

"I'll tell you what harm the girl does."

His voice is tight, barely under control. "She has brought many souls back from death: the Child of the Clouds in her temple in the land above, and now these Shades enslaved in trees."

Who is this child of the clouds? What did I do?

"Will this girl defy the gods? Run wild in my realm?"

His bristling rage that stuns us is shattered when Zeus, god of thunder and lightning, laughs, a raucous burst that shudders the charred land. "Play for us, Pan's chosen. Bring us sunshine. Play!"

I lift the panpipes tucked in my sash, but before I can play, Hades says to his brother, king of all the gods, "We drew lots, and the result was fair for you. You were well-pleased, I imagine, when you were named king of the whole kosmos, while I was sent to rule here beneath the ground in this land where no one lives, where there is no time or love or Helios' light. Do you have any idea what it's like to be banished here to this dismal land? Do you? Do you care? So, leave me to rule my dominion as I see fit! You owe me that, at least."

He whirls to confront me. "You've gone too far. You, the intruder. You broke my most sacred rule: Only for me to grant here life or death. Not for you, never for you to bring these trees back to their human lives... and you will pay!"

As if Demeter stands beside me and strengthens me with soil and wild barley seed and all that is earth's bounty, a great calm fills me. "If what you say is true, let me ask Queen Persephone if she is here of her own desire. If you have nothing to hide, let me ask her that question."

Rather than answering me, the Lord-of-Many-Names places his gold helmet, crested with black horsehair and shining like Helios at dawn, on his head and roughly pulls it over his ears. With one last scowl, as if never having stood by his brother's side, he's simply gone.

A look of annoyance flashes across Zeus' face, before he smiles. "Not many have succeeded in getting my brother to disappear."

With the dark god's abrupt departure, the farmers stop dancing and chanting and crowd close behind me. Their uncertainty brushes against me with gossamer wings.

Going to one knee, I touch the Thunderer's foot and wait with bowed head. When at last he speaks, his voice is kind.

"Do you know who you are, child? Do you know your destiny?"

He rests his hand on my head. Heat and joy course through me.

He lifts my chin so I look into his eyes. They are black as the raven, glowing like coals in Hephaestos' fire.

"Parmenides told me to find Tiresias. He knows who I am. He will tell me my destiny."

I can't pull my eyes away. There's knowledge in this god's gaze. He knows everything. The earth and starry heavens, the seas and men's souls. He knows hope before it blossoms. Every fear before it wilts. Every whisper my soul sings. But what roots me unmoving before this god is the understanding that he knows *me*.

"Do you know who your father is?" He asks gently.

I hold his eyes, willing him to say more. "Tell me, Lord-Thunderer."

"No, this you will discover for yourself."

With one loud thunderclap, the god transforms to a lightning bolt that sears the sky. His corporal body is gone, but his voice roars, "We will meet again. Know thyself, Oracle."

CHAPTER SIXTEEN
REVENGE OF THE FURIES

ne farmer steps from the circle and kneels before me. He touches his earth-worn brow to my feet then looks up with such longing, I catch my breath.

"My name is Koros. You wouldn't remember me, but I will always remember you. You are the child of our Pythia. The Forbidden One."

"I am a pythia's daughter?" The truth of his words stuns me. I lean closer to learn what he knows about me.

"I remember you on our mountain..." Tears fill his eyes and his words stop, choked and stolen. "Do you? Do you remember an old farmer who spent his days tilling rock and dirt, rolling sweet grain between his fingers to salt the earth with life? A man who prayed to Demeter the goddess? Do you remember me, child?"

I want to take his hands, turn them palms up to stroke his calluses, hands worked rough and hard, so they fear to stroke a wife's gentle skin, but they are only smoke and shadow. "I'm sorry, I don't remember you... but why? What memory haunts you even here, in this death land?"

"My baby. My daughter. She cried. Day and night. Until one day..." He drops to his knees. "You were so young running alone up the mountain—probably six or seven years old—looking for that old shepherd. What was his name? Hestos, they called him. You heard my baby sobbing and tiptoed through our door. The sunshine burst around you as if it wanted to never leave your side. You came in and sang a lullaby to her and placed a narcissus across her swaddling blankets. She hiccupped. Sighed. And was quiet. All her childhood from that moment, she laughed and sang and brought such joy to my wife. Who are you? Who are you to bring laughter to my baby? To free me?"

"You and I..." I look from face to face. "All of us live our lives; sing and dance our songs... and together we weave the kosmos. I am no different from you. Or you from me."

"You are different, child. You are the child of our Pythia. I will never forget her." He folds his large hands around mine with great tenderness, then stands. "And there is power in these hands." Though Shade without flesh, the strength in his muscles from hours of tilling rocky soil and sowing seed vibrates through my own.

"I didn't remember you, Koros." My voice is a trembling whisper. "But now I will never forget you. When I pass a field of wild narcissus, I will hear a baby's cry; I will sing a lullaby. When I finally return to the Land-of-the-Living, I will carry you there in my heart. Our song will stretch from this land of darkness to the light."

Gently, with ghost fingers, he kisses my fingertips and releases them, then backs away without ever taking his eyes from mine. One step. At last another. Another.

The dancers gather around him and with happiness shining from their eyes, they cast timid smiles at me. It seems a long time that I sit. The farmers touch my shoulders and wish me well as they scatter into the shadows. A hand brushes hair away from a young woman's eyes so she can see me, until she takes one last step behind the limestone cliff. Until they are gone. Every woman and child and last of all Koros, with a wave and a tremulous smile of farewell.

I should be triumphant, joyful with my victory against the two most powerful Olympian gods... but I'm not. I feel shaken. Dread settles around me with the mist. Hades will want revenge.

I know what *I* want. I want to go back to the riverside and build the bed of grasses and smell the wild poppies and rest. Please, just rest, with Poet there to hold me. And eat apples and swim.

Is that so much to ask?

But Poet is with that *kore*. Medusa.

Suddenly, unable to control my agitation, I pace from oak to oak. Pausing only long enough to rest my palm against each one to be certain every prisoner is freed. But my mind races, and I mutter out loud as I stride to another tree. "I can't do this!"

As I rest my hand on the rough bark; it trembles. I stop and concentrate on the oak. "Is someone there? Are you trapped?" I don't feel or hear an answer. The tree is solid and rooted... only a tree. "The gods are playing with me in some sick game." I look around the forest. It feels so empty now with the farmers gone. Shadows leap and disappear as the sky flares. It's disorienting, without the sun or a full moon casting shadows that seem to grow in tandem with a day, this perpetual night lit only by a sky that broils and flames... "Enough!"

I run out of the forest. Push myself faster, my feet flying from boulder to dry creek bed, across another field of ghostly asphodel flowers, until I can run no farther. I stop, bend over, gasp for breath. I want to run farther. Get away from the gods and Shades. Just leave!

But, as I lean against a boulder with trembling hands, a girl's Shade—seemingly slipping though solid rock—smiles at me, as if happy she's found me. I think it's the girl from my vision. The one killed by the priest.

She stands. Smiles. Waits for me to say something. Do something.

Every fiber of my being wants to gather her hand. Shades sweep high above me across the sky and shadow me like hunting raptors. A black wind, soot and moans and a sorrowful heartbeat, wraps around me as if I've returned to the cocoon.

"Who are you?" I ask.

"Leave."

"Why... what do you know about me?"

Her only answer is laughter... a laughter colored with sadness. The Shade leaps into the blistering sky and spins round and round above me. Her screams shatter me.

She points down the trail, past ghostly flowers, abandoned oaks. Then disappears. Dissolves like salt in water until all that's left is her sigh.

Nothing is real in this Land-of-Death. "What am I supposed to do?" I shout and sink to the ground, trembling. Shadows laugh. Gods threaten.

I have to find Tartaros, find the blind seer, but I don't move. All I really want is the river.

The river.

Some peace.

I throw my hands to the sky and shout. "Pan, help me!"

The river. The god shoot apple. My heart aches with yearning for Poet. A buzzing is born in my ears, quiet at first. I don't pay attention, don't notice it until it grows so loud that it fills my head like hornets and my chest tightens. Blood rushes to my face. I'm dizzy. While I clutch the dirt and stones until everything stops spinning, vultures slow in their lazy flight, until they are suspended in the red sky. Flames freeze solid like blood painted against the high heavens. Everything goes black.

Whirling laughter surrounds me, a roar like water colliding against rocks and tumbles and flows.

Pressing both hands over my ears to muffle the screaming wind, I clench my eyes shut. The rumble is deafening. I'm so dizzy, I flatten myself on the dirt as the ground beneath me trembles. The wind is a meltemi raging and blowing...then abruptly stops. Everything just ceases—shaking, roaring, whirling. Songbirds sing a sweet and plaintive call.

I open my eyes. No one's here. I'm beside a wide river. "Where am I?"

"Now, that's a foolish question."

Pan squats before me. Everything about the satyr radiates. There's joy and mischief in his eyes, his full lips. Strong muscles ripple across his sun-bronzed chest, smooth and hairless. His missing tooth endearing. He waits for me to decide what to do as if he has all the time in the world.

"You summoned me?"

"I'm back at the river? How?"

"You wished to be here, did you not?"

"Is Poet here?"

Pan's smile fades. "Well. In a word. No."

"Where is he?"

"You know as well as I do... a little distracted."

"He's off following that *kore*."

Reflecting my anger, the river roars over boulders, its rushing water deafening, then quiets.

"Pan, why am I here?"

He walks over to Poet's last nest of grasses, and I follow him.

"Consider for a moment. What do you already know? Don't think constantly about what you don't, or what frightens you. How did you get back to this riverbed?"

"You brought me here?" I feel suddenly shy at the idea.

"Yes. And why?"

"More riddles, Pan? Now?" I sigh, exhausted. "I defied Zeus and Hades, the most powerful of all the gods... I'm in no mood for enigmatic questions."

"Well, yes, about that... you don't really think your little episode with King Thunder-gatherer and the Lord-of-Many Names is over, do you? I think what you did was very ill-advised."

It probably goes without saying that I very much agree. "So, why did you bring me here?"

"Love." His smile is so broad that I can't possibly stay angry with him.

"But you just told me that Poet isn't here."

I pick up an apple core I left beside the nest. It's covered with black ants. "There is no love here... only memories."

"Could we get back to my question? Since you in your vast wisdom thought it a fine idea to cross Zeus and Hades... well, let's just say we might not have a lot of time to philosophize about love and loss and stolen kisses."

I feel myself blush and look upriver to hide my face from the satyr. A warm wind blows my hair and stirs the grasses. I bend over and run my hand through a clump of poppies. "This place makes me sad, Pan."

"Sometimes sadness is a good thing. Sometimes if you know what you feel, then you know what you know...does that make sense?"

I look toward the distant shore. The water races strong and dark, sweep past swaying rushes. The river's sheen is brittle like a flat-bladed sword, the sun glances high against tree shadow.

One blink, and everything transforms. My time as a butterfly lets me see the beach in a different light. Burnished yellow shimmers from every rush and every grain of sand. An aurora of color sparkles like crystals in the reflected light.

A sudden shift, and the shadows and light return to a harsh gray, river that never ceases, a dead river without fish or snake or water turtle.

I take a deep breath and, glancing at Pan, understand he's waiting for me to know the meaning of my vision—the river and light and desperate separation of the two.

It's the girl and the butterfly. I've learned to see as a human and insect. From both their eyes. It's confusing. I shake my head and look closely at the satyr. My butterfly vision explodes once more into brilliant greens, like emeralds outlining his horns. Bold red like garnets halos his shoulders and crystal white spikes from his head.

Pan squats on the riverbank and plays trills and low melting notes. His mischievous eyes smile at me.

And his music! I can see the melody soar across the river. The notes are blue and green and deep, deep indigo. The beautiful song turns wild.

The butterfly in my heart wants to fly across the river with the colors and never return. The girl wants to curl up on the nest and never walk another step.

"Pan, please stop. Don't play another note. Tell me what I'm supposed to do."

He drops his arm and doubles over with laughter, eventually collapsing to the ground. At last, he calms enough to say, "You will be visited by a goddess. She will give you four tasks. If you fulfill them, you may be able to avoid the gods' wrath. You may bring your poet back to you."

"I don't know what's so funny about all this... what goddess?"

"Sorry. A child of Zeus will visit you."

I frown. A frown that quickly changes to a smile as the satyr's hummingbird flits between my poppy hair. Sips from one flower, caressing my chin with its wings, then flits off. Trying to gather my thoughts, I point out reluctantly, loath to shatter my hopes, "Zeus is not pleased with me. Why would his daughter help me?"

"She is the goddess of love."

"Aphrodite?"

"Yes..." He nods in a rare show of solemnity. "She may be your only hope. Really, isn't this Underworld challenge enough? You crossed Zeus *and* Hades? I don't know that even I can help you... but maybe, just maybe, you can help yourself."

"Parmenides tells me that only I can find my way to Tartaros." I toss a pebble at the water, watch it sink. "Now you tell me that I am the only one to... what, fight for myself? Pan, don't the gods *ever* help?"

The satyr picks up his panpipes and resumes playing. I'd swear that the river slows to listen. The wind stills.

"Pan, I remembered something. Well... partly remembered something."

The satyr smiles and squats before me. His eyes look like he already knows what I'm going to say, but he waits.

I turn my palm up and stare at three red stains. "You gave me three pomegranate seeds. We were in a cave... I remember a fire. You removed the seeds from a small chest and placed them in my hand." I look at Pan and try to see if this really happened. I don't trust any memories now. But he purses his lips kindly and waits and doesn't move a muscle.

"The seeds grew into a pomegranate..." My voice trails away. "Did this all happen? It must have. Just now, when the Olympians wanted to force me to leave... I knew it wasn't the first time."

He gathers both my hands and holds them palm up. The moment he touches me, everything changes. The river wind fills with bird song, and a light shines around the satyr's head and shoulders. Though he sits completely still before me, I hear his flute music, more beautiful than anything I've ever heard. It fills me with peace and a sense of belonging. "You're beginning to remember. That is good."

"Why, Pan, why am I here in the Underworld... alive? Why did I pay Kharon two pomegranate seeds to cross here?"

"You came here to rescue someone. Don't worry. You will find your destiny. You'll be fine."

He leaps to his feet and turns his back to me, then splashes across the river and disappears on the opposite bank, leaving me completely amazed... and alone.

I walk downstream, wishing the rushing water could calm me. Every step along the pebble bank, up the trail to the apple trees, reminds me of the time I spent with Poet. Our time together seems unimaginably vivid. I sink onto the nest of twigs and smell the pine straw—tart and earthy.

Everywhere I look, I see Poet. I smell the pine tar on his hands. I hear a small sparrow sing from a high branch, and my heart flies to Poet's laugh, the way his eyes shone when he looked at me. Then. Before the *kore*.

CHAPTER SEVENTEEN
THE GOD'S REVENGE

Have you had enough? Are you done trying to do it all on your own?

"Who's there?" I hear a woman's voice, but there's no one.

One you refuse to call upon.

"Are you the goddess Pan told me would help? Aphrodite?"

There is your answer. There is your help. You knew this once. Have you forgotten?

I wait another long, endless moment. A smell like sweet honeysuckle envelops me. "I am ready to face my destiny."

And?

"What do you want me to say? To do? What do you want from me?"

Nothing. At last a whisper—Διος δἐτελειετου βουλη. Dios deteleitou boulei.

"The gods do not seem willing to help. If you're the goddess Aphrodite, please tell me what I must do."

"Are you simple? Why do you even ask?" A new voice, cold as venom, is as shocking as a harsh winter wind on a balmy day.

I freeze, wishing I could disappear.

"You think you can hide?!"

"Who said that? Where are you?"

As if forming from tree gloom, great wings—black as night—

shadow me. There's another on the opposite tree. Three ancient hags with black, leathery bodies and talons emerge, perched on boughs. With unexpected grace, they swoop down to surround me, and fold their wings.

Silence sits heavy between us, a stillness quiet and long.

I try to focus on the fact that I am a girl with long legs to run, no longer a butterfly. I stand tall before these raptor women with taloned feet and harshness for eyes.

"Do you think you can escape a god's wrath?"

"No one will. No one can. We do their will, when murder's at play. Revenge for the mother, killed most foul."

"Revenge for the brother or father who dies when honor dies."

I'm stunned. The light alters. Red and blue, orange and yellow vanish... as if the river's beauty is assaulted by these three. There's an absence of light. A void. Even their leathery wings reflect black like a night sky empty of stars or moon. Hate creeps up my back.

"Murderer."

"Murderer."

"Murderer."

"I'm not! I am blessed by the gods."

Snakes hiss and slither through their black hair. "Aww, why didn't we know the girl is blessed?" Monstrous and reeking of excrement and rancid blood, they press close on either side of me. The third sits on a boulder. With inhuman screeches like wild children gone mad, they mock and taunt me.

Who are these vile creatures? Parmenides... Pan, if you can hear me, who are these madwomen?

But it's not the Oracle's or a satyr-god's voice that whispers in my ear. It's the woman's... Soft and loving. *Stay calm. Do not show fear. These crones are Furies, vultures of death. They serve us gods to exact revenge. They know no pity or compassion—only thirst for blood.*

"Goddess, help me."

I cannot. Zeus sends them. I am not to meddle in his plans. Stay calm.

The Furies pant with high, hysterical laughter. "The girl looks guilty to me. What say you, sister?"

"I've done no wrong."

"That is for the gods to decide. Zeus and his brother Hades and the warrior goddess Athena will know your fate." Their laughter shrieks and whispers in sobs simultaneously old and childish.

"Once you cross the River Styx."

"Once you enter the Land-of-the-Dead."

"You will never leave alive."

"Ne...ver."

"Ne...ver."

The Furies. My mind stumbles over tales of vulture women without mercy who pursued Orestes. Like trying to repair broken pottery shards, I remember parts of the myth. Apollo ordered him to murder his mother. She'd laid a trap for her husband Agamemnon. He returned from Troy, from the battle, seeking his wife—and found her with another man. Orestes took vengeance.

Oh! These are Erinyes. Death hags.

Their wings brush my back, sending shivers up my spine. "If you've done no wrong, why are you here?"

I quickly think of Pan's words. "I'm looking for someone."

Their laughter unsettles me more than their words.

"This breath and the next... so short this life."

"What god cut your life ribbon and left you in this land for only the dead to walk?" They lift black wings and circle around me. The air pulses red.

"I'm not a god's victim. I'm alive. I must find the blind seer Tiresias. He will tell me who I am. And I'm... there's something."

The Erinyes throw back their long necks and laugh. Is it laughter? It's screams and cries and harsh disdain.

"She doesn't kno...ow. Magaera, the little girl doesn't kno...ow." Like cruel children playing, they circle and mock. Cackle and flap their wings up and down in a slow rhythm, like a dirge. "We know something that you don't," they singsong. Dip long necks so their beaks, red tongues, and black, ruthless eyes whirl around me. Their game is sinister like death. Like hate. At last they stop, so close that I gag on their rank breath.

"You believe that you control fate?"

"Your destiny?"

The Furies fold their wings, cock their heads sideways to peer at me with bleak eyes.

"We kill. We claim loved ones."

"For the gods."

"For honor."

"From chaos comes order. All alone you became butterfly? Without a god's assistance?"

"Alone you will find the blind seer? Alone you walk this land of revenge and lost hope?"

"I don't need the gods. I can find Tiresias by myself."

"Ha! Only a fool believes she walks alone. Separate." Their voices jump one to another like a ball thrown round a circle in a child's game.

"I hope you find..."

"what..."

"you're looking for."

"A blind seer you trust to show the way?"

One hag's black-skinned hand snakes from beneath her rags and holds out a red cup, circled with black figures: a warrior with sword raised to kill a fallen woman, a spider, and a goddess, imposing with wide-swept wings.

"Here, sweet girl."

"You don't need the old man." Her voice is light, cajoling. "We help you find your destiny."

"Drink and know who you are."

"Drink." A second Fury steps back as if to let me decide. She tucks her wing feathers close to her side and looks at the third sister who also steps back, bows her head to me.

"Drink and remember, girl."

No, kore. They are vile. They only know revenge. Don't trust them. The mysterious woman's voice startles me, brings me back to my senses.

The dark red liquid looks viscous. "It's blood? You offer me blood? Revenge is all you know. Your world is dictated by gods' will. You kill for them without question."

"We destroy for honor."

"To avenge a mother's death."

"A brother's oath."

I refuse to cower. "What if the gods are wrong?" I demand.

"Justice vindicates us."

"What about Orestes? Apollo told him to murder his mother to seek revenge for his father's death. A god told him to murder his own mother! Where is the justice in that?"

"Apollo was wise," the hag-bird screeches. "Clytemnestra murdered Agamemnon, because he sacrificed their daughter... *their daughter!*"

"On the god's command, I might add. He sacrificed his own daughter Iphegenia to claim fair winds to sail to Troy... *because the gods told him to!*" I spit out the words.

"Διος δέτελειτου βουλη! Dios deteleitou boulei!"

"We do the gods' will."

"Their plans are fulfilled!"

I take a step closer to the tallest Fury, so close, I smell rotting meat with her breath and a stench of corpses as she lifts her wings, but I don't back away. "When does it end? Blood honor to avenge blood honor. Will it ever stop? Or just be passed generation to generation?"

"You question the gods? A girl who doesn't know who she is?" The Fury eases back and stares down at me. "The Fates weave your destiny."

"We give you a great gift. Drink and know who you are."

"Sweet girl. We can help."

"We know all."

"Take the cup."

"Take the cup."

"Take the cup."

Overwhelmed with an urge not my own, as if in a trance, my hand reaches out, brushes the hag's scaly finger, wraps around the clay cup and seizes the smooth rim. I claim the cup. I claim my destiny.

I lift it to my nose and smell. And smile at its unexpected sweetness, honeyed as berries.

How can I possibly find Tiresias alone like this? What did I think? It's crazy. The Erinyes do the god's will. They can help me. My head swoons with the aroma of nectar and honey and wild poppies. I close my eyes and try to imagine. *Parmenides always disappears when I need him. Poet is off chasing the* kore. *Whom do I rely on? I'll drink and know. One sip.*

"No! Thea, don't!"

"Who is here? Sister, I smell murderer!"

I jump back and look in the direction she points. Poet rushes from the trees.

He pushes past the Erinyes, shoving them aside, and knocks the cup from my hand. It shatters on stone and spills crimson into the river. It bubbles and steams.

"What are you doing? You followed Medusa... and now, you think you can tell me what to do? How dare you!"

Poet shrinks back at my words, but there's defiance in his eyes. We glare at each other, as the Furies whirl around us, screaming, flapping leathery wings spotted with blood.

"She's ours now!"

"The brother gods sent us to claim her!"

"Go away... you be murderer."

"Thea, I want to help. Please..."

"You want to help? Then go back to Medusa! They know my destiny! Do *you*? How dare you come here and tell me what to do!"

"Thea... I do." When he rests his hand on my shoulder, memories wash over me. The god's apple he picked for me. The raft he wove for us to float together into the unknown. Our nest in the Elysian Fields.

"Poet," is all I can say.

He takes my hands. "I know *our* destiny."

The Furies flap their wings wildly and fill the air with accusations of murder and revenge. They push between us and circle Poet.

"We claim you, murderer most foul!"

"Poet!" Red light throbs around his body. *You came for me.*

The air vibrates with the Furies' rage. Poet's fear.

"Go back to Medusa," the Fury leans so close to Poet that one viper slithers from her hair and wraps around his neck.

Poet seizes the snake with both hands, ripping it off. With a quick motion, the Fury scoops up the viper and wraps it lovingly around her neck.

"Medusa waits for you."

"He betrayed his oath to you, sweet girl? Never will he escape the dark gate."

"Revenge is ours for those who betray. For those who murder."

"You are murderer. You are ours."

I shut my eyes against the red shards of light flashing from Poet's body. Red like blood.

"It's not like that, Thea."

"Ratnakara! Murderer! Vengeance is ours."

"Is it true? Are you a murderer?"

He stares at the ground. "You know I don't know who I am... any more than you do."

The air around us is spiteful. The Furies' hatred shimmers between us. I glance over at Poet for reassurance but see only doubt. And that does it. These vulture-bat...whatever they are... birds rile me. I shove the hag closest to me so hard that she lurches into the air, only to land on the other side of Poet.

"No. Leave him alone! He's no murderer. He wouldn't... couldn't have intended to kill anyone."

"Death is our concern."

"And honor."

"Revenge."

The Erinyes circle us, their power like a storm wind, a *meltemi* hot and violent. But I no longer care. I'm swept up by my own words. I just don't care.

"Oh is it? When will it stop? Well, I say it stops here. Now! You can't have Poet!"

Abruptly, they're silent. Too silent. They ease closer.

Poet clutches my hand.

My head spins with a sharp buzz like furious hornets. I drop into a vision—

A wind swirls around me, honey-thick and alive with girls' voices. Chanting and dancing and laughing, young girls join hands and whirl around us, carefree, joyful.

Hope and laughter fill me. I *belong* with these sisters. And there's another thing: I feel powerful. Filled with new courage.

The girls fade, and there are only the hag-women hunched around me. Their fury is palpable.

I lift my head and stare from malevolent eye to malevolent eye.

The Furies step back but don't leave. Hatred blazes from them, timeless, vast. Revenge. Claim Poet. Judge Poet. Kill him. Kill us both.

CHAPTER EIGHTEEN
WHAT IS BETRAYAL?

To steady myself, I clutch Poet's fingers tighter, until my mind drinks their flesh and strength. Once again, the air around me fills with singing and chanting, honey-thick and alive with droning hexameters to Apollo, as the girls caress my hair and laugh in my ear.

My heart begins to understand. They are the spirits of all the pythias, a chain threading back to the ancient prophet who first communed with the Python deep in the earth's womb.

The girls' voices grow louder, more insistent. "You must never forget. We are linked mother to daughter like moonrise to sunrise and again to moonrise. And you, sister, you are one of us."

"Poet, do you hear the pythias?"

He glances at me, without taking his eyes off the hags who circle round and round, their breathing rough and wheezing as they lift and lower their wings, casting shadow, light, shadow and light. Poet's confused look is all the answer I need. He doesn't hear them.

Only the Furies. Only his death.

Sinking to my knees, I lift my arms in supplication and pray, then stand and face the Furies, my heart full.

They stop circling.

"As Pythia, I bring Apollo's light to this Land-of-Darkness. Like my sisters—" I sweep my arm wide and smile at the pythias above me, their yellow robes a-swirl. As if satisfied that I've heard and understood, their robes and smiles and laughter dissolve into a sparkling cloud. Dancing motes that dissipate, until only their song remains. "I am not alone. This day, you will leave. You will not claim Poet. He is here under my protection."

Poet glances from the hags to me, his eyes still wide and unsure.

I reach my hand across to him. The song swells. The sky turns yellow and lavender and then a deep indigo as the chanting crescendos and soars.

Poet hesitates to take my hand. The Furies step back as I smile one to another. Each glaring eye locks with my own, but I don't look away. I let their hate and venom flow into me... and then release it into song. I play the pythias' melody with my panpipes and let the music bring me hope.

The hags hunch and shuffle side to side, their black robes flapping, tangling in their gray hair. They lift their wings across ashen, wrinkled faces, their mouths wide in screams.

With my free hand, I take Poet's and entwine our fingers. Lifting our hands, I play, forcing my mind to imagine the sun's white power. The music turns black shadows beneath the Furies' wings to lavender, then searing white.

The hags screech and twist.

At last, the three crones howl and flap their powerful wings, lifting into the sky. They disappear beyond the sooty cliffs.

My song swells and fades. I drop my arm to my side and look into Poet's eyes.

We stand together holding hands with only the burbling of water washing over the stones and a warm breeze with a faint scent of apples. We stare across the river. I wonder for a moment what he sees... and what he *saw*. Did he see the pythias? Did he hear their song? Or only mine?

Pan's hummingbird dips its beak in the water and flits playfully around the poppies in my hair, as Poet rests his hand for one brief moment on my shoulder before kneeling beside the river and letting his fingers trail in the spray.

Quietude sits between us. It feels right. He is safe, and here. At last, I sink down beside him and cross my legs; place my shaking hands on my knees. "Poet, you came back."

"Did you think I would not?"

"How did you know where to find me?"

He laughs and nods at the tiny bird still dipping and bathing in the river. "He found me."

"Who?"

"Pan's hummingbird, in the forest near our campsite. He dove and careened right in front of me. Took off. Came back. It was clear he wanted me to follow, so I did... and here you are."

With that, I can't help but smile. At him. At my own stupidity. "I didn't think I'd ever see you again. I guess I thought you'd gone off with Medusa..." I finally look up at him. "She is very beautiful... and don't tell me you didn't notice!"

He wraps his arm around my shoulder, his grasp strong. His smile wide. "Thea, I may not remember who I am. Or why I'm here, but there's one thing I know... if only one... we are here together. For each other."

His olive-skinned face flushes amber, and he looks off, pulls his arm away and cracks his knuckles.

"Poet, I didn't even care who I was...who I am... I only wanted to stay here with you. We should never have left. I defeated the Titan, the Furies..."

"Thea, why did the Erinyes spare me? Your music has powers?" He grasps both my shoulders and turns me so I have to look at him. "How did you change back from a butterfly?"

"A lot happened while we were apart. I don't know if I can explain. I... remembered something. I am one of generations of pythias. Oracles who have the power to know the future. Sybils who speak with the gods... or really, they, well *we*... listen to the gods."

He stands and steps away. "You're an Oracle dedicated to Apollo?"

I nod.

"Then your life belongs only to the gods..."

I can't bear to talk to him about that. Not now. "Poet, there's another thing... I rescued souls—farmers and their wives and children. They had been enslaved in trees. That's the reason the Furies tracked me... the Lord-of-Many-Names... no! I'll say his name. Hades! Hades wants me dead. I betrayed his laws."

Poets face grows dark and concerned. He tilts his head to the side and studies my face. At last, a light kindles in his eyes. Understanding. He lifts one poppy from beside my cheek and smiles so broadly that his whole being seems to shine. "Thea, you are a Pythia. So, that explains these. A gift from a god?"

"It's not clear, but I think so. From Pan." I brush the flowers away from my face. "Poet..."

"You can ask me anything." Suddenly serious, he leans back and waits for my question.

"The Furies said they came for revenge. They called you Ratnakara. They called you a murderer." His face is blank and hurt by my accusation, deeply bewildered. "I don't believe them. I *know* you." I jump to my feet and look down at him. "I will not play their sordid game. My heart would know if you could kill. I don't believe it, Poet. Poet, that's who you are."

"Am I? What if I'm everything those hags said? The gods sent them. They must know."

I hesitate. That blood-red light around him. I saw it, harsh and accusing. Am I stupid to ignore the warning?

Poet sees me wait. He nods, as if answering my unspoken answer, and stands. "I should go. It's dangerous for you if I'm here... and you..." He stares at the poppies.

With his look, as if it's a caress, the flowers dance. Poet watches the flowers lift and twirl. His smile is so sad, so lost.

"You are touched by a god, Thea, you deserve better than what I can give you."

He turns away and walks slowly upstream.

My vision shifts to butterfly vision. Like my confused thoughts, the sand and wind fracture. Light casts off the racing water—flame red changing to lavender and indigo, sparkling light motes dancing like gnats.

Unable to move or decide what to do, I try to unscramble the honeycombed images of Poet. Like the faceted vision I have of Poet as he walks away, as he becomes a black dot in the distance, I have just as many thoughts of who he really is. Murderer? Friend? Betrayer? Lover? Are any of us any one thing?

Why can't it be simpler? Why can't he only be the man I love? The man I hold in my arms and forget everything else? My mind is a tangle. I should run after him. Will I lose him again? Even from this distance, his despair beats at me. He loves me, and I am letting him walk away... but what about my vision? If I am Pythia and he is a murderer? There is no together for us. I have to let him go, but I can't. I don't care what he's done before we met.

My legs tense to run after him. He is about to disappear around a bend in the river.

While I hesitate, out of the corner of my eye, I see something move. The Furies stand spread-winged like statues of black marble before heavy pines. The sky above me fractures with fire and smoke.

"Poet!" I scream. He can't hear me over the river. I run toward him, shouting and waving my arms. "Poet! The Furies!"

The hags flap from across the river with a sound like storm winds. Huddled together as one monster, they carry with them a shadow. A black shadow that encases him like a shroud.

Lost in despair, Poet doesn't hear my screams or the hags' shrieks. Only when the shadow envelops him does he turn toward the river. Too late.

All I can see is the bird-women, like scavenging vultures, huddled around him, screeching and thrashing their prey. My Poet is lost.

I run and run. Stumble over river stone. Jump to my feet and run harder. But there's nothing I can do. He came back for me. He loves me?

I didn't trust him. I didn't trust my own heart.

Like one beast, the Furies seize Poet's shoulders and lift into the air. He punches one hag's throat and kicks. His limbs are a windmill flailing against the Furies.

I scream until my throat is raw and run harder. The rocks bruise through my sandals, and I limp a step, then rush on.

At last I bend double to catch my breath, to relieve the sharp pain in my side.

Time slows. The shadows are rancid bat wings churning the air. Screams and curses and Poet's arms pummeling bird bodies. Beaks ripping away cloth and hope.

Though my rage matches theirs, there's nothing I can do.

They carry Poet high and away, black coal against the sky, and vanish beyond the high cliffs.

I try to follow, race once more along the river's edge. The blood-sky is empty.

"Where is he?" I scream at dead oaks, dense and tangled.

A searing wind rattling charred branches is my only answer.

I search the sky for any movement that might be Poet in the Furies' clutches. Shades slither between flames. Vultures squawk as if directing their dance. "Death-birds of this Underworld, tell me!"

The dance never falters.

"Tell me! I am Pythia. Tell me where they've taken Poet!"

I shake my fist at them and spin in mad circles. "I will destroy every stone and river... every bird of this land, until I find him. Where is he? Where did they take him?"

Poet is gone.

I believed in my courage and iron-strong will. I believed I could keep him safe.

I was wrong.

The sky is empty. He came to help me, and because he did, they found him and claimed him. If he'd stayed with Medusa, he'd be safe. I would rather lose him to her.

My heart is empty. I have no idea what to do.

The Furies will kill him.

It's my fault.

There's no thought to my flight, only raw will. I run an erratic path along the water's edge. As if the Erinyes left their evil path for me to follow, I see a sparking luminescence weave between the rushes. In the distance, I hear Poet's last faint cry and struggle to catch up. I run so far, I'm sure the gods cannot reach me.

A mantra repeated over and over pounds the path in time with my feet.

Save Poet.

Save Poet.

Save Poet.

I fail at everything. How can I possibly hope to save anyone?

At last, I sink down in river grasses and watch the water rush past. A cry comes from above. I jump to my feet, but it is only a bird circling me.

And Poet is gone.

Does time pass? Perhaps. My heart constricts with the waiting. Is that how we measure time? With loss and struggle? Do we sit in a Void with only our tears and triumphs marking it passing?

I hate the gods! "What use are you? I'll force you to bring him back! He did nothing!"

I pound my fist into the stones wet from the river. I cry and scream and strike the rocks, until my hands bleed.

And Poet is gone.

CHAPTER NINETEEN
GODDESS OF LOVE

For days, I wander aimlessly along the river.

When I stare at the current racing past, I remember Poet splashing me. I remember us laughing together. I can taste the apple we shared. So many memories. In the empty sky, I can pick out his smile.

And all the while, as I pace and wait and fume at everything in my path, I feel like I'm being watched. Back and forth I tread the shore and never arrive anywhere. How can I, when I have no idea where to go?

A branch cracks in the woods behind me, and I whirl around. "Poet?"

A young woman walks out between two pines. It strikes me for one short breath, a gasp so sharp that it hurts, that she reminds me of someone I knew. No, someone I *know*.

But the feeling disappears as she steps up to me with the grace of a dolphin slipping beneath the waves. I can't stop staring at her. Her confidence shimmers with a white light. Long golden hair curls below her waist. She's dressed in gossamer robes, a gold brooch carved like clamshells pinned at each shoulder. A wide belt, iridescent with blues and turquoise like the sea, wraps several times around her slender waist.

"He calls you Thea. The boy the Furies took away. He calls you a goddess... he's a fool."

It's the same voice. It's Aphrodite.

I feel as if I fall into her eyes, cerulean like a morning sky, indigo as dusk, I can be lost there. Forget the last shred of myself... but I won't, because there's another feeling about her. I don't like the way she makes me feel like a rancid taste of rotting olives. Repulsed and yet drawn to her beauty, my tongue is bitter, when I say, "You think he's a fool?"

I tense as a rushing wind like a sea wave sweeps around us. The goddess says nothing.

She lifts her arms high, leaving a sparkling trail of foam.

A chill runs through me. She smells of the sea... a deep ocean strewn with sweet narcissus. Something about her speaks of Mt. Olympos and power. There's overwhelming beauty in the lift of her chin and glow of sun-stroked skin. I want to fold my body in her arms like a child, stroke her hair and bawl to her about losing Poet.

A dove lands on her outstretched hand and sings a low and gentle melody that tugs at my heart. But at the same time, something is false about her smile.

There's a whisper in my ear. "I'm Aphrodite, goddess of love."

"Aphrodite, Pan said you can guide me. Those foul hags... the Erinyes... claimed Poet."

"Those *foul hags* are my sisters, all of us born from Ouranos' death at Kronos' hand."

A shudder runs through me at the mention of the Titan's name. "Aphrodite, Poet is gone. They took him. The *gods* took him."

Here I go again, crossing the gods. I know I should keep anger out of my voice. But I can't.

Aphrodite scowls at me.

She's a goddess. Love and desire, the stars and longing seas move with her power. I draw a deep breath and square my shoulders.

"You're the goddess of love. You understand how I feel." My words come out without thought. Their truth stifles my breath and erupts in tears. "I love him, goddess..." I choke back a sob. "He's gone. It's my fault the Furies claimed him." I kneel before Aphrodite and grasp her knees in supplication. "Please, I will do whatever you ask." Bowing my head, I let tears drop on her sandaled feet.

She looks down at me, hesitates before she draws me to my feet. "I may help you find Poet. Do you know the story of Psyche, the maid who loved my son Eros? Who betrayed him?"

You pretend to be a goddess of love? All I can think of is this goddess telling her son to make Psyche fall in love with a monster. Goddess of revenge maybe... or jealousy. Not love.

She tosses her head back and laughs, crows with the certainty that I will honor her. That I will love her as all mortals do. But adoration is not my game. She glares at me. She knows what I'm thinking. I lower my gaze and hope to appear humble.

"Do you have the will to fulfill my tasks? How much do you love the boy?"

Her touch stuns me, as if a lightning bolt shoots through my chest.

"You want to find Poet." Her voice trembles with venom. Her anger gnaws at my core, like a black mist that will suffocate me. "If you want to reclaim that boy you love, you will complete four tasks... and first, you will follow me... yes or no? Do not waste my time!"

"Yes, goddess, I will do your bidding. For Poet, I would fly the path of Zeus' eagles and circle the earth. For Poet, I would travel to Tartaros." Rays of yellow and white light flare and flash from her body. She waves her arms above my head. A deep purple mist haloes from her fingers.

"But Aphrodite, do not think me as helpless as Psyche."

Back and forth like a shuttle weaving woof and warp, I dance, crisscrossing the purple, waving and dipping my red poppies through and back, until a gossamer cloak of red—diaphanous and shimmering—drapes the goddess' shoulders.

Touching the delicate shawl with gentle fingers, she gasps. "How did you do that?"

"Let's just say it's my song of the universe. Now, about those tasks?"

She looks at me with new eyes. Curious eyes. For an instant, respect shines from them, before the moment fades. Her face hardens into a gold mask, she draws herself tall to tower over me. "You failed the boy. You mocked the love you say you have for Poet.

You betrayed him just as Psyche betrayed my son's trust." Her voice drops to a threatening whisper. "So, you are Pythia. And you believe that is more important than your love. Your *hubris* destroyed Poet, left him alone and vulnerable to the Furies. You call that love?" She screams her last question, and the world stops to hear. "You must now prove you love him."

Humbled by her accusation, I bow my head. "Tell me what I must do."

"First, you will spend the night in a room filled with wheat, barley, and rye. If you hope to find Poet, you must have each grain sorted upon my return."

The air where the goddess stood shimmers with a gold light like fireflies dancing their mating dance on a summer night. The sparkling motes that were Aphrodite swirl and lift and dissolve. The goddess of love is gone.

Poet is gone.

A fire-seared wind lifts my poppy hair. I look back into the pine forest, peer into the shadows. I turn in slow circles. There's no bird song. Not even any vultures above. The sky no longer flames but is iron gray and dull. Even the river churns by soundless. Black cliffs tower high.

I will find the grains and sort them. And then I will demand to know the next task and the next. I will find Poet and tell him that I love him.

I walk along the river, until the endless twilight shatters all sense of reality. Until there is only one reality, and it is so pathetic that I laugh. Occasionally, my fingers stroke the panpipes in my sash, but my hand and arms are numb, senseless to their swinging as I force myself to keep going. Just keep going. All I'm really aware of is my tired and stinging feet planting on pebble and sand and clay, plodding one after another.

Somewhere ahead is a chore demanded by a goddess. Somewhere beyond the river mist is what? A barn? Cottage? Stone shepherd's hut? I have no idea. I only know that I must find the grains. And sort the grains.

I can't think about what I've lost or hope to find.

I will only think about the task set for me by Aphrodite.

What other choice do I have?

With each step, growing more and more tired in this land of semi-darkness that never grows light or fully dark, I force myself to imagine only one thing: I'm sitting on a stone floor with a tangle of grains piled before me. Sickly light filters through deep stone windows, barely lighting the room. I stop there in my vision, take another step along the shore, and re-imagine the cottage: stone floor pile of grains. My reaching hand scoops up a handful of grains.

I have no idea how I will sort the grains... if I ever find them... but first I must locate them. Maybe if I picture a cottage and the pile clearly enough, this Underworld land will reveal them. Over and over I envision them. My feet are so tired now that I stumble. I want to stop. Just sink down in the grasses here along the shore. Just stop.

But the Furies have Poet.

I can't stop. I won't stop. I will find Poet.

CHAPTER TWENTY
FOUR LABORS: THE FIRST TASK

t last it's there. Just as I imagined it... because I** imagined it? Across the river, tucked beside a massive boulder that forms one wall, is a stone cottage.

But it's on the other side of a wide raging current.

Without hesitation, remembering what Poet had built when we needed to get away from the Titan, I head upstream toward thick rushes. Beyond loom the black snags—trees long destroyed by the rushing water inundating their roots. I wade out, bracing myself against the current. The water comes up to my waist and it's hard to balance. Twice I'm pushed over into the river and come up sputtering and choking. I fish around, square myself against the current with my knees bent and legs spread wide enough to steady me.

At last, the dead and brittle branches break off when I pound them with the biggest boulder I can lift. With one movement, I drop the rock and grab my prize before it's swept away. I throw the branch to the shore, search for the stone, and do it all over again.

Before I can gather the branches I think I'll need, my arms tremble, my knees quake.

"Poet, I will find you." I chant with each double bash of rock against wood. "Poet, I'll save you. I'm sorry. I'm sorry. I'm sorry."

When I finally wade back to the closest shore, there's a sharp pain between my shoulder blades and my hands are lacerated. I squat on the river's edge and dangle my hands in the water, while I stare across at the hut. I push on my knees to stand and wade over to the rushes. They don't look like the lush, green grasses that grow along the river that flows by Pan's meadow.

These are rough and brittle. Purple and black. I thought I'd be able to snap them off with my bare hands, but they're tougher than I imagined. I fix my feet in the mud, seize a rush with both hands, and tug. At last, one plant comes up, roots, and stem and leaves. Again and again, I pull up the river plants by the roots, until I gather enough to weave the tree snags together.

It takes forever. At last, I jump on and let the current carry me downstream. Using several rushes I twisted together as a paddle, I guide the raft to the opposite shore.

Exhausted, I climb a slight hill to the hut. Push open the splintered wood door, with hinges of goat skin stiff and cracked. The door scrapes across a dirt floor and hangs askew.

It doesn't take long for my eyes to adjust from the perpetual twilight outside to the quiet, utter abandonment of the hut. A shaft of gray light slants through a solitary window, slithers its way between the dust motes. Rising from the room's edges to the rafters, barley and wheat and rye grains tumble together. How can I possibly sort them? By morning? It's like a cumulus cloud swallowing the raindrops and then demanding I organize them.

I sink to my knees.

"Poet."

Despairing, I scoop up a handful of grain from the pile, and one by one, pick out the dark rye and start a new pile to my right. Another handful.

There's a subtle shift of light against the wall. The room grows darker with shadow but never completely devoid of light. I switch to the light wheat, because it's easier to see in the dimness. My wheat pile grows to the size of my thumb, my fist, but the original pile never shrinks.

Out of the corner of my eye, I see movement. It looks like a slender thread the Moirai weave, the silk strands that the sisters, the Fates, spin out to create our destiny.

But it's not a silk thread. It's ants doggedly pacing a chain, one behind another, toward the massive grain pile.

Each ant turns back with a grain of barley, wheat or rye in its mouth, almost as big as its body. The ants' nature compels them to tread day after day in their struggle to find food, to feed the queen, to support the farm... and am I any different? A goddess tells me to sort the grain... so here I sit. Is this how the gods control us?

This is hopeless! How will I find Poet sitting here?

In my rage, I crush several ants with my thumb. But killing the poor, pathetic ants doesn't make me feel better. I find another kernel, focus on the colors, try to make each pile exactly right. What else can I do?

Beyond the door, a wind gathers. I'm not at all sure how long I've been listening to it, but at last, I sit back on my haunches, push my hand against the small of my back. I stand slowly and walk over, push aside the planks.

No, it's not wind. It's singing. A woman's voice low and soft... and familiar. From where? Could it already be morning and this is the goddess come to mock me? I panic at the thought and peer into the gray world.

It's not Aphrodite, but the old woman who defied the Shades when I was a helpless butterfly who thought it would be a good idea to argue with the brother gods. Her head wrapped in a blue scarf, her eyes dark and smiling, she sweeps dead leaves from the path beneath an oak sheltering the hut. With each stroke of her rush broom, she hums and sings the same refrain over and over.

"Girl... hmmm... white.

Girl... ran.

Not stay...

... wedding... hmmm... day." Each broom swipe brings her closer and closer.

She stops singing and sweeping less than a stride before me. Grabs her broom with both wizened hands to lean on it and looks up at me. There's a light in her eyes as she waits for me to say something. To recognize her.

"No kill ants."

"What... how...?"

"Ask in?"

Her voice is frail and halting as if it's hard for her to form words, but her eyes fill with love.

I stand aside and with an exaggerated sweep of my arm, usher her in. Always welcome a stranger to your home, someone told me many times... my mother?... for any stranger at your door may be a god in disguise. This old woman's arrival from the shadows and mist certainly feels like a divine visitation.

A corner of her blue scarf brushes me as she slips past. No, it doesn't touch me. It slithers through my finger holding aside the door planks with a sensation of both heat and cold. I shiver involuntarily, but don't back away.

I follow her in to the tower of grains. A slight smile lights her face as she looks at me and then down at the ants, still meticulously pacing in line. I watch with her. It's mesmerizing. The tiny insects scurry toward the mound, seize a granule, turn and hurry back the way they came. They pass the other ant line without a glance sideways.

"You see? Understand?"

She sits beside the pile and looks up at me with expectation.

"Are you here to help me?" I squat beside her.

"Kill ants?" She pierces me with a look filled with surprise and anger. "Stupid!"

I jump to my feet. "You call me stupid? I have to sort these grains. The goddess told me I have until morning." I point to the door. "If you're not here to help me, please, leave. I have no time to waste with you, old woman!"

"Stupid!"

I'd expect her to be angry, but her eyes implore me to understand. With a wizened finger, she points from the grains to the ants and then

ORACLE OF THE SONG

at last at me. "Granddaughter."

"What?" A shiver of understanding runs up my back but fades before my forgetful mind can grasp it.

She points once more at the ants. "Help you."

Her finger jabs again toward the ants that have never stopped trudging between the pile and a crack in the stonewall where they disappear.

"What are you trying to tell me?"

She looks at me with such pleading in her gaze. "Ants work." Her breath comes in gasps now, each word forced from her cracked lips—an obvious effort. One that is also stealing what strength she has to maintain her form. For it is fraying and drifting like smoke from a fire. She is almost gone.

And I'm desperate to understand why she came. "Wait! Please."

I am alone in the room. There is the grain mound. The ants.

At last, a disembodied whisper, "Ants." Hoarse and strained, it fades into the shadowed stone. "Help. Help. Help."

I slump to the floor.

The ants scurry one after another up to the heap and then away. I'm sorry now. Why did I hurt them? I place one grain of barley in a pile. Rye over to my side. My fingers move on their own while my mind goes wild.

The ants march past in line.

I pluck another grain and another.

One ant, loaded with a barley grain as heavy as its body, pauses and looks up at me.

With that one look, that one break in his line and work and routine, I suddenly understand. The ants! They sort and carry and never question their lot. The role life's given them... or do they?

I lie on my stomach and watch the insects hurry past. From this angle, they are a blur before my eyes. They are also my hope.

"I'm sorry," I breathe, afraid my voice will startle them. "The old woman was right. I am stupid. I am deeply sorry I killed your friends... and my friends. They are my friends too, aren't they?" I feel a little crazy lying on the floor talking to ants, but suddenly it all makes sense.

"Can you help me?"

The ants pace past, segmented bodies brushing a line on the dusty floor, eight legs in their steady march.

Suddenly tears pour down my face, relentless and purging. "They took Poet... the goddess said... please, will you help me?"

The two lines of ants shift. A new pattern forms. Three lines, as if by magic, approach the mound from three sides. One line walks back with rye. Another wheat. Another barley.

My efforts are feeble at best, but I smile and cry and pluck grains as fast as I can.

The mounds grow in three corners. The only sound for long hours is a scrape of grains against the dirt floor and my breath. Time passing is our enemy. The ants scurry back and forth to the dwindling pile and their growing mounds faster and faster. With each moment, I fear the goddess' return.

"Thank you. Thank you." I whisper over and over, like a work chant to aid in completion.

The light shifts and plays and fills the damp cottage. The goddess.

"Girl, there's no time to waste. If you would find your beloved, then come over here. Sit before me and be quiet."

My throat is dry with worry, but something about her tone, some new tenderness distracts me. "As you wish, Aphrodite." I kneel before the goddess and rest my hand on her sandaled foot. "I finished separating the grains."

Her eyes narrow as if she sees inside me. "*You* separated them, girl? Without help? Such *hubris*!"

I flush, as I bow to the goddess. "Not alone." I look up into her stern gaze. "I am never alone." Gesturing behind me without turning around, I let my words rush out as if they could escape. "What is the next task?"

"As well you've asked. Bring me the Golden Fleece. It hangs in perpetual sun in Colchis on a barren oak branch. Deep in a thicket lurks the sleepless fire-breathing dragon, as vast in width and breadth as a fifty-oared ship, whose teeth can become armored warriors. There you'll find the resplendent pelt guarded by bulls with hooves of brass and breath of fire."

"How do I reach rocky Colchis, Goddess?"

"Find a ship and sturdy sailors, and navigate through the Symplegades, the channel where the rocks are alive, where huge cliffs crash together. No one may sail between them." At my puzzled look, Aphrodite sees fit to bestow upon me a smile. "No one, that is, who does not have the help of a goddess. You simply do as Jason was advised: release a dove as you approach the islands. If the dove makes it through, then have your men row with all their might... why do you look so pale?"

I bow my forehead to touch her knee. My throat constricts. Looking up into her calm gaze, I swallow. "Divine Aphrodite, I may not leave the Land-of-the-Dead."

"Then you will never find the boy."

I pace back and forth. "But if I leave, will I be able to return?"

"Stop pacing!"

At her sharp tone, I sit on the ground in front of the goddess of love. "For love, I came to this dark land. Now for love, I must leave?"

"Yes. You must. You must travel to Colchis."

Aphrodite lifts her arms and sparkling sea foam flows from her golden hair, until it envelops her like a mist growing denser. The mist frays and drifts in a soft breeze, and with the last chime of melodic laughter, she's gone.

I rush outside and turn in circles, but there's no sign of her. A snake looks up at me, then slithers off between charred rushes. "Aphrodite?"

Back inside the hut. The piles are gone. And the ants. Pulling my panpipes from my sash, I sit in the doorway and play, hoping the music will guide me. There's only my growing awareness that it's been a long time since I ate beside Parmenides' fire, a long time since my drink of sweet mint tea. My stomach cramps with hunger, but I continue to play. Songs the satyr played in his meadow, while the hummingbird flitted flower to flower. Songs that come to me that feel like I've loved them all my life. Were they my mother's songs? With every one, I catch quick glimpses of a woman in a moss-green chiton bending over a fire to stir a pot of soup, smiling over her shoulder. My heart believes she is my mother. I play the melody that twines with hers. I play a song soft and cooing like Aphrodite's dove. And another that is the river's rush. I play every cry of this forbidding land and then play each one again. The song I heard the pythias sing is droning hexameters, sonorous like a wind between cliffs. Then high and laughing like the cliff swallows.

With each song, I'm sure I will summon help. But no one comes. At last, I tuck my flute away. "Pan, where are you?"

CHAPTER TWENTY-ONE
THE SECOND TASK

I **thought you'd never ask."**

"Pan!" The satyr crouches on a black rock covered in lichen and nestled between thorn bushes. "Did you forget so soon?"

I jump up a rush over to him. "What?"

"You wanted to return to the apple tree... uhh, to the nest, and just who was it that brought you there?" He licks his full lips and plays a lively dance tune on his flute. His eyes narrow with a knowing smile.

The blood rushes to my face. "You did. Pan, you brought me back to the river."

He lowers his pipes and smiles at me. "Yes, well, and why?"

I stare at him until he gives in. Must everything with the gods be a riddle?

"The answer is simple... you asked me to."

"Oh."

"And?"

I grab his shoulders. "Please, Pan. Four tasks..."

"Child, tell me one thing at a time. Tell me how you plan to find the boy."

The satyr and I sit side by side on the hut's stone threshold, and I explain about Aphrodite's demands and the ants and the Golden

Fleece. When I finally finish, he rubs his curly beard and stares at the ground.

As if the ants have returned and climb up my legs, I jump to my feet in impatience. "Pan, don't you see? You travel between the Land-of-Light and Land-of-Dark. You travel where I can't." I reach out for his broad fingers and pull him to stand. His tail and ears twitch, but he doesn't speak. "Please, Pan. Go to Colchis."

"There's the small problem of the dragon. The bulls that breathe fire. Not to mention the fact that if a goddess gives you a chore, then *you* are supposed to fulfill it." He pulls his hands from mine and squats before me, his arms wrapped around his knees drawn up to his chest.

"I'm not allowed to leave the Underworld and return. Pan, please help me... us."

"I believe I have already. Why should I defy the goddess?"

"She's the goddess of love. She will understand. She knows I love Poet."

"Love? The Oracle of Delphi loves a Hindu poet?"

I can't meet the satyr's gaze, and glance away sharply as a vulture lands atop the hut and peers down at me. The tilt of wrinkled skin surrounding piercing eyes... it's as if he listens to us...

"What will you give me in return?" Pan interrupts my thoughts, and I refocus on him.

He smiles, leaning back against the oak, arms crossed. Waiting, as if he has all the time in the world.

"Anything." My voice is more strident than I intend. I try again. "Pan, please."

He bursts out laughing and leaps up; his cloven hooves dance staccato on the earth. "Be careful, child! It would not be wise to promise a lecherous old satyr a gift without restrictions. I should say yes, and bind you to your oath." He skips two leaps closer, until he is so near that his breath, sweet with wine, blows warm against my lips.

"Pan, we're wasting time. The Furies have Poet. And this is my next task. I promise you anything you request... but will you go?" I drop to one knee and bow my head.

He grabs both my hands and pulls me up. Mischief fills his eyes.

Round and round he spins me, until I'm so dizzy, I can barely stand.

"Pan, what are you doing?" I laugh despite myself. "Poet. I have to find Poet."

He spins me around once more and lets loose; I go flying, then land in rushes and roll and roll. Weeds tangle my poppy hair as I stop at last face down.

I look up just in time to see Pan disappear with one high leap across the grasses leading down to the river. His voice drifts back to me. "You still owe me that favor." His laughter and flute music fade across the field.

Walking slowly back to the river's edge, I play Pan's melody over and over, willing the satyr to return. Wind blows through the grasses. There's the rush of water over boulders. And nothing.

"Gods! You play me for a fool! You come and go, help and curse. Tell me who I am! Tell me where I am!" I sink to my knees beside the river and pound the gritty soil. "How will I ever get the fleece?" I snap a branch that drifts onto the bank.

My anger spent, I sit back on my heels and let my tears fall into the river. Watching the current, I remember my mentor's words. *Are your tears separate from the river? Can we say: These are my tears and this the river's current? You are wrong, if you believe we stand apart from the trees, the river...the gods. Our senses fool us, Thaleia. Touch, sight and smell tell us we are alone. But do not believe your senses. Water is water. The kosmos is the kosmos... a universe that we are all a part of, though we think we are not.*

I chuckle and raise my arms to the fire sky. "Will I ever learn? Gods, I honor you and humbly ask your guidance. Only my hubris would urge me to think I can help Poet alone." I bow my head.

Five massive vultures swoop down, forming a half-circle around me. Red leathery heads sprouting bulbous eyes shift side to side.

The hair lifts on the back of my neck from their death stench. Gray dust covers their shiny feathers.

"The ants were my friends. Did some god send you? Can death be a guide?

I look from bird to bird... and at last settle my gaze on the largest.

"Please, bring me the Golden Fleece."

The massive bird tilts his head and stares at me. Honeycombed vision creates hundreds of vultures from the one.

I repeat Aphrodite's words.

Nothing.

A slight wind lifts the bird's shiny feathers.

I urge my vision to shift to the butterfly's, until the scavenger's ink-black feathers shimmer with rainbow colors. A memory of butterfly flight sweeps over me. I remember... no, I feel once more the wind lifting my wings.

In the distance, the river roars. Lavender, yellow, red and green swirl around the circled birds, pulsing with my breath.

Dancing colors fill me with a memory—the pomegranate tree sprouting from my palms. Black seeds hidden within the red flesh. My fingers tingle with their memory of the spider web stranding between laughing farmers and treebark and the gods.

I laugh, jump to my feet and spin in wild circles. "What a fool I am!"

Looking from bird to bird, I wonder... not for the first time... what destiny led me here to sit with vultures?

"My fear makes this Death-Land Real."

As if to prove me wrong, the scavengers flap wide wings and lift into the twilight sky. They fly higher and higher, until they are nothing but black specks.

"Divine Immortals! You live for time everlasting, but someday I will die. Now *I* choose my destiny!"

My vision shifts. Swept up by the hunting bird, as one, the largest vulture and I circle higher and higher. Far below, beside a racing river, I see a girl grow smaller and smaller. I am the pythia earth-bound and at the same time, I am the vulture with its thirst for death, for carrion.

There's no time to waste. I must guide the vulture to claim the fleece. Together we can escape the Underworld, seize the boon and with the grace of The Song, return with our prize.

Fly to Colchis!

With each turn, there is power. Power I have to control. Power I have to direct. I urge him higher.

We break through smoke and fire to sun-drenched blue. A song fills the honey-sweet sky. My heart leaps with longing. A thirst to stay and never return to the Land-of-Death.

Over there. Do you see the Sirens singing?

The vulture flies on a straight path as if deaf.

No, they're calling to us. Over to the right. Or is it there... the left? Suddenly, their song swells around me from every direction.

The vulture screams a harsh call that jolts me back to my senses.

We push on, until we fly high above a wine-dark sea and rocky shores lined by towering limestone cliffs. The cliffs are moving!

The vultures twist, darting between the massive limestone as it crashes together. There is a sound like thunder and earthquake as they collide just behind us.

Without hesitation, our feathered band soars high once again, flying straight toward an endless sun. At last, I see the oak rooted beside a clear stream.

Draped over a sturdy branch, the Golden Fleece shimmers with its own light—bold and brilliant.

Pacing round and round the tree are three bulls, black as a moonless night. They bellow fire when they sight us and paw the ground with brass hooves that flash in the sun. Gold-tipped horns rip the air as they lift high on muscled haunches.

A dragon jerks its indigo-scaled head high above laurel bushes and spits flames at us.

The vulture shrieks and plummets toward the oak. We twist and soar and dive... but it's hopeless. No matter how we approach, we can't get close to the fleece.

I urge the vultures up again. The air lifts us easily, so we can draft in circles without effort. The dragon and bulls rage far below.

I scream against my fear and direct the vultures lower.

"I can live my life with honor, and I will die."

We circle closer and closer to the dragon and bulls.

"I can live immobilized by fear... and still I will die."

Dragon-fire lashes so close that our feathers singe and curl. The vulture veers up and away. This is nothing like butterfly flight. My heart... our heart beats wildly, but I won't give up. I urge the bird to attack. *Now! Faster!*

There's a catch in his breath. A beat of fear.

We push on. Closer to the dragon's fire and raging bulls. Closer to our death.

One bull slashes with his horns but misses.

The vulture twists, swoops... clutches the shining pelt. We lift with one thrust of wide wings. Higher and higher into the sun-drenched sky.

For what seems an endless time, we fly, until the sky darkens with smoke, then flames hot and stinking. The vulture draws his feet close, so the fleece is nestled and safe in his feathers.

At last, a sharp descent past limestone cliffs lands us beside the hut. Beside a girl laughing and dancing and lifting her arms to the black scavengers.

Her laughter draws me back to my own body.

Once more the vultures circle me.

The Golden Fleece shines and glistens with its own light at my feet.

I bow my head to the bird. "Thank you. There are no words to express my joy. Thank you!"

The birds lift high in the sky as I hold the offering with outstretched hands and turn in circles. "Divine Aphrodite, I have the fleece. Come claim your boon and tell me my next task."

A light that smells of the sea and a warm summer wind envelops me. Before I see the goddess, I hear her voice, redolent and kind. "You have the hide of the ram. How did you claim it? The Sirens, the Clashing Cliffs... how, girl, did you claim this prize?" Huge and shining, Aphrodite appears before me and gently, as if it may shatter, takes the cloak from me. She holds it up to study it before turning those deep-sea eyes on me. "How did you do this, girl?"

"What does it matter, Goddess? I completed the second task. The

Golden Fleece is yours. What is your bidding? Tell me what I must do now?"

From beneath her silver robes, the goddess pulls a crystal jar. "This one may be the simplest yet. Return to the River Styx and fill this jar with its waters. Bring the doleful water to me. If you do, there will remain but one chore. The most challenging. The one that will take you to Hades Realm, the heart of this death land. But for now, return to the black river. Beware of the boatman, he will not take kindly to your return. I will find you by the shore if you succeed."

Clasping my hands together, I say, "It will be as you ask. I will return to the black river. I will challenge Kharon... but I don't know the way. I don't remember, Goddess."

Maybe my tears soften her. Maybe she finally sees how I feel about Poet. She takes my hands. "Child, Thumos and yearning—θυμος will lead you to the river. Trust your heart."

Without waiting to hear more, I grab the container from the goddess' hand and head back downstream. I walk until my legs are afire and my hunger is like a rat gnawing my insides. I walk and wait for my heart to guide me.

I'm just walking to walk, looking to find some direction.

My one hope is that the racing water will join with a larger river. But will it? Where? Have I even picked the right direction? Why, oh gods, do I trust this world? There's no light, only perpetual dusk. And no time. The Shades come and go and taunt and betray. The Furies steal Poet, and Typhon screams with a hundred animal heads and arms.

With slow deliberation, I lift the panpipes high to the roiling sky teeming with smoke and fire and mist from the waterways flowing one to another. But which one leads me to the River Styx?

The river bank is alive. What I thought was solid is dancing particles. As understanding dawns on me, I remember Parmenides' words. *But will the droplet be separate from that roaring river?*

Or is it also the river's rushing and swift current? The river's song?

Water is water.

The song is the song.

Every grass blade, flower and cloud dances like summer fireflies. I think of the vultures., beginning to understand.

I wet my lips and play a song of the wind. It lifts with a memory of rain on meadow grasses. It cries with a memory of poppies sprouting at my initiation. It sobs with the loss of my Poet.

I play until my throat is so dry, I can play no more.

I stop playing and whisper out loud. "I didn't sort the grain alone. I didn't claim the Golden Fleece alone. The gods helped me."

I slip a poppy between my fingers. A yellow light shimmers from the flower's stem and my fingers. "Everything is. Divine is."

At last, I know what I have to do. Laughing with relief, I close my eyes. Quieting my breath, I listen for the river's roar. At first, there is only the wind sweeping the grasses flat. And that? Oh, the vultures calling to me. I breathe slower and try to ease my hunger and tension from my shoulder. A breath in. Out. There. I hear something, but when I try to focus, the sound slips away and becomes the rushing river.

"Wind is wind. Water is water. Everything is and shall not, not be." I chant in a low monotone to the rhythm of the wind.

Breathe in. We are not separate from the gods. Out.

Suddenly, the wind roars in my chest and heart. My head swims with its lusty song, louder and louder. Caught in the song, there's flute music. At last, it all fades.

I open my eyes to the same sparkling grasses and mist, until that also fades, and I breathe in and out.

My right hand is shaking. My hand that holds the crystal jar.

Without a second thought, I jump to my feet and run over to the shore. "Water is water." I fill the jar to the brim. "The kosmos is the kosmos, a universe that we are all a part of. It's futile to struggle against ourselves."

I hold the jar up to the sky.

"Aphrodite!" Instantly, she stands before me.

"This water from the River Okeanos is no different from water from any river. They are one. Water is water... therefore this jar is filled with water from the River Styx as you bid me find."

The goddess' chuckle echoes from the cliffs. "Now, pythia, aren't you clever? It did not take you long to figure that out." She laughs long and loud, so I have to laugh with her. Abruptly, she stops. Her voice becomes serious again. "The final task, child, is the most difficult. You must travel to Hades' Palace; go to Queen Persephone's personal chambers. There, beneath her bed of gold, you will find a small chest filled with a sleeping potion. Bring that to me. And beware. Do not let the queen see you." Aphrodite laughs again, but this time the sound is more sinister, joyless. "And under no circumstances are you to open the box and look in!"

CHAPTER TWENTY-TWO
WHAT...NO, WHO IS A HERO?

The goddess is gone. The air dead and muffled. Even the river seems sluggish. A pine-wind sighs. I hear a cry in the distance and whirl to look back upstream, but the sky is empty.

One last chore. Pan said that Tiresias is the only one who can show me the way to Hades' Palace. And so, on to Tartaros? I let out an explosive sigh. Do I have any choice?

What do I know about the deepest pit in the Underworld? There's a faint smell like stagnant water or slime or fear. My stomach twists with the thought. But before I head off, I have to be smart. I can't go any longer without food. Turning back, I retrace my steps to the apple orchard.

The air is sweet and a warm breeze whistles through the leaves of the oldest tree. The matriarch with the god shoot, a simple limb reaching to mist and flashes of fire. The apple with its first blush is gone. Poet is gone.

I sink to the ground and lean back against the tree. At last, I allow myself to cry, until there are no more tears. Only an iron resolve to find Poet... or die trying. I climb the tree barefoot, looking for knobs and rough bark, just enough to offer a grip. I hang out as far as I dare, grab an apple and twist, slip it into my bodice, and climb higher. By the time

I scramble back down the tree, I look like a lumpy basket.

Back at the river, I tug rushes from the silt shore and weave them into a sling bag to carry the fruit, wishing I still had the pack I left with Parmenides when he turned me into a butterfly. I laugh at the thought of a butterfly carrying a backpack and immediately cry. How can I find anything funny now? But I smile again, realizing that Poet would find it funny too.

I have to rest. Without a second thought, I head over to our nest and lie down, drawing a deep breath. Hoping to smell Poet.

The pine straw is damp and musty.

Sleep and exhaustion claim me.

My dreams are the hags clutching Poet and ripping him from the ground and into flames. I start awake. The river rushes through the perpetual twilight. Some small animal scuttles in the dry asphodel stalks behind me. My eyes won't stay open. Just a little longer. Then I'll go.

I don't know how long I've slept when a hand on my shoulder shakes me awake. I jump to my feet and slip on an apple that lands me flat on my back. A man smiles down at me. A man in full armor—horsehair crest on a gold helmet. The nose guard and cheek coverings are etched with eagles. Their lustrous sheen makes his dark eyes bold.

"*Kore*, from what rocky shore do you come? Who are your excellent parents?" He extends his hand to draw me to my feet. He smiles, but there's tension around his mouth and eyes.

I can't decide what to think about this warrior. His eyes are both fierce and kind. His grip so strong, that I admonish myself not to gasp. Once I'm standing, his height finally makes an impression. His broad chest is protected by gold armor, his shins with gold greaves.

"I drank from the River of Forgetfulness. I cannot tell you my land. Or my parents. And you, brave warrior? Which rocky soil claims you as son?"

"I am Perseus. The all-powerful Lord Zeus is my father. And lovely Danae my mother."

"Zeus?"

"So my mother told me as a child. And the gods have since claimed the truth of it."

"Why are you here in the Land-of-Death? You're..." I lightly touch his shoulder. He is no Shade. Flesh and blood warm the skin beneath his tunic. "You're alive... like me."

"I am."

"Why are you here then?"

"My pride, sweet *kore*. My rash pride was my undoing."

"Well, Perseus, I'd hear your story, but I must go."

He raises his eyebrows and looks around. "What dire task would take you from this lovely meadow?"

"There's someone I have to find... someone who trusted me."

"Perhaps I can help. As far as I've seen, we alone are alive in this land."

"Why is that, Perseus?"

"I, too, search for someone. The Gorgon Medusa." When he speaks her name, my butterfly vision flares to life. Bold red flashes around his head, warns me to be careful. *Is he the man Medusa said was following her?*

"I've seen her." The image of Poet following her into the forest rises unbidden. I hurry on, hoping to hide my guilty blush. "Not long ago. And not too far from here... I think."

His face hardens.

Should I lead this warrior to Medusa?

"I'm not sure I remember the way though. This land is confusing. Skies that should be blue are fire red. Rivers that flow with flames, that should be hot, are cold. And I warn you; time is endless with no beginning or end, no day or night, just perpetual gray. Not morning. Not dusk... but tell me..." I clear my throat and take one step back.

This warrior is powerfully built, strong-armed. His muscled legs are planted, balanced as if ready to spring in any direction. Dark eyes bore into my own, daring me to challenge him... so I do. "Tell me why you seek Medusa."

His jaw tightens and there's a moment where I see rage, but his eyes become vague. As vague as his answer. "The gods send me to find her."

"Which gods send you to find the Gorgon... and why?" My mind races with thoughts of Hades threatening revenge and disappearing. "Is it Zeus? Does he bid his son find the *kore*?"

"Hermes and Athena."

"Athena! She cursed Medusa." My hackles rise with suspicion. "Why does she send you to find the girl?"

"Should we question the gods?"

I guess my scowl persuades him to not ask more.

He suddenly launches into his tale in a manner so quick and breathless, as if the very gods are watching, and though I am desperate to be on my way, I don't know how to stop him. He is overwrought and big, a dangerous combination when you are a girl, alone, on the bank of a rushing river. "My mother is the daughter of the goodly King Acricius of Argos. His only child. My grandfather despaired of not having a boy and went to seek counsel of the Oracle of Delphi."

"What did the Oracle tell him?"

Perseus draws a shining sickle from his belt and carefully brushes his fingers across etched wings that flutter across the blade as if a flock of birds in flight. "This sickle is a gift from the god Hermes, did I tell you?" He won't look at me, only swipes it back and forth before him as if the sharp blade can slice the winds.

Perhaps if I hurry it along, he will leave? "Perseus, what did the Oracle tell your grandfather?"

"It is the very blade that Kronos used to unman his father Ouranos." He glances at me, swipes the blade high above his head. His face flushes. His jaw is so tight that I expect his teeth to fall out. "The Titan Kronos ate his children. One by one at birth."

He shoves the curved blade back into the belt with a harsh swoosh of finality, turns to face me. His face is dark, angry. "Fathers can be cruel."

Father, the word conjures a smell of roasting lamb, distracting me. My head swims with a memory of lamb fat dripping on hot coals. I shake my head to clear it. "Are we talking about Zeus' father... or your grandfather? What did the Oracle tell him?"

"Her answer was that he would never father a son... but there was more. She told him his daughter's child would murder him." He steps so close that his breath blows hot on my face. "Do you understand? She told him that *I* will kill my grandfather. I would never do that!"

"What did the king do? Your grandfather?"

"My mother told me the story when I was still young. According to my grandfather's version of things, the Oracle told him that he must murder his daughter, before she conceives a child. But he didn't. I'd like to think he couldn't kill his own daughter. Maybe he feared the Furies and the gods' revenge..."

I gasp.

He stops mid-sentence. "What? You look pale."

I don't know what to say. I'm not ready to tell this stranger about Poet. "I've met the Furies. They are wild and filled with only one desire—revenge."

I look across the river. One, two lightning bolts sear the sky, followed by a distant thunderclap, as if Zeus himself is angry. Or is it only my guilt? There's that bitter taste in my mouth, an acid bite that convinces me that... whomever I search for was lost because of me. And now Poet.

Perseus' lips move. "What?" I say a little too loud, with a little too much enthusiasm.

"How shall I call you?"

What can I say? I don't know my name. To ask him to call me Thea, like Poet called me, seems a sacrilege. "You may call me Oracle. I am a pythia. I know that much."

"Pythia, the Goddess Athena told me to find the Graeae, the..."

"Three sisters who share one eye between them."

"Yes. She said that they guard Medusa's cave."

I breathe out a sigh of relief. "Then here our paths diverge once more. I travel to Tartaros to find the blind seer Tiresias. Aphrodite sends me to The Lord-of-Many-Names' Palace."

"Hades' own realm? Then the Goddess sends you to your death."

Be careful, Thaleia. Think what you will and will not tell this warrior. There's death in his gaze. "Does any mortal question the Fates?"

"I will travel with you."

"You have your quest, and I have mine. We part here." I gather apples in the sling, nod my head, and start off, before he can answer.

The wind smells of smoke and ash that fills my mouth with acrid dust. Shadows beneath oaks lurk like the Furies. And always, always each crack of a branch behind me or crick of shattered asphodel blooms convinces me that the warrior follows. My neck aches with listening. What does he want with Medusa? With me?

I pace down and down the path, until the cliffs tower so high that there is nothing left but shadow. The trail narrows and becomes a ravine that slices its way between basalt rock. Vague outlines. Smoke. Sifting ashes drifting down on the wind off the stone, so thick that my hair-poppies are white as Shades. And still I put one foot in front of the other and try not to think.

Not about Poet.

Not about Perseus.

But it's hopeless. I know he follows and watches.

When the path twists around a solid rock slab, I sink down on a patch of lichen. I'd rather confront the warrior than wait for him to come upon me unexpected.

So, I kneel on the side of the trail, nestled in dead brush, and trace Poet's face in the dirt.

I don't have to wait long.

With long strides, the warrior rushes past without seeing me at first. Gray dust lifts from the path as an emerald snake slips across and into the brush. Dead flower stalks rattle and whisper. Heat lightning sparks and crackles in dense mists that smell of smoke and bitter death. And still I crouch in the weeds.

When I no longer hear his footsteps, I stride up the path.

CHAPTER TWENTY-THREE
WHAT IS TIME?

Instinct tells me to veer off on a side trail that climbs steep and jagged up a cliff rising black and rubbled, so high I can't see the top.

At last, the way drops abruptly, threads between steaming bogs, clings to a thin rock shelf with putrid water on either side.

No wind stirs the air. Or bird cry. I should stop. Get my bearings. Decide which way to go. With every step, I listen for Perseus. At last, I clear the bog and just walk. Everything about this land oppresses as if the rocks are hard with accusations, black with remorse, jagged with loss.

I push on. The path grows steeper, and though it doesn't seem possible, the awful stillness grows. The air is dense, heavy and hot. I can hardly breathe. My mind grows confused.

"Pythia." A voice whispers from a great distance.

Laughter, sweet as a child's, bubbles around me.

"Where are you? Who are you?"

"I am the friend you lost. I am Sophia."

Sophia… I remember that name now. Sophia, my best friend.

"Sophia, I've come to bring you home."

"Never."

"Let me help you, Sophia!"

"Where was your help when I needed you? You laughed at me.

Mocked me. Told me to run up the mountain after the gods... well, I did. While the villagers honored your great victory..."

Her bitter tone shames me.

"They thought you were so noble...if they only knew..."

"Sophia, I've come to save you."

"Ha! Save yourself, Pythia!"

Her laughter shatters like ice. And she is gone. Chittering surrounds me, this of a fleet of Shades. Only one or two at first, then three and four become many, but I have no sense if they are men or women or even human at all.

"Sophia!"

There is no answer.

Stunted, twisted trees stud the basalt crags like rotten teeth. A mist thickens to yellow. Its sulfurous smell stings my eyes and tightens my chest, but I never falter. Just place one foot after the other and climb, trusting my body will find a way that my mind no longer remembers.

Angry voices shatter the shrouded silence. Gods? Mortals?

"Give her to me!" A man's voice demands.

I step through the fog. Three hags loom before me. Old women with withered arms jutting from flowing *chitons*, two tattered and ripped, but the third wears yellow silk robes, flowing and flawless. Their upper bodies are shriveled dugs and wrinkled faces perching on the stalks of thin and sagging necks, but their lower bodies are black swans. They spin and screech—round and round—their wings frantically flapping.

I catch glimpses of a girl in the middle of their circle.

A shadow figure steps closer to the swan women. Hidden by a large boulder, I hadn't seen him at first. "Give me Medusa, or I will kill you all!" His voice is threat and raw violence. He brandishes a curved scythe engraved with thunderbolts.

"Perseus!" I step into the clearing.

The warrior, though shocked at first, lowers his weapon. His smile is strained and careful. "It seems destiny brings us together, Oracle."

"Leave her alone!" The hag in yellow says.

Without taking his gaze from me, Perseus says, "The Graeae, these foul, worthless creatures, are protecting someone the gods sent me to claim."

"She is our sister." They shuffle back from the warrior, sheltering the woman.

"I've come for Medusa. I do Athena's bidding. Give her to me!"

The hags cower and screech but do not obey him.

"No, Perseus." Resting my hand on his arm, I hope to calm him like I'd quiet a wild horse.

"Enough, sisters! Move aside!" Medusa admonishes and squeezes between the Graeae.

Perseus whirls toward her as I frown, confused.

"Medusa, I thought you were with Parmenides. The last time I saw you..." My memory is of the *kore* disappearing into the woods with Poet; of my jealousy turning me into a caterpillar; of my mistrust... the Furies... Heat rushes to my face. I don't know what to tell the girl. "I feared I'd never see you again."

She smiles at me. "I was afraid at first. I ran away, looking for escape. Parmenides and your Hindu poet helped me find the courage to do as you asked. To stop Athena... it seems she sent this *warrior* to kill me." She spits her last words with disdain. The air between her and Perseus is charged, broken only by the bird-hags' whispers.

"Medusa, stop. Don't go any closer."

"Stay with us! We will protect you, our sister."

"Deino. Pemphredo. Be still!"

"Enyo, let us see. What's happening?"

"Be patient! Don't you see, it's..."

"Of course we don't see..."

Medusa glowers at Perseus. "Death travels with this one."

She and I edge closer to one another, careful to stay out of the scythe's reach.

"You have our eye. How can we see? Who is there, sister?"

"Silence!" Enyo's anger cuts through their questions. She takes one long look, then digs the eyeball from its socket, rests it alive and turning to look at me in the palm of her hand. She steps close before the sister in yellow. After much grumbling and fumbling, Pemphredo pops the eye between fleshy flaps; blinks a few times, and stepping around her sister who is now as blind as she had been, peers at us. "The girl with the flute." She glowers at Perseus. "And a warrior."

"Give me our eye, so I can see!" Deino whines.

Pemphredo also plucks their pitiful prize from its socket and reaches out to give it to the third sister.

Perseus pushes me aside and snatches the eye.

"No! Perseus, give it back!" I lunge to grab the eye. It rolls in his palm as if to glare at the warrior, but he closes his fingers over it as all pandemonium breaks loose. Three blind hags flap their swan wings and screech. Circling us, bumping into one another, they push and shove anything in their way.

"Where's our eye?"

"Sister, give it to me?"

"I don't have it. He does!"

"Perseus! Give it to her. Right now." I try to keep my tone firm.

"Yes, give it to us."

"You must give us our eye!"

"Stop!" His voice is so deep and forceful that we all stop mid-stride. The sisters turn as one and tilt their heads to one side like birds listening.

His voice drips honey-sweet. "Of course you must have your eye back. And I will return it to you." There's a sigh from the three hags as if they'd been holding their breaths. "But first..."

Pemphredo jumps toward Perseus, but he snatches his arm away, and she misses and sprawls on the ground.

"Like I was saying, first you must give me something."

She scrambles to her feet and whirls to face me. "You... you! You brought him here!"

I glare at Perseus. "How dare you barter with their only eye? Have you no pity?"

"Athena, goddess of wisdom, sent me to find her priestess Medusa." Perseus opens his hand and stares at the eye twitching and spinning like some caught bug.

"Give us our eye!" The Graeae shuffle closer so they surround us.

Perseus closes his fingers back over the eye.

The three women peer blindly up at Perseus, who is at least two heads taller than the stooped hags. Their eyelashes flutter over empty sockets, and each head tilts at the exact angle as they wait for his answer.

Turning his back to the Graeae, he smiles at Medusa, then me. "You haven't asked why the goddess wants me to find this *kore*."

I'm supposed to answer all questions brought to me by pilgrims. Questions posed by kings. And generals. Wealthy merchants with five daughters will ask if they will sire a son. Only now I cannot ask the one question that needs to be asked. Now that it is my turn, I am speechless.

Perseus whirls around and grabs my arm. "Where is your courage, girl? Don't you want to know what Athena asked me to do? Don't you want to know why?"

I square my shoulders and look deep into the warrior's dark eyes. They hold power and determination. His brow is tight. As I hold his gaze and try to understand what I am to do, I realize that I also see myself reflected there.

"Ask me what the goddess demanded I do."

I take a deep breath. "What did Athena, patron goddess of Athens, goddess of wisdom and war... what did the mighty gray-eyed goddess demand of you?"

My reflection in his eyes grows very still with waiting. Even the Graeae are quiet.

"She told me to chop off the Gorgon Medusa's head. She told me to stuff it in a sack so that never again can she turn men to stone. She told me to bring the head to her."

The Graeae screech and batter Perseus with their wings, blindly thrash around trying to protect Medusa.

"Stop! I'll kill you all!"

"No!" Medusa's outcry quiets her sisters. "I was her priestess. I was devoted to Athena! She cursed me. Banished me to this death world... and now she wants my head? Why? I loved her. I worshipped her. Why would she want this?"

"She would place your head on her breastplate to claim a Gorgon's power for her own."

"Never!" I grab for the sickle, but he's too quick.

He clutches my wrist. The smile never leaves his face. He squeezes my wrist tighter, until I think it will break.

"I won't let you murder her."

"You talk like she's an innocent *kore*."

"She is!"

"How can you say that? She's horrible! She turns men to stone. She's a monster who betrayed the goddess, seduced her rival Poseidon!"

"No! You're wrong. Poseidon was to blame. It. Is. Not. My. Shame! I do not accept the goddess' blame. It's Poseidon's shame... not mine." She steps closer to Perseus. "How dare you! Give them their eye."

"What will you give me if I do?"

A disquieting hush gathers like a mist over a hero, three hags, and an oracle... silence that strangles a priestess who would challenge a goddess.

Medusa's whisper cuts through. "Warrior, Athena orders you to claim me. That you will never do. The goddess can never claim my honor. My duty to the gods." She strokes each of the hags' heads as she would a young child. "These are my sisters. I give you my life willingly to save theirs. Return their eye and promise you will not harm them... or the Oracle."

Perseus opens his hand to peer at the confused eye turning and turning. Without tearing his gaze from it, he says, "Do you swear by the gods that you will honor your word? That you will willingly sacrifice your life for your sisters?"

The eye twitches and spins, like a butterfly pinned to bark. As if unwilling to touch the wet eyeball, the warrior tilts his hand. The eye rolls from his hand to mine.

I'm startled by how alive it feels, thrumming with an anxiety that tickles my palm. As fast as possible, I open Pemphredo's hand and nudge it onto it, then gently close her fingers over it.

She turns her back to me. When she spins around to face me, her eye is in place. It glowers at the warrior before shifting its gaze to me.

Medusa bows her head to Perseus.

The Graeae batter his face and shoulders. Their anguish is beyond words as they screech and sob, stumble across one another. At last, out of breath and beyond hope, Pemphredo sobs, "Pythia, don't let him murder our sister."

Before I can move, Perseus averts his eyes and tilts his shining shield—gift from Athena—with his left arm, so it blocks his view of the *kore*.

Forcing myself between the warrior and the girl, I scream. "Stop! What if there is a better way? A braver and kinder way? Would you choose it, even if it wasn't exactly what the goddess told you to do... but yet accomplished the same thing?"

He stares into the shield's shining surface. Hatred tightens his lips.

Forcing myself between the warrior and the girl, I scream. "Stop!"

With both hands, I pull on his arm, throwing all my weight into it. His arm doesn't budge. "She is beautiful! Look at her, Perseus. She is no monster! Would you murder this innocent girl?"

Medusa pitches her arms straight out to ward off his attack and steps back. She never takes her eyes off Perseus.

The hero holds his shield steady between him and Medusa but looks down at me with wide, incredulous eyes. "What in the name of the gods are you saying? Look at her!"

"I am! Look at her hair black as night."

"Vipers. Her hair is alive with snakes."

"Just look at her eyes. Can't you see?! She's beautiful."

Perseus stares into the polished shield at Medusa's reflection. "She is vile! A monster with boars' tusks protruding from purple lips. Her face is scaled like a lizard's. Her bulging eyes filled with hate! She wants to kill me... to turn me to stone like the others." He jerks his arm free from my grasp and swings the scythe high in the air, staring all the while at Medusa in the shield. To be sure his aim is true? So her stare cannot turn him to stone?

"No! Perseus! You can't! Stop looking at her reflection. Look at *her*! Look at the girl, Perseus. You see what you want to see. You see what the goddess told you you'd see. Don't let this reflection in Athena's shield tell you who she is." I grab his arm again, but he's too strong.

He tenses but doesn't swing his weapon.

"At least look at her if you would murder her! You call yourself a hero? Do you have the courage to look at this girl you would kill?"

His muscles quiver.

"Perseus, she is a beautiful girl who was seduced by Poseidon. Would you view her only reflected in the goddess' shield? The goddess who cursed her? Would you?"

"I do the goddess' will. Athena sent me to destroy the one who betrayed her. I ask you, Pythia, will you defy the gods?" He jerks his arm free. "Athena, I honor you!"

This time I grab his hair and jerk his head back.

A huge owl with darting gray eyes, mottled feathers, and wide-spread hushed wings lands on the hero's shoulder, glares at Medusa, then twists its head almost completely around to stare at me. Contempt, like icy hatred, commands silence from the wind, fire, smoke, and wailing Shades. Like poison spreading in red wine, her rage and jealousy consumes my breath. "You dare to interfere?" A woman's voice roars from the owl. "I sent him to kill my betrayer!"

The owl shimmers, expands as chest feathers become gold armor, gray bird eyes glare from a human... no, godly face, her crested helm shining with its own light, every inch of her body shielded in unforgiving metal. Her breast that might suckle a child, arms that never held comfort, strong legs planted wide—all speak one desire: revenge.

Athena, the warrior goddess, pulls the hero free from my grasp, seizes Perseus's arm, and lifts it to strike. "If you would be a hero, you must prove yourself. Kill her!"

A dark cloud seeps from the cave mouth. This is no ordinary sea mist. The air shimmers as if the world will disintegrate. Black snakes slither out. Blood flows, carving rivulets in the dirt where poppies sprout.

"Not even Zeus of the thunder bolts will cross me!" A woman's deep voice bellows from the cave shadows.

The snakes glide through the blood toward Perseus.

CHAPTER TWENTY-FOUR
A GODDESS' WRATH... A GODDESS' LOVE

A **goddess steps from the cave. The air between us is** charged as if before a thunderstorm. At her feet, a crystal mist is alive with spirits of owls, snakes, and rats. "I am Nyx, Goddess of Night, older than the Olympians. Older than the Titans. Goddess of Earth and Air." She flaps her wings up and down, dispelling the mist and unsettling the *kosmos* caught between them.

She moves between Medusa and Athena in a motion that is beauty, power, and mystery. Her voice is deep and filled with threat. "Free your priestess."

Releasing the warrior's arm, Athena steps close to Nyx. "You dare command me?"

The black goddess never hesitates or backs away. "Even your father fears me. The girl is under my protection."

Perseus' shield arm is frozen, ready to strike... but there is fear in his eyes.

"The girl is *my* priestess, Nyx. She betrayed me. Do. Not. Interfere."

Nyx—dark with fury, beautiful in her rage—lifts her wings revealing whirling nebula and constellations. Stars and planets and vast swirling dust clouds spin faster and faster.

The goddesses are beautiful in their vast power. Darkness and light.

Athena, surrounded by darkness, spins in circles gathering every bright spark and hurling the light into the night, the darkness, the Void.

"Where is your compassion, Athena? How can you curse this gentle child? She was your priestess devoted to honor only you."

The goddess stops spinning and glares back at Nyx.

"I condemn the seductress. In my own temple, she used her beauty and wiles to lure the powerful god of the sea. Poseidon, my rival, desecrated my sanctuary because of this girl!"

"How can you blame her? This jealousy does not suit you, goddess. Will you accuse your own devotee because of a god's lust?"

"Of course you would speak up for Medusa... two of the same cloth... you think you control men, gods, the kosmos..." Her words spatter like sparks from a fire, until at last, she chokes on them. Athena steps closer to the dark goddess, her voice low and threatening. "There are those who understand how you use your beauty, how you manipulate."

Nyx is furious. A raw, dark power—a divine breath of a cave hollowed deep in the earth, a river's roar as it carves channels through towering rock, wind howling and sighing between ancient trees the moment before dawn—is focused on Athena like a crow's eye as black as wisdom with winter snows all around.

Stepping beside Medusa, I wrap my arm around her and pull her close.

"Don't worry, Pythia," Medusa whispers. "Nyx is ancient. Older than the earth and seas, child of Chaos. Athena cannot overpower her."

But someone forgot to tell Athena. She stands proud and determined, a goddess of a different wisdom. Her intellect is piercing like sunlight on the winter solstice that shoots straight as an arrow into a cave's dark. She narrows her eyes and glares at the goddess of Night. "Gods and mortals may fear your power, Nyx. But I see through that dark mystery you throw over their senses, as you confuse them with a veil that clouds their thoughts, sweet musk that entices. Your sensual beauty is the way you control... but I see through it all! You love none but yourself!"

Faster than I can react, Athena grabs Medusa from me and shoves her into Nyx's arms. "You don't love this girl!"

Medusa drops to the earth and throws her arms over her head.

"How would you know anything about love?" Nyx raises a wild wind with her wings. The air shimmers with lights—green and yellow and orange and red. Red like pomegranates. Red like sunset. Red like blood. "You've never known your mother. You've never taken a lover. Love? What is love to you? You accuse me of seeking power? Control is all you've ever cared for."

The goddesses' struggle is fearsome. Laments drift from the crystal mist. Shades whisper like seeking bats in a cave. The world around me stirs and breathes and waits for a warrior to strike or for a goddess to wield her power.

"What do you know of womanly love or a goddess's gentle compassion? Warrior and fighter and destroyer... that is all you know. You live inside your gold armor and battle the world to prove to Zeus... what?"

With a frustrated howl, Nyx bends close and whispers in Athena's ear, her words fill with barely restrained fury. "You're *jealous* of your priestess. Poseidon came to your sanctuary to find her... not you. You wear metal armor, brandish your spear to preserve your chastity, and keep suitors away. Is your sword and breastplate all that you have to show the Olympians your power and courage? In your heart, you know the truth. You are a goddess never touched by her mother's hands, never loved by a god's or mortal's caress, never one to suckle a babe, to offer comfort."

"I am Zeus' beloved daughter! The one he cherishes above all others. I alone was born from his mind, his brilliance, his courage!" Her words are an almost unintelligible scream.

But instead of screaming back, Nyx lowers her voice more, her words fill with threat. "You will never be truly courageous or wise or powerful, until you let go of your fear.

You hate the girl.

You hate me... because we are everything you deny in yourself. Be Athens' guardian, strong and chaste and wise. Be the giver of the fruitful olive tree. But ignore at your peril the dirt and mud and darkness that gives life to the olive."

"I am the most powerful of all the goddesses!" Athena steps close to the goddess of night.

Nyx lowers her wings and stillness descends around us.

The stars and nebulas fade into the Void.

Nyx's voice is hoarse as if she barely restrains her emotions. "Why do you hate Medusa? Your curse made certain that one look from her turns men to stone. Why?"

"She betrayed me." Athena says.

"Did she? Or did you betray yourself? Every time you dressed in harsh armor and brandished your sword and believed the only way to prove your power and courage was in war, fighting alongside gods in bloody battle... where is the woman in you?

Where is the goddess?

Be a powerful warrior but be a wise warrior. Don't fear setting aside your breastplate to free the woman's heart that beats with power.

With love.

With compassion.

With wisdom."

Athena grabs Medusa by the scruff of her neck and pulls her to her knees. "Perseus, do you ignore my command?"

The deities circle one another. Arguing. Shouting so the ground shakes. Rage unravels them, until there is nothing left of the goddess of night and goddess of gold. Now primordial winds, they swirl around Medusa and Perseus. Light and dark like a storm at sea, a wild hurricane, opposing forces as ancient as chaos.

The hero stands frozen, his arm holding the scythe raised, prepared to bring death... but unable to. I clutch the dirt, dig fingers into unrelenting rock.

"Kill her, Perseus!" Athena screams.

I close my eyes. Quiet words thread through the goddesses' roars.

Τοι παντ ονομ εστει...

Toi pant onom estei...

The whisper grows clearer and louder with each repetition, a chant filled with wisdom and power, the Oracle. Parmenides.

GAIL STRICKLAND

Your fear makes this land of death real. Your fear makes this land of death unreal.

I force myself to look up. An image of Parmenides floats before me, his hands clasped together, his body a shield between the goddesses and me, his eyes calm and kind.

The Land-of-Light may fracture and confuse, but there is only a single darkness. Imperishable; whole.

A sharp cry from Athena shatters his likeness. I strain to shut everything else out. *It is now. Altogether. One continuous.*

"Parmenides!"

Listen to me. Your time is now. You don't need me.

"But..."

Remember, child. You must remember! The kosmos is the kosmos, a universe that we are all a part of, though we think we are not. You fear this rage-driven hurricane, but remember: water is water. Everything is. Divine is. Here is your power.

Medusa takes my hand and stares at me with wild eyes. I shake my head and try to focus on my mentor's vision.

You believe you are separate from the gods, but you are not.

The truth of his words calms me.

What-is is. Without beginning or end.

"I think I understand. I'm the eye in this mad hurricane. The solitary eye that does not exist without the wild wind that surrounds me."

Yes, now you see. I leave you to find the blind seer.

Parmenides' form fades, but I no longer feel alone. I wrap one arm around Medusa. The other I throw in the air. "Stop, both of you!"

The miracle is that they do. Both goddesses, stunned by my command, stop their crazed dervish and turn to me. Their gazes hit me like the unleashed power of lava stifled by stone.

I hurry to speak, trusting my words will find their own way. "You are both right. Athena, if you suppress your feminine side, that power found in caves and moist hidden places, dark wisdom found beneath the earth..." My voice falters. I have a sense of what I want to say, but no idea how to say it.

They step closer. Do I dare defy two mighty goddesses? One glance at Medusa, and I know I have to find a way.

"Nyx, your world is this dark land, a domain of Shades, a world so terrifying to souls passing from the world above, that only the dubious blessing of River Lethe allows them to survive it. You live here hidden away with Kronos. Child of Chaos and the Void, in darkness, you are at peace."

"I am the kosmos. I am the Void. Never will I hide from god or mortal!"

"I honor you, goddess of Night. If you will, hear my words." I turn to the warrior goddess, her face tight with fury.

"Athena, daughter of the sky god, lord of thunder and lightning, you fear the threat of darkness. You fear a dark beauty and power that exudes from this land without time. You would place the *kore* Medusa's severed head as a crest on your shield."

"How dare you..."

I turn back to Nyx. "You mock Athena's chastity, her intellect, sharp as her sword, cutting as her tongue." As I look from one to another, they move in. Blood red flares from them, but I can't stop. I have to save Medusa. "Each of you blames the other... but I say you do so at your peril!"

A roar tears from the goddesses, but I lower my voice to force them to listen, clasp Medusa's hand tighter and talk slower. "A mighty oak must have sunlight warming its leaves as well as rich dirt for its roots that wander into darkness. The Land-of-the-Living needs you, Nyx. And yet you hide in the dark with Kronos, your grandson, the Titan who mutilated your son. Even the goddess Athena needs you, though she knows not that she does. Do you believe you can hide the *kosmos* away here in this dark cave?"

CHAPTER TWENTY-FIVE
A CHOICE

No! No, words are not enough. I have to do something. When the hero, still wavering in horrified indecision, glances back at the girl's reflection, I snatch the sickle. He grabs for it.

"Perseus," I say.

He doesn't move.

"Perseus, set aside the shield. Look at the girl."

For a long breath, Perseus stands frozen.

"How can you fulfill your destiny as hero, if you cannot look at the one you would slay?"

At last, he lowers the tall shield with trepidation, then turns toward Medusa, his eyes averted from the girl huddled against me. He gasps, when he finally looks up. His eyes widen. He smiles, and Medusa, the beautiful *kore*, smiles back at him.

"Do you defy me?" Athena pushes between the hero and the girl.

"I..." Perseus starts.

"All is the will of the gods! You will regret this, Pythia!" Athena's scream echoes off the cliffs, scatters the stars like snow falling around us.

"Athena, even the gods must know their true natures. We are all... gods and mortals... woven into the fabric of the eternal Divine. Love is the weave. Be honest with yourself. Acknowledge the reason for your hatred of the girl." I raise her arm high and wait. Wait for silence. Wait for quiet understanding.

"She betrayed me!"

"Poseidon betrayed you both. The sea god betrayed you. You have the power to cleanse that stain. If you would heal the sanctity of your temple, then you must heal yourself. And to heal, you must let go of your jealous rage. Athena, forgive your priestess!"

"Never!"

I whirl around to face her rage, but she is gone. An owl hoots from the crag high overhead, its call snagged by the sighing wind, until it fades and is lost.

"Goddess Nyx, Athena will return. There is no time to waste. I have to find my friend... and save Poet."

Medusa's eyes are wide with terror.

"Can you protect Medusa?"

"Yes. What you say has great wisdom, Pythia." The goddess bows her head.

Perseus motions for Medusa to stand beside him. "As will I. Go, Pythia. Follow your destiny. We will both protect this *kore*."

All I can do is smile at them. Nyx enfolds me in her embrace. I have never felt so alone as when the goddess releases me.

Stepping away, Nyx waits for me to speak.

I take a deep breath. "Aphrodite told me to fulfill four tasks. I've completed all but the last."

"To secretly steal a box from beneath Queen Persephone's bed." Nyx speaks quickly. "First, child, to enter the queen's private chamber, you must know who you are. Only with knowledge of your power, will you be able to gain access to her most sacred room."

I shake my head in wonder that she knows my mind.

"In Tartaros, there will be many to stop you. Not only the queen, but her companion Hekate. Her husband the dark lord... and now... Athena."

"So there will be. Yet, if... no, *when* I accomplish this, Aphrodite will help me rescue Poet." I straighten my shoulders and step back to face the goddess more fully. "The Furies seized him."

"Ah, my willful children."

"They carried him off... I doubted his friendship..."

The goddess laughs. It doesn't feel pleasant. Her laugh is derisive, almost threatening, definitely challenging. Waiting for me to be more honest.

"I..." My words choke in my throat. Taking a deep breath, I hold the goddess' gaze and almost shout. "I doubted his love."

My hands tremble before me. "I betrayed him. Now I must save him."

Nyx holds my gaze, as if probing the truth of my words and my courage. It's uncomfortable, but I refuse to look away. Stars whirl around her head, constellation of dogs and bears, gods and goddesses.

A lynx scrambles up her black gown and sits on her shoulder. It stares at me with beady black eyes. Two green snakes slither from beneath the lustrous cloth and twine themselves around my feet. Out of the corner of my eye, I see Medusa step toward me, and motion for her to stay where she is. Perseus holds the massive shield against her back.

"Adrasteia, play for us," orders Nyx.

A pale girl steps from the cave, her fragile arms and slight frame barely holding the drum out before her, but when she plays, the melody is powerful—steady and slow. Mesmerizing. Blue and green star-fields fill the air, roiling like storm winds with the music.

The goddess picks up the rhythm, swaying from side to side, chanting a refrain over and over. "You can't kill the Song. You can't kill the Song." Stars spin faster and faster as the Goddess whirls in time to the drum, until she is a swirling Void. Her voice deepens, softens. "It is Pan's song. It is the gods' song, and the stars and sun and earth and wind. It is all of us."

Raw power flows from the chant and black, unending swirling. The planets and constellations breathing between her wings spin and spin. "You can't kill the Song, girl. You must remember. Do you believe you can tell us goddesses what must be done?"

With her last words, everything stops. The stars suspend in the black sky. The drumbeat pulses steady as a heartbeat. The goddess wraps soft-feathered wings around me, and whispers once more. "You are brave. You saved Medusa. But do you think you can control the gods?"

"Zeus and Hades want me dead..."

"Why would I worry about Hades *or* Zeus? Zeus is a coward! When Hera asked my son Hypnos to put Zeus to sleep, so she could meddle in the Trojan War and *interrupt* Herakles' return from Troy, the Thunder-bearer was furious." Her voice drops to a murmur like lava throbbing down a mountain, slow and seething. "He went after my son. He should never have done that."

"But Goddess of night, he's the ruler of all..."

"I dare Zeus to confront me! I am the dark mother of all—the earth and heavens, this realm." She growls. "I sent the Furies after Zeus. The Lord of all begged... he *groveled* at my feet, pleading for me to call them off."

Bowing in wordless supplication, I touch my forehead to Nyx's knee. "Goddess, you are The Furies' mother?"

"Child, I am ancient, mother of many—Keres, the daimona of fire and death, The Fates, Aether, god of the air, and even Thanatos, death himself. With my consort Erebos, the dark lord, I gave birth to many children of the dark and light... so many more..."

"The Furies... they are..." My throat tightens. Pulling my panpipes from my belt, I look over at Medusa. Watch Perseus stripping petals from an asphodel stalk. They return my stare. It's all come to this. To now. If I will save Sophia and escape this Land-of-Darkness, I understand it will only be with this goddess' help. But what can I possibly say to persuade her? I turn the flute over and over in my hand, stalling for time.

The goddess wraps her wings around me. Her heart beats steady and loud.

Her feathers are suffocating.

I'm dizzy and disoriented, desperate to cling to any shred of courage.

There is no sound other than her heartbeat.

There is no color but black.

My breath comes quick and shallow and strained. My heart beats, skips, and stutters, then slowly and relentlessly pulses in tandem with the goddess' bold heart. She is goddess of night. Older than the Olympians. Is she here to stop me or guide me? Do the gods assist us? Aphrodite offered help, but demanded impossible tasks as her price. But Pan... he is old like Nyx, an ancient nature god. Am I caught between the gods old and new? Are they using me? Mocking me?

No, I have it wrong.

Once I stop fighting the goddess' embrace, her feathers are warm. Her heartbeat comforts.

Here is my power, my courage.

I quiet my mind. Here is *Hesychia*—The Great Stillness. In the heartbeat, Parmenides says, *Toi pant' onom' estai. Its name shall be everything.*

"Goddess, it is not for me alone to find my friend. To escape this dark land."

Nyx smiles and her night eyes shine with love. "No, child, it is not. You are beginning to understand. *You* helped the men and women trapped in the oaks. *You* helped Medusa."

"But I didn't save Poet."

"No, you didn't. But think, girl. Were you afraid when you confronted Hades? Were you afraid when you faced the snake-haired Gorgon? Were you afraid when you taunted Typhon with a riddle? When you confronted the warrior Perseus and persuaded him to look directly at the *kore*? When you stood up to mighty Athena? To me?"

I square my shoulders. "No, I was not afraid. They needed my help."

Nyx whispers, leaning close to my ear. "And were you afraid when the boy told you he had murdered for money?" The goddess flings her wings wide and constellations scramble and spin between them. The lynx leaps between us and snarls. An owl lifts from Nyx's shoulder and shatters the air with a war-screech. "Were you thinking of Poet then, or only of your miserable self?" The fury in her voice cuts through me.

When I don't answer, her voice softens with kindness. "I will give you a choice, because you were brave and helped Medusa, not once but two times. You may choose: I will help you escape this Land-of-Darkness. This land that no living being may enter and leave alive. With my help, you will return to Delphi and your parents, you will claim the sacred tripod and live a life respected and honored. Without my help or the help of another god, you will never leave. This Land-of-the-Dead will destroy you. My son Thanatos will claim you, and you will wander these mists as Shade."

"Why would I consider not accepting?" I bow and clasp the goddess' knee. "I pray you help me, wise mother."

The goddess sighs. And with her sigh, the darkness shudders. The stars and nebulae shake and scramble, until it seems a new kosmos settles into place. Is that how the gods play with us? Do they sigh in exasperation or relief and our world shifts and changes?

I focus on the goddess of night, realizing that she is saying something. Something important.

"There is a secret tunnel known only to me... and my grandson. This tunnel leads to Tartaros. To Tiresias. To Hades' Palace and Queen Persephone and the gold box beneath her bed." She grabs my hands and draws me to my feet. "You will have to travel this tunnel alone. Like the birth canal gives life to a baby, it will take you to the darkest pit in the Underworld. Tartaros may give you back your name and your destiny. But like so many before you, it may trap you in unceasing horror. To honor you, I offer you life and escape from Hades dark land... but if you choose to continue on your quest, to honor you, I will show you the hidden way. Pythia, it is yours to choose."

"I could be home right now?"

"Yes, child. With your mother and father, honored by all. You can return to the moment of your triumph, when King Xerxes and his army ran from the earthquake and storm, ran from your power."

Home. Fragments of memories bring tears to my eyes. Smells and laughter and a lullaby caught just beneath a woman's breath, while she bends into a hearth and stirs barley in her pot. I'm sure all this love and beauty must be Mama.

"Yes…" my mouth starts to decide for me. "I want to escape Lord Hades and his kidnapped, murderous queen, the fire and Typhon, the Furies and their rabid need for revenge…"

The goddess lifts her wings to send me home.

I look at Medusa and wonder about my friend, whom I followed into this Land-of-Death. I remember Poet fighting the Furies.

"No, great goddess. No, I won't abandon them. I will find the blind seer and the box beneath the queen's bed. I will reclaim my name and rescue Poet. Together, we will find my friend. Thank you for your offer, but I will travel to Tartaros. Please, Nyx, please show me the hidden way."

"As you wish. Once you enter the tunnel, I will no longer be able to help you. Are you certain that this is what you want?"

As if the pit of the Underworld answers, a belch of sulfuric smoke gasps from a fissure to my left.

CHAPTER TWENTY-SIX
THE TITAN

here are no more words. I trail Nyx into the cave.
Adrasteia plays the tympani in a slow, solemn beat, leading the way. Perseus and Medusa look at each other with suspicion, then follow.

I'm assaulted with a damp cold as I enter. Nyx turns slowly in a half-circle and points with her long fingernail. A yellow candle, thick with melted wax, lights, then another, and another, until the high-ceilinged chamber dances with shadows. There're animal skulls wedged in crannies in the stone, jawbones resting on shallow ledges, dried asphodel and poppies dangling from their fangs.

The candlelight reveals a thick, red rug in the middle of the chamber. I bend to place the scythe on the carpet and remove my sandals, but freeze when several snakes slither toward me.

"Girl, you'll need your sandals in the tunnel. And those snakes? You'll need your courage. You must bring two to the blind seer. He struck a male and female snake with his staff on Mt. Cocytos. Bring them to the seer so he can ask their forgiveness. Only then can Tiresias speak your destiny."

The snakes are vipers—triangular heads storing poison, black tongues tasting the cloying air, sweet with death. One forked tongue flicks my hand. I shudder as if the poison already sweeps fire up my veins.

"It's not too late. My offer holds, Pythia. I will help you escape and return home."

With both arms extended, palms up, I wait completely still while the snakes crawl up and wind a scaled body around each of my arms. Two heads sway side-to-side and four black eyes stare into mine.

"It is my fate to claim, great goddess."

As slowly as I can, I rise and walk toward her with my palms straight up before me like a priestess bringing offerings. The snakes wrap their coils tighter around my arms. My veins stand out like blue rivers.

Forcing my breath to slow, I stand before Nyx and wait.

One snake jerks its head as a bat flies above us, its leather wings stirring the air.

The goddess points with her taloned finger. She is silent. Calm as death.

As my eyes adjust to the darkness, I realize the cave is massive. Its ceiling disappears into a night sky with constellations and swirling nebulas, all dancing in time to the nymph's drum beat.

I walk deeper into the cave, past the staring skulls, past candles dripping wax like pus festering from a wound. Amid the death and shifting darkness, an oddly sweet smell fills the air.

As if breathing and alive like a lurking god, the cave walls throb with loud snoring. The snakes start. They tighten and spin higher up my arms; lick red tongues in and out as if testing the echoing rumbles that bounce and career off the stone.

I take one step and another and force myself to only look ahead. If I look at the snakes, I will freeze. *Follow the snoring. Follow the smell. Follow your heart.*

Another step. I ease toward the roar and cough and snore. Snore and laugh. Another step.

Chains rattle as a heavy body shifts beyond a gash in the wall that leads to the back chamber.

One viper slithers up my arm, through my poppy hair, and over my bare shoulder. My skin flicks in response, but I don't stop. I pace another step and stare straight ahead. Torchlight flickers and shadows from the opening, goes dark and flares bright as if something... or someone crossed before the flame.

Another step.

The snake eases from my right shoulder to twine itself with the snake on my left. A living caduceus.

I reach the opening. Before I step beyond the threshold, I stop and finally allow myself to study the snakes. Two diamond heads turn toward me. Shining black eyes glare, daring me to enter the chamber. Daring me to face what's within.

The snoring stops. Whatever's in there is waiting. Whoever's in there knows I'm here.

Adrasteia thumps a furious tympani beat. My heart responds and pounds in tandem. With her drum. With the stars and diving bats.

Nyx's voice chants low and sonorous. "You can't kill the song. It is the wind." She lifts her towering wings, casting black shadow over me. "It is the stars." Her wings flap up and down, sweeping the Dog Star and Draco high to the ceiling. Crushing a spinning green nebula. With her curved black fingernail, she points at me. "It is all of us... even what lies beyond." She brings her wings down with a rush that seems to leave a deathly calm in its wake.

Her divinity is raw and earthy. Never before have I felt power like this. Not with Aphrodite or Pan. Not even quaking before those mighty brothers, Zeus and Hades. Like the sun's core, her stare is chaos and light. It overwhelms me.

Before I know it, Medusa is at my side. Her lip snarls as the viper hisses a warning. For an instant, she reminds me of the snake-haired Gorgon she was. Her hand rests comforting on my shoulder, but I don't look at her. I'm afraid I'll change my mind. It would only take a little love to persuade me to turn around... and I can't. Poet needs me.

"Goddess, who is in there? Whom must I face?"

"My grandson. Only my grandson."

She's not telling me everything. There's more. I don't drop my gaze from Nyx. "And...?"

"Honor him, child. He was the ruler of the Universe. The king of earth and sea and the vast Void. Kronos."

Not trusting myself to speak, I nod and duck my head to step into the next chamber, another stone room carved by time and water. I thought it would be smaller, but it is also huge with stalactites jutting from the ceiling like massive teeth.

It takes a moment for my eyes to adjust to the dimmer light. Only a couple of candles flicker. Yellow wax covers the rough stone beneath them, like vomit. A phlegm-wet cough draws my attention. I strain to make out who else is here in this chamber.

Something shifts in the shadows. I pull a candle from its wall holder and raise it so I can see. Chained to the back wall and staring at me is a giant. Fleshy and black like a slug that digs through soil. His skin hangs off huge arms and hands that clutch an amphora in his lap. Though he sits cross-legged on a tattered rug with nothing beneath him but cave stone, he is so massive that he bends his neck slightly to allow room for his head.

The giant coughs and farts so that the chamber is an unpleasant mixture of sweet honey, mold, and gas, but I stay still and wait for his answer. And wait. Only when I hear him snoring, do I look up into his face. His chin slumps into his chest and jiggles up and down with each breath, all his fat shuddering. Jerking with a dream, the power is palpable in his arms as he clenches a fist and throws it toward an invisible enemy. His dream startles him awake and eyes swimming in sagging flesh open and focus on me. His face is huge.

"I asked you not to forget me… dinna say to come back." His words slur with drunkenness. He hoists a clay jug high to slurp a golden liquid into an almost toothless mouth.

A cloying smell fills the chamber. He glares at me over the amphora rim; licks his fat lips, then sets the jar back onto the stone floor, too hard, too fast. It rocks and tips. Honey pours out, but he ignores it and brushes lanky, gray hair off his sweaty forehead.

"I knew you would, of course. Come back, that is. So boring always knowing everything that will happen… but girl, you've been busy. All the gods? Let me think... Zeus, Hades, Athena... not to mention the Furies and Typhon. You thought it was a good idea to make them all mad at you? You're a feisty one, you are." He snorts. "Well, come closer then, so I can see you better."

Taking one small step, I hesitate... only for a breath, then I stride across the chamber so fast that bats scatter and chirp above me. When I'm so close to the giant that his breath blows my poppy-hair, I kneel in supplication. "I pray to you for safe passage. Please tell me how to find the seer Tiresias, so I may discover who I am and find the way to Hades' Palace."

"What took you so long to return?" he slurs.

"I drank from the River Lethe—"

"Ha!" He takes another slurp of honey and starts singing. "Zeus, my son, bring me the scythe. I'll give to you as you gave to me. Zeus, my son, return home. Set me free. Now, set me free." His voice echoes brazen and loud off the cavern.

I summon my will and shout to be heard. "I. Must. Find. Poet."

Kronos stops singing and looks at me with annoyance, as if at a bothersome insect. At last he says, "I helped you once. You ignored my warning." A wet cough gurgles in his throat as he resumes his song. "Zeus, my son, bring me the scythe..."

The scythe! Bring him the scythe! I rush back to the cave antechamber and snatch the blade from the startled warrior and stumble back to stand before the giant.

"Here it is! Here is the scythe that stole your manhood!"

Kronos' eyes grow wide, he roars, but he takes the blade from me and stares at it as if it would come alive.

I'd almost forgotten the snakes on my arms, they've been as still as armbands, but when the Titan roars, they both slither up into my poppy curls. I shiver with the feeling of them nesting there, but force myself to ignore it. I must hold the Titan's gaze and make him help me.

Without tearing his eyes from the shining blade, Kronos speaks in a hoarse whisper, overcome with emotion. "You did remember me, girl." He lifts the edge of his dirty tunic and polishes the scythe. "This

weapon stole my manhood, my power... and you've returned it to me."
When he looks up, there are tears in his eyes. "My son attacked me. But
I deserved it. I destroyed all my beautiful children. I murdered my
father. I deserve imprisonment here in the dark. But I will keep this
scythe with me, so it will never again be used to maim... or to murder."

Kronos rolls his lumbering body until he is on his knees. There's not
enough height in the chamber for him to stand, but he nudges over
little by little.

Behind the Titan there is another opening, a small, dark crevice in
the stone. Kronos points at it with the shining scythe, dancing and
gleaming in the candlelight.

"Tartaros. The way to Tartaros is here."

I don't hesitate to plunge into the tunnel. At first, it's only darkness.
No, not really black... but something unknown to me. A living thing
that seems to glow with its own light as if the stone is a sea creature
swimming the sea's deepest depths, where no sunlight reaches. A
pulsing red like blood in my veins shows my way.

The tunnel is so narrow that I have to feel my way through. It takes
me awhile to understand that the walls I touch, the stone my fingertips
caress hoping to find some purchase, to make some sense of these cold,
mossy, slick slime, pulse with a heartbeat.

The passage narrows yet more, so I can only crawl through on my
hands and knees. The throbbing intensifies. Pushing, pushing me
forward. There's no thought to before or behind. Only the tunnel
urging me onward, like a snake gorging on a mouse.

On and on. The walls scrape my shoulders. And the air. When I set
off, it was hot, sulfuric, rank with death... but this. This is worse. It's
grown so cold and brittle, so fierce that I'm reluctant to breathe it in. I
can't think of what's ahead.

I imagine Poet at the tunnel's end. Terror threatens to imprison me.

The walls press closer, and my breath comes in tight short gasps. I'm certain each one will be my last.

My nails claw rock that scrapes my knees and shoulders. One more breath that burns me with searing cold. All I want is warmth. To escape. To be able to draw a breath without fearing that it will be so harsh, so frigid that all life will be stolen from me.

I can't stop.

I won't stop.

I crawl on.

When I think I can go no farther, when there is only grit scraping my hands and knees and the passage is so tight that I twist and turn to squeeze through, the visions begin: The hook-nosed priest just ahead in the darkness, laughing and taunting. Blood drips from the stone above onto my face, but when I reach to wipe it away, it is only sweat. I ignore it all and try to close my ears to the constant whirring that is more terrifying than all the rest.

My frigid limbs push and pull me on.

Abruptly, the tunnel ends. The wall pulses and throbs. Darker red. Then yellow. Then a sickly green. But there is no opening.

I twist myself around to look back down the tunnel. Did I miss another passage? The stone behind me tightens to a rusty red.

Scrambling backward as fast as my frozen limbs allow, I try to retreat, but the passage is too narrow now. I'm intensely aware of my breath in the cold air, in this stone chamber in the earth's belly, coming in short, useless gasps. I know it shouldn't. I need to stay calm and think.

I try to pray to the gods, but entombed here, all I can think of is the men turned to stone... and the *kore*, Medusa, ravaged by Poseidon, betrayed by Athena. Her fear... and *rage* turned men to stone. Pray to these gods?

The faster I gasp for air, the more the earth constricts around me. The darker the light.

And though my terror threatens to engulf me, as the passage pulses and tightens, I will myself to slow my breath and close my eyes. *Let go of your fear, Thaleia.*

As if the earth will swallow me, the chamber shrinks, until stone touches me on all sides. Unable to move or turn, I can barely draw a breath.

But I do.

The stone constricts my shoulders and head and thighs crossed tight against my chest. Is this what it feels like to be birthed? This terror? This raging against the womb that entombs us, that expels us when our time has come?

I breathe slower and slower and the stone stops shrinking. With each intake of air, I hear a heartbeat. It pulses in my chest and arms. My head.

"Child?"

I'm afraid to open my eyes. Is it death come for me? Hermes ready to lead me to be judged? But it's a woman's voice, frail and gentle.

"There's no time to waste. Open your heart and you will find me there."

One more breath. One more heartbeat. Behind my closed eyes, a white light flashes and my grandmother seems to float before me. Small and stooped, dark eyes laughing and peering from under the same blue scarf.

"Grandmother, how did you find me?"

"Love connects us, child."

"You're here to teach me what I must learn?"

As she nods, her eyes smile.

"I can't move."

"So you believe. And that is what frightens you? That you will lose your life? Yet you and I stand one on each side of death... and still we love. What is it you fear, granddaughter?"

"I'm trapped."

"So you said."

"Look at me! Would you tell me I'm not?"

With my flaring anger, the walls tighten and the vision of Grandmother flickers, shatters. "No! Please don't leave me here alone!"

The more my terror seizes me, the darker my tomb.

I take two deep breaths to calm my racing heart. Light and warmth swell inside my chest.

Her voice seems to fill my head. "Is there life here in this tomb or only death?" She is impatient, tired. "What is your answer? Is there life in this tomb?"

"What life—" And then... "Oh yes! Yes." I urge myself to understand. To trust she is here to show me the way to freedom. "There is."

"What life is here?"

"There is my life."

"Will you abandon it? Will you destroy it before your thread ends?"

"What can I do?"

"Do you believe you can banish the dark? Don't struggle against it. Reconcile with it. Roots from the Land-of-the-Living find nourishment even here, in this dark Land-of-Death."

"I am your grandmother." She is fading, tired. But determined. Oh, so determined. "Your mother's mother. My blood and hers flow through you. As the pythias live on in you—sister to sister. We are never separate and alone. There is our greatest fear! But it is never warranted. Don't you understand why you have visions? Why you dream the future and your heart yearns to help and soothe? Think, child! Now you must understand, or forever be trapped by your fear."

I breathe slower. The stone light glows brighter with sun-filled yellow. The walls ease back.

"Yes, you begin to understand." The smile in her voice encourages me. "And what of your father? Your mother, your mother's mother, a long chain of women has given life to you... but what of your father? He is also a spark of life in you, is he not?"

"I remember a kind man. His smile..."

"He is not your father."

The walls tighten around me. The light grows red and angry. My breath is squeezed from my chest.

"Ask me who your father is. I am the one who knows. I've waited in this dark land for you. For one purpose. My *psyche* does not rest and has no peace. Because you have to know. You have to understand. You have to have the courage to know the truth. Ask me who your father is."

"And if I do, will I lose the papa I know is kind and gentle?"

"Never. He will always love you."

"If I do, will your soul at last find peace?"

"Yes. Only then."

"Grandmother, I am afraid." I tense my muscles. Relax. "Who is my father?"

CHAPTER TWENTY-SEVEN
TIRESIAS

No!" A deep roar, like the earth shifting, explodes around me. My ears ring. A flash of white light blinds me. Adrift and entombed with no sight or sound, I can only kneel in prayer. The hush that follows is hollow, until it is once more filled with a whirring like a thousand hummingbirds' wings beating against the rock walls. I feel a change before I can see anything. Air surrounding me opens, freeing me like I was liberated from the butterfly's cocoon.

Deaf. Blind. I have no idea if Hades lurks here. All I can do is breathe in. Try to hear beyond the ringing in my ears. Breathe out, my skin shivering in anticipation of a god's touch.

Slowly, my eyes see the creviced darkness of stone walls. My ears fill with silence.

Grandmother is gone.

The narrow tunnel shifts like a leviathan in the sea's depths. I jump to my feet and rush down a corridor that opens before me. With every step, the way broadens until at last, just beyond a stone archway, there is a towering cavern. Without hesitation, I step inside.

Stalagmites jut from the floor like rotting giant teeth. Shades fly just below the ceiling, weaving between dripping rock formations, hanging down, almost touching the floor.

A young woman dressed in flowing purple stands before me as if she waits for me.

She is beautiful. I want to gently trace the soft fabric of her chiton and brush her long, lustrous hair off her face. Eyes dark as black pearls shine with love... enough love to hold the world. A love, deep and powerful as a sea, calm at night with a heaven of stars above dancing and reflecting in water as brittle and shiny as onyx, emanates from her. I would no more turn away from her than my own relentless heartbeat. Yet, the gods lock her away in the darkest and most vile crevice of the Underworld. They've shut her here in bleak Tartaros, where rock walls imprison her. Scabby mold drips from jagged stalactites.

And still her beauty and love shimmer like a soft light, the waves of it washing over me with a scent of vanilla and honey. Her smile is so compelling that I know I would do anything, face any monster or uncaring and jealous god to protect her.

"Who are you?" I whisper, unwilling to startle the girl. But she's not startled. As if she knew all along that I stood in the entrance and watched, she turns slowly toward me.

"A long time I've waited for you, Pythia."

"How did you know I'd come?"

"You are the bringer of snakes."

I lift my arms before me, and the vipers pulse and slither across my bare skin. Skin that shivers with their scaly touch, though I try not to show my fear. My body does. My body wants them off and gone.

But my will is stronger. I stand like stone with my arms outstretched before me and wait.

Here in Tartaros, all will begin or end.

Instead of looking directly at me, the woman stares off over my shoulder. It's then I realize that her blind eyes do not see me. Or the snakes. "Tiresias?"

She looks at me and then smiles with gratitude and relief. "So, you know who I am."

Stepping closer, I bend to one knee before her and let the snakes slither off my arms onto the cold stone. The chamber floor is slimy from rot and mold, and the snakes are soon lost in the green. Their movement all I can see, as they slip in tandem, weaving through the sludge until they reach the woman's feet.

Just before her, they stop and lift their heads, swaying side to side. Side to side.

She crouches before the two serpents and tips her head as if listening for their approach. Addressing them like long, lost friends, she says, "You've returned to me. My boon. My blessing."

With a finger from each hand, she lightly strokes the snakes' heads. "Forgive me. I did not understand. I was young. Stupid. I did not mean to hurt you."

The snakes don't move. As if the air around us is empty and venomous, there is nothing. In a distant recess, water drips.

Then another drip.

Tiresias does not move. The snakes weave their heads before her.

A stunned look sweeps across her features, and she stands. There is shock in her sightless eyes, raw terror.

Though I can't believe what my own eyes tell me, she sheds her skin. Slender arms turn burly and hairy. Long hair transforms from black to hoarfrost gray. High cheekbones and long neck shift and expand and stretch, until a man with broad brow, stubbled cheek and deep-set eyes stands before me. His crossed arms are muscled, his legs planted on the stone. When he speaks, her honeyed voice has dropped to a gravel growl. "Do I repulse you now?"

I'm shocked to my core. She was everything that is beautiful. Like summer sunshine on poppies and grasses. Moonlight across a silk sea. She was the song of the kosmos... so lovely. Yet, even so, even now, he is the same—only strong as an oak, rooted and bold.

My heart overflows with compassion for this being. A woman? A man? With everything that I am, I know that it does not matter.

"No. No, you do not repulse me." I take his hand and place it on my chest so he can feel the truth in my heart. "You are Tiresias. The only one to walk our Greek soil as man and woman. And you are blind, blinded by Hera."

"Thank you for seeing me as I truly am, child. Why are you here? You have traveled far. Do you seek me?"

"I've looked long for you, wise Oracle."

"Then you seek a prophecy?"

"I seek wisdom. The truth."

He stares over my head as if he might find my eyes just before him. "What would you learn from me then? Kingdoms won? Kingdoms lost? The birth of a child? Lies and deceits of mortals?"

"Please, Tiresias, only tell me who I am."

"Ahh."

"Parmenides sent me to find you. He said only you can tell me who I am."

"But, child, you know without me telling you. You know all these things: the fragrance of a poppy flower, the rainbow light of a butterfly's vision, the power of a living tree sprouting from your hand and freeing those enslaved... You must know that you are the one who sings the Song of the Universe. You burst with life."

"What does it mean, Tiresias?"

"Who you are, the one who bursts with life."

The moment he speaks those words, it's as if I hear my mother say, "Thaleia. It means to burst with life. We named you wisely, daughter."

"Tell me your name, child. Claim your name. Seize your destiny."

I open my mouth to speak but am overwhelmed by my tears.

"Claim your name, child."

I dry my tears and with a shudder of recognition, I whisper. "My name is Thaleia."

"I can't hear you."

"My name is Thaleia," I shout and laugh. "It means to burst with life. My destiny is to bring life to The-Land-of-the-Dead." My words fill me with so much strength and determination that I gather both of Tiresias' hands and say it again, "My name is Thaleia."

With the claiming of my name, a rush of memories drops me to my knees. Every doubt I carry seems to crowd around me: Poet hauled off like carrion—a black speck in the fire underbelly of this land, a sword screaming through night air, chanting and drums and an acrid smell of sulfur that oozes from every dead plant stalk and rock crevice... everything about this land that is loss and fear and darkness that threatens to sever my hope to ever find him.

My heart jolts with another memory. I'm dizzy and confused. A black vision envelopes me.

Birds, shadow vultures cast wide wings in a wind that blows through me. My body is gone. There are shades in the wind. And the mocking laughter of a girl. A girl I know. A girl I love.

They are all here. Warriors who sacrificed their lives on some bloody battlefield. Men and women in armor, shrieking war cries, moaning death-throes. They surround me.

And then the girl is with them. Her laughter flows through me. She is in me, and not. We are both this black wind, joined in the Void. Shame alone connects us.

She is the girl I came here to find.

I would cry, but I have no body to cry with. I would reach my hand to her and pull her back to the world above, to the trees she loves, wild laurel, sweet smelling along the River Pappadia.

But she is inside me, and we are both this dark, ill wind. Nothing is—not stone nor tree nor a soft poppy.

"Pythia." The blind seer's voice whispers from a great distance. "Come back."

Nothing is.

Laughter surrounds me. Fills me. There is no joy in this laughter. It mocks and taunts. It is outside me and inside my heart as if it could shred me like myriad stars in the night sky.

I breathe in the dark wind as if I can call her to me. A name drifts through me.

Sophia. Her name is Sophia.

We are joined like two sisters in a mother's womb. We float together in a world that is dark wind and bird cries. A world that is alive with death. Shadows of men and women and children and wild animals.

All who walked in light. Now lost.

Laughter, sweet as a child's, bubbles around me.

Sophia. I'm here. We will return to the Land-of-the-Living.

As if she hears me, the laughter breaks off like an icicle off a roof tile. And she is gone.

I come back to my body and Tiresias's shaking. "She's gone."

"Who?"

I'm too stricken to say anything at first, but he won't accept my silence. His strong hands tighten on my arms. He stares into my face as if he can *will* me to answer. "She is... *was* my best friend. I've lost everyone I love. Sophia. Poet. They're all gone because of me. That is the reason I am here. I am Thaleia. I came to this Land-of-Death to reclaim my friend. To beg her forgiveness."

A name carved in a limestone block drifts through my memory. Sophia. Her name is Sophia.

"Sophia." My heart feels like it will shatter. I exhale her name as if I can call her to me. Like a tidal wave, my guilt, my horror, my shame wash over me.

"Now you know. Now you understand."

I nod.

"Where is Sophia? You are the blind seer who knows all. Where can I find my friend?" Tiresias turns and points to a far wall.

"And Queen Persephone's box. I must bring Aphrodite the *kiste* hidden beneath the queen's bed. Only then can I save Poet. Poet... I remember now! His name is Valmiki! My Hindu Poet. Will you show me the way?"

"Look carefully, girl."

At first I see nothing out of the usual. A woman's Shade dips and moans. And another. The mother I freed from the oak. Faster and faster they swoop and whirl, until the rough stone blurs with their vaporous forms. At last, they split apart from one another to reveal a long stone corridor that appears then as if a mirage, vanishes, only to appear again.

I laugh and race toward it as the opening grows wider and brighter and slip through just before the doorway starts to fade.

Beyond is a hallway with black alabaster tile walls. Diamonds sparkle from the ceiling, with emeralds and garnets scattered among them catching firelight from torches that light the way.

Walk. Walk. Don't turn back. At last, there's an end. A heavy tapestry, deep sea-blue decorated with dragons and poppies and twining vines spun from gold thread covers the entire wall.

I push it aside.

And step into beautiful palace grounds. Huge Doric columns painted yellow and red and aquamarine-blue tower over mosaics. An open-aired chamber, with darkness beyond. But here is a warm wind and torchlight and girls holding hands dancing and singing. Desperately, I look at each one, hoping to find Sophia, but no luck.

At last there are fewer girls, until there is only one standing a little aside from the others off to my right where the gold trail curves around an ebony boulder, sharp and angular and shining like molten glass. She holds up one imperious hand for me to stop, and startled, I do.

Her dress, diaphanous like all the other Shades, shimmers with yellow sunlight. I can see through her. Black stone is harsh and solid behind her body and chiton that ripple like water over river stones.

"Stop. Think before you take another step." She glides over, until she is directly before me. "Look where you are." She points above her to draw my gaze.

I look up. Consumed by my search for Sophia, I hadn't noticed the huge gate that towers over the girl. Gold and black ebony, carved with serpents. The girl turns and points just beyond, where flaring fire lights jagged boulders, silhouetting vultures in the smoky sky. The gold path winds its serpentine way, shimmering and inviting.

Barking dogs shatter the fire's hiss. Ten, twelve black mastiffs lunge from the gate and surround me, snarling and growling.

"Be still! Leave her alone!" A pale woman dressed in black robes steps across the threshold. She holds a flaring torch high with one hand and rests another on the alpha dog's head. Once he's calm, the others, too, grow quiet. "Down!" At her command, all the dogs crouch, still shaking with the hunt. Baring their teeth.

The woman and I study each other. She appears startled by my poppy hair. I'm equally amazed by the twisting branches that form hers... and by something moving there—snakes. Small, green snakes wind round and between the oak twigs, interwoven like an eagle's nest.

"What brings you to the Gate to Hades Realm? Who are you? Who are your parents? From what rocky shore do you come?"

"Goddess, my name at last I know and will gladly tell you. I am Thaleia, Oracle of Delphi, sacred center in the Land-of-Light. Hipparchia is proud to call me child. My father... my father, with your permission, I'll divulge, when I know you better." I kneel and touch my forehead to the woman's knee. When I stand once more, I say, "What goddess are you? Will you allow me to pass through this portal? I seek Queen Persephone."

"I am Hekate, protector of women and girls. Guardian of all crossroads and thresholds. Companion to the Lord-of-Many-Name's great queen."

"Hekate?" I look back at the pale girl standing off to the side. Am I imagining it? Or do her eyes plead with me?

"I've come the same as you, wise goddess. I've come to help a girl."

"Why should I believe you?"

At the tone of suspicion in her voice, as one, the dogs jump to their feet and tighten their circle. The hair rises on the leader's back. He snarls a warning.

I keep my words soft and firm. "You can trust me, goddess of the dark moon. And if you do not, send your dogs with me. May they tear me limb from limb if I bring any harm to the Queen."

"I believe you, Thaleia, Oracle of Delphi. The dogs will stay here and guard this Gate to Hades Realm. For Persephone is my friend... just as Sophia is yours."

"How do you know I'm looking for Sophia?"

The goddess smiles as the snakes twist in and out of her oak-limbed hair. They slither down her bare arms and coil around the columns forming the threshold. "Two days ago, I took a lone girl to drink from The River of Forgetfulness. As she drank a cup of the cold balm, her memories fled like drifting spirits. I saw them all: waiting in the cave for you, afraid you would abandon her forever. Writing Timon's name in poppy petals on the dream stone. Yes, your dream stone. The way she betrayed you to the old priest... I saw it all, Thaleia." Her voice is low and husky as she leans close and whispers in my ear. "Her death. I saw how she died. Girl, I saw why she died."

My mouth is dry. I swallow twice, trying to speak, but words won't come.

Hekate waits a long moment. "I can show you where she is... but she will not remember you. And *that*, girl, will be her blessing."

I stumble twice as I try to stay apace with the goddess, stunned by black marble towers jutting into a starless void. Searing lightning bolts and fire flashes shatter the dark—momentarily blind me. Each bolt roars like a monster blacksmith bellow. The silence left behind is still as Death.

Ahead, at the end of the gold path, is a palace. Peaked windows, too many to count, stare down on us. As if thousands of voices welcome us, men, women, and animals chant and cry out with joy. It's confusing and so overwhelming that I stop at the first step.

But Hekate never slows, and I hurry to catch up. The singing stops the instant we cross the threshold into an antechamber that unfurls above us open to five or six levels. Hekate's feet pacing quickly across the shiny marble floor make no noise, but each tentative step I take echoes from the walls. I have no doubt that I am the intruder. It's as if the castle is alive and would frighten me off.

I laugh out loud in defiance and run after the goddess, my steps thundering with me.

We walk up stone staircases, wide and inlaid with symbols from every land—Egyptian hieroglyphics and ancient runes. In one stone step, there is the imprint of a hand, so large that it must be a god's or giant's. I'm careful to avoid it and hurry on. Long, high-ceilinged halls pass door after door. Each one is gold-etched with scenes from myths. I don't recognize many of them—we're rushing past too fast for me to study them—but in one I see Pan handing his panpipes to a young girl.

My heart races. My story has come even to Hades' Realm? I recognize another as the battle between the Olympians and the Titans.

We turn another corner. Hurry up another staircase and down a long hall lined with mirrors, so the dark goddess and a girl are rushing through an endless universe. We are like stars in the sky—too many to count.

At last, out of breath, I stop beside the goddess at a simple door at hall's end. This door is not marble or gold or even decorated. It is oak, adorned only by the wood's grain, yellowed and polished with age. It is beautiful.

Hekate smiles at me and knocks twice. The oak door sings out like a tympanum.

A vast tiled courtyard, dotted with wide-fanned palm trees, ponds alive with carp swimming beneath soothing waterfalls spreads out before us, crossed by flower-lined paths, studded with sapphires and emeralds. Hundreds of girls and young women dressed in bright chitons of yellow and blue and deep red chatter and flit like butterflies around the ponds.

I scan the girls for Sophia. Despairing, I search again past dark girls of Egyptian heritage and tall Amazons.

She's not there.

CHAPTER TWENTY-EIGHT
THE QUEEN'S BEDCHAMBER

midst all the confusion and laughter, a goddess—
Queen Persephone, my instinct tells me—stands tall and
stern. Dressed completely in white. Thin arms and face, a
long aquiline nose. Surrounding her, but leaving space, the girls are a
tapestry of color, constantly moving.

Desperate to find Sophia, I plunge in their midst and squeeze my
way between them. One strong girl with almond eyes whirls to face me
and shouts a protest. Another shoves me back. But I push on. She has
to be here. Tiresias said she is, and he would know.

At last I see her. Standing with her back to me and addressing two
girls, both older than Sophia, but listening intently to her with nods
and smiling eyes. In that instant, I understand that they respect her. I
weave my way through two more groups, until I'm right behind her.
The girl facing me looks up, a question in her eyes. Sophia stops talking
and turns around.

"Sophia!" I move to hug her, but she steps back.

"Who are you?" She must see the hurt that I try to hide. She reaches
out and strokes my arm like she might a frightened colt. "I'm sorry. Do
I know you?"

I can only nod at first, then find my voice. "It's me. Thaleia. Your
best friend."

The girl who first spotted me over Sophia's shoulder steps up and wraps her arm around Sophia's shoulder, a scowl creasing her forehead. "*I'm* her best friend."

"Sophia, I've come to bring you home."

She steps back and shakes her head a quick up and down of denial. "What are you saying? I am home. I live here." She sweeps her arm wide. "With my sisters." And points over to the stern woman in white who has noticed me now and is making a stately way over. "And Mother."

"No, Sophia, this is not your home. Please, come with me! I've fought the gods to save you. Giants and fire rivers and even Hades and Zeus... what are you saying, Sophia?"

The woman seizes my shoulder. Her grasp is stronger than I'd imagine it could be, but I'm desperate. I whirl around to face her.

As if to get a better look at me, she pins my arms to my side. "How do they call you?"

I lift my chin and stare directly into the woman's eyes. "Thaleia."

"From what rocky shore do you travel deep into Hades' Realm?"

"I am Oracle of Delphi, Pythia in the Temple of Apollo on Mount Parnassos."

"And who are your parents?"

"Icos and the wise Hipparchia who was Oracle before me."

She scowls. "The Forbidden One."

Though I worry it will enrage the queen, I spit out my answer. "If you would believe the priests who wanted to destroy her!"

The woman steps back to study me. She draws away my hood to reveal my poppy hair. "Why are you here disturbing my daughters? Did my mother send you?"

The anger roughens her voice and know I should be careful, but I have to ask. "Demeter?"

With my question, sadness washes over her face like a cloud covering the sun. "Yes, Demeter. Goddess of fields of grain and mighty oaks, goddess of wildflowers, meadows filled with sunshine and narcissus. All that is lost to me for most of each year."

I drop to my knees and bow my head to honor the queen.

ORACLE OF THE SONG

"Rise, child, and tell me why you've come to this Land-of-Darkness."
She takes both my hands and pulls me to my feet.

"I've come for Sophia. To take her home, but she no longer knows
her name. Or home. She no longer remembers those who love her."

"Why would she? No one remembers once they drink from the
River Lethe. It is a blessing, not to remember. To leave behind the
pain of death."

"She has to remember. I drank from it, too. I also forgot, but now I
know who I am, and why I came to the Underworld." I gather Sophia's
hands and kiss her fingertips. My words come out in a jumble. "Sophia,
we were friends. We've been friends all our lives. You're engaged to
Timon, and I'm engaged to... oh, none of that matters."

I can't go on. Choking and sobbing, I can only say over and over,
"Forgive me. Forgive me." Throwing my arms around her knees, I can't
stop crying. "The priest murdered you, struck you down with his sword
on the night of the Agrionia. Oh, Sophia!" I throw my arms around her,
bury my face in her neck.

But she stiffens and gently pushes me away. "I don't know what to
say. You clearly came here thinking you would help me." She paces
away, then back. She takes the woman's hand. "This is home." She
kisses the woman's cheek. "This is my mother, and these are my sisters.
Do you understand? Why would I want to leave here?"

When I grab Sophia's hand and try to draw her to me, the Queen
shouts, "Let her go!"

I drop my friend's hand and whirl to confront her false mother,
speaking between clenched teeth to control my anger. "You rule here,
but I have come to save Sophia. To bring her back to the Land-of-the-
Living. No one will stop me now. Not even you, Queen Persephone."

I expected to be assaulted by a queen's anger. Instead, her smile for
me is filled with so much love and understanding that I am
dumbfounded. When she rests her strong and gentle hand on my
cheek, tears rush to my eyes. "You... you don't understand." I stutter.

"No, Thaleia, you do not understand." She crosses her arms and
draws herself tall. Her face reclaims its hardness, stern and cold like

marble. Unyielding. "You have absolutely no idea why your friend is here." She sweeps her arm wide to take in all the girls.

They've circled us and stand with protective arms thrown around another's shoulder. Everyone watches us to see what will happen next. I see in their eyes that they are lost. Confused.

"What have you done to these girls? Are they your servants? Enslaved to do your bidding?" I step close to the queen. She is just my height. Just my build. We could be sisters. "What have you done to them?"

Persephone rests both of her hands on my shoulders, but I jerk away.

"You don't understand the way things are, Thaleia."

"Then tell me!" I clutch Sophia's delicate fingers and pull her close. She doesn't resist but stands still as death and stares between her mother and the friend she doesn't remember. Waiting. Only waiting for her path to be decided for her.

My rage rises with bile in my throat. "What is there to understand? I am taking her home!"

Gently, reluctantly, Sophia pulls her hand from mine. "I won't leave."

"Sophia, come home with me. Come home to your mother and father. Come home to Timon, your betrothed."

"These girls are her sisters, Thaleia. Come with me to my chamber, where we may speak in private, and I'll explain."

I hesitate, unwilling to leave Sophia and afraid there is some trick, but I'm torn. If she takes me to her inner hall, maybe I'll have a chance to find the secret box beneath her bed.

The queen of the dark land smiles. "Come with me, and I'll give you the box beneath my bed. It will be my gift to claim your beloved." Did she read my thoughts? Well, she's a goddess, a queen. Why did I think I could fool her?

She doesn't wait for my answer, simply spins on her heel and walks up a gold path that appears before each sandaled foot just before it touches the earth.

What can I do? My heart is torn. Sophia is here. Can we run while Persephone's back is turned? I grab Sophia's hand. "Come with me. Now's our chance!"

"Why should I trust you? Why should I leave my home, my mother, my sisters?"

Beyond Sophia's shoulder, I see the Queen Persephone's receding back. Will I lose any chance to save Valmiki?

"I'll explain later, when we can talk in private. There's something I have to do first." I grab her hand. "Come on!"

We hurry after the goddess who knows my mind, the goddess who returns to The Land-of-Light each spring to summon the grasses and flowers and gentle rains. The goddess who murdered the nymph.

As we run up the path to the shining mansion, the girls step aside to clear a way. Their eyes follow us, questioning, worried. Many of them are about my age, golden-skinned with sun-kissed beauty, tall with ebony skin from the eastern lands, but some are much younger, tiny and pale as if hidden indoors all their lives. Something about them haunts me. Though their faces seem smooth and content, unlined by worries or struggles, their eyes tell a different story.

Hidden in the dark iris of each eye that follows me is hurt.

Fear.

Betrayal.

What has happened to these girls? More than ever, I'm convinced the queen enslaved them. I hurry after her, determined to put an end to it. Determined to reclaim Sophia.

At first, I'm so angry that I don't see where I'm rushing. There is only my furious racing after the goddess, but I never seem to gain ground. Her form recedes on the gold path that winds between the silent girls, then disappears behind a golden door decorated with poppies and narcissus.

When I knock, Persephone opens it immediately. Her smile is bemused and a little surprised? Her beauty not quite hidden by a stern gaze strikes me.

"Good, you've come." She opens the door wide and gestures for us to enter, then leads us down wide halls, laid out like a labyrinth, lit by gold stanchions holding candles burning with an unnatural light. Sapphires and diamonds sparkle in spiraling patterns along the walls.

At last we come to the widest door, situated at the end of the hall.

When the queen opens it, I pull a reluctant Sophia in behind me. The queen looks a question at the two of us, then motions that we follow her to a circular table carved from oak with dragon legs and sit in high-backed chairs crowned with narcissus carved from red-veined marble.

While the queen busies herself with a silver teapot on a side table, I look around the room, more luxurious than I could ever have imagined. High-ceilinged and bright with torchlight, everything is gold. Frames for gigantic mosaics of dragons and pythons, lyres and cavorting nymphs. The floor is highly polished marble tile grouted with seams of gold. And at the far end of the chamber is a canopied bed with green silk, draped and hanging from each gold column.

I shiver with the thought that the box I need to rescue Valmiki is beneath it, but force myself to look away.

"May I offer you pomegranate tea?" Hekate has slipped in behind us without notice and stands here with the teapot in one hand and the most beautiful gold cup I've ever seen in the other.

I start to smile at her joke, but remembering Sophia and the other girls, turn instead to Persephone. "You live here in luxury as Hades' queen with everything you can possibly want. I'm sure the great Lord-of-Many-Names will do anything to keep his lovely bride happy. Why those girls? Why have you made them your slaves? Why do you keep Sophia here? Stolen her memory?"

Scowling at my tone, her companion grabs my shoulder hard enough to make me wince.

"It's alright, Hekate. The child does not understand why I gathered *my daughters...*" She smiles gently and moves to stand beside Sophia. "And brought them to this place. Sophia is her friend. Thaleia has a right to know."

I can barely breathe, I'm so angry, but I force myself to sit still and say nothing.

"Thaleia, contrary to what you believe, those girls are not my slaves. They are not even my servants. I honor them as daughters."

I jump to my feet. "Your daughters! Slavery is the way you'd treat your daughter?"

Sophia frowns at me and wraps her arm around the queen's waist. "Please, sit and let me explain."

When I'm once again seated, the pale queen paces back and forth before the fire as if trying to gather her thoughts. Hekate takes the chair opposite me. We wait.

"You think I live here in this golden palace, queen to Lord Hades with hundreds of beautiful young girls at my beck and call... first, you must understand, I am not only his queen."

I start to stand in protest, but she motions for me to sit, and I do.

"My Lord Hades is a kind man."

Now I can't sit still. I hiss, "How can you say that? He kidnapped you and dragged you to this dark land. He keeps you here a prisoner!"

"I can't deny it. He kidnapped me while I was gathering flowers in the far-off Nysan Meadow. I later realized it is known as the Garden of Dionysos. I sometimes wonder... But no matter, Lord Hades carried me off in his chariot to this realm, but once he knew, let's just say my father Zeus has reason to be ashamed of the way he treated me."

"What happened? How did Zeus dishonor you?"

The pale, forlorn-looking queen shrugs. "Zeus is my father. My mother Demeter is Zeus' own sister, and still he treated me with disrespect." She stares at her clasped hands, before she looks up at me a long, silent moment. "Why would a father give someone permission to abduct his child? He didn't even tell his sister. It's as if I am something lowly, a beast not worth anyone's attention. But it matters not. Hades... he is my friend. Do not judge him too harshly. Together, we rule the Underworld. He helps us save the girls."

"What do you mean?"

"So many girls are treated horribly. Many end up as Shades in this bleak land, because men are taught to think a girl is not as important as a boy. Boys' lives are honored, even those tilling the land, or sent to perish in battle. Girls are expected to keep the hearth and marry whomever their parents deem fitting... they have no choice! They have no love!"

"Yes, I know." I quietly sip my tea. "My parents arranged a marriage for me. I ran away." Smiling, I remember the rest of it. The way I kneed the priest in the groin and climbed the mountain to join Sophia in our secret cave. "My betrothed was a disgusting fisherman, a traitor who betrayed the Greeks at Thermopylae. A man twice my age!"

"Then you were one of the brave ones, the fortunate few who escape. We live in a world where females are ridiculed, ignored, even abused because every boy grows up with the idea that they are more important. And girls?" The queen paces before a massive fireplace, the logs crackling and spitting sparks. "Girls' lives?" She leans with both hands on the hearth and stares into the flames. "They are worth nothing."

"But aren't you guilty of doing the same thing to these girls you call *your daughters*?"

When she turns back to look at me, her face is solemn and sad. "No. That is where you are mistaken. How did Sophia die? How did she end up here in the Land-of-the-Dead?"

"A priest killed her." I look away, unwilling to look Queen Persephone in the eye.

"How?" She says. "You've come to the Underworld for her. Why?"

"It was the day I stopped the Persian army. I was exhausted."

"Why does it already sound like you're making excuses, girl?" Her bitterness stuns me. I take a deep breath and glance over at Sophia, wondering what I can say. What I should keep secret. "Start at the beginning and tell us what happened. Tell us the truth, Thaleia."

CHAPTER TWENTY-NINE
DEATH

I take a deep breath. The truth, yes. But what truth? "I'd been asleep. But Mama and Papa's voices woke me. They were talking about Sophia." I gather my friend's limp hand and kiss her fingers. "Don't you remember, Sophia? We promised each other not to, but you left in the dark of night to attend the fertility festival up Mt. Parnassos... you must remember."

Her face is blank. She shakes her head in denial but says nothing.

"Tell us what happened, Thaleia." The queen urges me.

"I ran outside, raced through the village. I remember running past homes lit brightly with oil lamps from the day's celebration after the defeat of the Persians; others were dark and closed. I remember every moment, every frantic step... if only I didn't.

I ran past Hestos' goat pen, the animals crowding against the railing, bleating for me to release them. Without stopping, I rushed up the back path toward the Cave of Pan. All I could think about was bringing Sophia home to safety.

But the path was empty. No sign of Sophia—or any of the celebrants.

I ran higher and higher up the mountain, scrambling over boulders and under low-hanging branches... Sophia, I was desperate to find you!"

Tears fill my eyes, when she smiles and brushes my cheek. "Now, do you remember?"

"No, I'm sorry. But I believe you are my friend. What happened? Tell me how I came to be here with Queen Persephone."

She would offer pity. I sigh. This is Sophia. "At last, a torch flared just ahead, dancing and flickering through the trees. I heard laughter—girls calling for the god Dionysos in nervous excitement. It wasn't your voice, Sophia, but I ran up to them. Ino, Asteia and Hippia, your friends. They were dressed in fawn skins, and sitting by the cave mouth. Like one creature, they whirled around to stare at me. I saw fear on their faces, as if I was Thanatos himself come to claim them. I yelled at them, had them jump to their feet. Bones fell from their laps and scattered to the ground. 'One of you will die. Don't you understand? Go home! Run!' I urged them.

At that moment, Asteia... do you remember, the small-boned girl, barely crossed into womanhood... She said, 'We're casting knucklebones to find our fortune.' The firelight left black hollows around her eyes as she backed away from me, looking at others. 'The priest Diokles ordered us to play games and search for Dionysus. The matrons were to throw a wicker god into the Kastalia Spring to enter the Underworld to find the god's mother. He said it would be fun.'

Yet, no, she didn't believe any of it, I could tell. But she came. She didn't want to be different, to cross the priest... Even at the expense of being sacrificed to honor Dionysos. How could she, how could they *all* go up the mountain year after year like lambs to the slaughter?!"

My chest heaves with sobs. "I don't want to remember. I can't say more. I can't!"

"Please, Thaleia, only you can give me back my memory."

"I couldn't help them, Sophia. I couldn't help you. They trusted me, and I couldn't help them. I tried! The girls circled me as if I could keep them safe. I am their Pythia. The gods talk to me. It was my duty to protect them. I tried. 'Leave. Go down the mountain,' I yelled at them. I thought I saved them. They gathered their shawls filled with figs and nuts and turned to leave. 'Wait,' I said. I asked them if they'd seen you, Sophia. I'd maybe saved these girls from the sacrifice, but where were you? Ino, the goldsmith's daughter, told me you went looking for Dionysos up by our dream stone."

"Our dream stone." Sophia squeezes my hands. "I remember. It was white, high up the mountain..." She smiles. "We went there together, and I spelled his name on the stone by licking poppy petals and pasting them to spell... I spelled Timon, the boy I loved."

"You and Timon tried to save me from the old priest, to run away with me to Korinth before I faced my judgment." I gather her hands. "You were willing to leave your home, your family to save me."

"Tell me why I'm here, Thaleia, and not with Timon." Her eyes glisten with tears. I nod, letting the cathartic words burn their way out. For Sophia.

"Ino's eyes grew wide, terrified by what she saw behind me. I whirled around.

The priest I kneed in the groin to escape my wedding day grabbed my *chiton*.

'Release me! I am the Oracle!' I screamed, but he pulled me against him and whispered in my ear. 'Not this time, *Pythia*. You will marry Brygos. He will control his wife.'

'No. *I* am your true Oracle. I will never marry. And would *never* marry that traitor. He betrayed us all. Showed the Persians the hidden trail. The Spartan king is dead because of that vile fisherman. I will not marry Brygos!' I stomped my foot hard on the priest's and ripped free from him, but we were surrounded. Yellow robes emerged from behind the trees and boulders. There were screaming and running girls, total confusion. The priest grabbed me again, tore my gown. Angry, terrified, instead of trying to pull free, I stepped closer to the priest, so close that I felt his breath. 'You dare touch me! I am your Pythia. Apollo is my protector.' Like a Shade from this Underworld, his face turned white, and he stepped away from me and bowed his head.

It was my chance to save you, Sophia. I ran straight uphill to our dream stone. The priest raced after me. My foot slipped, and I almost fell as I leapt down into a gully wet with moss and spring water, his ragged breath close behind.

I screamed your name as I got close to the clearing... to our stone.

I'll never forget it, white and gleaming as the moon cleared the cloud cover. A girl jumped up, ghost-like in the moon's shimmer. Sophia, do you remember? It was you. You shouted at me, just as the priest caught up to me and grabbed my sash. I ran so hard that I pulled him along with me..."

I cover my face with both hands as if I can abolish the memory. In the hushed room, I hear only my tortured breath and Sophia's gasp and running water beyond the deep-set window.

"Thaleia, tell us the last." She strokes my poppy hair. "Tell me."

"Against the white stone, I saw a shadow—the priest's arm, the thrust and strike of bitter edge of bronze..."

"I thought he was chasing you, Thaleia. I thought he wanted to kill you..."

I can't look at her. Staring at my folded hands, I tell the story's end... but not the middle. I can't answer her question.

"I rushed the priest. I remember that look of shock, his eyes wide with surprise, when I shoved him hard with both arms. He screamed, his cry shattered like rock splinters, sharp, cutting... until there was only silence and the night wind from the cliff's bottom."

"What happened to me?"

I can't answer her at first. Overwhelmed with my memory of kneeling beside Sophia; cradling her in my arms; her blood warm against my skin as it soaked her leopard skin-robe and my yellow one, warm and sticky.

At last I whisper, "You were still alive, but there was too much blood. You moaned. Your eyes were half-open, unfocused. And I knew... I didn't want to... but I knew. 'I won't let you die, Sophia,' I said. 'Even if you travel to the Land of the Shades, I will find you. I will bring you back.'

But your eyes locked with mine, and without fear you said, 'Pray to Hermes for my safe passage, Thaleia.' That was the last thing you said. 'Pray to Hermes.' You grasped my hand, until your fingers released mine. I thought I could bring you back. I thought I could bargain with the gods. 'Divine Apollo the Healer, do not claim her. Take me.'

I lifted my arms as if I could reach Mt. Olympos with my will. I rested my hand on your heart. For a moment, a fire stirred in my palm and there was hope. I tried to summon the pomegranate tree. Passing my hands over your head and along your body, I prayed to Asklepios and divine Apollo to heal you.

The gods did not answer. Not Apollo. Not Asklepios... the gods abandoned me. The gods abandoned us, Sophia!"

I glance up at the goddesses. Queen Persephone stares at me and runs her finger round and round her cup rim. Hekate coughs. But they say nothing, so I go on.

"I don't know how long I held you. I heard shouts and a fast-approaching scrabble of feet on rubble. Several priests—followed by Diokles panting to catch them—rushed up.

'We need the girl's body to offer to the god,' Diokles said.

I tried to stop him but had no answer for what he said next. There was truth in his words, and I knew if I interfered..."

I look a painful moment into Sophia's solemn stare. "If I interfered, I would lose you for all eternity in limbo. I would never find you here in Erebos. You would be with the lost souls, unsanctified, beyond my reach."

"What did the priest say?" Sophia whispers. I can barely hear her.

He said you were the divine sacrifice. That your death honored Dionysos. He told me to get out of his way, his voice growling with authority, and motioned for an acolyte to lift your body. I stepped between them."

For a moment, I can't go on. Twice I open my mouth to speak, but choke on the words. But at last, looking at Sophia's innocent face and wide, fearful eyes, I push out, "The priest sidled up to my side and hissed in my ear, 'Will you betray her again, Pythia?'"

If possible, Sophia's whisper is softer than before. "What did the priest mean? You didn't betray me, Thaleia, not you. It was the priest."

"Yes, but... what could I do? There needed to be a death ritual, so you wouldn't be caught between two worlds. Every muscle in my body didn't want to let them take you. It took all my will, but I let them carry your body back to the temple.

I waited outside. I remember thinking an owl's call was a message from a god. I hoped Pan might help, but he never came. I sat cross-legged on the bottom step listening to the priests' incense-laden chants."

"Thaleia?"

I no longer look at Sophia. I'm drained by the memory. At last, I force myself to finish. "Finally, the night sky fragmented to dawn. I don't know how long it had been quiet inside the temple. The chants and scattering melody of finger cymbals and tympani long since faded. I didn't want to move. All I could think was that your body was inside. Covered with laurel and pine? Scented with frankincense? Cinnamon? I didn't go in to look. You were gone.

Slowly, I unfolded my stiff legs and walked beneath the wide portal; paced the Sacred Way back down to Delphi, past the cistern and bake oven—the somber path soft and gray with the early light. Pine needles whispered in the morning wind. A peaceful morning, but not for me. All I heard was the rush of the Kastalia Spring growing louder—mouth of the River Styx—mouth to the Underworld..."

"Pythia, there's more you haven't told us." Queen Persephone's gaze is sharp and discerning.

I catch my breath but quickly add, hoping they won't notice my hesitation. "I knew I alone had to find you, to bring you back to the Land-of-the-Living. I dove into the black waters."

"There's something you're hiding, Thaleia. But what of the priests, the men in power who did not listen to you? They killed Sophia. She came to me as a daughter... now do you understand who these girls are?"

In response to my blank stare, she goes on. "Every one of these girls died because someone treated her like her life had no value. Every one of these girls lost her life in shame. A shame that was never hers but an oppressor's!" The queen gives me a knowing look. "I understand these girls. I know dishonor. When I told my lord that I wanted to help them, he offered his wealth, his power... he aided in every possible way."

Hekate gathers both my hands and strokes my fingers. "She sends me out to every hidden corner of the Underworld to find them. I lead them to the River Lethe so they can forget their past. So they forget their sorrows. Then, with their hearts pure and untroubled, I bring them here to live in Hades Palace."

"It's the least we can do for them, Thaleia. Give them a little peace and perhaps some love."

I look from the queen to Hekate and again at the queen completely at a loss for words. At last I stutter, "I... I thought they were slaves."

"You couldn't have known. No one knows, not even the other Olympians. It's how I keep the girls protected. I stick to the myth: Lord Hades kidnapped me and ravished me. I am his slave, doomed to nine months a year in this dark land, where I live frightened and lonely with only my slave girls for company. No one troubles them as long as they think they are my pathetic servants."

Queen Persephone walks over to her bed, kneels, and pulls a gold box from beneath it. The *kiste* is as wide as a seed gourd, decorated with interwoven myrtle and poppies etched in gold.

"This is my gift to you. My gift for you to give the goddess Aphrodite, so at least one girl may find love. But know, Thaleia, there is a delicate line between love and hate. Life and death. The gods and the mortals."

"Are we so alike, Queen Persephone? Do the gods also suffer from jealousy and hatred?"

Queen Persephone nods her head almost imperceptibly.

"You attacked Minthe... I saw it..."

"And I'm ashamed of what I did. These girls..." She sweeps her arm wide to indicate her daughters, her realm. "These girls are my atonement for my weakness, my rage. And what is atonement? Think for a minute, Thaleia, before you would judge me. At-One-Ment is the word. We are all One. We are all part of the *kosmos*, separated by a whisper, a breath. And you, Thaleia... *every* mortal is that thin line between us. So, decide, child. It is not the god's choice to save your beloved. It is yours. What will you do?"

I take the box. I expect it to be heavy, but it's as light as a small bird.

"Thief! I gave that to my queen. Now you are mine forever! You will never leave Tartaros!" A man's deep voice rumbles, shatters my vision. "You were warned but did not listen! She who crosses the River Styx, will never leave alive."

The voice fills the darkness. *Is* the darkness. It is the Host-of-Many, the dark lord.

CHAPTER THIRTY
HADES' DUE

I **won't back down. With this box, I can save Valmiki.** "Lord Hades, will you let your helmet of invisibility hide you? Are you afraid of a mere girl?"

He roars with rage and materializes from black crystals in the air. First red eyes, then muscled arms and clenched meaty fists he shakes in my face. "No one takes the souls in my realm. No one! Sophia stays here! Companion to my queen."

Zeus appears quickly beside him with a lightning bolt and resounding thunderclap to support his brother.

My heart catches. I step backward, away from the gods. Persephone and Sophia quickly take my side.

"Now, you are in Tartaros, heart of my realm. Pathetic girl, still you challenge me?" The air shimmers red around his body, red like fire reflecting from his gold armor, red like coals burning for eyes.

"Open the box, Thaleia," Queen Persephone says in a low voice.

"The goddess Aphrodite ordered me not to."

"Sometimes we must ignore a god's warning." The queen smiles at me, a smile filled with a question. "Perhaps it was a test? Will you claim your destiny? Are you ready?"

With trembling hands, I unclasp the gold latch and lift the lid. Darkness sweeps over me like a thunderous wave. My head spins, and there is only black. *Sophia and I drift in the dark Void. Together. Separate. There is no time. No form. I would hold her hand and calm her. I would wrap my arms around her and protect her. But we are lost in nothingness. A darkness where stillness roars, and hope collides with fear. My ears ring with hissing like a thousand snakes. I feel my shame tattered in the dark.*

Nyx emerges from a swirl of stars and nebulas. They spin in time to a drum, the heartbeat of the kosmos, pulsing in time to my own. "There is truth in the darkness. Will you seize it?"

"I'm not ashamed of anything." *I reach for Sophia's hand, but she drifts just out of reach.*

"Do not lie, child. Your chance is now. Your hope is now. Speak the truth now or lose her forever."

Sophia cries out and spins helplessly, caught in a receding galaxy. "There is truth in the darkness. There is shame. There is guilt."

As my vision thins and frays, I shake off my fear. Inside the kiste is truth I must face. It is my shame—my guilt unspoken—that prevents me from saving Sophia. From freeing myself.

The stench of sulfur fills the room, swirling in clouds around the god, so thick they obscure his form. Only his voice rages from among the smoke. "No one can steal life from death!"

"I can. I have." I keep my words even and calm.

"You've been allowed to wander my land, but now here you will stay, never to return to the Land-of-the-Living."

There's finality in his voice. We stare at each other.

A hand rests on my shoulder. Hekate stands behind me.

"If so, Lord-of-Many-Names, do not imprison Sophia. Take me in her place."

In my mind, a sword catches moonlight to glint with fresh blood and death. A rock splits from the cliff and crashes and bounces down the rock wall. My mind swoops unwillingly to an image of me shoving the priest off the cliff, his flailing body striking limestone boulders.

I kneel before Sophia. Drawing her fingers to my lips, I say, "I didn't tell you everything. Not the whole story... not how... not *why*."

I've held the shame so long; the guilt has eaten my heart. At last, tears pour down my face. "Sophia, it is my fault that you died. Everything I told you is true. Rage propelled me up the mountain with the priest chasing me. He grabbed my hair and jerked my head back. You jumped on his back trying to help me, scratched his face and tore his tunic, until he let go of me and whirled around to face you. I grabbed his knees and dumped him to the ground, but he got the better of me. Just as his sword flashed in moonlight, terror overcame me. I didn't mean to."

"What happened?"

My heart aches to confess, to clean away the shame, but I can't make myself admit my guilt to Sophia, to Hades and his queen, Athena and Aphrodite. Can I really announce to the world that I am a coward?

While I hesitate and Sophia stares at me, waiting for me to speak the truth of her death, a Shade appears in the queen's chamber, drifting like smoke between us. Recessed eyes glare at me over a hooked nose. His lips a red snarl. The priest I killed. In a venomous voice he says, "Issss ssssomeone dead? Maybe it be you to blame?"

"Yes." At last, I answer. I will not hide from his accusations, not now, never again. "Yes, Sophia died. You killed her, priest." Rage chokes me. My hands clench.

Sophia whirls around to confront him, her mouth open in shock.

"Know thysssself, little girl. In your heart. What be your nature. Know thysssself..."

"I know many things. I know I am Thaleia, Oracle of Delphi. I know none of us are alone, that together with the gods, we fulfill our destiny. I know I hate you!"

"Pythia, you murdered me. You shoved me off the cliff."

"You killed Sophia!"

"Ahhhhhh, revenge. You sssseek revenge, little girl?"

"Yes!"

"Yeeesss..." He bows at my feet. "I forgiiive theeee."

"What? You forgive me? I murdered you!"

"I am change, little girl." The priest-Shade floats before me. Transforms before me from snake-man to a celebrant with yellow robes and eyes shining with compassion. A feeling of love overwhelms me. "I forgive you for my death. And now, I beg your forgiveness. Tradition commanded that I kill. My superior Diokles ordered me to fulfill my duties. Can you forgive me? Proud Oracle, are you without blame?"

The compassion and wisdom I feel from this priest, this man I blamed and hated, and killed, shocks me to my core.

"Not what will change, Pythia. Who. Who will change?"

"I forgive you, priest."

Long-silent, my friend gasps, and I turn to her. "I forgive the priest, Sophia, because it is my fault that you died."

"What do you mean? You said this priest murdered me?"

I let silence sit a long moment between us. Silence in which the gods are waiting. I rest my hands on Sophia's shoulders and plead for her forgiveness with one look. Blood fills my vision. "Just as he lifted his blade to strike, I jumped behind you. Hoping to kill me, he murdered you." I've said it. At last, I honor the truth.

Sophia's face is blank, white. She shakes her head. "I remember now. I know who I am. How I died."

"Forgive me, Sophia." Once again, I pass my palm across her heart. "I am a coward. It is my fault that you died. It is my shame."

Sophia wipes the tears from my face with a sad smile. "All of it was the priest's doing, Thaleia. He wanted to murder you. Could I have stood up to his sword?"

"You jumped on his back. You tried to save me." Now I can't stop sobbing. I sink to the ground at her feet.

"You came looking for me, Thaleia, when I promised not to go!"

"I hid behind you. I was a coward, and you died." I stare at the ground as the truth of my words sinks in.

Sophia bends down and takes my hands, pulling me to my feet. "Remember what Hestos told us?"

"No, what?"

"He said, 'Fear is a terrible enemy.' Now I understand."

"I'm the Pythia. I'm your friend. I betrayed you and my sacred duty. I beg your forgiveness, Sophia."

"I do forgive you, Thaleia. With all my heart. Out of fear, you jumped behind me. But, Thaleia, you're here now. You came to this Land-of-Death; you risked your life to save me, and as for your sacred duty, there is still time. I forgive you, and now I need you. We all need you!" With a wide gesture toward the door and courtyard, Sophia reminds me of all the girls waiting outside. "The past is gone. Be brave now!"

"Lord Hades, Sophia died instead of me. It's me the priest wanted to kill, and I didn't stop him. I didn't save Sophia. Take me. Allow me to save my friend at last."

Before he answers, the Furies burst through the door and fly into the room pursued by Aphrodite. Valmiki hangs lifeless from the vulture hags' talons. The queen's gold chamber fills with screeches and flashes of black, leathery wings. Thrashing and twisting, soaring like one creature to the high ceiling and swooping back down just above me. Their raucous accusations assault me. One hag's voice indecipherable from another, like scattering lightning and thunder crashing over me.

"Do you hope to escape The Lord-of-Many-Names?"

"King of this foul Underworld?"

"Lord of Death's Realm?"

"No one will. No one can. We do their will, when murder's at play. Revenge for the mother, killed most foul."

"Revenge for the brother, the father whose honor dies."

"You, pitiful girl, escape a god's wrath?"

Valmiki's body flops from their claws. His head whips from side-to-side.

"Poet!" I jump to grab his foot, a hand... but he is helpless in their clutches.

Aphrodite glides over to stand between Hekate and Persephone.

I run to her and hold out the box. "I have what you've asked for. My task is complete."

"So I see." She takes the chest and peeks inside before quickly closing it. A smell of honey and summer flowers warmed by the sun fills the room. The goddess of love smiles at the queen. "I did not imagine that you would give the child assistance, but no matter."

The Furies land on a high crossbeam and drop Valmiki. He lands with a sickening sound on the tile floor and lies there, splayed and crumpled.

Before I can think, as if my body leaps before my mind, I am beside him. Gently, I cradle his head in my lap. "Valmiki, please, Valmiki." There's no breath in his chest that I can see. His eyes are closed and still. I hold two fingers to his neck and gasp. There! A faint pulse. A long pause. So long that I think I felt his heart's last beat. But no. There's another. I look up at Aphrodite. Then Hekate. And last, Queen Persephone.

"You will never leave alive." The hags chant.

"Never."

"Never." The Furies surround me. Their hoarse laughter fills the chamber with a stench of rotting flesh. Like mad children, they spread their leathery wings wide and circle me slowly, chanting. "She doesn't kno...ow. The little girl doesn't kno...ow."

Round and round they spin their game of life and death. Mocking and taunting me with their child's verse.

"Once you cross the River Styx."

"Once you enter the Land-of-the-Dead."

"You will never leave alive."

"Ne...ver."

"Ne...ver."

"Persephone, please, brave queen. You helped the girls. Now help Valmiki." I cover his body with my own. The Furies circle us and shriek and laugh, slower and closer, slower and closer. Death and blood and rotting flesh. "Tell me what I must do!"

"I gave you the box. They returned the boy to you. I cannot do more. It is up to you, Thaleia. This boy's fate is in your hands."

Hekate steps between the hags to tower over me. Stars shimmer around her head. The oak branches tremble and her voice, though hushed and calm, fills the room with its power. The Furies step back and fold their wings, cock their heads like ravens over carrion.

"Thaleia, Persephone gifted you her sacred *kiste,* and Aphrodite fulfilled her promise. Will you ask more of the gods?"

"This is how they bring him back? More dead than alive?"

"Come to me, child," Aphrodite says.

I gently rest Valmiki's head on the hard floor and look from Aphrodite to Persephone and last to Hekate. When I stand, the startled Furies move back, but soon crouch and spring to surround me. I back up, until my heel touches Valmiki's leg. "Pythia to pythia, god to goddess, I am chosen." I glower at the Furies. "Let me pass."

The hags resume their slow dance. "You will never leave alive."

"Ne...ver."

"Ne...ver."

I straighten my shoulders and take a deep breath. "Iiachos! Iiachos! As Initiate into the Mysteries, I call upon you!" With great care, I draw the panpipes from my sash.

The Furies screech and flap their wings. The oldest reaches a taloned foot to snare Valmiki. She pulls him close to her with a jerk and continues circling, his body dragging limp across the floor.

Is it too late? Have I lost him?

"Ne...ver. Ne...ver.

The girl is lost for...ever."

I play a melody that spins and weaves with the Furies' chanting.

"Ne...ver. Ne...ver."

The flute sings high, tender notes.

Aphrodite sweeps her arm high and a milky-white dove lands on her hand.

"Ne...ver. Ne...ver."

My panpipes mourn and howl. Hekate's muscled mastiffs surround the vulture-hags. Their chant scatters and halts. One dog growls and steps closer. The others follow.

I play Pan's melody. It is sunshine and grasses. Bees and sweet honey. It is laughter and filled with such yearning that Queen Persephone catches her breath then drops to the floor, wrapping her arms around herself as if she could spare her heart.

The Furies screech as if they could drown out my music. And still I play.

"Thaleia, it is the meadow. Dionysos' Meadow where Lord Hades dragged me down to this dark world. I went there for three days... until each day's light faded." Queen Persephone pleads for me to understand, her voice high and frightened like a girl's. "I could not stay away... it was this music. This is the song the flowers sang. And the wind carried these notes. Thaleia, no more. No more."

But I don't stop. I won't stop until there is breath in Valmiki. Until there is hope.

Queen Persephone throws her arms high. Her stare stills me with its power. Resting one hand on Hekate's shoulder and the other on Aphrodite's, she pulls herself up and leads them to stand before me.

"She is Initiate into the Mysteries, sisters. Goddess of love, it is time she look once more into the sacred *kiste*. It is time for her to share our secrets."

In awe, I drop my arm to my side. My song fades away.

Aphrodite nods and hands the box back to me. She holds my gaze.

Hades voice rumbles like earthquake and tidal wave. "She is mine!"

A queen, a goddess of darkness, and one of love stand together as myth changes and the Fates rewind their thread. Who am I that I have the power to change myth and history? Oracle? Child of a prophecy? Is that enough?

I look at the Furies still hovering over Valmiki.

Hearing the queen's words as if from a great distance, a plan sweeps through me like wildfire. My ears roar as blood rushes to my head as if it would burst. "My queen! I will save them." I circle the queen and Hekate, my mind racing. "I can do it! I know I can."

The queen touches my arm as I pass the third time. "What are you saying?"

I stand still as stone before the queen. "I came here determined to save Sophia and to bring her back to the Land-of-the-Living. That is not enough. I see it now. Sophia does not want to leave her sisters. I'll take them all home. Every one of them! I won't leave them in this bleak Underworld! Together, we'll cross the threshold! I will fill their lives with sunlight and meadows."

I can barely breathe or think. Bowing before the queen, I wipe the tears from my eyes and touch my forehead to her gold-sandaled foot. "You rescued them from their sorrows, but that, too, is not enough. I will bring them their *nostos*, their return to the sun-soaked sea and stone paths in their villages." I jump to my feet. "Do you hear me, Queen Persephone, I will bring them home!"

The air between us shimmers with a frigid light like ice crystals in a winter sky. Fear chills our breaths and quiets my hope.

"They are companions to my queen! They will never leave my realm. Nor you!"

"I don't seek your permission!"

I expect to be assaulted by Hades' rage, but instead his voice lowers and his eyes narrow. "There is a law here. No one may be returned to the Land-of-the-Living unless another relinquishes his life. I have brought hundreds of girls to live with my queen. How do you hope to save them?"

"I will save them all or forsake my life trying."

Hope and despair and defiance simultaneously pass through the queen's gaze. "I believe you, brave Oracle of Delphi. It will be lonely here without the girls, but, yes, take them with you." She lifts her chin and glances over at Hades who glowers, but holds his tongue. "They deserve some joy. Some love." Her eyes brighten. "Return them to their homes, Thaleia!"

"I am Initiate in the *Kore's* Mysteries. Lord Hades, you can't stop me! The Song is older than you or your queen! Older and more powerful than all the gods!" Pulling my panpipes from my sash, I play a melody of summer winds and honey-swept meadows sparkling with sunlight. The poppies in my hair dip and swirl, twining like circling partners in a dance. I whirl round and round; throw my head back; and play with love and yearning like never before. At last, my melody calms and trills like a nesting bird and settles into Pan's melody.

Glancing at The Dark Lord, I see even he is mesmerized. His eyes have a far-off, dreamy cast. While I play, the shouting outside grows louder and closer.

With hope filling me, I whirl faster and faster, allowing my melody to lift and cry as it will. The girls. I only know I have to help them. It may be too late for Valmiki, but I can still save the girls. I can still save Sophia. Maybe Persephone's girls are my last hope.

With my melody turning fierce, not wanting to waste an instant, I clutch the box tight beneath my arm and rush over to the chamber door.

Just as I reach for the handle, it bursts open.

My music has summoned them all.

Two hundred frightened girls.

I look from girl to girl—each staring at me with fear, with hope—and understand what I need to do.

I play my melody, the low, sorrowful notes painting colors and shapes like diamonds and shattered crystal in the Shade-filled air, sweeping the spirits away like scattered storm clouds. Gray shadows change to yellow and red and iridescent green. Like shears cutting through wool, the fear and silence are sundered by one girl's laughter. The same girl I met by the gate to Hades' Realm. Her laugh is infectious and soon followed by another and another, until all of them throw their arms in the air, grabbing each other's hands and swinging in circles, singing for the sheer joy of the music.

Pan leaps through the girls, prancing and playing his flute in counterpoint to my melody.

"Pan! How did you find me?"

"You made a promise to fulfill any wish I have." He grabs Sophia's hand and prances around me, playing his own flute melody that weaves in and out of mine. At last he stops just before me and steps close. "I've come to claim payment."

"As you say, Pan. What is it you want?"

"There will be time to say, first there is much to do."

Persephone's chamber fills with our music and laughter.

"Stop!" Lord Hades bellows so loudly that we immediately quiet.

"Listen to my godly brother in his own realm!" Zeus glowers at each of us.

Pan and I drop our arms. The girls look anxiously one to another. Sophia slips to my side.

CHAPTER THIRTY-ONE
SEED OF LIFE

A **door bangs hard against the wall behind us. I hear** chanting and a steady drumbeat before I see anything. A woman's voice, deep as the earth, fills the room. I strain to understand the rumbling words mixed with a tympani drum. My entire body throbs with the beat. My heart lifts before I understand... but at last I do. "I am Nyx. Goddess of Night. Born of Chaos. Older than the Olympians."

Stars brush the high timbers; nebula and imploding galaxies tumble and swirl above us, as the goddess' power fills the room. Adrasteia and Medusa follow close behind, adding a cymbal's ringing to the chant, seemingly unaware that the goddess Athena has suddenly appeared in the shadows and glares at her erstwhile priestess.

But before I can warn Medusa, I'm stunned to see Kronos lumber into the chamber behind them, one hand still clutching his honey jug.

"How dare you bring that foul Titan to my palace?" Lord Hades grabs Nyx's sleeve as if to yank her around. But the goddess rises to her full height. "If I choose to bring my grandson here..." Her black wings tangle stars and planets above us in the chamber's ceiling, an endless kosmos. A universe she controls. "You do not frighten me, Lord Hades!"

When Hades steps back stunned, Queen Persephone seizes the opportunity. She steps up before me and lifts my chin and smiles. "We are sisters, child. You are Initiate in my sacred Mysteries. In your heart, you already know what must be done."

"Do I?"

Kronos belches a stench of cave and rancid honey.

"Child, you do. You are wiser than you know. You were not afraid of me. You offered me revenge for my imprisonment."

Medusa takes my hand and kisses my fingers. "I was foul and ugly and hateful. Consumed with self-loathing. You returned my beauty to me. You taught me that shame is Poseidon's, not mine." The beautiful girl drops to her knees. "You freed me from Athena's curse."

Athena strides before the girl as if she would curse her again, but Medusa never falters. She glances quickly at the warrior goddess then says, "She can no longer shame me or condemn me, because I know my own power. Thaleia, look around you. This dark realm is no more real than was my shame. Hades' Realm is created by your fear."

Parmenides' words echo in my head. *Your fear makes this land of Death real.*

Pan joins Medusa, Persephone and Kronos to stand before me. "It is time, Thaleia. It is time to grant my wish."

"Enough!" Lord Hades roars. The chamber shakes as if struck by an earthquake and even the constellations of the dark goddess' *kosmos* shimmer and fade, then reappear.

"I'm hungry," he says to me. "And you promised me anything I wish."

"Stupid satyr! Nothing but insatiable appetite. Apples and wine... nymphs." Hades snorts,

but the old nature god ignores him.

"I wish for a pomegranate seed." He holds out his hand expectantly.

"What?" I can't help but laugh. "A fine time you've picked to eat. A pomegranate seed is what you wish? Oh."

Suddenly, I understand. I know how to save Sophia. I know how to save all the girls.

I hold my hand out before me palm up and stare at it.

The room is quiet, filled with a tense, restless waiting.

My hand tingles. I focus on my palm's hollow and envision the pomegranate tree. Once more I hear Pan's melody, but it's not the satyr playing. He stands with crossed arms and smiles at me. Am I the only one who hears? The flute song fills the queen's chamber like laughter and sunlight. Understanding makes me smile. Here is the Song of the Universe that connects us all. Here is the joy. Drawing on the music's power, I stare at my hand and will the tree to grow.

First a seedling, then a sprout thickens to trunk and limbs. At last, red pomegranates hang from delicate, miniature branches. The rough trunk grows roots that dig into my palm, but I feel nothing. Two snakes—brown of earth and blue of Apollo's sky—twine around the tree.

I glance up to see Hades' expression. With furrowed brow, as if confused or amused, he studies me but doesn't speak. I don't wait for him to decide what to do. One pomegranate is bigger than the others. Plucking it, I tear it open with my teeth and extract one blood-red seed.

"Sophia, in legend, three pomegranate seeds doomed Queen Persephone to stay three months a year in this Land-of-Death. This fruit trapped the queen, but the sacred pomegranate also brings renewal and birth. Eat this seed grown in Tartaros and know the One. Know there is no beginning. There is no end. There is no threshold separating life and death. Step outside your ego and know that you may cross from the Underworld to the Land-of-the-Living, when you choose."

I give each girl a seed. As I pluck pomegranates from the tiny tree, the snakes entwine the branch, and another fruit grows. Turning to the goddesses, I slip a seed on each tongue. Even mighty Zeus bends on one knee for me to place a kernel in his mouth.

At last, I place a pomegranate seed on Hekate's tongue, then Nyx's.

"And what of my children, the Furies?" she asks.

"They are vile, Goddess of Night. How can they be your offspring? They kill and maim. They stole Valmiki... a loving and harmless poet," I say, barely able to restrain my fury.

"Ratnakara? Harmless? Was he always so harmless?"

I look over at Valmiki lying crumpled on the floor. "No, but that was long ago. He was like a spider trapped in a web of poverty and hunger. He is forgiven!"

"Ah, the spider web. And where is your web that connects us all? Show us!"

I'm startled by the power in her voice. An uneasy stillness shrouds every child and god.

"Thaleia, you are Pythia. You've wandered without fear through Hades' own realm... do you believe you are alone? Show us the web."

In my palm, the tree fades away. I quiet my mind to touch *Hesychia*—The Great Stillness.

A spider web strands from each of my fingers, my toes, my head and shoulders—a great web sparkling with dew and light shimmers between us. A strand from the center of Nyx's palm to my own. From the center of her brow to mine. From her heart to mine.

"Now, show me exactly where on this web I am separate. Or our Queen Persephone? Pan? Hades?... Sophia?" Her voice rises with urgency. "Is there a place that this web does not connect to Valmiki?" She drops her voice to a whisper. "To my children the Furies? Tell me, child, whom exactly do we cut out? Whom do we forgive and whom do we not? Is it for us to decide?"

"Toi pant' onom' estai. Its name shall be everything." I whisper, remembering Parmenides' words and truly understanding them for the first time. Understanding my duty.

I approach the Furies as they spread their leathery wings—an evil shadow over Poet. As one, they screech and flail to keep me away, but I take one slow step, then another. Extend my fingers with the tiny seed. "Don't be afraid. Let me help you."

A black hag spreads her wings wide, blocking my view of Valmiki.

"Listen to me. You defend honor and in return, receive fear and loathing and hatred from mortals. Mortals are disgusted when they look at you."

Another sister Fury steps beside the first, throws back her head so her wrinkled throat is revealed, and screams.

I don't stop. I take another slow step. Only two arm's lengths away, I lower my voice to say, "What if they could see instead your unceasing devotion to the gods, to what is just and true? Would they see your determination and glorious power?" Now I'm directly before the two Furies. I hold out my hand with three pomegranate seeds bright against my pale skin. "With this offering, I, Thaleia, name you no longer the Furies but the Eumenides, the Kindly Ones." My heart aches. These vultures dragged Valmiki away. They tried to poison me. They're ugly, hateful.

And if I hate them? Judge them? Am I any better?

"I am Thaleia. Oracle of Delphi. Pythia for the entire world. I am a vessel, filled with Apollo's wisdom and the god's words. When I sit upon the sacred tripod, I am one with the god. As Initiate into the Mysteries, I know that there is no wall between us, no barrier to stand behind and throw stones at one another."

I take a deep breath. I want to spit in their faces for hurting Valmiki, but I have to stay true to myself. My power as Oracle is found in forgiveness. "With these pomegranate seeds, I forgive you. I honor you."

I feed a blood-red seed to each of the vulture hags who dragged Valmiki away.

Each seed disappears with a slurp of a long, red tongue into their beaks.

They step away from Poet. Stand to one side in a line.

"With gratitude, we honor you, Pythia."

"You are wise."

"You are courage."

"Hestia's fire is your eyes..."

"... your heart."

They bow their heads and kneel before me and chant as one, "Honor. Honor. Honor to our Oracle. The gods speak through our Pythia."

Closing my eyes and crossing my arms over my heart, I nod to the hags.

Finally, all have eaten. Only the Dark Lord and Valmiki remain.

With tears in my eyes, I kneel beside Poet, my friend. "Valmiki?" His eyes are closed. His chest neither rises nor falls. His face is pale and gaunt. I shudder at how like a death mask it is... Is he alive? Dead? Am I ready to know?

The girls and goddesses back away, forming a quiet circle. I cradle his head in my lap and brush damp hair off his face. "Valmiki, I'm stupid. Selfish. I doubted your honesty and lost you. Valmiki..." My words choke in my throat. I rock him back and forth, letting my poppy hair fall over his ashen face. I want to hide the death shadows beneath his eyes, cover him in the red flowers of Demeter, of fertile fields and sun-filled meadows. I want to hide him from Death.

Nyx lifts her wings wide to shelter us. Her oaken hair crisscrosses shadows across Valmiki.

"Thaleia?" The Goddess of Night whispers. "Thaleia, you know what you must do. Trust your own..."

But Hades interrupts. "Thaleia, you've forgotten me." His powerful voice shakes the queen's bedchamber, as he leans his massive frame over us. "You did not give me a pomegranate seed."

"You? I have no forgiveness for you." Forcing my voice to stay low and even, I face the god. We are eye to eye as he kneels, and I stand. "You enslaved men, women... innocent children in oak trees. You kidnapped your queen. You..."

"My brother Zeus, all the handmaidens, these goddesses... even these loathsome vultures were given the seed of life." When he sweeps his arm wide to gesture to the hags, they cringe back. "Will you avoid me? Are you afraid? Give me a seed. Trust me." Hades' voice cajoles as if sweetened with honey.

I don't trust him, but somehow the girls will have to get past him to leave this Underworld. I will either have to trust him or outwit him.

He stretches out his hand for a seed.

Something shifts in the stars above. Nebulas swirl and hum. A whirring trembles the air.

I feel Nyx's power merging with my own. *What will I lose if I trust Hades?*

Out of the corner of my eye, I see Persephone shake her head no, but I rip one last seed from the fruit and move to place it in Hades' hand. *How can I hope to outwit this god in his own realm?*

Pan leaps between us. "Trust your power, Thaleia."

The whirring stars hum and race in wild circles above me. A murmur like spinning chariot wheels swells, grows. Three snakes slither from Nyx's hair and circle me.

"Lord Hades, your queen granted me permission to return to the Land-of-the-Living with Sophia... with all her daughters."

Hades glowers at Persephone. "This time you've gone too far! I gave you the dark goddess' companionship. I humored you in your loneliness and allowed you to gather the girls." He whirls around to confront me. "Choose, Pythia! Give me the seed of life if you ever hope to leave my realm!" The Lord-of-Many-Names towers over me. The weight of his dark land thickens around me. My butterfly vision engages, and now five gods menace me, each wearing a gold crown that glows red and purple and searing white. I blink, and again he merges into one angry and threatening god.

Hades narrows his eyes. "Only I can help you here in my realm, Pythia. So, hear me. I will let you and Sophia and all the girls return to the Land-of-Light."

I try to stifle my gasp, but the dark lord notices.

"And... I will bring Valmiki back to life." He smiles, a mocking grimace filled with threat. "But Valmiki stays here as a son for me... and my queen." He smiles at Persephone winsomely. When I don't immediately answer, he screams with rage. "You must choose: their lives or his!"

"No, give me another choice. Any choice but that."

"The choice is yours."

"But, to choose for you to save him... only to lose him. Please!"

"So, you are selfish once more," he drawls. "You'd rather he remained dead..."

"He's dead?" I drop to my knees, wrap my arms around my body. "He's dead?" I whisper, but saying the words cannot bring any truth to them. *He can't be.*

"He will be my son." Hades' smile is both sad and treacherous. "A son whom I can trust to not claim my throne... but enough! You must make your choice!"

I jump to my feet, anger racing through me. "I don't need your permission to save Valmiki's life, Lord Hades."

"What! You defy me? A god?"

The hall shakes as an earthquake erupts from Hades' rage. Nyx's constellations shatter with Zeus' thunder and flashing lightening. The girls scream, cover their ears, and cower together.

I look over at Poet's unmoving form.

I will save you, Valmiki.

Strong winds rip poppies from my hair. Petals swirl like drops of blood in a whirlwind that threatens to expel me out the door.

I lean into the maelstrom, struggle away from the Lord-of-Many-Names, and kneel. "Valmiki, forgive me for not trusting you." I press the seed between his limp lips. "I vow to remain forever in Hades' realm. I trade my life for yours. I, Thaleia, Oracle of Delphi, grant you life!"

"No, Thaleia, you must return home!" Sophia cries out. She and the queen drape their arms over my back as if they can protect me from my words.

Hades' roar shakes the room, but all I hear is Valmiki's groans as he rolls over and opens his eyes. A storm rages around me with lightning and wind and the power of gods who ruled the kosmos for millions of years... until now.

Valmiki is alive. He lives because I defied the gods. He breathes and smiles and returns my love with his eyes.

With care for his bleeding wounds, I hold him and kiss his cheek, his forehead, both hands. With a light caress, I kiss his mouth.

He tries to say something, but can't form any words. Instead, he smiles and takes my hand. His once strong grasp is weak. His face is pale and his eyes are sunken dark circles... but he's alive.

Tears pour down my face as I lean close and whisper, so he can hear above the storm. "I love you. Poet, I'm so sorry. I love you." I rest my head on his chest.

Valmiki's beating heart fills me. Gives me courage to do what I must.

At last, I sit up. "Lord Hades, when I entered your realm, you told me a price would be demanded, and I promised to pay that price. I vow to remain forever as your servant here."

"No!" Valmiki struggles to his knees. With screeches, flapping wings, and grasping hands, the Furies... no, the Eumenides... rush to support him.

I stand slowly, throw back my shoulders, and raise both arms in the air. "Dark Lord, you don't fool me with your rage and bluster!" I shout above the storm.

The winds and thunder stop as abruptly as they started. Both Zeus and Hades stare at me. Silence fills the room.

"I've seen into your heart. I know who you are, Lord-of-Many-Names. I understand now why you are called in different ways. You are Plutos, the god of wealth, and Aides, the unseen, who wanders throughout Erebos in your helmet of invisibility to oversee your realm. But you are Eubulos, too, the giver of good counsel... and as such, I honor you."

"There is much power in you, Thaleia." Hades stares a long time at me, narrows his eyes, at last, shakes his head. "Are you mortal?" He looks over at Nyx. "Are you the child of Nyx that you have this power to give life... and the courage to honor me after my threats?"

"She is not my child, Lord Hades, though I would gladly claim her as such," Nyx says.

"The Pythia Hipparchia is my mother, King Hades."

"I tried to destroy you, Thaleia, why do you return my hatred with honor?"

I bow to the god. "There is much about you to honor, Dark Lord. Wearing your helm of invisibility, you wandered throughout this Land-of-Death to gather together all the lost girls. The dishonored. The abused. You brought these forgotten maidens to your queen that she may do her penance. She told me that you even hid the truth from the Olympian gods."

Hades glances sideways at his brother.

"She explained how you continued the myth of her forced abduction... and all the while you helped her save these girls."

I bow lower to Queen Persephone. "And about your queen. I honor your wish, Goddess, to help these abandoned girls. You brought them here to give them a loving home. Now I will continue your good work. I will give them their homecoming to their mothers and fathers, their lives reborn to the skies and fields they love."

Hades kneels before me so we look eye to eye, then takes up my hands in his large ones and stares at them as if pondering something. "You say your mother is mortal, the wise Hipparchia, The Forbidden One. Tell us now. Who is your father?"

"Icos the kind tavern keeper is the man I would claim. The father I know. The father I love. Yet, my grandmother told me a story... about a god. Apollo knocked my grandmother to her death with one sweep of his wing as he pursued my mother."

"Why? Why would a god pursue his own Oracle? Murder her mother?"

"She told me..."

"Who?"

"My grandmother. I saw her here in Erebos. I think she tried to warn me. Help me."

Lord Hades sweeps both his arms high and shouts. "Summon her!"

And with his one command, my grandmother stands before us. Old. Frail. The blue scarf draped over her hunched back. There's fear in her eyes, when she looks from god to goddess and last, to me.

"It is my wish that you tell us who this child's father is." Hades voice is low and ominous, the anger threaded beneath his words.

Without stopping to think, I step between them and lead my grandmother over to the table, where the cup shards are scattered through a puddle of tea. I help her into a chair. "Grandmother, please, I understand now. Though I don't want to believe it, I know Papa is not my true father. Please, tell me. Who is?"

CHAPTER THIRTY-TWO
KNOW THYSELF

er whispered answer is quiet. Too quiet. I bend close and ask again. "Grandmother, who is my true father? It's not Icos, is it?"

"The god of sweet wine and wild abandon is your father. The god of nature and rebirth."

"Dionysos? Do you mean Dionysos? But Mama was Oracle of Apollo…"

"Dionysos is your father, Thaleia."

"Dionysos! That upstart!" Hades protests.

At last I remember what all this time I chose to forget. Something Mama told us as she paced restlessly back and forth before the hearth and a sparrow sang outside from a grapevine. *They say, Thaleia, and Sophia, that the god's possession is pure love. They say you don't hear the god's words, but feel them infused with your breath as hope and dreams, as if anything imaginable is possible. Nothing needs to be explained or spoken. The Pythia feels the god's words in her bone marrow. She knows.*

My memory sends shudders through me as once more I see fire spark from Mama's body as she speaks the god's name.

The gods vie for power. Apollo is the most powerful god of Delphi, but in the cold winter, another god is worshipped—Dionysos.

I saw—but on that long-ago day, didn't want to understand—

when her eyes smoldered to dark coals as she told us the god Dionysos visited her.

Apollo and Dionysus are like two brothers. Two sides of a coin. The earth and the sky. Apollo is the god of light and reason, but Dionysos is wild and untamed.

The truth of her next words jars me. *Imagine the Pythia communing with that bold god of pine trees and the sacred vine.*

Mama told me about her forbidden love for the god Dionysos. A love that betrayed Apollo. Here was the god's jealousy; not for a mortal. For another god. Apollo and Dionysos, light and dark, insane with jealousy and in love with one human woman.

Mama told me who my father was, but the young girl I was didn't want to hear it. Didn't want to understand.

"Dionysos is my father." I whisper at last, and cover Grandmother's hands with my own. "You sacrificed your life to save Mama. To save me. But I have to know, did Dionysos take Mama like Poseidon claimed Medusa and Hades is purported to have seized Persephone?"

"No, Dionysos loves your mother. And she him. She risked everything for that love, and for you. Even Apollo's wrath. She is The Forbidden One, banished from the sacred tripod, stripped of honor and power... and she willingly gave it up for that love. For you, child."

"My father is a god?"

"The immortal elixir runs through your veins, Thaleia."

"I am half-Immortal? That must be why..."

"Yes."

"My visions. The reason I could save the men and women and children trapped in the oaks. The spider web connecting me..." I touch my hair. "The poppies. Demeter's poppies."

And then, there are tears. At long last, as if I could wash away all my loss, all my guilt, all my shame, I hold my grandmother's hands and cry. And understand it all.

"The god Dionysos is my father. I am the child of the prophecy. The reason I can summon life from death. I am the thin line between gods and men."

I shake. Papa, the man who sang to me and tickled me and threw me high in the air, until I laughed so hard I could barely breathe... he's not my father? A god is? Dionysos, whom the maenads follow on wild nights? This god who demands virgin sacrifice? This god whose priests killed my friend? And me? Am I immortal? Where has he been all my life? One thought after another race through my mind. But one repeats itself: *My father, a god, demanded my sacrifice!*

With one last look at Valmiki, one last smile, I turn to confront King Hades. "The god Dionysos is my father. His power to harness nature is in me."

"You may have a god's blood running through you, Thaleia, but there must always be a price. You are in my kingdom. My domain. What will you give me if I allow you to trade your life for Valmiki's?"

"I give you freedom."

"Freedom?" He laughs. "I'm a god. I am free."

"Are you? Even though you are a god, your life is marred by petty fears and anger. You are jealous because your brother drew the heavens for his lot. Athena is jealous of Nyx's dark beauty and Medusa's. And you, Queen Persephone, you still pretend you are bound to this realm, you still relive the horror of your fight with Minthe. Is this freedom?"

Do I dare touch this god?

I rest my hand on his arm. "You've been helping these girls all along. Now, as I guide them home, I beg you to search your hearts and forgive one another."

Medusa, more beautiful than ever, wraps her arms around my shoulders. "Lord Hades, for many years I lived in darkness. Cursed by a goddess. Shamed and disgusted by my guilt." She steps away from me and walks over to stand before Athena. There's a fire in her eyes. "Athena, I appeal to your wise counsel. Thaleia returned my beauty to me, my honor, she helped me understand that when the gods quarrel out of all-too-human emotions—jealousy, envy, greed, and anger—they are no better than we mortals. And no worse."

"You betrayed me with Poseidon in my own sanctuary! I curse you forever..." Athena says.

"And I forgive you, goddess." Her words are soft, but their power stuns us all.

I smile at Medusa and look from Athena to Hades to Nyx.

"My daughter," Zeus says with gentle but firm words. "Athena, you are the goddess of wisdom. Surely, you hear the wisdom in your priestess' words. When mortals are courageous and wise, they are touched by the Divine." The Lord-of-All smiles at me.

Athena bows to Medusa. "Loyal priestess, I am honored by your forgiveness."

"Athena," Nyx says. "You claim a woman's heart at last. Is there more you would tell your priestess, an innocent girl you cursed?"

Athena strokes the owl that sits on her shoulder, preening his feathers.

"Athena, here is freedom. Jealousy and hatred are chains. What do you say?" Nyx tries to persuade the goddess.

"Medusa, I am humbled that you set aside your anger, though I hurt you grievously. Will you return to my temple atop the acropolis? An enemy approaches. A massive army from the east led by King Xerxes, who would destroy our Sanctuary. Will you stand with me to protect Athens?" Athena rests her hand on Medusa's shoulder.

Medusa bows before her. "Yes, my goddess. Our city needs us."

When Medusa smiles at me in triumph, I stand on the table and shout. "Listen to me, all of you! I, Thaleia, Oracle of Delphi, set you free from the hatred that divides you. Today I liberate you. No god, no mortal, no stars are separate from each other. Our *kosmos* is unceasing, undivided, endless. Today I acknowledge my initiation and my Night of Pan."

I jump off the table and gather the surprised satyr's hands. "Today I fulfill Pan's prophecy: A beetle will crawl from earth-stone, no longer grasping the sun of immortal sun-god Apollo. Between its black pincers, the scarab will carry a child sacred to Dionysos, a girl who will bind mortals and immortals for time everlasting."

Dropping Pan's hands, I walk from Hades to Zeus to Athena and Aphrodite and Nyx. Slowly, one by one, I look each in the eye. "I am sacred to Dionysos. I am the girl who binds mortals and immortals. The time is now!"

At last I find myself before the Titan Kronos. "Kronos, father of Zeus, you have the power in this very moment to end this cycle of hatred. You unmanned your father Uranos. Your son Zeus imprisoned you. When does this thirst for revenge end? Will you end this lust for power? All of you! Do you want to be free?"

Kronos heaves his heavy body up and lumbers over to stand before his youngest son. He holds out the scythe, its stone blade glowing in the candlelight. "Zeus, ruler of the skies, with this sharp scythe I reaped my power... now I give it to you. I forgive you for the violence you wrought upon me. I honor your destiny as determined by the gods." The Titan bows his head and hands the reaper to Lord Zeus.

The Thunderer holds the scythe before him as if a venomous snake. With slow tread, he walks over to Nyx. "Free him, wise Goddess of the Night. Never chain your grandson again in the earth's bowels. I allow him freedom to walk beneath the sun, or, if he prefers, under the skies of Pan's Elysian Fields. I forgive him for rising against me in the War between the Titans and the Olympians. I grant Kronos, my father, his freedom, at last."

I bow to Zeus, and look up into the dark lord's fire eyes next. "Release Valmiki. Set Sophia and the other girls free from this Land-of-Death, wise Hades." There is only palpable waiting in Persephone's hall. With a nod to the queen and all present, I intone in a loud voice that echoes from the gold beams to the tile floor, from crystal and precious stones. "I will pay this debt with my life."

There's a scraping and scrabbling of claws against tile as the hags hold onto any arm or shoulder or thigh that they can grasp on Valmiki. He can barely hold himself up, but they flap their leather wings and like one beast, supporting him as he hobbles across the room.

"Thaleia. No! You must return home." Valmiki's words are gasping and quiet, but all have heard him. "You are needed in Hellas. King Xerxes will destroy Athens. He will destroy the League. He will destroy democracy." His strength spent, Valmiki crumples into the hags' waiting arms.

Sophia and I pull a chair over and ease him into it.

He smiles up at me weakly. "Don't you remember? I promised to protect you."

"And you have. Now, return to Delphi. Take Sophia and the girls with you. I'll show you the way to the temple. And, Valmiki, when you see Mama and Papa, tell them I know the truth. Tell them I understand now why they arranged a marriage in the village to protect me. A marriage they hoped would allow me to live a village life. A mortal life. A life the enraged and jealous god Apollo would not destroy, as he did Kastalia's...

"Tell them I thank them. And that I'll love them for all time."

Tears glisten in Valmiki's eyes as he tries twice to speak. At last he says, "Thaleia, I'm not only staying for you. There are debts of my own to pay off. My soul to redeem. Until I am no longer Ratnakara, murderer of innocents, until I am Valmiki the poet, your beloved." He touches my cheek. "There is much truth, much wisdom for me to find in this shadow land. I will write an epic poem here to guide others on a true path. I will call it The Ramayana to honor Lord Rama. There is a need for you to return to Delphi to fulfill your destiny. There is a need for me to stay here."

Before I can answer, before I even take one breath, Parmenides stands before me. One minute I face the dark king alone, face the prospect of losing Valmiki—and then he's just there. In his regal robes and comforting smile.

"Most honored Lord-of-Many-Names, I thank you for welcoming me to your magnificent home." He bows low and long before turning to look at me.

"Thaleia. Child of Pan's prophesy. Have you forgotten?" He waves his arm over my head, and I'm plunged into a vision.

The honeycake is never eaten. Athena has left her sanctuary.

Priests whimper in the dark temple shadows. Flaming arrows fly into the sanctuary, burning barricades and the ragged robes of Athenians too poor to flee the city, too drunk with the hope that the goddess Athena will keep them safe in her temple.

While the Persians' arrows assault the citadel, the sacred olive tree dedicated to Athena burns until nothing is left but a charred trunk.

Parmenides' words seem to come from far away. "Will you deny your destiny, child?"

Valmiki takes one step and wraps his arm around me. He whispers in my ear, "We must both fulfill our destiny, Pythia. I must stay here. One day, you will return for me." He touches the spider web necklace. "You must not forget why you came to this Land-of-Death. You came to bring Sophia home."

My vision blurs with tears, as I look from girl to girl, waiting and hopeful.

A shadow falls over me. Nyx. Stars and nebula and whirling planets spin around me so fast that I am dizzy. The goddess wraps her arms around me to still my trembling. When she speaks, her voice, deep and rich like warm honey culled from a hive, sings and thrums through my chest. "Girl, you are brave, and courage leads you wisely. But there is no time to waste."

I take both of Parmenides' hands. "The Song will carry us home?"

He smiles and nods.

I look back at Valmiki and rush to his arms. "I don't want to leave you, Poet!"

"Such is your duty, Thaleia." He lifts my chin and kisses me, a caress of my lips so swiftly over. A shiver runs through me. "I love you... now go. And promise me you won't look back. Do not deny me my destiny. Or you yours." He pushes me gently from his arms and turns me around. "We came here to save Sophia. That was our vow. Take her home to safety, Thaleia. When it is our time, when I've completed The Ramayana to help mankind and you have made sure Hellas survives, then, I know, I believe, you will return for me. This is not a goodbye."

I walk away from Poet.

I don't turn around.

I lift the pipes high and swing them side-to-side like a harvester's scythe. My melody is the earth's heartbeat and Medusa's stare. It is Typhon's roar and the River Cocytus' rushing despair. My melody is

Poseidon's Seas and Zeus' Thunder. It is the *kosmos* caught between Nyx's swan wings and the Graeae's poor pathetic eye searching, searching for compassion.

And last it is my yearning to find my father. My father who is not Icos, no matter how much I love this kind, simple man. My father—the god Dionysos—who has left me alone, forsaken. Who has demanded my sacrifice. How many of Persephone's daughters are abandoned by their fathers?

My music is their solitude.

It is Valmiki lost behind me.

My music is their suffering. It fills me with determination.

CHAPTER THIRTY-THREE
THE MYSTERIES—PARMENIDES

Parmenides here one last time. At last she knows—the god Dionysos is her father.

A god who demanded sacrifice. A god who never revealed himself to his daughter.

In her victory, Thaleia taught the gods to forgive. She healed the rift between gods and mortals. We are not separate. We are not alone.

The song is almost done and the melody fades. But at last Thaleia understands: The Song of the Universe is the gods' song and the stars and sun and earth and wind.

It is all of us.

That is the reason that you can't kill The Song.

She understands that only her fear can make Lord Hades' realm real.

And only her compassion for others brings her salvation.

She understands what it means to lose love.

The last part of this puzzle that she does not know is the mystery.

Shall I call it by its true name? The Eleusinian Mysteries?

None may speak of these secret rites. None may divulge the sacred ceremonies... but in my heart I know. I understand. And now the girl must as well.

Thaleia walked in dark night to the Cave of Pan and became

Initiate. She drank the sacred *kykeon* and spoke with the ancient nature god.

She has heard the prophecy. Communed with the divine fire.

And then, at that moment of understanding, it must have been then that she and Mother Demeter and Daughter Persephone were One. It must have been then that the poppies sacred to the Mother, the *Kore*, and the Child of the Prophecy grew wild in Thaleia's hair.

Even I am not allowed to know the Sacred Mysteries.

Now truly she understands.

And, so, it is time. Let the girl close her eyes. Let darkness fall, a moment's blindness like the wise Oracle Tiresias.

For only a breath.

When you open your eyes, fair Thaleia, you will be in the heart of this dark realm.

CHAPTER THIRTY-FOUR
THE VOID

I **whirl in circles, the gods and goddesses a blur, stunned and** solemn.

I play my dreams and the girls' dreams. For dreams are beyond time, dreams are The-Land-of-the-Living.

Nyx, Athena, Medusa, Hades and his Thunder-god brother, the ants and vultures, the drop of water that is every river, I bind them all—friend and foe—with the spider web and song. Was Kronos only a vengeful son who mutilated his father? This Titan beyond time who knows all and yet lives his life chained to a moldy wall, drunk and despairing. Does the scythe destroy or create new hope?

Our destiny is the butterfly's vision. Chaos becomes beauty. Despair, looked at as guide, becomes hope.

My music carries me to a living darkness that engulfs me. I feel its warmth. I hear its breath like it's alive. I feel the girls close around me and Sophia's hand in mine. We move ahead into oblivion, together, unafraid. Out of the reach of time.

Abruptly, like a waterfall's stone lip, blackness falls off into blackness. A different one. Though black is black, it feels changed. One moment there is a ledge, then there is not. Black. Only black. No sensation against my skin. No sound in my ears. No touch of Sophia's hand... Sophia! There is nothing at all. I have no body, no sense of anything around me. There is only the Void.

It's impossible to keep any sense of direction.

I can only trust the gods.

I go on.

How far?

How long?

CHAPTER THIRTY-FIVE
DELPHI

linded by the brilliant Greek sun slanting off the Shining
Cliffs, I shut my eyes.

When I open them, I am home. We are home.

Marble columns cast long shadows across us, the columns I once transformed to mighty oaks—the Temple of Apollo. I was a girl then unaware of my powers. Ignorant that a god is my father.

"Thaleia, you brought me home. You brought us home." Sobbing and laughing, Sophia wraps her arms around me.

The girls huddle close, circling us silent and wondering. I will help them return to their homes. Those with no home, their family destroyed by war or famine or tradition that values them less than they are worth, will stay here with me as priestesses. At long last, the choice will be theirs.

My gaze is drawn to the carvings in the stone lintel high above me.

Know Thyself.

E...Divine is.

ACKNOWLEDGMENTS

In my acknowledgements for *Night of Pan,* book one of the *Oracle of Delphi Trilogy,* I first spoke of thumos (θυμος)—heart and yearning. I wrote: Thumos is "my passion to understand an ancient world peopled by bold mystics and philosophers and poets."

I still feel the same way.

But the world has changed—at least it feels that way to me—grown ever more chaotic than when I launched my debut novel, Fall 2014. In this book, my Oracle Thaleia encounters monsters and challenges in a bleak Underworld of fire-rivers and vengeful gods—a chaotic world in which she seeks hope where there is fear, forgiveness where there is hatred. Wars, mass killings, corrupt and dishonest politicians make us feel like we are also wandering through a dark Underworld. It would be easy to despair and lose our way. I find myself clinging to the ancient Greek maxim: Chaos is inherently good. Only out of chaos can we form a new order.

There's been my own personal chaos these last few years. My beloved father Robert Strickland, Sr., who inspired me more than I can express, passed away peacefully in his sleep after 96 creative and loving years. His loss makes me feel like I've wandered into that bleak Land-Beyond-Time. Also, my health has been less than great. But through it all, I don't feel lost.

Why not?

Because my overwhelming feeling is one of gratitude. I feel grateful. So grateful for my friends—my Willful Writing sisters, my entire Left Coast Writers community, Chris Guidry, (my IT hero who saves me from hackers and my own technological demons... and then designed my website!), The Birthday Club and Lauri, Debbie, Mary, Penny, Roxie and Diana Dillaway (my adventurous mountain friend), Ken and Karen who have been my friends forever... I am blessed with more friends than I can name... you know who you are... all those hugs and smiles and encouraging words. I'm so grateful for my family and the way my phone rings, and it will be one of you "just checking in" when I need it most. I'm grateful for my publisher. (Alisa Gus is the best editor in the world!) So grateful for all the new friends I've made along the way in this crazy and wonderful writing journey. I've learned from all of you. Speaking with you in bookstores and conferences and wandering into classrooms via Google hangout, more and more I realized the truth of the wise seer Parmenides' words: "We are never alone."

So I have to end by saying, I am grateful that you have all taught me that even in the midst of chaos, we truly are not alone. And for that... with all my heart... I thank you.

ABOUT THE AUTHOR

Gail Strickland—classicist, poet and musician—was born in Brooklyn, NY. After immersing herself in the classics in college, Gail lived on a Greek island, where she discovered her love of everything Greek: their song culture, the wine-dark sea... and retsina.

November 2014, Curiosity Quills Press published her acclaimed debut novel *Night of Pan*—a mythic journey of a young Oracle in ancient Greece. In *Oracle of The Song*, book two of *The Oracle of Delphi Trilogy*, Gail weaves a tale instilled with Greek myth and a dark, defiant spirit of an ancient time.

Thank You
for Reading

© 2017 **Gail Strickland**

www.gailstrickland.com

Please visit http://curiosityquills.com/reader-survey to share
your reading experience with the author of this book!

Burning Bright, by Melissa McShane

In 1812, Elinor Pembroke wakes to find her bedchamber in flames—and extinguishes them with a thought. Her talent makes her a desirable match in Regency England, but rather than make a loveless marriage or live dependent on her parents, Elinor chooses instead to join the Royal Navy. Assigned to serve in the Caribbean, she turns her fiery talent on pirates preying on English ships. But as her power grows, Elinor's ability to control it is challenged. Could her fire destroy her enemies at the cost of her own life?

Kiya: Hope of the Pharaoh, by Katie Hamstead

To save her younger sisters from being taken, Naomi steps in to be a wife of the erratic Pharaoh.

As Naomi rises through the ranks of the wives, Queen Nefertiti seeks to destroy her. To protect herself, Naomi charms the Pharaoh, who grows to love her. But when Naomi conceives his child, Nefertiti's lust for blood is turned against her.

Made in the USA
Middletown, DE
14 September 2022

10495521R00175